THE SCENT OF WATER

She dropped her hands into her lap, straightened herself and sighed deeply, but more with relief than sadness. Somewhere, at some deep level, she had made a decision. Or it had been made for her. Yet she felt she had something to do with it for it felt like an act of obedience. She was giving up her work and going to Appleshaw as soon as possible, to live there. It would mean losing her pension but with the small legacy from Cousin Mary, and her annuity, she would manage.

She picked up her pen and wrote her letter to the lawyer but it was not the letter she had meant to write. She asked him to send her the name and address of the village woman who had looked after her old cousin. She would, she said, ask this woman to keep the house in order for her until she came. She would come in the spring, in May, not to view it but to take possession. She stamped the letter, put it in her "out" basket, and turned once more to her work, this time with entire and successful concentration.

The Scent of
Water

Elizabeth Goudge

CORONET BOOKS
Hodder Paperbacks Ltd., London

Copyright © 1963 by Elizabeth Goudge
First published by
Hodder and Stoughton Ltd. 1963
Coronet edition 1966
Second impression 1966
Third impression 1967
Fourth impression 1968
Fifth impression 1971
Sixth impression 1974

Printed in Great Britain
for Coronet Books, Hodder Paperbacks Ltd.,
St Paul's House, Warwick Lane, London, EC4P 4AH,
by Richard Clay (The Chaucer Press), Ltd.,
Bungay, Suffolk

ISBN 0 340 15104 8

FOR
AUDREY

For there is hope of a tree, if it be cut down, that it will sprout again, and that the tender branch thereof will not cease. Though the root thereof wax old in the earth, and the stock thereof die in the ground; yet through the scent of water it will bud, and bring forth boughs like a plant.

The Book of Job

Still ran Kangaroo – Old Man Kangaroo. He . . . ran through the long grass; he ran through the short grass; he ran through the Tropics of Capricorn and Cancer; he ran till his hind legs ached.
He had to!

Kipling: Just So Stories

"SHE'S gone, dear," said the district nurse.

The elderly woman on the other side of the bed sighed and said, "Well, poor soul, it's a happy release."

Both were silent a moment out of respect for the dead and then Mrs. Croft, the nurse, said briskly, "Well, dear, we'd better get cracking for I'm pressed for time."

The old-fashioned room was filled with the quietness of the deep country and the light of a marvellous sunset. Mrs. Baker, who had loved the dead woman, was touched to awe by the tide of gold. It was like water, she thought, flooding into the room, and she was unusually silent as she and Mrs. Croft performed the last offices with the gentle yet swift dexterity of long practice.

"Nothing on your mind, dear?" asked Mrs. Croft, for Mrs. Baker was by nature chatty. "The way you looked after the poor old dear, year after year, you've nothing to reproach yourself with. A few hours a week were all you were paid for, as well I know, and you were here morning, noon and night."

Mrs. Baker, a wiry, doughty little countrywoman, said simply, "I was fond of her. No, I've nothing on my mind. I was remembering her last words."

"What did she say, dear?" asked Mrs. Croft soothingly. Mrs. Baker, she perceived, was in her own fashion taking this death hard, and it was always best to let them talk.

"She said something about sailing out on living water."

"Wandering," said Mrs. Croft.

"She had been, but not then. She was quite clear in her mind, like they so often are. Living water, she said. This gold puts me in mind of it."

Mrs. Croft returned to practical matters. "Do you think she would have wished to be laid out in her wig?"

"Of course," said Mrs. Baker tartly. "She was always one to make the best of herself."

A little later, their work done, they stood back to admire their handiwork, in which each took the pleasure of an artist.

"Looks peaceful," said Mrs. Croft. "Funny how quickly they change." A few hours ago a very grotesque old woman had been dying in the curtained bed but now the sculptured face already wore the stamp of beauty. "Must have been a lovely woman once."

Though life and death were equally all in the day's work for both women the mystery held them for a moment. Then Mrs. Croft turned briskly to the door. "Well, dear, I must be getting on. I've a baby due any time up at the farm."

Mrs. Baker was not listening. "It was herself that she meant," she said.

CHAPTER I

I

"Mary, you will regret this."

Mary Lindsay settled herself in the driving-seat of her small car and pulled on her gloves. She looked apologetically at her friend and said, "It's not irrevocable, Catherine." Yet she knew it was and so did Catherine as she said irritably, "You'll go to seed."

"Things do in the country," said Mary. "They have to, for there is seed-time and harvest there. Catherine, this may be my last chance to live it."

"What?"

"Country life. I've never known it. I'd like to before it and I disappear from the English scene."

"You talk as though you were seventy," snapped Catherine. "And why must you go alone? You might at least have let me come with you."

"Catherine," said Mary gently but forcibly, for they had had this out before, "you know, for I've told you. I have to go alone. You'll come and stay when I'm settled. Goodbye my dear. Thank you for helping me pack. Thank you for everything. Good-bye."

She was far too disciplined a woman to cry but Catherine was not very clear to her as she waved and moved off down the familiar London street. They had worked together for six years, Mary in an executive post in one of the ministries, Catherine as one of her subordinates, and it had been wordlessly understood that they would live together when they retired; in London, where they would have music, ballet and good plays, all those things that until now had been so necessary to Mary. And now she had already retired at fifty, and Catherine would not do so for another ten years. The parting was harder for Catherine, Mary thought sadly, for she herself was sustained by the madness of her adventure.

For the woman that she was, both urban and cosmopolitan,

it was indeed mad. A few months ago a cousin of her father's, whom she had not seen since she was a child, had died at the age of eighty-five, leaving her a little money, a small house and all that it contained. The house was in a remote village in the Chilterns of which she possessed only a few memories, and they had been almost totally submerged until that morning when the lawyer's letter had come. She had had no time to look at her post before she left her flat, and she had taken the letter to her office and opened it there. She had read it over and over again, marvelling, passing with each minute a little farther away from where her body sat, a little farther back in time, and then suddenly that day when her father had taken her to see Cousin Mary had been alive again, with the memories no longer memories but present experience. Her comfortable office, the roar of traffic in the street below and the woman at the desk had all vanished, and Mary Lindsay had been a child again.

2

She was driving with her father in a pony trap along a country lane bordered on each side with trees. They were like no trees she had ever seen in the London parks, they were tremendous, august and unearthly. Far up in the blue sky there was a faint rustling of leaves, a movement of branches in the May wind, but below there was a motionless, shadowed, possessive stillness. Yet though she pressed closer to her father she was not afraid of them. She thought they were good trees, pleased to see her and glad her father was taking her to see her namesake, Cousin Mary Lindsay. She had not been called after her cousin on purpose, she had understood from talk between her father and mother, merely by accident; but poor Cousin Mary had been so pleased to have a child of the family bearing her name that they had not liked to undeceive her. And now she had asked that the little Mary might be brought to see her so that she could show her "the little things". She had sent the trap from the pub to meet the London train at the nearest station, six miles away. There was a boy at the pub who could drive it.

"Fine trees," said her father to this boy, whose piercing

blackbird whistling had been momentarily hushed by the grandeur of the trees. "What are they?"

"Limes," said the boy. "Ain't another lime avenue like this in all the county."

And then his whistling broke out again as the trees drew back. Mary heard them moving and felt their mysterious hold releasing her. To her left now were cherry trees at the edge of a wood. Within the wood were bluebells and she heard a cuckoo calling.

Between that memory and the next the cuckoo called in a warm darkness, its note changing imperceptibly to the pealing of a bell, for the clock in a square church tower was ringing the hour. The grey rock of the church towered above a graveyard where the buttercups were gay about the slanting gravestones. There was a village green with thatched cottages about it, one of them the village shop and post office, and opposite the lych-gate of the church lilacs grew in a tangled mass behind a garden wall. In the wall was a green door under a stone archway. It had a round brass handle and beside it was an ancient rusted iron bellpull. Cut into the stone on the other side of the arch was the name of the house. It was called The Laurels, though there wasn't a laurel in sight. The lilacs had grown so tall that their branches hung over the wall and over the arch above the door. Four steps led up to the door and they were very worn in the middle. What could be behind the door Mary couldn't imagine. Not the world she knew. The thicket of purple and white blossom, the door and the steps, were like a picture painted a long time ago, and it horrified her to see the boy dragging the bellpull out of the wall and hanging on to it while a solemn peal sounded far away, muffled and sad, as though it rang at the bottom of the sea. One did not ring the doorbells of painted pictures and if there should be a door ajar one did not push it and go in. The world inside a picture was a hidden thing.

She realized that her father was speaking to her. "I expect to find her very odd. You must not laugh and if your surroundings seem unusual you must not say so." Of course she would not say so, thought Mary, as she climbed out of the trap. Of course things would be unusual inside a picture. What did her father expect?

The door opened inwards very slightly. The boy had jumped into the trap and driven away and her father, his hand on her shoulder, was urging her gently forward. She hung back, then grabbing at her courage she pushed through with her father behind her. The door shut behind them and they were in a scented darkness. At least that was how it seemed to her at first as she stood on worn paving stones with her back to the door, and to the little man in a leather apron, a gardener perhaps, who had opened it and was now talking to her father. She took no notice of them for they did not seem to exist for her. She was alone in the world inside the picture. It had seemed dark but now the light was silver. The paving stones were those of a narrow paved passage with four delicate fluted pillars on each side. The roof was made of wooden beams holding the weight of a great wistaria vine that entirely covered them and hung down in curtains of scent and colour on either side. Beyond the leaves and flowers Mary was dimly aware of birds singing in a garden.

At the end of the passage a little old woman in a black dress, with snowy mob cap and apron, stood at an open door smiling and holding out her hand. Mary went to her and took her hand and passed with her into a dark stone-flagged hall where a silver tankard of lilies of the valley stood on an oak chest. The flowers and the polished silver gathered all the light to themselves and Mary gazed at them entranced, noticing that a bird with spread wings was carved upon the top of the chest, and that across the front of it interlaced strappings formed a cross in the centre, and suddenly she was no longer an intruder in this world inside the picture. It was her own world.

After that the memories were clear but not consecutive. They fell together, lovely and confused like the bright fragments of a kaleidoscope. She was upstairs and the old maidservant was pouring water out of a brass jug into a basin patterned with honeysuckle, and washing her hands and face. The soft towel smelled sweet against her face and even when it momentarily covered her ears she could still hear the birds singing. Looking out of the window she saw through veils of greenness a boy standing in the centre of a pool. Then she was standing on a dark, uncarpeted staircase and the worn treads sank in the middle like the steps outside the green door. She walked down very slowly, carefully placing her feet on the hollowed wood that shaped itself like a curved hand to hold her safely. She was seated at a mahogany dining-table eating roast beef and Yorkshire pudding, and later apple tart and custard, while her father talked to the tall gaunt woman in the wide-skirted flowered dress who was sitting in the chair with the carved back at the head of the table. She did not look up from her plate, and she did not speak, for she was very frightened of Cousin Mary. She did not think her funny, she thought her terrible, with her light eyes bright as a bird's, her red hair piled untidily on the top of her head and her deep hoarse voice. Her hands were so thin they were like claws, covered with bright rings, and the long necklace she wore chimed when she moved. But the fear Mary felt then was nothing to what she felt later when the door of the small panelled parlour clicked shut behind her father, going out to smoke in the garden, and she was alone with Cousin Mary. But she was a brave child and she did not pull away when her wrist was nipped between a cold finger and thumb. She followed where she was led, over a mossy carpet scattered with roses, through the dim shadows of the room to where a sea-green light illumined a small round table with a plush cover, and set upon it a tall domed glass case.

"Look, Mary Namesake," said Cousin Mary and the child-like eagerness in her voice contrasted oddly with her deep voice. "Look there, my dear!"

At first Mary could see nothing, for the shadows of the green vine leaves in the little conservatory outside the window flickered over the glass case, but then Cousin Mary lifted it away and she saw the circles of velvet-covered wood, diminishing in height and held together by a central upright, making shelves for the display of a host of miniature treasures, fairy things of silver and gold, jade, pinch-beck, glass, ebony and ivory, all so small that only the eyes of a child could fully perceive their glory. But Cousin Mary's bright eyes were still as keen as Mary's. She knelt down, bringing herself to the same level as the child, and they were equals. Mary was no longer afraid of her. She had forgotten that she ever had been afraid. She had forgotten everything for time had stopped for her. She stood and gazed at the little things and it was the greatest moment of her life until now, more wonderful even than that moment when she saw the lilies in the silver tankard. Perhaps five minutes, perhaps a hundred years went by, and Cousin Mary gently touched a few things here and there with the tip of her finger, and talked to them softly, but Mary did not dare to touch. She scarcely dared to breathe. In their London home, a doctor's house where people were perpetually in and out, her father's patients and her mother's guests, and where she was one among five noisy children, there was no place for things like these; still, fragile and silent things.

"An ivory coach, you see, Mary," whispered her cousin. "It's no bigger than a hazel nut but it's all there, the horses and the coachman and Queen Mab herself inside. Do you see her inside?"

Mary nodded speechlessly. She could see the fairy figure with the star in her hair, and the tiny delicate features of the child-like face. It did not occur to her that human fingers could possibly have made Queen Mab and her coach for she seemed timeless as Cousin Mary herself. They had always lived here in this world inside the picture and they always would.

"It's Dresden, my dear, this little tea-set. Dresden."

Mary had just been trying to think herself small, and smaller and smaller, so as to get tiny enough to sit beside Queen Mab in her coach, but she courteously allowed herself to get large again so as to gloat over the tea-set of frail white china patterned with forget-me-nots. The cups and saucers and plates and teapot looked as though they had been fashioned out of thin egg-shell. There were several of these tea-sets, of glass, china, gold and silver. There were birds and animals, a dwarf with a scarlet cap, candlesticks and lanterns, and telescopes with microscopic pictures that you could see when you held the telescope up to the light. There were wooden dolls no larger than Mary's little finger-nail, with chairs for them to sit on and a cradle for the wooden baby. There were so many things that Mary lost count of them. But it was Queen Mab and her coach which she loved best, and the smallest of the tea-sets, the one made of clear blue glass, airy as a blown soap-bubble. She yearned to possess these two and her eyes clung to them, yet when Cousin Mary said, "Would you like to have something for yourself, dear?" she shook her head. They would have no place in the London house, Queen Mab would die there and the tea-set dissolve at the first crash of a banging door. "It's noisy in London," she said. "There are no trees in our street, and the birds don't sing like they do here. They wouldn't like it."

"Perhaps not," said Cousin Mary. "No, I don't think they would. I've never wanted to give anything away before, except once when I wanted to give the dwarf to a little boy, but you're different. You're my namesake. You're Mary Lindsay like me. My dear, I want to tell you——"

But Mary never knew what her cousin wanted to tell her because the church clock struck four, the door opened and her father came in, followed by the old maidservant with the tea. Cousin Mary lifted the glass case back over her treasures and turning round said to Mary's father, "She has seen my little things." She spoke gravely, in awed tones, as though something tremendous had happened, but he only nodded pleasantly and standing with his back to the fire he began to chat about the weather, and he did not even glance at the little things. But Mary knew that he was wrong and Cousin Mary was right. Something very important had happened.

Then tea was over and they were saying good-bye in the hall, and Mary was in Cousin Mary's arms and they were both crying bitterly. "Bring her to see me again, Arthur," sobbed Cousin Mary.

"Yes, we'll come again," said Mary's father. "Cheer up now, both of you. We'll come again."

But they did not come again for soon after that Mary's father died, and her mother, hard at work launching her clever children into the world on the wings of scholarships, lost touch with her husband's family. She had never liked them anyway. They were a queer lot.

3

Mary was once more sitting at her desk, very much shaken by the wave of forgotten memories that had broken

over her, and slightly scandalized by the way she had
abandoned herself to them. She had, literally, forgotten
where and who she was. She had been again that little girl
of, how many years ago? She must have been about
eight years old. Forty-two years ago. All that time gone
by, and now those flowers in the silver tankard were more
real to her than the pile of official letters waiting on her
desk. She straightened her shoulders, took the first one off
the pile and then dropped it on the blotter. Was the child
she had been five minutes ago an imaginative child? I must
be, she thought. I mean, I must have been, or I wouldn't
have felt like that about the trees, or thought as I did about
going into a picture, into a hidden country. Father was
imaginative, I think, but not Mother. I've always thought
I was more like Mother.

It had been her father's brains but her mother's drive that
had taken her to a good school, to Oxford, where she had
won a first in modern languages, to the top of the teaching
profession before the war and after it into government
service. When she retired it would be on a good pension,
augmented by an annuity left her by a man who had died
in the war, and she would have all she wanted. But she
would not want a house in the country. When she had her
next leave she would go down to Appleshaw and sell the
house and dispose of any furniture she did not want to
keep. She would write to the lawyer now and tell him, and
then it would be off her mind and she could concentrate on
her work. She pulled a piece of notepaper towards her, and
then suddenly found herself with her hands covering her
face, remembering a frail blue glass tea-set and an ivory
coach. Were the little things still there after forty-two years?
It did not seem likely but if they were she would bring
them back to London, to the flat. No. How could she? She
had not been able to do it before and she could not now.
They belonged there, not here. There and here were two
different worlds. Though could you call that a world, that
enchanted country in which a child had lived for a few hours
forty-two years ago? *This* was the world, her world, the
other was merely the shadow of a dying way of life. The
shadow was moving over the grass slowly, while the birds
sang their cool ringing song in the trees at the bottom of the

garden. Presently it would be gone. Then they would cut down the trees and build a nuclear power station there. You sentimental fool, she said to herself, but her hands were still over her face and she was wondering whether the wistaria still hung over the pillared way that led to the front door.

Why did she take such a fancy to me? Why did she leave me her poor little bit of money, her house and all she had? I forgot her but she did not forget me, and she was what the world calls peculiar and I'm supposed to be eminently sensible. Yet her memory was better than mine. I thought she was old, that day, but she wasn't much over forty. When I go back it will be the other way round, she will be young and I shall be old.

She dropped her hands into her lap, straightened herself and sighed deeply, but more with relief than sadness. Somewhere, at some deep level, she had made a decision. Or it had been made for her. Yet she felt she had something to do with it for it felt like an act of obedience. She was giving up her work and going to Appleshaw as soon as possible, to live there. It would mean losing her pension but with the small legacy from Cousin Mary, and her annuity, she would manage. She picked up her pen and wrote her letter to the lawyer but it was not the letter she had meant to write. She asked him to send her the name and address of the village woman who had looked after her old cousin. She would, she said, ask this woman to keep the house in order for her until she came. She would come in the spring, in May, not to view it but to take possession. She stamped the letter, put it in her "out" basket, and turned once more to her work, this time with entire and successful concentration.

CHAPTER II

I

BUT why didn't I go down at once to see the place? she wondered, as she drove smoothly through the London traffic. She drove well. She was in all things capable, as in all things honest. She did not often ask questions of herself, for she was not introspective and there was not enough time, but when she did the answers were generally truthful. This one astonished her, though she knew it was the truth. She had been afraid. She, a courageous woman, had been afraid, and there had been several strands in the twist of her fear. She had been afraid that the Appleshaw she remembered no longer existed, and that she would not find again the old enchantment. Or that she would find the village unchanged but the house a ruin, and in despair sell it out of hand. Or that if she went there uncommitted she might, when she went home to London again, let herself be overborne by Catherine's disapproval. But now, with her boats burnt behind her, she was committed. But why is it so important that I live there? she asked herself. I'm a Londoner. I don't know about country things. What will I do all day?

But she couldn't depress herself, and as she left London behind her, with her friends, her work, her interests and all that she loved, her spirits were actually rising. She had left home much later than she had meant to, and after a scrappy breakfast, and by the time she reached Westwater, a country town by the river which was the nearest shopping-place of any size to Appleshaw, it was twelve-thirty and she was hungry. She drove slowly up the beautiful High Street, looking for the best place to eat. She chose an old half-timbered house called the White Swan, with a bay window of diamond-paned glass and the swan painted upon a swinging sign. She went in and sat at a table against a wall. There were as yet only a few people there and they were all by the window, women in from the country, doing

THE SCENT OF WATER 21

their shopping. They seemed to know each other and they talked together, enjoying this weekly break from their home chores. One or two were well-dressed but most of them looked comfortably shabby in their weather-worn tweeds. I'll soon look like that myself, thought Mary, and feeling a pang of dismay she looked at herself in a long mirror hanging on the opposite wall.

The sight reassured her for she was a miraculously preserved fifty. She had kept her tall slender figure and straight back and did not sag either at the shoulders or in the middle. The bones of her face were good, broad across the cheekbones and narrowing to a small, firm chin. Her dark eyes were bright and lively under eyebrows whose mobility, combined with her resolute mouth and short determined nose, had often struck terror to the hearts of her subordinates. Her hair was thick and iron-grey, and her smooth ivory skin, only faintly lined about the eyes, needed little make-up. She wore no jewel, apart from her gold wrist-watch, and her plain black dress and short jacket, with a vivid flame-coloured scarf, cast a slight blight upon the women in the window. Their conversation faltered for a moment or two, and then in resolute self-defence they turned their eyes away and picked up the broken threads of their conversation.

Mary chose the best the menu could suggest and ate it with resignation, hoping the coffee would be better. That glimpse of herself in the glass, looking so surprisingly young, had suddenly sent her thoughts back over the past. The struggle of the years after her father had died, very hard work, very little money, but a great deal of fun when the children were together during the London holidays and entertainment was cheap and easily come by. The happiness of school and college days, the thrill of early love affairs, which she had always ended before they became too serious because in these matters she could never feel as she would have liked to feel. Her years of teaching before the war, with the pride of being house mistress in a famous school before she was thirty, and her holidays abroad. She had liked teaching. She knew the trick of discipline and taught well. And she had loved the children steadily and patiently, taking pains to understand them. Then the war,

return to London and work at the Admiralty, the blitz and
the fear and pity and raging anger of it, and the deaths of
two of her brothers.

And then her engagement in her early thirties to a sailor
whom she had met at the Admiralty, a man older than herself and so infinitely her superior in intellect and power of
love that the glowing, deeply emotional months of their
engagement had made her feel a little unreal, for the first
time in her life unsure of herself, carried along by a tide
too strong for her. He had been killed a week before the
date fixed for their wedding and her shock and grief and
disappointment had darkened her life for a while. But not
enough grief. Paradoxically she had broken her heart
because her sorrow had not been the overwhelming anguish
she had seen in others. She had realized with shame that
the deep affection which was her way of loving had not
been enough. Overwhelming love between man and
woman, a symbol perhaps of some deeper mystery, she knew
nothing whatever about, and she had been haunted by
Rupert Brooke's sonnet,

> "*I said I loved you; it's not true.*
> *Such long swift tides stir not a land-locked sea.*"

She was land-locked in herself. For a time she had sor-
rowed because not only was she bereaved of the man but
also, by reason of what she was, of her birthright of true
grief. Then her resilient nature had come to her rescue
and when the war ended she had given herself with energy
to the business of clearing up the mess.

She had gone out to Germany with a Red Cross unit and
worked with and for the shattered men and women coming
out of the concentration camps. Nothing she had seen in the
blitz had been more fearful and at length even her good
health had broken down. She had come back to England
and after a rest, and on the strength of her war service and
knowledge of languages, had obtained her government post
and risen slowly and steadily to as high as she could well go.
She had enjoyed post-war London, in spite of the noise, the
rush, the luxury and the undercurrent of perpetual fear,
and she had been so busy that she had not thought a great
deal about John.

But now she remembered him with extraordinary vividness. Why should he suddenly be so real to her at this moment? Why should the memory of their days together be rushing back on her in this teashop? They've come out with the others, the Cousin Mary ones, she thought, because those two loved me and whatever I gave in return was not enough. She paid her bill, accepted a cup of coffee and lit a cigarette. Not here, she thought, and not yet. There's a lot to do. Not yet. She pushed the thought of John away from her and looked out of the window at the beautiful street. It was old and dignified, and had the gentle windings of a stream, but between the tall, quiet houses went cars and lorries and restless people in a stench of petrol. It's a sort of meeting-place here, thought Mary, it's where the waves break. The tide is coming in over the old ways but I shall find quiet inlets still, and pools and rocks that only the spray touches. She went out of the shop and as she stood beside her locked car, feeling for the key in her bag, she thought briefly of London and the work she had done there. It seemed to her far away and not very important. She got into her car and drove off.

2

She was very soon in the country, and driving slowly lest she lose her way. She had studied her map carefully before starting but the twisting lanes were confusing, and she felt a little stunned by the beauty about her. Her love of going abroad had caused her to know little of the English countryside. She had spent week-ends with friends in their country cottages, week-ends of good food, good talk and good bridge that might just as well have taken place in London, and other friends had motored her down to lunch in country hotels, to Henley regatta and to Oxford, but again good talk and good food had predominated. She had seldom been alone in the country and she had not realized that anything quite so remote as this existed so near London.

She did not know that she had stopped the car until through the lowered window she heard the ring of bird-song in the tall trees. She was in a silver-stemmed beech wood roofed with green and gold. The floor of the wood was tawny with beech-mast beneath the polished darker green of low-growing hollies, the silver, green and tawny faintly veiled by the gauzy blue air of spring. And the birds sang. That piercing clear deep ringing and ringing seemed thrusting though her almost intolerably. She believed she had not heard such birdsong since she was a child; yet every year they had been singing like this in the tall woods of England, those that remained.

"*Through the echoing timber thrush doth so wrench and ring the ear, it strikes like lightning to hear him sing.*"

John had loved that poem and she was grateful for it at this moment. The poets did at least put it into words for you and ease the pain of it.

She drove on, for time was passing. She came out presently on high ground and looked down over a great plain and across it to a far line of blue hills. She saw a city, so alchemized by distance and blue air that its towers and spires seemed drifting on the plain like the vision of Lyonesse that is seen floating out at sea. Between her and the city she saw villages and farmsteads and the gleam of silver where river and stream wound through the water meadows. Against the steep slopes below her apple blossom broke like spray.

The lane took her away from this far view, keeping on high ground but going through woods again and giving her a sense of penetration. She remembered an Indian toy she had had as a child. Many-coloured boxes were placed one within another, and at the end came a small golden box that was the heart of the matter. It was so small that it could have been placed with Cousin Mary's little things. Her heart began to beat fast for she believed she was coming to that extraordinary avenue of trees; if they were still there after forty-two years. She steeled herself to see a caravan site where once the trees had been, and when she got to the village a row of council houses replacing the thatched cottages round the green.

She was within the avenue almost before she knew it, and the trees were the same. She stopped the car and got out and stood in the deserted lane looking up at them. If they were not quite as tremendous as she remembered she had expected that, for the scenes of childhood revisited always seemed smaller in reality than memory, but even so they were immense and she felt their power just as she had as a child. And their possessiveness also. Who had planted these giants in their ranks? They turned the country lane into a gracious avenue that looked as though it must lead to a great house. There was a small, lovely manor house away to the left but it did not match the trees.

As she walked back to her car a stout little woman in the uniform of a district nurse came towards her on a bicycle from the direction of the village, pedalling vigorously. As she passed Mary she gave her head a jerk that sent her spectacles down her nose. Over the top of them her bright kind eyes took Mary in from head to foot. With a half-smile, and a nod of brisk approval, she jerked her glasses back into position and pedalled on.

Mary got into her car and drove slowly down the avenue. It ended abruptly, as she remembered, at the bluebell wood, where the lane ran steeply downhill between the wood and some fields where she heard the cuckoo calling. She had forgotten this lane but she remembered the cuckoo. Some bungalows had been built beside the lane but they were not too blatantly modern and pretty gardens had grown up around them. At the garden gate of one of the bungalows an old man stood propped up on two sticks, a battered hat on his head. His shabby clothes hung loosely on his shrunken body but they had once been good clothes and there was about him, in spite of his feebleness, an air of alertness, of discipline, that attracted her. As she came opposite him he transferred, with infinite difficulty, the stick that was in his right hand to his left, lifted his hat and smiled at her with shy courtesy. She returned the smile with a sense of warmth about her heart, for it was almost as though he had been watching for her. But the moment she had passed him she was seized with panic. People! Of course there would be people living here, and the small community of a remote village was welded together like the different parts of a body. The hand could not say to the foot, I have no need of you. But why am I feeling panicky? she asked herself. I have always liked knowing people. Whom now do I want to know? The odd answer came back at once. Cousin Mary and John.

She turned the corner, the bell pealing the hour over her head, and there was the square church tower above the grey rock of nave and chancel, and the slanting gravestones and the thatched cottages about the green. She drove at a snail's pace. I believe it's twelfth-century, she thought with awe, looking at the church. Father did not tell me it was so old. The churchyard was no longer filled with grass and buttercups, for it was well kept, and on the other side of it she could see a small Georgian house in a garden full of trees that might be the Vicarage. It must always have been there but as a small child she had not noticed it behind the tall grass and buttercups. There was a telephone kiosk in front of the village shop and post office, and two of the cottages looked as though those who lived there now had not been born and bred in Appleshaw. But those were the only changes. After forty-two years this was still Appleshaw.

People? To her relief there were only two to see her arrival. An elderly lady was coming out of the post office as she passed it. She wore dark glasses, a grey tweed skirt longer at the back than the front, a home-knitted cardigan of bright pink and a sad black straw hat. She was tall and tremulous and when she saw Mary she was so startled that she swayed a little, and put her hand to the side of the post office door to support herself. She had the soft, crumpled face of a lost and frightened child, and Mary found herself giving her a quick smile of reassurance.

In front of the smarter of the two modernized cottages, with rose-pink walls and a small, elegant wrought-iron gate leading into a trim little garden, a slim, dark-haired woman wearing green slacks and a yellow pullover was giving her front door a new coat of turquoise paint. She turned round as Mary's car came by. She had clear-cut features and faultless make-up but her face was thin and prematurely hardened, and when her dark eyes met Mary's with a cool appraising stare the unhappiness in them was somehow shocking on this day of sunshine and singing birds.

Then abruptly Mary forgot the shock for there in front of her was the thicket of lilacs behind the garden wall of The Laurels, taller and wilder than ever. The arched door in the wall was still green, though the paint was peeling off it, and the bell was still there too. Mary got out of the car, went slowly to the door, took the old brass handle in her hands and turned it. She was aware of nothing in the world at this moment except that she had come home.

3

The door had dropped yet more on its hinges and it screeched wildly upon the paved path beyond when she pushed it, opening only enough to let her through. Inside there was no gardener in a leather apron and she missed the old man. But the curtains of wistaria were the same, and beyond them was the garden, green and wild. The fluted pillars on each side of the path were mossgrown and two of the beams above had cracked with the weight of the vine. The front door stood open but there was no friendly figure to welcome her, and when she came to the threshold there were no lilies of the valley in a silver tankard to make light in a dark place. She had forgotten just how dark this hall was. It seemed like a cave, and from the depths of it there came a dank breath of mildew and mice.

It was then that Mary had her one moment of panic, frightful panic, as though the earth was suddenly opening under her feet. What had she done? Exchanged her comfortable modern flat for decay and mice. It would probably cost a small fortune to make the house habitable again. But it was too late to turn back now. She was committed. If she gave up now she would break faith with Cousin Mary and John.

Mrs. Baker had promised to meet her here. Where was she? She called aloud but there was no answer. A mouse scurried in the wainscot and in the depths of the wild garden a thrush was singing. She stood and listened to him for a moment and his song, twice repeated as though in reiterated welcome, made up to her for the loss of the lilies in the silver tankard. Was the oak chest still there? She stepped over the threshold of the house and came into the stone-flagged hall, and it was gone. In its place stood a hateful little bamboo table. She was growing accustomed now to the darkness of the hall and she stood and looked about her. As a child she had not noticed the position of the rooms. She saw now that the staircase was in front of her, with that remembered curving dip in the centre of each tread. There were two doors to the left, the dining-room and parlour she supposed, and to the right two stone steps led up to a door which like the one in the garden wall was set within a stone arch. It drew her, it was so attractive, and she went quickly up the steps, lifted the latch and stepped suddenly into warmth and light.

It was a big old-fashioned kitchen, stone-flagged like the hall. There·was an oak dresser filled with cheap china, a large table covered with a scarlet cloth and a low, white-washed ceiling. She saw to her relief that the original range had been replaced by a modern Rayburn that was alight and filling the kitchen with warmth. A kettle was singing on the hob and a white cloth covered one half of the table. On it was set out an exquisite Staffordshire tea-service, deep mulberry-colour with a pattern of vine leaves. One plate was filled with door-step slices of bread and butter and another supported a grocer's cake of a strange shade of yellow. There was milk and sugar and a painted tin tea-caddy. Mrs. Baker's tea? Or hers? She had left the door into the hall ajar and the smell of lilies of the valley was drifting in to her. Yet there had been none in the hall. She told herself she must be getting tired and confused. There was a window opening on to a small walled kitchen garden, beside the half-open back door, and she went to the door and looked out. There was a bed of lilies of the valley growing under the window, nearly strangled by weeds but smelling like heaven. She was tired and confused indeed, for the next thing she knew she was outside on her knees grubbing up the weeds to give the lilies light and air. And then she was picking a bunch of them.

"There now," said a voice behind her. "I'd just gone down behind the apple trees to bring in the tea towels, what I washed this morning, and just that minute you come. Would you believe it? And I've been to the front door ten times if once this last hour, to welcome you like. Had a good journey, dear?"

Mary got to her feet and found herself confronting a little woman whose head scarcely reached her shoulder. Sparse grey hair was done up in an old-fashioned bun and very bright hazel eyes twinkled in a brown wrinkled face. She wore a white apron over an electric blue cardigan and a purple skirt, and her hands were full of clean tea towels. Her smile was wise and loving and there breathed from her whole person that sense of comfort and security, spiced with severity, that in the days of Mary's childhood had characterized the best nannies. She knew in one glance at Mrs. Baker that she had met her best friend, the best she had ever had or would have.

"Yes, I had a good journey," she said, "but it seemed a long way and I'm dying for a cup of tea."

"Come along in then, miss," said Mrs. Baker. "It's all ready."

Mary paused for a moment to look at the kitchen garden. Gooseberry bushes, a few apple trees, an old fig tree growing against the wall and the rest a tempest of weeds. But it appeared that someone had tried to do something for in one place there was a cleared patch. "Taties," said Mrs. Baker, following her glance. "Baker put 'em in on Good Friday. Thought you'd like 'em. He's done what he could in the garden, mowing the grass and such, for love like, but he couldn't do much, not with his tubes affecting his heart. And he's a bodger by rights, not a gardener. But he'll carry up your luggage later. I've told him to come along."

They were in the kitchen now and Mrs. Baker was making the tea. What is a bodger? Mary wondered. And what did Mrs. Baker mean by saying that Mr. Baker had mowed the grass for love? "You'll have tea with me, Mrs. Baker?" she asked.

Mrs. Baker's sallow face flushed a little and she answered with quiet dignity, "If you wish it, miss. Or would you prefer me to say madam?"

"I'd rather you called me dear, like you did at first," said Mary. "It made me feel at home."

"It slipped out," said Mrs. Baker. "You had a look of poor old Miss Lindsay, standing there." She regarded the elegant woman pouring out the tea. "She had your figure and kept it to the end. Lonely she was, poor old soul. People were scared of her but in her good times she was as sane as I am."

"And the bad times?" asked Mary.

Mrs. Baker hesitated. "She suffered," she said. "But

afterwards, she never spoke of it. There are those who tell you the sick in mind don't suffer like you think they do. Well, dear, all I can say is, they lie."

"Most of us tend to belittle all suffering except our own," said Mary. "I think it's fear. We don't want to come too near in case we're sucked in and have to share it." She was silent, but she did not feel the shrinking of which she had spoken. She wished she could have shared Cousin Mary's bad times. She was ashamed that she had not and presently she said to Mrs. Baker, "I only saw my cousin once. My father brought me to see her when I was a little girl. Then he died and I never came again. When she left me her house I could not believe it."

"She knew what she was doing," said Mrs. Baker. "Such as poor Miss Lindsay, they've their own wisdom. Often they'll know what's right when a normal person would only know what was expedient."

Mrs. Baker's understanding both astonished and supported Mary. She was aware that her new life was not going to be altogether a pastoral idyll. She was going to need Mrs. Baker. "You will help me as you helped my cousin, won't you?" she asked. "How many hours a week did you work for her?"

"Miss Lindsay's lawyer, Mr. Judson, paid me to come for two hours three mornings a week, dear," said Mrs. Baker. "Would that suit you?"

"Could it be every morning just at first?" pleaded Mary. "Could you manage that, or have you other people to work for?"

"I don't work for anyone else," said Mrs. Baker. "I do oblige occasionally here and there but nothing regular. You see the old lady——" she caught herself up. "Yes, I could come every morning until you're straight."

A suspicion began to dawn in Mary's mind and she remembered that Mrs. Baker had said her husband had worked in the garden for love. "I believe you worked for my cousin for many more hours than you were paid, Mrs. Baker," she said.

"Well, I was in night and morning," agreed Mrs. Baker. "She needed me, poor soul."

"We must put that right," said Mary.

She had said the wrong thing for Mrs. Baker stiffened. Her mouth tightened and her eyes flashed. Mary inwardly quailed before her and she was not by nature a quailer. There was steel and fire in Mrs. Baker, she realized, and a sense of what was right and proper that could not be outraged. This indigenous country pride was something she had not encountered before and she would have to learn about it. "I understand," she said gently. "I'm sorry. You loved my cousin, of course. And Mr. Baker, will he be so good as to continue to do a bit in the garden?" She smiled. "Not this time for love."

"You could ask him," said Mrs. Baker. "He'll be round soon to carry up your luggage. Come to that he's here now."

Mr. Baker was knocking at the back door. He was as tall as his wife was tiny, and cadaverous as Don Quixote. He had ginger hair, a walrus moustache, a sad thin mouth and receding chin. He wore corduroy trousers tied below the knee with string and a strange duffel coat that hung so loosely from his gaunt shoulders that Mary was sure it had been bought at a jumble sale. When she smiled and held out her hand his answering smile was so gentle and deprecating, and the stare of his china-blue eyes so sweet and blank, that for a moment she wondered if he was perhaps a little childish. Then his great hand took hers in a fearful grip and his eyes abruptly focused upon hers with a hard and penetrating look that seemed to come out at the back of her head. She was extremely alarmed but she managed to ask him if he would continue to help in the garden. There was a long pause and his Adam's apple began to work in his long thin throat. His voice, when it came, was that of a bronchitic corncrake.

"Might do," he said at last.

"I don't know the rate of pay here," said Mary, "but you and Mrs. Baker will tell me."

Mr. Baker's Adam's apple was again working. "I've never worked in this garden for pay," he brought out.

"But you will now?" Mary pleaded.

"I think the lady would prefer it, Baker," said his wife.

He ruminated over this for a long time. "Might do," he said. Then suddenly he stumped into the kitchen and went

stalking through it like doom, his coat swinging behind him,
out through the hall to the front door and down the passage
to fetch her luggage.

"Could I put these in water, Mrs. Baker?" Mary asked
shakily, picking up the lilies. She felt shaky, so awe-in-
spiring was Mr. Baker when set in motion. "Is there, do
you think, a silver tankard that I could put them in?"

Mrs. Baker opened the door of a cupboard in the wall
where a row of jugs and mugs hung on hooks. The tankard
was among them. "This do, dear?" she asked, taking it
down.

"Thank you," said Mary with extravagant gratitude. She
filled it with water, arranged her flowers in it and carried
them out and put them on the bamboo table in the hall.
Then she had to move hastily aside, for Mr. Baker was
coming back into the hall with her hat-box on his back,
hung round his neck by the strap, two heavy suit-cases one
in each hand, and two more cases, her dressing-case and
writing-case, gripped to his sides under his armpits. Thin
as he was the weight seemed nothing to him. He tramped
by like a prophet, not glancing at her, his head up and his
eyes probing the darkness of the staircase as the eyes of
Elijah probed the thunderclouds. He mounted the stairs
two at a time and strode heavily down the passage above.
Then she heard him enter a bedroom and there was a re-
sounding crash as he dropped the lot.

Mrs. Baker was beside her. "I've put you in Miss Lindsay's room, dear. The other bedrooms, they're not really
habitable now. It's a comfortable bed. She died in it and
it's well aired." Mr. Baker came tramping down the
stairs. "That's right, Baker. If there's anything else in the
car put it in the hall. Then you can go. You can get the
tea for me at home if you've a mind. There's kippers in the
larder. I'm taking the lady upstairs. Leave your car outside tonight, dear, and we'll find somewhere to put it in
the morning."

Mr. Baker tramped away with a muttered, "Good night,
miss," but without a glance in his wife's direction. But
Mary did not doubt that he would get the tea. That Mrs.
Baker was accustomed to be obeyed she could see already,
yet she felt that Mr. Baker was no yes-man. He obeyed

under no compulsion but because he had deliberately chosen the path of peace.

They climbed the stairs and came to the room where Mr. Baker had dropped the luggage on the floor. Mrs. Baker gathered it together and put it tidy, while Mary looked round the room, with its two windows looking east and south on the garden. She thought it must be the same room where she had washed her hands because on the old-fashioned marble-topped washstand stood the honeysuckle china she remembered. "Has it always been there?" she asked Mrs. Baker. "It's not been brought from another room?"

"It's been there as long as I remember, dear," said Mrs. Baker. "And I was always in and out of this house even as a child. I used to help my father bring the milk round and I was very friendly with Mrs. Kennedy who looked after Miss Lindsay."

"Did she wear a white mob cap, very old-fashioned even for those days?" asked Mary, and as she poured out the hot water that Mrs. Baker had put beside the basin in a brass can, and washed her hands, she could feel again the soft scented towel against her face.

"Yes, dear. She died fifteen years ago, and then I came to look after Miss Lindsay. Mr. Postlethwaite the gardener, he lasted longer. You could see their graves from your window if the trees wasn't so tall and thick."

Drying her hands Mary went to the east window. It looked out over the lilacs to the church. The square tower rose straight in front of her, against a sky that was now golden, but the trees hid the gravestones. She leaned at the window, with the covered way just below her to her left, sniffing the scent of the wistaria and gazing down at the rose garden directly below her. There was a flutter of wings down there, and the blue and rosy hues of chaffinches and tits. She went to the south window and saw a garden held between tall old walls of rosy brick, with the remnants of what had once been a herbaceous border against one wall, flowering shrubs, overgrown and wild, against another and a green lawn between them. A mulberry tree and a weeping willow grew in the lawn and at the bottom of the garden was a copse of hawthorns, cherry trees and tall old crab apples in bloom. A mist was rising now and the shadows tangled in the trees were blue and mysterious. She fancied there was another garden over there, and another mulberry tree beyond her copse, and that she saw the chimney of a house, but it was difficult to see with the shadows so blue. They were as blue as the lawn was green, an intense and almost burning green in the evening light. Just at the end of the lawn, poised between the green and the blue, was a winged boy with bow and arrow raised, delicately beautiful and very strange. He stood in the centre of what had once been a lily pond, but there was no water there now. Mary heard again the ringing of birdsong. They were singing in the trees behind the cupid. Then she had the curious feeling that eyes were watching her from the depth of the copse. And the eyes were hostile. She drew back and turned and faced the bed. The eyes had given her a creepy sensation and the bed did nothing to reassure her.

It was a high bed with damask silk curtains. Those at the side hung from brass rails that could be folded back against the wall or drawn forward to exclude draughts. Behind the bed-head they hung in long folds. The many pillows were piled high and an old patched bedspread of the same silk covered the bed. Mary looked fixedly at the pillows and could almost see the old dying woman propped against them. Don't be a fool, she said to herself. A bed's a bed however many people die in it. What's a bed for? Sleep and death and each is as natural and right as the other.

"The curtains and bedspread have been cleaned," Mrs. Baker encouraged her. "The carpet the same. And Baker and I, we've papered this room, seeing the old paper looked a little dingy." She gave Mary a glance of kindly reassurance. "And we kept the bills for the paper, and for the cleaning, for you to pay. We knew you'd wish that."

The paper was white, patterned with small golden stars, and looked strangely bright and innocent against the worn old carpet, made of little pieces stitched together. It had once been the same red as the curtains and counterpane but like them it had faded to a soft dingy rose. The dressing-

table, wardrobe and chest-of-drawers were of heavy
mahogany, polished till they shone like glass. Suddenly
Mary realized that she was happy in this room, happy in
spite of the bed. It was a long, low-ceilinged room, quiet,
filled with the scent of flowers and the echo of birdsong.
"I shall like sleeping here," she said to Mrs. Baker.

CHAPTER III

I

On the top of the wall that divided the two gardens three children were sitting. It was not difficult to get to the top because their old mulberry was the easiest tree in the world to climb, and you just had to step from the fourth branch to the wall. And then, if you wanted to go down on the other side, there was a crab apple tree to help you. The trees, with their fresh and heavenly blossom, made the same sort of magical pattern about the children that the birds made, weaving their gold and silver songs in and out, but they could look through it and see the pond, the lawn, the willow that was now golden green and the window where the woman had been, leaning and looking out.

But they hated her. Sitting there in silence they would have done murder if they could. For this was their garden. The one behind them, utilitarian and impeccably tidy, was Father's garden, but this was theirs and they had played in it ever since they came to live here. The old lady hadn't minded and after she became too ill to leave her room it had become more their own than ever. Provided they avoided the times when Mr. and Mrs. Baker came they had had it all to themselves, and what it had meant to them, with its wild beauty and deep quiet, only Edith of the three of them would be able to express in years to come.

For only she would really remember this garden. The other two with their happy, objective minds would always be absorbed in the moment but she would look backwards and remember, and look forward and be afraid, and the present would always confuse her because she would never entirely live in it. She sat a little apart from the others, her chin cupped in her hands. She was a brown girl with smooth acorn-coloured skin, no colour in her cheeks and straight dark hair cut in a fringe across her forehead. She was small for her nine years, her body all sharp angles, her eyes a greenish-hazel fringed with dark lashes. She was the adopted sister of the other two, and though the children's parents took great care that it should make no difference yet it did. She felt unsure of herself and she hated her old-fashioned name, Edith. People said it suited her and that made it worse. It was difficult to remember that Rosemary, whom they called Rose because she was so round and pink, glowing and good-humoured, was a year younger than herself. It was always Rose who seemed to be the eldest for it was she who decided what they should do. Jeremy was six, sandy, fat and freckled. He was a comfortable child at present but he had a will of his own and might not be so comfortable later.

"It's been our garden for years," said Rose. "And now *she's* come. I'd like to put poison in her tea." She tried hard to speak venomously but venom being foreign to her nature she could never manage to sound nasty however nasty she wanted to be.

"I could shoot her with my catapult," suggested Jeremy.

"Perhaps she will let us still play in the garden," said Edith.

"What will be the good of that?" demanded Rose. "It won't be ours any more."

Edith wondered. A garden had to be your own before it would let you in, and even your own garden did not give up its secrets unless it liked you. But if a garden had once been your own did it disown you when somebody else took possession of it? She did not think so.

They were silent until Jeremy turned his head towards home and sniffed. The open kitchen window was not very far from the mulberry tree. "There's a cake baking," he said hoarsely. He was always hoarse when desire consumed him, and just at present in his growing state he yearned after food like a saint after heaven. Luckily he had the kind of mother who did not use her palette knife too efficiently when transferring her cake mixture from the mixing basin to the tin. The forefinger of her youngest, if washed first, was expected to have a good wipe round. Jeremy silently disappeared. Though possessed of an astonishing capacity for noise he could be as silent as a Red Indian in pursuit of food.

"I think I'll put Martha to bed," said Rose. Martha was her hamster, who lived in a mansion with stairs on top of the bookcase in the living-room. And Rose too disappeared, leaving Edith alone.

She got to her feet, walked along the wall and climbed into the branches of a stout crab apple tree. She could climb trees as nimbly as a cat. Even now, all sharp points and angles as her body was, she could move with a sure-footed ease that would presently be grace. She climbed down the tree without even faintly disturbing the thrush who was singing in the highest branch. The birds seldom took any notice of her as she came and went smoothly as a sunbeam among them. At the foot of the tree she was on the rough grass and primrose leaves that carpeted the little copse, spun round with birdsong and gossamer shadow. In her smoke-blue slacks and blue jumper she looked like a shadow herself as she slipped through the trees, ran a few steps over the bright green grass and sat down on the edge of the pool.

She sat with her hands linked round her knees and her feet in the empty mossgrown basin. She did not look to-wards the house for she knew it was all right. There were no faces at any of the windows. They had gone away. She always knew if she was being looked at for she felt at once awkward and unsure of herself. When no one could see her she was relaxed and happy. She looked up at the boy, one of the best friends that she had, for he could be relied upon never to look at her. He looked only westward for he aimed his arrow always at the heart of the sinking sun, that on some evenings would poise itself like a flaming orange on top of the garden wall. His smooth limbs were of greenish bronze and his face was absorbed and remote. Close curls covered his head and his wings were spread. As soon as he had loosed his arrow he would be gone. Yet Edith was sure he knew she was here and liked to have her sitting on the edge of his pool. She had shared the ownership of the garden with him only, for though she had acquiesced when Rose and Jeremy said the garden belonged to the three of them yet in her heart, with a small secret scorn, she had repudiated their ownership. And with an angry leap of the heart she denied even part ownership to that woman with the clear pale face and grey hair whom she had seen at the window. I was here first, thought Edith. She can walk in it if she likes, I'll let her, like I let the old lady, but it's mine, not hers. And the little things are mine. All of them. Not only Queen Mab and the ivory coach and the tea-set of blue glass but all of them.

She looked towards the house, remembering the day when she had first seen them, when the old lady had been still alive but upstairs in her bed. Jeremy had sent his ball in through the open door of the little conservatory where the vine grew and she had crept in to retrieve it for him, and through the window she had seen the little things. She had gazed at them with her heart beating in her throat, and then she had picked up the ball quickly and gone away again because she did not want the other two to know. They must not know for they'd want them. And they were hers. No one must know about them but her. She came back again when she was alone, came back again and again. Kneeling in the green shade of the vine leaves, her arms propped on the low sill of the closed window, she would go into a sort of trance, staring and staring. She knew every one of the little things by heart, knew the number of them and how they looked when the sunbeams came through the vine leaves and how they looked when there was no sun. She adored them all, but especially Queen Mab in her ivory coach and the blue glass tea-set. They were more to her than anything in the world.

And then the old lady became very ill and soon after that she woke up one morning with a sense of threatening danger. She had been dreaming about her little things and it had been a confused and unhappy dream. Were they safe? Had anything happened? She had felt sick with fear and later in the day she had been able to escape from the others, climb over the wall and run to the conservatory unseen. They were there. As she sank to her knees she felt as sick with relief and joy as before she had felt sick with fear. They were there and for the first time since she had found them the window was open at the bottom. She climbed in and removed the glass shade. Now she could not only see them but with the tip of her finger touch them. She touched the ivory coach and the blue glass tea-set, and then somewhere in the house beyond the little parlour a door closed and she heard a step on the stairs. Her heart leapt and then sank. Someone was coming to take away the little things.

It was then that she had committed her crime, the sin that had been secretly corroding her ever since, making her thinner than ever, giving her nightmares and sudden unexplainable attacks of sickness, and making her afraid of going to church because of that phrase "descended into hell". Sometimes she forgot it and was happy, as she had been happy just now sitting by the pond, and she tried hard to forget, and then suddenly she would remember again. Yet she was glad she had done it, and she would have done it again, for when she had next crept up to the window the little things had gone.

Had they been put back to greet the new lady? She must know, for if they had not been put back then perhaps they had gone for ever. She got up and moved towards the house, a wraith in the gathering dusk. Her way led her obliquely under the branches of the willow tree, for she would not have dreamed of crossing the lawn without going through the willow tree. Inside it was another of her special places. She stood for a moment with the gold falling all about her, as though she stood in the secret place under a waterfall, and then she parted the golden water and went on to the conservatory and kneeled down at the window. The table was empty. She felt very desolate and getting up she drifted sadly away through the willow branches, through the copse and over the wall, and the boy was left in sole possession of the garden.

2

I'm too tired to do any more, thought Valerie. She put down her brush and paint pot and straightened her aching back. Then turning round she leaned her arms on the top of the gate. There was no one to be seen, and nothing to be heard except that thrush singing in the little copse between the Talbots' garden and the garden of The Laurels. For a moment she thought she saw a gleam of blue in the Talbots' mulberry tree and thought, Those wretched children, but then it was gone. The silence oppressed her. They might all be dead, she thought, and then with a pang of bitterness, I wish they were. Paul too.

A few years ago, when such thoughts had trickled into her vacant mind, it had shocked her that she of all people could think such things, she whom everyone admired so much for her selfless devotion to her blind husband. She had pushed them down to wherever they had come from but they had kept coming up again and now she no longer cared. What did it matter? They were not really her and no one knew, for Paul couldn't see her face or read her thoughts. So long as she cooked his meals and slaved for two, that was all he cared about. Other blind men did things, earned good wages. With all the wonderful gadgets invented for them the blind could be as useful these days as the sighted. But Paul was idle, content to spend his days tramping through the woods with his dog or drinking with his cronies at the local, and his evenings droning into his tape recorder in the tiny room he called his study, or just mooning, imagining he was working and pleased as punch if he was paid a small sum for a poem or article once in six months. Meanwhile they were poor, with nothing but his disability pension and the bit of money that Grannie had left her. They hadn't even been able to afford a child, but for that she was thankful for Paul would have been a rotten father. She flattered herself no one knew about the poverty. To keep the cottage and its tiny garden pretty as paint, herself smart and up-to-date and Paul as tidy as was possible for a man who had been born untidy, was what she lived for. But unable to afford any help in cottage or garden she was sure the work was killing her. Let it. She didn't care. When she was dead Paul might be sorry.

She glanced across at The Laurels. What was that woman like? She had caught a glimpse of her passing in her car. Old, like they all were. There was no one young here except Joanna and Roger Talbot and they were so rapt up in each other and their wretched kids that they were no use to anyone. Old, it went without saying, but good looking and a marvellous suit. But probably she was no use, and anyhow she wouldn't stay. Anyone would go round the bend living in that ghastly house. No, she won't stay, thought Valerie, and if she does I wouldn't have time to be friends. I'm too tired to bother.

She picked up her paint pot and carried it to the little garage beside the cottage. Their car was a second-hand one and she was ashamed of it. However much she cleaned and polished the thing it still looked awful. But it was all they could afford and she had to have a car for the shopping. She wasn't strong enough now to bike everywhere. She wished they could move to the town but Paul would not budge. A blind man was best in the country, he said, it was less confusing and he needed the quiet for his work.

Valerie came round to the front of the cottage again and her habitual mood of sullen endurance was warmed by a glow of pride. It really looked very pretty, with the new turquoise paint against the pink walls, the small latticed windows and the steep hillocky old roof. It was a tiny place, and sometimes when Valerie complained of the vast amount of work she had to do her friends silently wondered why. For the garden was as small as the cottage. Behind the clipped escalonia hedge and the wrought-iron gate there were only two flower-beds, filled now with tulips, and a paved path to the front door, and at the back of the cottage a little vegetable plot bordering on the orchard of the Dog and Duck. Yet her friends had to agree that there was never a weed to be seen in Valerie's garden, or a speck of dust in her perfect rooms. One had to hand it to her that she did everything she did supremely well.

She went into her sitting-room, with the charming chintz curtains and covers that she had made herself and the horse brasses hanging over the old fireplace, consumed by a longing for a cup of tea, but when she glanced at the little gilt clock on the mantelpiece she saw there was no time if she was to have supper ready punctually. She cooked exquisitely and elaborately. In the early days of their marriage Paul, who had simple tastes and a shocking digestion since the war, had put in a plea for steamed fish and an occasional rice pudding, but Valerie had been so terribly hurt that ever since he had dutifully eaten whatever she set before him, and taken bi-carb. afterwards.

In her dainty kitchen-dining-room, tying on her flowered overall, Valerie said to herself, No time even for a cup of tea. That's married life. What's to happen to Paul and me? Do we just go on and on like this till we go mad? Or I do, for he won't. I don't think I'd find him so maddening if only he'd realize how rotten our life is. But he never realizes anything. He's self-centred as a cow. Her thoughts ran on in this habitual manner, a tragic Greek Chorus to the central figure, until there came a sudden check. . . . I liked that woman, she thought. She looked as though she's had an interesting life. Not like me. . . . And then the Chorus was back and telling her what rotten luck it had been that she, at nineteen, not long out of school, should have married a man who a few months after their marriage was back on her hands a blind and nerve-shattered wreck. And his plane had been shot down in the last two weeks of the European phase of war. If it had ended a fortnight earlier it wouldn't have happened. She could remember as though it was yesterday standing in the hospital corridor on VE-day, waiting for permission to go in and see Paul, trembling and reluctant, for suffering in any form terrified her, thinking that it was VE-Day and everyone had been happy and rejoicing in the streets, and this had happened to her and Paul. Of course it had been awful for Paul but it had been much worse for her. It was always worse for the wife. Everybody said so. And it got worse still as time went on because people did not sympathize with you any more. They couldn't do enough for you at first, and that helped, and then they got bored with your troubles. But your troubles went on just the same and you had to bear them alone. Again came the check. . . . That really *was* a marvellous suit. I wonder what she gave for it?

3

"A very good-looking woman," said Colonel Adams to his wife as they sat over their late tea. They did not have supper, just cocoa and bread and butter when they went to bed, cocoa being cheap, so they had a late tea. It helped to pass the evening for happy though they were together the evenings did sometimes seem long, especially in the winter. The fact was that by the time they had done the work that had to be done in the cottage, cooked and eaten their frugal lunch and washed up afterwards, they were tired and

couldn't do much more for the rest of the day except sit;
out in the garden in warm weather, in front of the fire in
winter.

Colonel Adams was eighty-two and crippled with
arthritis. He had suffered with a grim and humorous hero-
ism for many years but now the joints were fixed and he was
in less pain; but it was difficult to get about on his two sticks.
Mrs. Adams was younger, a little creature who hardly
reached to her husband's shoulder, but her physique had
not been equal to the strain of bearing her four sons, losing
three of them in the war and having the fourth turn out so
disappointing. Then there had been the perpetual planning
and contriving that had been necessary with the cost of
living ceaselessly rising and Service pensions staying where
they were. And so now she was delicate. They had had a
little private money once but Charles's debts had swallowed
most of that long ago. One couldn't refuse to help one's own
son, especially one so beloved as Charles.

But if life had been hard for Mrs. Adams it had never
occurred to her to think so, and her soft face was serene as a
kitten's. It had never occcurred to the Colonel to complain
either. His lean brown face, with bushy white eyebrows and
white cavalry moustache, was wrinkled in lines of perpetual
good humour. It was only their evident exhaustion and the
faded blue eyes of both of them that suggested suffering.
Nothing else. They had each other. An unusually happy
marriage, its selflessness strengthened by shared tragedy,
had grown into something more, an identification so close
that each could be said to have passed beyond the barriers of
self and to live in the other with an immediacy that very
largely shut out thought of the future. Largely, not entirely.
The thought of death did come at times and they would
smile at each other and say, "We'll go together." But in
each was the fear, never expressed to the other, that it
might not be so. They hardly realized the uniqueness of
their love, and their good fortune in its possession, though
they did know they were happy. The discontent and unhappiness of others was a great puzzle to them, especially
if those others happened to have television. At the heart of
their mutual content was this mutual longing for a TV. It
was not an acquisitive longing, it was almost the mystical

longing of a child for the morning star. On the few occasions when they had seen it, and had sat before it spellbound, it had seemed to them an unbelievable magic. And so their longing was not a corroding one, because no one expects to possess the morning star. They did not speak of it to each other because neither liked the other to think that they wanted anything more than the riches they had in each other.

"A very good-looking woman indeed," repeated Colonel Adams, who had always had a harmless eye for a pretty woman. "And looked as though she could play a good hand of bridge."

Now there was another thing that it would have been nice to have, more frequent bridge, and of this they did sometimes speak to each other because it was an attainable thing. It only needed a little change in the village population to bring it about. Colonel Adams played a first-rate hand and Mrs. Adams, who had not liked the game originally but had taught herself to like it for her husband's sake, was adequate, the Vicar was more than adequate but not yet quite first-rate, though Colonel Adams had hope for him. But the Vicar had other things to do, and a counter passion for chess, and they hesitated to call upon him too often. Valerie Randall could play a good hand, and when commanded by the Vicar to come with him to Holly Cottage she would do so, for she was scared of the old Vicar. His manners were exquisite but he could be sarcastic and she was not at all sure that she liked her. He liked her husband and she was always uneasy with those who liked Paul. So her bridge too was uneasy and she always had her eye on the clock, haunted by the thought of all the things she had to do at home. Valerie as a fourth was better than nothing but she was not quite what one wanted. And the three old people sitting round the table with her knew quite well, as old people always know, that she thought all old people a damned nuisance. There was Mrs. Hepplewhite at the manor, of course, but they couldn't appeal to her because she was so extraordinarily kind. Had she known of their desire she would have whisked them in her Bentley to every bridge party for miles round. That was the trouble with Mrs. Hepplewhite's kindness. Once let loose it was

like a roaring cataract and one had to be very strong to
stand against the current and live.

"Not a young woman," Colonel Adams assured his wife.
"Grey-haired. Fiftyish. Looked as though she'd enjoy her
bridge."

"Perhaps we could call," suggested Mrs. Adams. It was a
tremendous suggestion for they hadn't called on anyone for
years.

"How do we get there?" asked her husband. It was not
far, only down the lane, round the corner and across the
green, but it was a long way for them.

"We get to church on our good days," said Mrs. Adams.
"And it's not much farther. We'll have an early lunch one
day, have our rests and then go. Does she look like the sort
of woman who will give us tea when we get there? That
would help for the going back."

"She looked like a woman who would do everything cor-
rectly," said Colonel Adams. "In the way we are accustomed to. Is there another cup of tea left in the pot?"

She poured him out a third cup of tea, smiling to think
how much he could still tell about a woman in one glance.
Then she turned her chair to the wood fire that was burning
in the grate, for though it was May the wind was in the east
and a little fire was comforting in the evenings. Their next-
door neighbour, Mrs. Eeles the gamekeeper's wife, was very
good about running in and doing the grate, and other jobs
that were difficult for Mrs. Adams, and her husband Bert
looked after their tiny garden for them though they could
pay him next to nothing for doing so. Everyone was so
kind. Colonel and Mrs. Adams never ceased to be touched
and astonished by the kindness and generosity that they
met on all sides. They couldn't understand it. It was
wonderful.

Colonel Adams finished his tea and turned his chair too
round to the fire and lit his pipe. The little room was
shabby and charming. The remnants of a beautiful carpet
they had acquired long ago in India had been skilfully
pieced together by Mrs. Eeles and fitted to the wainscot.
The yellow curtains and chair covers were faded and darned
but still pretty. There were books, photographs of their
children and a few bits of rare china that could not be sold

because they were cracked. And the card-table. It was Queen Anne, with candle-slides and elegant legs, the only thing of value left to them, and they were resolved not to part with it for anything in the world the antique shops of Westwater could offer them. Outside the window the evening light was turning the garden to magic and in the wood the cuckoo was still calling.

"Five months," said Mrs. Adams and sighed with satisfaction. Her husband knew what she meant and held out his hand to her. She meant that they could now expect five months of reasonable warmth. Their bills would go down, with no coal and less electricity. They would not catch so many colds and they would feel better. Above all that fear that each kept so carefully concealed would be laid to rest. It was in January and February that old people died, not in the summer when their blood was warmer and their heart-beats steadier. She took his hand and laid it in her lap.

"Tom," she whispered, her face alight with the joy of divulging a secret she had been keeping for this moment, "there's a fowl for lunch tomorrow, plucked and ready for me to cook. Gladys from the Vicarage brought it this morning while you were in the garden."

4

At the Vicarage too they were having a late tea, for the Vicar had been visiting outlying farms.

"I saw her as I was coming out of the post office," said Jean Anderson timidly.

"Who?" snapped the Vicar. His sister started at the sharpness of his question, tears came into her eyes and her tea slopped over into the saucer. They had lived together for ten years now and still she could not get used to the quickness of his speech, his unintentional sarcasm and the pouncing vigour of his mind. And he on his side could not learn to adjust himself to her weakness and incompetence, though he tried hard, and with resolute loyalty always refused to look back to those halcyon days when he had lived alone. Poor Jean. She was the one weakling in a brilliant and healthy family. Very odd. Their mother had had some illness or other just before her birth, he remembered, and perhaps that had had something to do with

it. She'd never been able to do anything much and had
lived at home with her parents, always ailing though never
with any specific disease. Nothing wrong mentally but
just slow in the uptake. And now she was fifty-six and
looked seventy, with a tall, thin frame that wavered like a
bending poplar as she walked, dazed blue eyes that she
protected when she was out with dark glasses, and thin
wispy grey hair that was always falling into her eyes. She
wore terrible wool jumpers and cardigans she knitted for
herself, for knitting was one of the things she had learnt
to do and she enjoyed it. And she loved her hens.

The Vicar recollected something. "Did that fowl go up
to Holly Cottage?" he demanded sharply.

"Yes, James," she said shakily, and the tears ran over.
She felt for her handkerchief and wiped them away. He
remembered suddenly what her hens meant to her, and
how deeply she felt the occasional necessary liquidations.
With compunction he got up and came to her, a piece of
Gladys's marvellous plum cake in his left hand, and put his
right on her shoulder.

"I'm sorry, Jean. I spoke sharply but I don't mean it.
It's my way. I'm always telling you." He gave her shoulder
a friendly little shake and went back to his place. "What
were you saying just now? You had seen whom?"

"The new Miss Lindsay. Coming to The Laurels."

"God help her," said the Vicar. "The state that house
and garden must be in. What sort of woman?"

Jean hesitated, struggling to find the right words. It was
all there in her mind, very clear, but she could never match
the right words to the vivid pictures that she saw.

"I think," she said at last, "she would be called smart."
And then she could have bitten her tongue out. That wasn't
the right word for that graceful woman who had leaned forward and smiled at her as she passed. She had had that
bright scarf round her neck. It was a wonderful colour
and Jean's slightly sentimental imagination had seen her as
a tall gladiolus. She had been afraid of her, of course, for
she was always frightened of strangers, but she had been
attracted too.

"Smart?" ejaculated the Vicar. "Then God help us.
Like the Hepplewhite?"

"Oh no, no!" said Jean, almost in tears again. "Oh no, not like *her*!" Mrs. Hepplewhite was the president of the Women's Institute. Her husband had bought the Manor House up on the hill after the old squire had died, but he was not at all like the old squire, dear old Sir Ambrose Royston. With her great kindness and capability Mrs. Hepplewhite knew exactly how to help everybody, including Miss Anderson whom with untiring perseverance she was endeavouring to cajole into "going out more". Jeant spent a great deal of time in her company because she was in all her nightmares, and she had constant nightmares. "No!" she said again.

"Well then, if she didn't scare you stiff go in tomorrow morning and see if there's anything we can do for her."

"Go and see her?" gasped Jean, and began to tremble. James did not know of course how terrified she was of that fearful house. She had never told him, or anyone, about that day when the queer old lady had popped out of the green door in the wall, like a spider out of its web, just as she was passing, seized her wrist and dragged her inside, up the stone-flagged path into the dark dreadful house and —and—— Her pulse was racing madly and the sweat started out on her forehead. "The Laurels?" she whispered. "Go to The Laurels?"

"Of course," said the Vicar briskly. "Say I'll be calling in a day or two." He pushed his chair back. "I'll go along to my study. Haven't dealt with the post yet."

He strode from the room. Walk was not a word that could be used to describe his mode of progression. He was a tall Scot, lean but with large bones, and moved always as though over his native heather, with long, steady strides. Yet only his youth and his holidays had been spent in Scotland. All his working life had been passed in Oxford, where he had been Fellow and Tutor at the same college where he had been an undergraduate, with only a few years break as a schoolmaster in between. For many years he had lived in rooms in college in wonderful comfort and seclusion, cared for by an excellent and devoted scout, Arthur Brewster, writing scholarly books, lecturing superbly, dining well, one of the institutions of the place and utterly contented with his mode of life. Then his mother

had died and to his intense annoyance and dismay Jean
had come upon his hands. But he had not shirked her for
he was not a shirker. He had taken a house in north Oxford,
installed Jean and prevailed upon Arthur and his wife
Gladys to come and look after them both. This had worked
reasonably well except that Jean had been very miserable
in Oxford. She had not been able to keep hens in the little
garden and she had been terrified of her brother's friends;
old men, sarcastic and brilliant, who knew their own
abstruse subjects inside out but did occasionally profess
ignorance upon other subjects, and even more brilliant
young men who knew everything. But young and old they
had been alike equally incomprehensible to Jean. She had
grown more frail, more muddled, and would not leave the
house and garden because the traffic frightened her.

Then had come the time for retirement and it had been
borne in upon James Anderson that for Jean's sake he must
leave Oxford. The prospect, for him, had been appalling,
for the roots he had put down in the place had gone under
the very walls of the buildings like the roots of a poplar
tree. Nevertheless, grim-faced, he had decided to hack
them out, for that was his duty. But where should he go?
It must be the country for Jean's sake, and not too far from
Oxford for his, so that he could go back now and again and
gently comfort the torn remnants of those root ends that
still remained under the buildings. But where? It was in
this dilemma that a friend had suggested to him that he
should seek ordination and a country living. He had been
all his life a convinced Anglican but this suggestion had
taken him by surprise. He had felt unworthy. But later,
after thinking it out and discussing it with those best
qualified to help him, he had come to see it as God's will
for himself and Jean. By taking a country living he would
be setting a younger man free for an industrial parish, or
one of the new housing estates into which the hordes of the
heathen English were now pouring in their thousands, or
the mission field. He had good health and private means.
He would be able to take a living with a small stipend,
would not find the work too much for him and would have
leisure for the writing of his books. So he had gone to a
theological college for a year, leaving Jean still in north

Oxford in the care of the Brewsters but much happier when he was away. After his ordination they went to Appleshaw, the devoted Brewsters going with them.

How fortunate he was in the Brewsters James Anderson did not perhaps sufficiently consider, for he belonged to a generation that had taken good service and comfortable living for granted, but he was grateful for the small dignified Georgian house in which he lived, his garden, his study and his peace. As a parish priest he was thankful to find that he got on reasonably well. The glorious church gave him profound satisfaction and to administer the sacraments within it, as so many other men had done before him, shook him as nothing had shaken him yet. For a man who had been lecturing all his life preaching only needed a little readjustment, and he barked out short scholarly sermons twice a Sunday with no trouble at all. He got on famously with the indigenous country folk, men like Joshua Baker and Bert Eeles. He found that he understood them as well as liked them, and they on their side liked his Scottish integrity and forthrightness. But the women! Not the countrywomen, whom he liked nearly as well as their husbands, but the Hepplewhite and those like her, and that appalling woman Valerie Randall. He had never liked women. They had souls to be saved, he knew, but his knowledge remained purely academic. But there were those in the parish whom he loved with a steady and reverent affection, Colonel and Mrs. Adams, Mrs. Croft the district nurse, Dr. Fraser, a gruff and sensible fellow Scot, and Paul Randall, and to them he humbly hoped that he was sometimes of use. If he was then he could be glad that he had come here.

At work at his study table he was aware of the Vicarage thrush singing at the bottom of the garden. The cadences of his song seemed to intensify the silence and deepen the blue of the spring evening. He laid down his pen and listened, not so much to the song as to the silence, and found it hard to believe that anything existed within it except himself and the thrush. He was Adam, in those days of blessed solitude before Eve came. Since he came to Appleshaw he had tasted solitude with more understanding than in his Oxford days, and for this knowledge also he was glad that he had come.

CHAPTER IV

I

MARY too, as she left her bedroom, was aware of the depth
of the country silence, but it was now her duty to turn her
attention to her bathroom. "Baker and I distempered it,"
said Mrs. Baker. "We felt we couldn't let you see it like it
was."

The bathroom was over the kitchen and looked out over
the kitchen garden. The walls were shocking pink and the
ceiling sky-blue. Tact was one of Mary's strong points and
as she smiled her appreciation there was no sign upon her
face of her inward recoil. The bath was an old-fashioned
one poised on four legs, with the enamel peeling off. It was
extremely small but on the other hand the mahogany
throne was approached by two steps. It seemed to Mary
that there was no wash-hand-basin, towel-rail, chair or
cupboard, but the light was growing dim and she put out
her hand for the switch. There did not seem to be one.
"There's electric light?" she asked.

"Oh no," said Mrs. Baker. "Lamps and candles. We've
only had the Rayburn the last two years. Those bills I told
you of are in the kitchen, and the bills for the tea and sugar
and eggs and that. I thought you must have something to
start you off, and I took bread and milk for you. It's all in
the larder." They were at the bottom of the stairs now
and Mary had gone down them stepping carefully in the
centre of the worn treads, as she had done as a child. "The
parlour and dining-room are clean but they've not been
lived in for some while, for Miss Lindsay was bedridden
at the last. They smell a bit damp and I laid a fire in
the parlour just in case you should wish to put a match to
it."

In the kitchen she gave Mary the bills and put on a
shrunken coat that hung behind the door. It must once
have been a child's and was as much too tight for her as
Baker's coat was too large for him. "I'll be round in the

morning at ten o'clock," she said. "You won't be nervous all on your own?"

"I don't think I've got a nerve in my body," said Mary. "I've been terrified, in the blitz, but never nervous. I slept alone in my London flat."

"Ah, you're used to it," said Mrs. Baker. "Good night, dear," and she banged the door behind her and was gone.

"Now I'm alone in my house," thought Mary. "Now it's beginning."

She went upstairs again and in the last of the sunset light unpacked her things, folding them carefully away in the drawers that Mrs. Baker had lined with clean white paper stopping sometimes to look at the room and get the feel of it, for she was one of those women to whom the privacy of her bedroom is as important as his shell to a snail. It was always a matter of astonishment to her that those religious who slept not in cells but in dormitories could retain their sanity. She supposed they abandoned their shell for love of God and in prayer found the sheltering of His hand instead. Mary herself came of an agnostic family but she had been confirmed at school, under pressure from her headmistress, had enjoyed singing hymns in chapel and still went to church at Christmas and Easter, finding herself deeply moved by the beliefs that were the rock beneath the charming traditions and practices. But where had she heard the phrase that had come into her mind, the sheltering of God's hand? She couldn't imagine. It had seemed to come from the room.

The light had nearly gone but she had taken possession of her shell. Many other women had called it theirs but they had passed and now it was hers. Her Chinese dressing-gown with the golden dragons lay on the bed and the silver-backed brushes and silver-topped bottles from her dressing-case, miraculously not smashed when Mr. Baker dropped it, sparkled on the grave Victorian mahogany dressing-table. John's photograph was on the mantelpiece and a volume of Jane Austen was by her bed. She liked Jane. She liked her cheerful sanity. She had expected no very great things of human nature, yet she had loved it, and in Mr. Knightley and Jane Bennett she had portrayed a quiet steady goodness that had been as lasting in literature as it would have been in life. And she had lived in a house much like this, in a village hidden in a quiet fold of green and rural England, and found her existence entirely satisfying. That's why I've come, thought Mary. To have a look at the few last fragments of her England before it is too late; that and to keep faith with Cousin Mary.

She groped her way down the stairs and struggled with the oil lamp that Mrs. Baker had put ready for her in the kitchen. She succeeded in lighting it at last and by its soft light ate a supper of cold ham, bananas and tea. By the time she had finished it was quite dark and she could see three stars in the window-pane. She was, she found, dreadfully tired and her limbs felt like lead as she washed up and stoked the Rayburn. But there was something she had to know before she went to bed. All day the surface of her mind had been obsessed with practical problems but all the time, in her heart and at the back of her mind, had been the little things. Were they still here?

Putting off the moment of knowing she took the lamp and went first to the dining-room. A blast of cold air met her face as she opened the door. It was a small room filled to capacity with the oak table, sideboard and chairs, one of them with a high carved back, that she remembered. A dingy Morris wallpaper was peeling off the wall and the brown oilcloth on the floor was full of holes. There was a scurry of mice and the smell of them. Mary shut the door again hastily and went on to the parlour. She stood with her hand on the door-handle afraid to go in. She remembered the mossy carpet strewn with roses, the sea-green light shining through the vine leaves and the table with the plush cover. Then she summoned her courage and opened the door.

It was not so changed as the dining-room, for the beautiful panelled walls were untarnishable by time, and the carpet must have been well looked after for though it was faded it was still pretty. As Mrs. Baker said, a fire was laid in the basket grate. There were a couple of spindly chairs with gilt legs, an escritoire against the wall and the table with the plush cover still standing in the window. But the little things were not there.

2

Mary was awakened at five the next morning by the birds and felt it to be incredible that such small creatures could make such a row. She got out of bed to see what could be singing with such abandon, like one of the beloved music hall stars of the old days, and it was two blackbirds in the lilac opposite her east window. Their wide-open crocus-coloured beaks looked like the jaws of crocodiles and from them song poured forth. Leaning out of the window with her dressing-gown round her shoulders she could distinguish the heavenly music of the seraph thrush singing in the copse, and when the blackbirds paused for a moment she could hear the lark singing high overhead and the cuckoos calling in the distant woods. These songs woven together were an almost visible web of music lifting the earth from darkness to light.

She went back to bed and lay watching the movement of shadows on the wall, shadows of the branches, of birds' wings, of her curtains swaying, and listened to the striking of the church clock, the rustle of trees, and cows lowing in the distant fields. For these things were a part of her room and she must learn them by heart. When she went away she would come back to them as surely as she came back to John's photo on the mantelpiece and Jane Austen beside her bed, and would find in them a measure of her peace. The light grew stronger and the birds went about their business but she could not sleep again and she stretched out her hand for *Persuasion*. It was one of the loveliest love stories ever written, she thought, quiet and yet exciting. Although she practically knew it by heart yet upon each re-reading she recaptured that first deep anxiety lest Captain Wentworth should not come up to scratch. Yet anxiety was not a word one ought to use in connection with Jane, who was so eminently trustworthy. Perhaps it was a measure of her genius that she could arouse it. Would you have found me trustworthy had you married me? she asked the man in the photo opposite. I should have found you so. You had honour and fire with gentleness. I liked you, admired you, wanted to love you more and know you better. Would you have made me love you as I wanted to love you? Was I capable of knowing you? And if not then, am I now? Can you teach me? There was no answer in the great emptiness of death and she got up feeling suddenly cold and weary. She had never known what she believed about death, whether it was the end or whether it wasn't. She knew there could be no certainty, only faith. Could she find faith? Was there anyone here who could help her?

She washed and dressed, and on her way downstairs looked into the two bedrooms that Mrs. Baker had told her were uninhabitable. They had dry-rot in the floorboards, fungus growing in the corners and not a stick of furniture in either of them. What had happened to the furniture? What had happened to the oak chest and the little things? Feeling now thoroughly discouraged she went downstairs to the kitchen and found the Rayburn out. Her stoking the night before could not have been to its taste. Looking into the larder she found milk and cereal, bread and marmalade for breakfast, but her whole being ached for hot tea. She must have an oil stove, or calor gas, or something that would ensure a cup of tea when she wanted it, and eventually she must put in electricity. But it was not a priority. There were things far more pressing in this house than electricity.

After breakfast she fetched her writing-case and went into the little parlour to make a list of these priorities. It was a lovely day but she was cold after a tea-less breakfast and put a match to the fire. She sat down beside it with her blotting pad on her knee. There was a small window beside the chimney breast that looked west into the kitchen garden, and she saw to her delight that just outside it was a blossoming apple tree. The light of the flames was warmly reflected in the panelling and the sound of them was a voice murmuring of pleasant things beside her. She began to feel more cheerful. Like all women she enjoyed making lists, and even a list of her lists, and she lost track of time noting down repairs to the house in order of priority. Then she made another list of those of her possessions in store in London which would be suitable here, and another of those that would not. She was hard at it when Mrs. Baker's head came round the door.

"The Rayburn's out, dear. Now that's a funny thing. It never goes out. You made it up?"

"Yes, Mrs. Baker. I'm sorry."

"It's your riddling that's at fault. I'll show you before I go. Now I'll light it again and bring you a cup of hot tea. But first I must get the fowl on for your lunch. A boiler, and should eat soft. Baker took the liberty of killing one of ours for you. Give you a good start, we thought, with soup from the bones. And he also took the liberty of inquiring of Jack Beckett at the pub if you could keep your car there, seeing as you've no garage. You're welcome, Jack says. There's plenty of room in the barn where he keeps his. We hope you don't mind, dear."

"Of course not, Mrs. Baker. Thank you very much."

Tired and cold, she felt near to tears. Strong and self-reliant woman that she was, no one had looked after her since John had died. Mrs. Baker looked at her. "A cup of tea is what you need, dear. And I'll get Baker to bring you down my little spirit stove and kettle. Then whether the Rayburn's out or in you'll always be able to get yourself a cup of tea."

The tea when it came in the beautiful Staffordshire teapot was placed beside her on the little plush-covered table. "Mrs. Baker, can you tell me of a good builder and decorator?" she asked.

"Well, there's Roundham in Westwater. But he'll charge you a pretty penny. And there's my husband's nephew Bill Baker in Thornton. He's a good worker, Bill is, and employs good men. Not so classy as Roundham but more reliable."

"I'll have Bill Baker," said Mary. She looked round. "Is there a telephone?"

"Telephone? No, dear. What would poor old Miss Lindsay have been doing with a telephone? Drop Bill a line. Twelve Mount Street, Thornton. Say I told you of him and he won't keep you waiting."

Mary put down her teacup and said hesitantly, "Mrs. Baker, when I was a little girl, and came here to see my cousin, a glass case was on this table and under it a whole host of little treasures. My cousin showed them to me and I loved them. Did she give them away?"

"No, they're here. I packed them away in one of the drawers in the escritoire, for safety. The glass case is in a cupboard in one of the spare rooms. Miss Lindsay would never have parted with the little things. They were for you. She's told me time and again how you loved them as a child."

"Did she part with many things?" asked Mary.

"She had to, dear. As time went on her money didn't go so far. She sold a lot of silver and valuable china, and the furniture in the spare rooms, and the chest in the hall."

"Didn't her lawyer get her an annuity?"

"He wanted to, but she wouldn't have it."

"But why not?" Mrs. Baker hesitated and with pity and compunction Mary answered her own question. "Because she wanted to leave something to me, a child she'd only seen once. I'm ashamed, Mrs. Baker."

"Well, dear, don't take on. It's a queer thing, but when I came to look at the little things, before I put them away, it seemed to me that there were a few missing. I couldn't say which they were, for I've never got the little things rightly in my head, but I thought there were one or two gone. It worried me."

"Perhaps Miss Lindsay gave them away."

"It wouldn't have been like her to do that, when she was keeping them for you."

There was a curious twanging sound, fumbling and a little eerie, and both women looked at each other. Then light dawned on Mrs. Baker. "Someone trying to ring the bell," she said. "That bell needs seeing to," and she left the room.

Mary followed her, for the weak twanging had almost sounded like a cry for help, and together she and Mrs. Baker dragged the screeching garden door back over the paving stones. Outside on the steps stood the woman whom she had seen coming out of the post office yesterday. She was dressed in the same clothes and carried a very large basket in which reposed a very small pot of blackberry jelly, and she was trembling so violently that the pot rattled in the basket. "It's Miss Anderson from the Vicarage, come to see you," said Mrs. Baker in encouraging tones, adding very low for Mary's private enlightenment, "Poor dear."

"Do please come in," said Mary. She had just been thinking of Cousin Mary, and now for a strange moment this woman seemed to be her. Yet there was not the slightest resemblance. She took her visitor's arm and they walked together up the paved path. At the front door Jean recoiled, as though at the mouth of the pit, and Mrs. Baker made encouraging noises behind her. "It *is* dark," said Mary, "but it's light in the parlour, and I've a fire there." She thought briefly that it had never occurred to her to call the panelled room the drawing-room or the sitting-room. It was the parlour and nothing else.

She installed Jean by the fire in one of the little gilt chairs, mentally adding two small armchairs of suitable period and repairing of the doorbell to her list of priorities, and Mrs. Baker fetched fresh tea. This seemed to revive Jean, though she had to hold her cup with both hands, and presently, while Mary talked about the beauty of Appleshaw, she set her cup down and removed her dark glasses. She sat facing the light and Mary could see her face, the most vulnerable face she had ever seen, with a taut look of suffering about the mouth. The eyes, blue and beautiful, were not the eyes of the woman whom Jean appeared to be, and looking into them Mary was aware of intelligence and courage. She realized with deep respect that this woman had always done what she had to do and faced what she had to face. If many of her fears and burdens would have seemed unreal to another woman there was nothing unreal about her courage. The dark glasses, Mary felt, were more of a psychological protection than a physical one. The lack of co-ordination between what she was in herself, and the jarred mechanism of body and nerves, had so deeply shamed her that she must hide. But with Mary she had taken her glasses off. Had she known that she had done it? Mary was afraid to speak lest she frighten them on again.

"My brother," said Jean, "wanted me to bid you welcome. He's the Vicar here, you know. He'll be coming to see you soon. He wanted to know if there's anything we can do." Her face was suffused with crimson but she had got it out.

"That's kind of you," said Mary, "but I'm settling down well and loving this house."

"Loving it?" whispered Jean.

"Did you know my cousin Miss Lindsay?" asked Mary, and was instantly aware that she had said the wrong thing, for Jean had begun to tremble again and was groping for her glasses. She was terrified of Cousin Mary, she thought, and she's still terrified of the house. "Let's go out into the garden," she said. "We can go out through the conservatory. We won't have to go back to the hall. The window opens almost down to the floor. Look, I'll help you."

But Jean resisted her helping hand for a moment while she groped in the basket for the pot of blackberry jelly. "For you," she said, holding it out. "I made it myself. Gladys helped me."

"Now I really feel I've come to live in the country," said Mary gratefully, as she put it on the mantelpiece. "There are trees and birds in London but not blackberries. I can't wait for the autumn in Appleshaw. Blackberries and the smell of bonfires, and the cherry trees scarlet along the edge of the woods."

"No, no!" cried Jean. "You must not hurry like that. I mean, it's spring. Each year, I mean—I want—but I can't do it!" She ended on a note of despair.

"You mean each year not to let the spring go racing by while you think of something else. You form your resolution and having formed it you look up and it's summer."

Jean nodded in astonishment and relief, as Mary helped her through the window. Mary had expressed it for her and the relief was physical as well as mental.

"The vine grows up through the floor!" cried Mary. This was the first time she had been in the conservatory. The trunk of the old vine grew straight up through the centre of the tessellated pavement of dim blue and green and spread out like an umbrella beneath the low domed glass roof. There was nothing else in the conservatory, though a shelf ran round it, waiting for flowers. Scented geraniums, thought Mary, and chrysanthemums in the winter.

The conservatory door was open and they passed out into the garden, breathless for a moment while spring broke over their heads like a wave. Jean was visited by one of her rare moments of happiness, one of those moments when the goodness of God was so real to her that it was like taste and scent; the rough strong taste of honey in the comb and the scent of water. Her thoughts of God had a home-liness that at times seemed shocking, in spite of their power, which could rescue her from terror or evil with an ease that astonished her. This morning, for instance, put-ting on her outdoor shoes in her bedroom to call on the new Miss Lindsay, terror had come upon her. The dread of meeting someone who did not know about her was one of her worst fears. They would try and talk to her, and she would not know what they were talking about, or if she did know, and she knew more often than people realized, and the answers were lucid in her mind, she would not be able to find the words to give them form. She would see the sur-prise in the face of the newcomer, the embarrassment, and then the relief with which he effected his escape. And to that fear had been added her terror of The Laurels, and the thing that had happened to her there. She had fumbled helplessly with the knotted laces of her shoes and got in a panic because she could not tie them. Because of course she had known she must go. She always did the thing because in obedience lay the integrity that God asked of her. If anyone had asked her what she meant by integrity she would not have been able to tell them, but she had seen it once like a picture in her mind, a root going down into the earth and drinking deeply there. No one was really alive without that root. And meanwhile she had not been able to get her shoes laced. She had stopped struggling, her hands sticky with fear and anxiety, and taking her shoes right off had turned back with blind trust to the beginning again, to the beginning of the action of obedience that always had a wholesome sweetness in it, though it was hard, a foretaste of the end with its humble thankfulness. And then, just as she had bent to pick up her left shoe, it had happened, and she had sat with the shoe in her hand and laughed. Just the sense of her own ridiculous predica-ment, only she had not been laughing alone. He had laughed with her. After that the knots had come out of the laces quite easily, she had put on her hat and gone. The fear had gone with her, of course, but it had become bearable. And now look how easy it had all been and how he had helped her.

Mary's next remark was another mistake. "Isn't that a lovely willow tree?" she said. "Like a waterfall."

"There's someone inside it!" gasped Jean, trembling with a new terror.

"Just a bird," said Mary, and stretched out a hand to pull aside the green-gold curtain and show her it was all right. But her hand dropped again. Ridiculous ideas are catching and she too now had the feeling that there was someone there, someone hostile to them. They would go and look at the beautiful boy in the pond, she thought, but when she turned and glanced towards him some trick of the sunlight, rippling down his smooth limbs, caused the illusion that he moved. "Come and see the rose garden," she said hastily. The rose garden, basking in warmth, was normal enough, but the curtain of wistaria hid the path beyond and anyone could have been there, pacing up and down, shabby silk skirts dragging on the paving stones, and Mary had to acknowledge that the atmosphere of her home, at present at any rate, was undeniably queer. She did not resist Jean's edging movement around the roses, her quick anguished glance towards the garden door. Indeed with her hand within her arm she helped her there.

At the door Jean, with her hand in Mary's, tried to remember what the other thing was that James expected her to say. "My brother and I—my brother—we hope you will be very happy here."

"Thank you," said Mary, and then, because she already loved this woman and must see her again, but not in a house which terrified her, "Will you come out with me in my car sometimes? I don't drive fast and with you I shall be driving just to look at the beauty around us, not to get anywhere."

Jean's face lit up with a joy out of all proportion to the normality of the suggestion. They had no car at the Vicarage. James, with his great physical strength, preferred his bike and his long legs; and in any case his brilliant classical mind was curiously inept when it came to machinery. Even had they had a car it would have been a torment to drive with him. But with this wonderful

gladiolus woman it would be heaven. She had not seen the
beautiful country round Appleshaw because her physical
weakness was too great for walking, and she had often
thought that if she could see it she might feel better.
"Thank you!" she ejaculated, and she was so happy that as
she turned away she seemed almost steady on her feet.

Mary waved to her and went back to the garden. She
walked slowly along the mossgrown path beside the jungle
that had once been a herbaceous border, her thoughts busy
with Michaelmas daisies, golden rod and peonies. In the
shrubbery on the other side, when she crossed over to it,
she found among the weeds japonica, guelder rose, escalonia
and actually a couple of laurels, all of them grown into
trees. She was afraid that the pruning and digging and
replanting that were necessary were beyond Mr. Baker
but he must choose his own helper. It would not be everyone who could work with him.

She went down to the end of the lawn and sat on the
edge of the empty pond, close to the pink and white blossoms
of the crab apple trees, and looked up at the boy with the
bow and arrow, remembering the glimpse of him she had
had as a child. He had waited for her a long time. She sat
by him lulled almost to sleep by the birdsong and the bee-
hum and the warmth and scents of spring. Then twelve
o'clock struck from the church tower. Twelve already?
Mrs. Baker would be wanting to leave and she got up and
went towards the house. As she passed the willow tree she
paused. She still had the odd feeling that there was someone there and again she put out her hand to part the
branches. Then it flashed through her mind; not yet.

When she reached the kitchen Mrs. Baker was already
putting on her coat and tying her scarf over her head. "I've
prepared the veg. dear," she said. "And I've stewed a few
apples and made a custard. Should last you over Sunday.
The fowl will be ready come one o'clock. If I were you
I'd just slip along with your car to the Dog and Duck. It'll
be quiet now and suitable for a lady. In the evening it's
more noisy. Down Starling lane, that turn by Orchard
Cottage, the Randalls' place, the cottage with the blue door.
You can't miss it."

"Thank you, Mrs. Baker," said Mary gratefully. "The

apples and custard look good and the fowl smells wonder-ful. I'll do as you say about the car."

"That's right, dear," said Mrs. Baker. "See you Mon-day. Bye-bye."

· She went out through the back door and down the path through the kitchen garden to the door in the wall leading to some lane that Mary had not discovered yet. The thought of discovery gave her a thrill of excitement.

3

She got into her car and followed Mrs. Baker's directions. Between the Randalls' kitchen garden and the inn there was an orchard, with beehives under the trees. The Dog and Duck was old with deep thatch and a painted sign. The lane went on beyond it, through gilded meadows towards the green-roofed splendour of a vast beech wood. She got out of her car and went into the bar, fearful lest it should have been modernized. But it was still much as it had always been, with an old black settle beside the wide fire-place, hunting prints on the walls and a huge cat heaped on the counter. Only this counter was modern, with rows of glasses on shelves behind it and leather-topped high stools in front.

She had expected to find the bar empty but it was full of a pleasant blue haze of tobacco smoke and two men, one of middle height, stocky and strong, the other tall and broad-shouldered, were smoking their pipes and talking to Jack Beckett behind the counter. A wonderful Labrador lay on the floor beside the tall man. The talk was of country things and Mary would have liked to stay unseen for a minute or two and listen to it, but though she moved quietly she was not a woman who could hope to enter a room unobserved and Jack Beckett at once stared at her in frank and delighted admiration. His three last remaining teeth, two top and one bottom, gave as much charm to his wide smile as the first three of a baby. The other two men were instantly on their feet. The one with the dog stepped back, his dog moving with him as though they were all of a piece, but the other turned towards her with a half-smile and a glance that took her in very efficiently indeed. He fetched a stool and placed it for her with an air. He had grey eyes, sandy hair and a broad, pleasant, snub-nosed face She could not place him at all. His clothes were those of a well-to-do farmer but not his well-kept hands or his sophistication.

"I did not mean to disturb you," she said in her unusually deep, cool and beautiful voice. "I came to thank Mr. Beckett for saying I may garage my car here."

"Ah, it's Miss Lindsay!" roared Jack Beckett. He had a very gentle and sucking-dove roar and Mary instantly liked him. "I thought as how it might be you, ma'am. What will you take, ma'am?"

Mary had not meant to take anything but she felt at home with these men, even with the one who moved all of a piece with his dog and whom she had not looked at yet, though she was very conscious of him. He seemed to have a gift of stillness. She sat on her stool and said, "A gin and lime, please."

"Paul and I are practically your next-door neighbours, Miss Lindsay," said the stocky man.

"If The Laurels can be said to have neighbours," said the tall man. "It's a place apart. A deep sort of place."

He had come back to his stool beside her, with his dog, and for the first time she turned to look at him. His face was disfigured with burns. Plastic surgery had done what it could for him but even so the marring of his face was grievous, and he was blind. She felt no sense of shock, rather of familiarity, as though she turned back, or forwards, she did not know which, to John. Yet this tall untidy man with his short rough greying hair and bowed shoulders was physically not in the least like John, always so immaculate and straight and easy on the eye. Nevertheless he was like him in some way that she could not define yet, and her sympathy and liking went out to him. And he was right about The Laurels being a place apart.

"I liked your cousin," he said. "In her good times she used to ask me to tea with her in that parlour that feels like a cave under the sea. Always cherry cake and tea so strong it nearly knocked you down. And in her bad times Mrs. Baker used sometimes to fetch me to help get her upstairs to bed. She used to kick our shins like a good un." His boyish grin made her realize that he was not as old as he looked. "But whether it was the good or bad times I liked her tremendously. She never complained."

"I'm glad you liked her," said Mary. "Do you live in the house at the bottom of my garden?"

"No, that's Roger Talbot on your right."

Mary smiled at the stocky man. "Nice to have you there."

"Long may you think so," he said. "My wife and I are quiet enough but the kids are at the tree-climbing stage. Should they fall out on your side of the wall I hope you will wallop them and send them back again."

Children, thought Mary, that's it. Children in the trees looking at me with hostile eyes. A hostile child under the willow. They played in my garden when Cousin Mary was ill. It's their garden. Aloud she said, "I like children. I taught them for years."

"You don't look like a schoolmarm," he assured her.

"Don't I?" said Mary coolly. "I'm sorry. I'd like to look like what I admire."

He laughed. "Touché," he said.

They turned then and drew Jack Beckett into their talk, until there was the sound of a car outside and Mary and Roger Talbot turned to look out of the window. A smart shooting-brake had just drawn up and a large man in immaculate tweeds was emerging from the driving seat. Mary only saw his back but she had an immediate impression of opulence and power. Two others, similarly attired, were climbing out behind. The two men with Mary wordlessly communicated and Paul spoke. "Jack, I'll take Miss Lindsay out at the side door and show her the barn. It's the one where you keep your car? I know. It's this way, Miss Lindsay."

The side door led through a short passage to the yard at the side of the inn, bounded on one side by the orchard. "That was Hepplewhite, the Squire," explained Paul. "He's in the city, directing companies or something of that sort, but I never do understand what these blokes do in the city. He spends his weekends here, shooting with his cronies, and they come and have drinks before lunch. Forgive us for hurrying you out as we did. The fact is you would have been cornered. You'd have had to dine there tonight and play bridge afterwards. He'd have sent the car to fetch you. He wouldn't have listened to any excuses. He's not a listener. Neither of them is. They're most awfully kind but their hospitality seizes you unawares like a spring trap. You know?"

"I know," said Mary. "Thank you. I'd rather not be trapped on my first day, and I didn't come here to play bridge."

They crossed the road to the orchard and leaned on the gate, the scent of the apple blossom coming to them on the light wind. From the crimson of the unopened buds to the white of the fully opened petals every gradation of rose-colour was present in flights and drifts on the lichened branches. The apple trees were old and it seemed a miracle that such misshapen age could support this airy light-ness.

"Just by our fence, where our garden joins the orchard," said Paul, "there's a fallen tree lying in the grass. But it still has a bit of root in the ground and every spring it breaks into blossom and every autumn it bears apples." He spoke with awe, from the depths of himself, as only one man or woman in a thousand has the power to do. What did that apple tree mean to him, she wondered, and what did this orchard mean? Far more than it meant to her, though she realized that each spring that she lived here it would mean more.

"I'd like to ask you something," he said suddenly. "If you haven't come here to play bridge then why have you come?"

The question shot out at her with a directness which she might have thought rude had she not already begun in-tuitively to understand this man. Suffering had had an effect with which she was familiar. The refusal of self-pity and despair had turned it from lead to fire, burning up the subterfuges and dishonesties below the surface of the inherited veneer of manners and thought that most men and women think are their true selves, and the veneer with them. He was forged now all of one piece, as he and the dog were of one piece, and spoke as he thought, rude or not. The blindness had helped perhaps. She imagined that if you were blind you must either live shut within yourself or seek with others a true and honest communication. Nothing else would be much use in the dark. It was this true communication he was seeking with her, and she with him, and the suddenness of this conversation did not surprise her. Paul was a man to know what he wanted instantly, and if it was right that he should have it he would take it at once if he could. She knew now why he reminded her of John, for coupled with John's courtesy, as with Paul's gift of stillness, there had been an alarming honesty, and his capacity for abrupt action, based on lightning decisions of great insight, had made him a naval commander of genius. She would find other likenesses presently, she believed, for already she was as much humbled before this man who was so much younger than herself as she had been years ago before the man who was so much older. With no premeditation she gave him the truthful answer to his direct question.

"Now that I am here, I realize it is to get to know Cousin Mary, Miss Lindsay, whom I saw only once in my life when I was a child, and also to get to know a man who died in the war."

He seemed to think this a reasonable answer and asked another question. "Before you realized that why did you want to come?"

"For a reason that still holds good. To get to know an England I've never known, the England of the deep country, before there's no deep country left. And also, and this must sound odd to you, it was an act of obedience. I had to come."

He turned from the gate. "We must get your car, and ourselves, out of the way before the Squire comes out. You've not lived in the country before?"

"Never. I'm a Londoner."

"There are people here you'll like," he said. "Miss Anderson, one of the three bravest people I know. The other two are Colonel and Mrs. Adams. When they turn up love them, please."

"How do you know I am capable of love?" she asked as they walked towards her car. "Steady affection perhaps."

"If by steady you mean faithful, there you have it; the kernel of love. I imagine men long for God because of that unchanging faithfulness. The rock under the quicksands. The psalms are full of it."

When she had put away the car and they were walking down the lane she said, "You are very direct. You haven't wasted time talking about the weather."

"Did you want me to?"

"No, but most people have sufficient caution to hover on the brink a bit before they take a header into friendship."

"The sighted do. The blind don't have to. One of the advantages of having been blind for a good many years is that you know almost at once what people are like, and if you're going to get on. Physical appearance, and trying to use it as a relief map to show you the lie of the land, can be distracting. Without the map intuition comes alive. But blindness has its disadvantages and one of them is that you don't know the time. Should you say I am going to be late for lunch?"

"It's a quarter to one," said Mary.

"Dead on time," he said, and there was profound relief in his tone.

"When I arrived yesterday," said Mary, "a young woman with beautiful dark hair was painting the front door turquoise. Is she your wife?"

"She's my wife."

He spoke in level tones but she was aware of bewildered grief. They had reached a small wooden gate opening from the back garden of Orchard Cottage into the lane, and the dog stopped. His master stopped too, as though at a voice, for the dog had not touched him.

"I think that's the most wonderful dog I've ever seen," said Mary.

"She's a good dog," said Paul, his hand on the dog's back. "We don't need the harness in the country, I know my way about so well, but you should see us dashing through the traffic in Westwater, when I have to go to the dentist or something. She and I trained together at Exeter. She's my second. When Sam died I thought it was the end, but Bess is even more marvellous. She's still only five years old." Mary could sense the relief. When the other half of your being can expect a span of life less than a quarter of your own the passage of time must be something you have perpetually to endeavour to forget. "Look out! Mr. Hepplewhite. Goodbye. I believe my wife means to ask you to tea. You'll come, please."

He and Bess were inside the garden with the gate shut, and she was leaving the lane for the green with long easy strides. The advantage of long legs was that you could hurry without appearing to do so. Paul had heard the car before she did, but she could hear it now behind her and feel three pairs of male eyes fastened on her back. She was used to this, and sorry for the interested parties when she turned round, for her back was a good twenty years younger than her front. She escaped into The Laurels with a marvellous sense of safety. As Paul had said, you could go deeply in, finding refuge like a cony among the rocks.

CHAPTER V

I

MARY was sitting under the willow tree writing letters. She sat on her travelling rug on the grass, her back against the tree, for the necessary garden chairs were still only on her priority list. It was still only Sunday morning yet already she felt that she had lived here for years, so happy was she in this place. Her writing-pad dropped to the ground and she let it lie there, for except in the evenings and the mornings this was the last lazy day that she would be likely to have for some time. The next few weeks would be full of business, workmen in the house, decisions to make and comings and goings of all sorts. She would enjoy this idleness while she could. It was quiet under the willow tree for the Sunday bells were momentarily silent. At seven-forty-five this morning they had been clamorous and had not allowed her the late sleep she had planned. They were fine bells, deep-toned, loud and lovely, and she had listened to them with acceptance, but their summons had been imperious, bringing before her mind's eye the strong square tower against the sky. The church was too big to be exactly a comfortable thing to have just over her garden wall. Who had built it and why had they made it so tremendous? She sat for some while in peace, aware of the trunk of the tree behind her back and the ground beneath her as living presences. Her hands moved over the rough grass and she could smell it, and smell the damp growing smell of the tree. I'm going to spend this day entirely alone, she thought, absolutely alone in this peace and quiet. It was the last time she started a fine day in the country with any such expectation.

And then the bells began again and they sounded louder here than they had done in her bedroom. They smote upon her temples and her eardrums and she sat enduring them as one endures the crash of thunder and the roar of wind, with exultation but also with alarm. The noise ceased, the clock struck eleven, and in the silence that followed she must have dozed, for suddenly she was awake and painfully alert. There was not a sound to be heard but she knew she was not alone in the garden. She waited, and beyond the willow tree she was aware of a shadow. This is bad, she thought briefly, but not as bad as if, yesterday, I had entered upon the child. Now the child comes to me.

The willow curtain was parted and a brown bare-legged girl in a shrunken cotton frock stood in the aperture. In a flash the expression of peace on her thin face was covered by one of alarm and she would have flown like a bird had Mary not been instantly ready to forestall flight. "Come here, please," she said. Her hand was held out but the voice was the one that no child had ever disobeyed in her teaching days. This child was immobilized by it. She stood where she was, shaking from head to foot. "Come right inside, please," said Mary. "Come and sit here by me."

Impelled by the kind, commanding voice Edith came closer. But she would not sit down. She stood by Mary, looking down at her, her eyes dark with hatred. Mary got to her feet and in turn stood looking down at Edith, for she must get the ascendancy now, quickly. Hatred, even in a child, or perhaps especially in a child, was a thing of such strength that if it was not overcome at once its growth was quickly a stranglehold. Smiling at Edith she said, "What is your name?" There was no answer, and she repeated the question. "What is your name?"

"Edith."

"You live next door?"

The child nodded sullenly, kicking at a tussock of grass with her sandal.

"Edith, I am sorry if by coming to live here I have trespassed in your garden. This is your garden, isn't it? And is this willow tree your special place? I am sorry. But the garden is not taken from you. We'll share it together but it will really be yours, and I will only work in it and sit on the lawn because you allow me to. But I won't sit under this tree again. This, under the tree, is all yours. I won't come here again. Come and look at the herbaceous border with me and we'll think what it would be nice to plant in it."

Edith followed her and they walked along the mossgrown

path together. She was unresponsive but when Mary talked quietly of the flowers they would have, looking down at the thin, clever, sensitive brown face, it was attentive and without hatred.

"Did you think I'd be in church?" Mary asked, when they had twice been the length of the border.

Edith spoke for the first time and her voice, as Mary had expected, was low and rapid with a timbre of music in it. "Yes. Everybody goes to church at eleven."

"Not you?"

"I was sick this morning. Mother said I needn't. I don't like church. Rose and Jeremy do. Rose likes wearing her hat and Jeremy likes the mouse."

"There are three of you?"

"Two really. Rose and Jeremy. I'm only adopted."

Mary took Edith's hand and held it firmly. She did not consider herself an intuitive woman but she spoke now without premeditation. "Will you help me with something? My cousin, Miss Lindsay, had a collection of little treasures that she used to keep under a glass case in the window of the parlour. Mrs. Baker put them away for safety. I want to unpack them and put them back where they used to be. Will you help me?"

Edith was transformed. The sun bursting out from behind a cloud or a leaping lark exploding into song, could scarcely have been more miraculously lovely than the change from misery to joy in her face. "Hurry!" she said, tugging at Mary's hand.

They ran across the lawn together, Edith racing ahead. Mary had opened the parlour window at the bottom that morning and the child was in the room and dancing with impatience by the time she had reached the conservatory. The night before she had found the glass case and the stand and put them on the table but she had waited for the daylight to unpack the little things. "They're here," she said, pulling out the top drawer of the escritoire. But it held only a collection of shabby leather-covered books that looked like old diaries. The two cardboard boxes containing the little things were in the second drawer.

"You have one box to unpack and I'll have the other," she said to Edith.

She lifted the glass case off the stand and they sat down together on the floor and began slowly to undo the tissue paper and cotton wool in which Mrs. Baker had wrapped the little things. It was hard to tell which of them was the more excited. One by one they appeared, the treasures of silver and gold, of jade, pinchbeck, glass, ebony and ivory, and Edith greeted each of them with delighted recognition. "Here's the mandarin who nods his head. Here's the peacock and the ivory mouse. Here's the little thimble and scissors in the silver basket. Here's the bluebird in the cage of golden wire. The lantern with the ruby glass. The dwarf with the red cap. The telescope with Brighton Pier at the end when you look through it. The elephant with a house on his back." Her voice murmured on in a happy monotone as she deftly put the little things back on the black velvet of the shelves. When Mary placed anything there she immediately altered the position, but without rudeness, and smiling shyly at Mary. Only she knew where they all had to be.

"Did Miss Lindsay show you her little things, Edith?" asked Mary.

Edith shook her head. "No. I never came into the house. I used to look at them through the window. By myself. Rose and Jeremy haven't seen them."

"I must have been about your age when I first saw them," said Mary, and she told Edith about that day of her childhood, making a story of it, remembering for Edith's benefit how the trees had seemed to move and the old wall and the door had looked like a painted picture. Edith listened gravely and when Mary had finished she said, "Yes, the trees move. I've never gone inside the green door, up the steps. I've never rung the bell."

"I'll ask you and Rose and Jeremy to tea with me," said Mary. "And you shall ring the bell and come in through the green door."

She had said the wrong thing. For the first time Edith's fingers fumbled and a minute tortoiseshell cat with emerald eyes fell to the carpet. Stooping to pick it up she whispered, "By myself."

"I must ask the others too," said Mary. "The first time. Other times we will be by ourselves. But if you want the little things to be a secret between you and me for the present I'll put them out of sight in my bedroom when you all come."

Edith looked up. "Not for the present. Always."

"It's not right to possess beautiful things by oneself," said Mary, "and presently you will want to share them."

"I won't!" said Edith.

Mary changed the subject. "We've unpacked them all," she said. "But I'm afraid my old cousin must have given some of them away. The things I loved best when I was a child aren't here. There was a tea-set of clear blue glass and a wonderful ivory coach with Queen Mab inside. They were the best of all. You would have loved them, Edith. I wish they were still here."

Edith's head was lowered. "I think," she said in a small voice, "that I'm going to be sick again."

They ran, gaining the bathroom only just in time. Later, under the willow tree with Edith wrapped in Mary's rug and imbibing warm milk with apparent enjoyment, Mary asked, "Does your tummy hurt at all?"

"Just sore."

"It didn't hurt before you were sick?"

"No, it never hurts."

Not appendix, thought Mary. What's worrying the child? "Keep still," she said. "I haven't got my books here yet, and so I can't read aloud to you, but I'll tell you a story."

Edith settled herself comfortably, looking up at the domed roof over her head. Mary looked too. The branches sprang from the central stem and curved outwards like the ribbed vaulting of some cathedral chantry, and between them the green and gold leaves were stippled on the blue sky. And it's mine, she thought with awe. This chantry is mine. And then quickly, No, Edith's. What story should she tell her? She didn't know the modern children's classics and she had to turn back to her own childhood. *The Cat That Walked by Itself*. That rather suited Edith. She was a good story teller and presently there was colour in Edith's lips, her eyes were bright and her body relaxed. Several times during the morning Mary had been aware of singing, but so muted that it had been no more than a

background to the music of birds and bees, but now twelve
o'clock boomed loudly and a moment later the story and the
quiet were torn in pieces by the clamour of human creatures
let loose. It was not the shrill noise of children let out of
school but it would have been but for the restraints of age
and good breeding. Then came the banging of car doors
and the purring of engines starting up. Edith leapt to her
feet and flew out from under the willow tree and down the
garden, Mary after her. "You've plenty of time, darling,"
she said when she caught up with her at the edge of the
copse and had her in her arms.

"Mother said I was to lie on the drawing-room sofa and
not move," said Edith.

Mary took her arms away. "Off with you then. And remember, it's your garden and your willow tree. Come and
go as you like. Good-bye, Edith."

" 'Bye," called Edith. She was already climbing up the
apple tree. She stepped nimbly from there to the wall,
turned to wave to Mary, then climbed into the mulberry
tree beyond. She's going to be beautiful, thought Mary,
watching her. She's going to be a remarkable woman.
Edith suits her. It's a grave, still name.

She went back to the willow tree and picked up the rug
and her writing things. It had been a rewarding interlude
she thought, and now she would go on with her solitary
day, though not under Edith's willow tree. The bell
clanged. She ran into the house through the conservatory
and went down the passage to the green door. She dragged
it back as far as she could, farther than she had ever dragged
it before, for the woman standing on the steps would not
have been able to squeeze through the usual aperture.

"Good morning," said Mary. "Please come in."

"May I? How kind. I felt I couldn't wait to welcome you
to our little community. You know we're just like one big
family here. It's so charming. My name is Hermione
Hepplewhite. My dear, I won't stay a moment, but my
husband and I want you to dine tonight. Now you mustn't
refuse us, for we'll send the car, and then you'll have no
trouble in finding the way to the Manor. I've just dropped
in after church. Unconventional of me but that's one of the
joys of the country. We're not conventional here. Not that

I ever was. I was a very unconventional girl. I like people. I like *knowing* people. How lovely your wistaria is. Your poor old cousin. Such a recluse. I don't believe I've ever been inside the house. I used to inquire, you know. Bring her flowers, poor soul. How old and strange this hall is. And this pretty parlour. My dear, I feel we're going to be great friends. It was in my stars yesterday that I should make a good friend and I took to you at once. I always know."

The kind flood of talk seemed to Mary to be slowly filling the little room, mounting higher and higher up the panelled walls like—no, not like honey, for there was strength and power in honey, but like warm very runny apricot jam. She pulled one of the little gold chairs forward, hoping it would bear Mrs. Hepplewhite's weight. Laughter was rising in her, and iron determination not to dine tonight, and at the same time a liking for Mrs. Hepplewhite, and admiration for the perfection of her presentation. That was the right word, Mary thought. To say that Mrs. Hepplewhite dressed well was true but inadequate. With her immaculate make-up, in her perfect tweeds, a wreath of soft blue feathers on her beautiful blue-rinsed white hair and a single string of fine pearls round her neck, she presented the countrywoman of wealth and taste as a great actress would have done, everything she wore as integral a part of her presentation as her movements and the inflexions of her voice. She *was* a great actress and it was the genius of the actress that Mary admired, though her liking was reserved for a woman now so buried that she might never know her. She did not believe that Mrs. Hepplewhite had been christened Hermione. What had made her choose the name? Did it symbolize for her the new woman she had put on so costingly? One could tell that the attainment had been hard for there was a look of strain about her kind blue eyes and her colour beneath her powder was too high. But for vigorous corseting, and probably dieting, she would have been stout, and Mary realized with keen sympathy that she would have liked to be stout, would have loved to let her tall upright figure sag in private moments of fatigue, but that she never did. The stiff armour of her corsets was a symbol of some dedication in her. To what?

To whom? wondered Mary, and returning suddenly to the surface realized that for the last three minutes Mrs. Hepple-white's conversation had been mounting about her without her comprehension. "Archer shall fetch you in the Bentley at seven-thirty," was the final sentence.

"Mrs. Hepplewhite, I'm so sorry, but I am engaged to-night," said Mary.

Mrs. Hepplewhite dived cheerfully into her bag, pro-duced a tiny diary covered in scarlet leather and flicked over its pages. "Tomorrow evening I've a meeting. I'm on so many committees. One likes to do what one can. Tuesday we dine out ourselves. Not Wednesday. My husband won't be home until late on Wednesday and he's dying to meet you. He saw you. Did I tell you? You didn't see him. Oh dear, we go away for a long week-end. Tuesday week?"

"Thank you," said Mary. "Tuesday week."

Mrs. Hepplewhite noted the date in the diary with a small golden pencil. "Archer, that's our chauffeur, shall fetch you at seven-thirty. And now, my dear, I must tear myself away. We've weekend guests. It's been delightful to meet you and I hope we shall see a great deal of each other. Who are you getting to do up this house for you? You must have Roundham at Westwater. We always have them ourselves. Ring them tomorrow. Tell them I recom-mended them. What did you say? Bakers at Thornton? But, my dear, they'll ruin the place. Cancel the order. Let me ring Roundham for you myself. I'll do it tomorrow. Oh? Oh yes, I see. Never mind."

They had got as far as the hall and for a moment she was crestfallen as a child, but then like a child she was happy again with a new idea. "Your hair, my dear. There's quite a good place at Westwater, when you haven't time to go up to town. A Belgian, a very charming man. I'll tell him about you. No, don't thank me. What are we here for but to help each other. Have you a dog?" They were under the wistaria and Mary speechlessly shook her head. "Oh, but you must have a dog. They're such companions in the country. I don't know what I'd do without my Tania, she comes everywhere with me, to meetings and church and so on. She does not mind how long she waits in the car if she has something of mine to lay her little face against, my gloves or scarf or something. It's so touching. You must have a poodle from Tania's kennels. They breed a wonderful strain there. I'll give you the address. Tania's here, outside in the car. Such a poppet."

Mrs. Hepplewhite's conversation, when she was in movement, dragged one in her wake with a species of suction. Mary did not want to go out to the blue Bentley and look at Tania but she had to. Tania, very white and very small, sat on her cushion and looked at Mary very intently for some while out of black, bright, unblinking eyes. Mary's gaze fell first, not so much because she was intimidated as because she was suddenly very tired; and Mrs. Hepplewhite, she realized, was writing out an address for her on a page torn from her diary.

"Not a poodle, Mrs. Hepplewhite. She's a darling but I've set my heart on an ordinary cottage tabby cat. For the mice. The house is full of them."

"Mice?" cried Mrs. Hepplewhite. "We'd a plague of them at the Manor when we moved in. I got some splendid mouse stuff. Now what is it called?" She pressed her hand for a moment over her tired eyes. "Now what *was* it called? How stupid of me."

"Tell me on Tuesday week," said Mary. "I mustn't keep you now. Good-bye till then." She moved back waving and smiling, for if Mrs. Hepplewhite were to remember the name of the mouse stuff there would be no escape, mounted her steps backwards with great skill, waved and smiled again and pushed the green door shut. She leaned against it, exhausted. It makes it worse, she thought, it makes it much worse, that Mrs. Hepplewhite is a darling.

2

Mary had not lied when she had said she was engaged that evening for she had pledged herself to spend it with Cousin Mary. The shabby old diaries that she had seen in the top drawer of the escritoire could only be hers. She had an early supper, lit a wood fire in the basket grate for the sake of company and loveliness and sat down beside it with the diaries piled on a chair beside her.

But she was in no hurry to open them and she sat with her hands in her lap, and gradually she became aware of a miracle. Through the west window beside her the sunset shone into the room, through the flowers of the blossoming apple tree that grew close to the window. Their moving shadows lay upon the carpet, and their scent, and the twin scent of burning apple wood, faintly filled the room. The flames gave their light and through the vine leaves came the cool blue of the garden where the birds were singing. Time not so much passed as was lost, and with it her sense of possessing herself, yet she felt no sense of loss for in the centre of perfection there is nothing wanting. Circle upon circle of unknown, invisible and terrible beauty stretched from her into infinity and yet it was all here in what now held her and filled her. She was in a state of happy shame. She guessed that many restless men had been driven to the ends of the earth to find this—what should she call it—this golden heart, yet it was hers in this miracle of light. Why should she among millions of women, some of whom toiled in great cities or rotted in refugee camps, be given this? She knew her worldliness and lovelessness. Why she? It was one of the unanswerable questions and there was nothing she could do about it except be thankful. Time returned and then it was as though a hand relaxed its strong and gentle hold. She could not have moved before, but she could now, and she got up and lit the lamp, for in the west the gold, like her own state, was now rather the remembrance than the fact of glory. She turned from it to the diaries.

They were not diaries in the technical sense for there were no printed headings with a particular day and date. They were blank-paged notebooks in which Cousin Mary had sometimes put the date of what she wrote and sometimes not. But she had numbered the books themselves in chronological order. The first entry began abruptly under the heading *June 14th 1897*. The handwriting was clear and beautiful.

"It has happened and I am home again. There's a sense of awe when the impossible thing that you refused has happened, and it's over, and you don't know whether you went on refusing and it happened just the same, or whether somehow you accepted. But anyhow it's over. But I am not as happy as I thought I'd be because when something you have dreaded comes to an end there's a sense of anticlimax, like dust in the mouth. All the crashing ruin, the falling and tumbling, are over, but the dust is horrible. They say it won't happen to me again but I expect they only say it to comfort me. But I must think it won't. I must be like the people who plant gardens and build houses all over again where the earthquake has been. At the back of their minds they know there may be another 'quake but with the front of their minds they plant gardens. I wish I had a house and garden of my own, in the country and quiet. Though it's the suburbs here it's never really quiet and all the people coming in and out make me so confused and sleepless and tired. I'd like to live in the deep country with my dear Jenny Kennedy, just the two of us; not with Father and Mother and their anxious looks, wondering what next. Jenny doesn't wonder what next, she just loves me and takes what comes. I can't marry with this thing hanging over me, and I'll never be able to do much because when I get tired the desperation comes. They've never understood that. They've always thought I was lazy. I'm not, only when I am tired it comes. It wouldn't have happened like it did if Mother hadn't made me go to Paris with her. It was the noise and the heat. All those people chattering, the traffic, and the dreadful din of the city pressing in on me. Father could give me a little house in the country if he wanted to. I've begged for it but he won't listen. And Mother says it's impossible, Father couldn't afford it. But I've that bit of money my godmother left me and he wouldn't have to add a great deal to it. If I were like Virginia and got married he'd give me a dowry and trousseau, as he did her. When God is cruel to you everyone else is cruel too. When he turns his back he turns the whole world with him."

The diary broke off abruptly and began again a few days later. "I oughtn't to have said that about God. I don't know enough about him. I don't even know if he exists. Only if he doesn't exist why did I refuse? When you say, I won't, you refuse somebody and when you say, yes I will, you say it to somebody. I remember now that I did accept, that night when I woke up in the hospital room and there was the nightlight burning, and the night nurse moving in and out, and I realized that I was sane again. I was so thankful that I said, yes, I'll do it. You might say that wasn't a real acceptance because what I'd refused had already happened to me. But yet it was. You can go on refusing even after it's happened to you, like the child who screams and kicks the door after it's been shut up in the dark room. Or you can sit quietly down in the dark and watch for the return of light.

"Now it's out. I have said I was sane again and that means that I was not sane before. I have written it down. For I'm to be honest in this diary. That's why I'm writing it. I'm writing this to help myself by speaking out exactly what's in my mind. I can't talk to people because this illness isn't like other illnesses; all that's worst in it you have to hide so as not to spread fear. And anyhow they wouldn't understand. I remember Mother didn't when I was a child, and screamed after I was in bed at night, and when she came and I said I was lying on stones, and the black walls were moving in, she said I was a silly child and gave me a biscuit. I threw the biscuit on the floor for I had wanted her to put her arms round me and tell me she knew about the stones and the moving walls. Only of course she didn't know.

"When did I begin to realize that other people don't wake up every morning in unexplainable misery, don't, as soon as they are ill or exhausted, become sleepless and desperate? People mean different things by desperation. I mean the terror of impending disorder. For disorder, of mind or body, is evil's chance. At least, I think so. It seems to me to be integration that keeps evil out. I don't know when it was, I only know I struggled to keep my difference hidden just so as not to be different. There is a sense of safety in being like other people.

"I scarcely remember how it happened, after we came back from Paris, for it's all a blur, but I do remember the insomnia and trying to get out of the window to escape from the evil. The time at the Home I only remember as a confused nightmare. But it's odd, I do remember one thing very clearly. I remember who among the nurses was kind to me and who was not. It would be awful to have to go back there and I'm going to ask Father once more if I may live in the country with Jenny. Mother will be furious because Jenny's her maid, and a good maid, but I know that if Jenny has to choose between me and Mother she'll choose me."

The next entry was some weeks later. "Father refused. It wouldn't be good for me to mope alone in the country. What I need is cheerfulness about me. Plenty of distraction. I tried to explain that what I need is just not to be tired, but I couldn't get the words out and suddenly I began to cry, and he kissed me lovingly and told me to go with Mother and buy myself a new hat.

"That was a month ago and it's been a miserable month until yesterday, when Mother thought it was her duty to ask the queer old man to tea. He's staying at the Vicarage taking the services while the Vicar is having a holiday. The Vicar apologized about him. The man who should have come got ill and there was no one to be found but this old man. The Vicar has cut his holiday down from three weeks to a fortnight, and only one Sunday, because of being so apologetic about the old man. He's very old and eccentric, and he doesn't shave very well though one can see that he's tried. At tea he was by turns very shy and very fierce and he mumbled sometimes and dropped cake on the carpet. There were other people there and Mother was annoyed and after tea she asked me to take him out in the garden and show him the sweet peas. He was like a child about the sweet peas, he enjoyed them so much, their colour and lightness and scent. He said he'd never had a garden and when I asked him where he lived I found it was in lodgings down in East London, and for years he'd been Curate at a church in the slums. He wasn't at all sorry for himself but I was sorry for him because he loved flowers and had no garden, and suddenly I burst out and told him how I longed to go and live in the country. He looked at our beautiful garden as though he wondered how anyone could want anything better, and then he looked at me very keenly out of his bright blue eyes and said, 'Why?' The question came out so sharply and suddenly that I answered with the truth. I told him everything. It was the queerest thing that ever happened to me because I take such infinite trouble always to cover it all up. I hide it like a crime. And yet here I was laying it all out in front of him. I was like a criminal emptying his pockets. I took out everything. He was silent for a long time, rubbing his chin, and then he said, 'You're afraid of it?'

"It seemed such a silly question and I spoke sharply I think when I said, 'Of course I am, I'm terrified.'

" 'Why?' he asked. 'If you lose your reason you lose it into the hands of God.'

"I said, 'Why does God let us suffer like this?' and he answered, 'My dear young lady, how should I know? Job didn't know, but he repented in dust and ashes.'

"He wasn't helping me at all and I said crossly, 'I haven't done anything frightfully wrong. Nothing that calls for dust and ashes.'

"He said quietly, 'No?'

"I said, 'It makes one hate God.'

"He said, 'Where you've put him?'

" 'Where have I put him?'

" 'On the gallows.'

"And then suddenly he caught sight of a tortoiseshell butterfly drifting down the path and he gave an exclamation of incredulous joy and ran after it. When I caught up with him he was standing in front of the buddleia tree, which was covered with butterflies like it nearly always is, and he was speechless with wonder, his face absorbed as a child's when the candles have been lit on the Christmas tree. It was almost as though the butterflies shone on him and lit his face. Or else it was the other way round. For a moment there seemed light everywhere, though it was a grey day. It was queer and I didn't want to move; until there was a sound of voices and we saw Mother and her guests coming out into the garden. The old man looked round at me and the light had been wiped off his face; it was puckered and distressed, like a sad monkey's, and he said to me in a hoarse whisper, 'My dear, I think I should be going,' and I realized that he was terrified of Mother and her guests. He must have been terrified all through the tea party, when he mumbled and dropped crumbs on the carpet.

" 'Come this way,' I said. 'Round by the greenhouse. I'll say good-bye to Mother for you.' We went into the house through the side door and when we were in the hall he said to me, 'I think I had an umbrella. I feared thunder.'

He had brought a baggy old umbrella tied with string and while he was fumbling to get it out of the stand he said to me, 'It's safe there, you know.'

"I said, 'The umbrella?' and he answered, 'No, no, no! Your reason. It's the only place where anything is safe. And when you're dead it's only what's there you'll have. Nothing else.'

"He had a round clerical hat, dusty and green with age. He put it on, gripped his umbrella in his left hand and held out his right to me. I held it and it was dry and rough and hot. 'My dear,' he said, 'I will pray for you every day of my life until I die.'

"Then he abruptly let go of my hand, turned his back on me and stumbled down the steps that led from the front door to the drive. At the bottom he turned round again and looking into his face I noticed that when he was neither eager nor alarmed his eyes had the most extraordinary quietness in them. 'My dear,' he said, 'love, your God, is a trinity. There are three necessary prayers and they have three words each. They are these, "Lord have mercy. Thee I adore. Into Thy hands." Not difficult to remember. If in times of distress you hold to these you will do well.' Then he lifted his hat and turned round again. I stood at the door and watched him go. He had a queer wavering sort of walk. He did not look back.

"I went to the garden, for I knew Mother would be vexed with me if I didn't go back to her guests, though I didn't want to. I walked soundlessly over the lawn towards two women who were standing in admiration before one of Mother's rose bushes, which was full of bloom. But they weren't looking at it. 'Horrible old man!' one of them was saying. 'Anyone can see he drinks. What was the Vicar thinking of to have him here? Better to have left us with no one. In and out of asylums for most of his life, I'm told.'

"I stood quite still. He hadn't told me. He'd stood aside, speaking only of God and me. I wanted to run after him but when I moved they saw me, and the one who had spoken blushed crimson and I had to go forward and speak to them and pretend I hadn't heard.

"And now it's night and I am in my room and writing

down everything he said before I forget it. He said so little and he explained nothing. He couldn't. But it has come into my mind that what he couldn't explain is that treasure hid in a field in the old story. If one were to spend a lifetime digging for the treasure, and in this time of one's life not find it, one wouldn't have wasted the time. There would be less far to dig in the next time. Only one must possess the field, whatever it costs to buy it, and it has again come into my mind that fields are quiet places. And so I've got to have that home in the country with Jenny. My old man had the quietness within himself and I'll never know how he came by it. Perhaps for him outward quietness isn't necessary, but for me it is. I've never got on with Father and Mother. I've always been the one of their children they cared for least, and now I've brought this trouble upon them. Once the tussle is over it will be as much a relief to them as to me if we can live apart. I'll start fighting again tomorrow."

The beautiful handwriting broke off and did not begin again for another three months. The date was "October 14th" and under the heading Cousin Mary had written, "The Laurels, Appleshaw. My first night here and I can't sleep I'm so happy. I'll sit up in bed and write a little. Fighting Father and Mother nearly cost me another breakdown, but I managed to keep saying the three words of the three prayers and though they didn't mean a thing to me I kept my head above water and I brought the doctor round to my side. He told Father to let me do what I liked.

"It was Jenny who found this house. She has a cousin, a Mr. Postlethwaite, who lives here, and he told her about it. She came down to see it, by herself without telling anybody, and she liked it. So when I was well enough she and Mother and I came down to see it and Mother thought it was awful but I knew it was home.

"And so here we are, and Mr. Postlethwaite is going to keep the garden in order and carry the coals for Jenny, and find someone to scrub the floors. But all the rest Jenny will do. She's always been a lady's maid and now she'll be doing everything. She's given up so much for me and there are times when I feel miserably guilty, and then at other times I realize that looking after me is as necessary for her as learning to be quiet and to dig are necessary for me. We just have to do it.

"I shall live and die here. Perhaps I shall never be well but this place will give me periods of respite that I would not have found in any other, and though I am able to do nothing else in this life, except only seek, my life seeming to others a *vie manquée*, yet it will not be so, because what I seek is the goodness of God that waters the dry places. And water overflows from one dry patch to another, and so you cannot be selfish in digging for it. I did not know anything of this when I began this diary and I don't know how I know it now. Perhaps it has something to do with the old man.

"It is quiet in this room. I've only been here a few hours and yet already I know my home so well. There are no curtains at my window for Jenny and I have only got the barest essentials as yet. I want to get the rest very gradually, old pieces of furniture to match this old house, just the right curtains and carpets. An old house that's come alive through the centuries is not just a shelter from the weather, it's a living thing and can be served. I could feel the life of this house as soon as I came through the door in the garden wall. And so there are no curtains at the windows and the moonlight is shining in so brightly that I hardly need my candles, and when I lean forward I can see a sky crowded with stars behind that great tower. I'm glad I've come here in still, mellow October weather. The great lime avenue was thick with piled gold when we drove through it, but when the trees bent to possess us and I looked up at them I could see the blue sky through the gold leaves because though there were so many of them they were worn thin, like very old coins. The fields were blue and hazy and when we got to the village green I could smell bonfire smoke and blackberry jam boiling. The wistaria leaves are a fall of golden rain on each side of the pillared way and on the south side of the house the virginia creeper is scarlet on the wall. Down in the coppice at the bottom of the garden there are crab apples and the haws are scarlet.

"I am learning it all by heart. I expect the winter will be hard in spite of the country snow like white fox fur wrapped about the house, filling the rooms with light. The snow will melt and it will be cold and wet and I shall be ill, like I always am, with the vile asthma and bronchitis, and I shall fall into black depression, and perhaps desperation too, but it will pass and the spring will come with celandines and white violets in the lanes, and then the late spring with bluebells and campion and the wistaria coming out. And I shall learn the spring by heart, and then the summer, and I'll learn the bells and bird-song by heart, and the way the moonlight moves on the wall and the sun lies on the floor. I'll grow older and lose my beauty but the spring will not grow old nor the moon nor the snow. Who will live after me in this house? Who will sit in the little parlour reading by the fire? And then she will put out her lamp and come up to this room and light the candles and kneel by the bed to pray. I don't know who she is but I loved her the moment I walked into this room, for that was a moment that was timeless. I shall have my sorrows in this house, but I will pray for her that she may reap a harvest of joy. I will pray for her every day of my life, as the old man is praying for me."

Mary closed the book for that was all she would read tonight. It was as much as she could bear. She put out the lamp and went upstairs to bed. In her room she lit the candles in the two brass candlesticks and knelt down beside the old-fashioned bed. It was only for the moment that it seemed strange to be kneeling, for those who had lived in this house during the past centuries had belonged to the years of faith and her body relaxed easily into their habitual posture. What should she say to her discarded God? Her childhood's prayers came to her mind but they were too infantile. But the old man's prayers were not infantile and she repeated them.

3

Paul, at work at this hour in his small study with Bess asleep on the floor beside him, needed no candles. It gave Valerie the horrors, when presently she looked in to say she was going up to bed, to see him sitting in the dark. "It's so morbid," she said. "Why can't you put the light on just for the look of the thing?"

"Why waste electricity just for the look of the thing?"

"You waste so many things, why not the electricity?"

"What do I waste?"

"Your time for one thing. When you're in here half the time you're not using your typewriter at all, or your tape recorder, you're simply sitting doing nothing." He smiled, his slow amused smile that so maddened her, as though he had a private joke with himself from which she was shut out. "And you call that work; I believe you think you're earning our living. Don't stay up late. When you come up so late, and wake me just when I've got off, I can't sleep again for hours. You know I can't.'

"I'll be quiet, Val."

"You never are. You knock into things. Why can't you work in the morning when other men do?"

"Because I'm no good in the morning. And there's no peace in this house in the morning." He broke off, for it was fast developing into one of their altercations. "I'm sorry, darling, but it has to be this way. One day, when I've written my best seller, I'll make it all up to you."

He was smiling at her but she wouldn't look at him. While they had argued she had switched the light on. Now she went away deliberately leaving it burning. It gave her a secret pleasure to think that he thought he was in the dark and he wasn't.

Paul sat for a few moments hunched forward in his chair, his hands locked together between his knees. It was almost the attitude of physical pain. Bess stirred in her sleep, turned and laid her chin on his feet. Valerie had been an enchanting and pretty girl. He was perfectly well aware of the change in her. Whenever he tried to visualize her the thin hard face slipped like a mask over the face that he remembered, and wanted to remember, and repulsed him as she herself repulsed him whenever he tried to restore again some measure of the love that had once been between them. Yet he believed it was still only a mask, not the reality as yet. If he could only get through he would find his girl still alive behind it. Would it have been all right if he had not been blinded, or if he had done what she had wanted and let himself be trained in one of the skills that blind men could practise so lucratively? But he had always wanted to write, and tried to write, even in his sighted days, and after he had been blinded he had wanted it with an obstinate intensity that had swept away every objection laid before him by parents and sensible friends, and even the pleadings of Valerie herself. He had had to do this thing, come what might, though as a naturally confident and hopeful person he had believed in himself and expected to succeed. He had never imagined that after years of hard work he would still be earning so little. Yet it made no difference. He wrote because he had to and for no other reason.. It did not even occur to him to give it up for Valerie's sake and even at this late date get himself trained for something else. Nor had he considered living in the town, as Valerie wanted, or going to bed at a reasonable hour. He always felt ill and without the quiet of the country and the night he would not have been able to write. There was possibly a streak of selfishness in his single-mindedness but though he did not much care whether he succeeded or not he still half-believed that he would. He had a small but growing reputation as a poet, a prestige reputation of which Valerie knew nothing but which he hugged to himself with secret joy, a couple of plays were even now hovering near to production and there was the book.

It was the book which it is said every man can write, that semi-autobiographical book which is as much a record of a man's spirit as of his life, and which he fondly imagines to be fiction from beginning to end. Paul, playwright and poet, had never even contemplated writing a novel until three months ago. A difficult poem finished at last he had been in the usual restless, nervy, miserable condition. He had been longing to get to the end of it yet without it he had felt intolerably bereaved. And he had known he would never write another line, and told himself that he never wanted to. Writing was an exhausting senseless business, a mug's game. Yet all the while he had been feeling frantically around in his dusty mind for ideas, like a miser who has dropped his gold in the dark, with desolation growing in him all the time like a bottomless pit. He should have recognized the symptoms as the first pangs of a new poem, for they followed each other regularly in the same order whenever he was not working, but he never did recognize them.

And then suddenly in the middle of the night it had happened again, and it had been new as spring, though it had happened so many times. It had not this time been a line of verse crying out like a lost spirit for habitation, giving him no rest until word by word and sound by sound he had built up the form it wanted. Nor had it been as when a play was beginning and a vivid scene flashed before his inward eyes, men in movement, in conflict, in some dilemma from which he must rescue them or neither he nor they would know rest again. This had been a presence with him, a quiet man standing at the end of his bed. He had seen him clearly, and seen too the foot of the bed that he had never seen. The man had been dark, physically unlike himself, his fine head and strong shoulders as magnificently sculptured as those of a statue. He had been suffering but dumb; like the Polish officer who had once occupied the bed in a hospital ward next to Paul and whose anguish had been locked within himself because those about him did not know a word of his language. He had seemed to Paul to represent all the men who suffered in war and, if they lived, came home again as speechless as they had gone out. Or if they tried to speak they found the common language had no adequate words; and so their sons must suffer all over again. "I'll try," he had said to the man. "I'll say it for you." But the man's suffering had been in no way relieved and would not be relieved until the book was finished.

And it seemed to Paul, sitting slumped in his chair, that it never would be finished. He was only a third of the way through and already he was played out. And the thing would not come alive. It lacked the vital fire. Yet he had to go on for the man's sake. What lunatics writers are, he thought. He was madder even than dear old Miss Lindsay. Get on, you fool, he said to himself. He sat back in his chair, and Bess lifted her chin from his feet and went comfortably to sleep again. He relaxed, trying to loosen the hold of every thought that still held him to time or place, to integrate himself for the effort of concentration that would set the spring within flowing. At first he had found it appallingly difficult to write like this, entirely within his mind.

In his sighted days he had thought with his pen in his hand,
writing a few words, then pausing to think again, able to
look back at will, checking what he had written with what
he was thinking. To create a whole chapter or scene in his
mind, remembering and co-ordinating it without recourse
to pen and paper, had seemed at first impossible, but now
that he had learnt the art of withdrawal within himself he
found it a more satisfying way of writing than the other
because giving more consciously from the depths of himself
he could feel that he had given all he had to give. But it was
more exhausting and it called for deeper concentration and
quiet. As to results, he tried not to worry. He would have
liked to have been in the first class but that was beyond one's
control. If one's intellectual equipment was not great, one's
spiritual experience not deep, the result of doing one's
damned best could only seem very lightweight in comparison with the effort involved. But perhaps that was not important. The mysterious power that commanded men
appeared to him to ask of them only obedience and the
maximum of effort and to remain curiously indifferent as to
results. For an hour he sat motionless, outwardly as relaxed as though he slept, inwardly at full stretch. Then he
pulled the small table that held his tape recorder towards
him, picked up the microphone and dictated straight
through without a pause. Then he repeated the process
and the clock struck twelve.

He had finished work for the night but he sat on listening
to the sounds of the night that he loved more than those of
the day. Intensely sensitive to the music of sound as he had
become, the crashing symphony of the day sometimes almost overwhelmed him; especially in the spring when the
birds and the children had gone mad, when the spring
rains rushed upon the new leaves and Valerie started her
spring-cleaning. But the night music was quiet as one of
Beethoven's gentler sonatas, the notes falling with grave
precision. There was the tick of his clock, the creak of the
tired old stair treads as they relaxed in the dark, the rustle
of a mouse, an owl calling and the slow deep breathing of
Bess. And other infinitesimal sounds that he had never
heard when he was sighted, the eddying of air on a windless
night, the tinkle of dew, the breathing of trees and the steps

of the moonlight. It might be that he imagined these
sounds. He did not know. But if he did they were none the
less exquisite for that.

It was time for bed and he moved in his chair. Bess was
instantly awake and standing by him, her silken tail swish-
ing expectantly. Every new activity, though it was merely a
repetition of daily routine, was hailed by Bess as a thrilling
occurrence. To eat, to sleep, to wake, to go upstairs or
downstairs, to go for a walk, to come home, it was all
equally wonderful to Bess because it was Paul's world that
controlled these things and she trembled to his will as a
compass needle to the north. She was trembling now with
eagerness to be put out, not for any need of nature because
Valerie had already put her out, but because he wanted to
put her out. They went together to the study door and Paul
turned off the light. He had heard Valerie switch it on and
knew why she had not turned it off. These small cruelties
now hurt him less than they did. His love for her was
tired he supposed. She made it difficult for him to love
her.

Bess took him to the back door and was let out, and he
stood leaning in the doorway while she chased her tail in
the moonlight. Beyond the tiny kitchen garden he was
aware of the orchard and the glory of motionless blossom
There was that apple tree there, just over their fence.
Fallen and broken it still lived and bore fruit. Suddenly
parting from routine, to the astonishment of Bess, he left the
door and walked down the short grass path to the low fence.
Here he only had to stretch out a hand and he could feel
the blossoms of the fallen tree. They were cool and wet
with dew and in his mind's eye he could see their pale
glimmer under the moon. There were so many of them.
This fallen tree bore fruit as richly as any in the orchard, a
round red little apple, crisp when one bit into it and very
fresh. The dew was heavy tonight, and most welcome in
this dry spell. As always after working too hard his scarred
face felt tight and hot, but the coolness of the dew and its
faint scent eased him. The scent of water, of the rain and
of the dew. It was difficult to separate it from the grateful
fragrance of the life it renewed, but it had its scent; the
faint exhalation of its goodness. It would still come down

upon the earth after man, destroying himself, had destroyed also the leaves and the grass. Its goodness might even renew again the face of the burnt and blasted earth. He did not know. But unlike Job's comforters he believed there was a supreme goodness that could renew his own soul beyond this wasting sorrow of human life and death.

Bess pressed against his knee. He fondled her head and it was wet with dew. They went back to the cottage and crept stealthily up the stairs, terrified lest a stair creak and wake Valerie. Paul no longer slept with his wife. Valerie had her wide bed and charming south room to herself and Paul had the small room over his study. When he and Bess had got inside, and he had managed to shut the door without its creaking, he sighed with relief. With any luck he'd get to bed soundlessly. But his luck was out for Valerie had left a tin of furniture polish on the floor and he trod on it and stumbled against the wall. He listened anxiously and heard the creak of her bed as she turned over, her cough and loud weary sigh. She never let him remain in ignorance of the fact that he had wakened her. He crept into bed and lay awake until a sudden burst of joyous music bubbled up from the throat of a small bird beneath his window. He could not see that first ray of light to which the bird responded but its song was all the more wonderful to him because he couldn't. Comforted, he turned over and slept.

CHAPTER VI

I

A FEW days later Bert Baker, two workmen and the inevitable boy took possession of The Laurels. Bert, a younger edition of his uncle but less impressive, possessed the calm and reassuring manner of all good builders and decorators. "It will be all right, ma'am, come the end," was a phrase frequently on his lips. And Mary needed reassurance as papers were stripped from walls, rotting floorboards were ripped from floors, tiles shattered from the roof and it seemed that her home would soon be lying in ruins about her. To escape from the noise she did some shopping and purchased the two little period arm-chairs for the parlour, and she took Jean Anderson for a drive and went to tea at the Vicarage and with Paul and Valerie. The week went by and it was Tuesday.

At five o'clock Bert Baker and his men departed in the roaring lorry and cradled in the deep peace they left behind them Mary moved about her room getting ready for dinner at the Manor. Out in the garden were Mr. Baker and his friend Joe Rockett but they did not disturb the peace for they were woodsmen, men of a different type, slow, taciturn, dedicated. Both lived and worked in the woods that Mary had seen beyond the Dog and Duck, Joe as a woodsman proper, Joshua Baker carrying on to the fourth generation the craft of making chair legs of beech wood. He was the last bodger in these parts, he had told Mary with melancholy pride, perhaps the last in England for he'd never heard tell of another. She now understood his air of tragic grandeur. He represented in himself the end of an epoch. When he lay in his grave the art of bodging would lie there with him. Mary, though thankful that she had lived to see a bodger, was saddened by the thought. She had come to Appleshaw only just in time.

Punctually at seven-thirty the Hepplewhites' car fetched her and swept her through the village and up the avenue

between the rhododendrons, swirled her around the gravel
sweep and set her down in front of the pillared front door
of the exquisite little Georgian manor house. The chauffeur
and the gravel sweep made her feel herself back in the era of
her childhood and she expected the front door to be flung
open by a butler. It was a shock when it was opened by a
lacquered, beautiful, slightly contemptuous young woman
who murmured that she was Mr. Hepplewhite's secretary.
Mary smiled at her and was glad of her own height. Few
things alarmed her but these siren secretaries of successful
businessmen were one of the things. Their slim palms held
too much power and power corrupted women far more cor-
rosively than men, she believed. She was sorry for Mrs.
Hepplewhite. When she was ushered into the drawing-
room, where her hostess stood to receive her with her
husband the regulation one pace behind her shoulder, it
did not surprise her that Mrs. Hepplewhite's eyes glanced
for one nervous moment at the siren. The movement
had been involuntary and at once the flood of kind
talk was rising upwards as before. This time Mary was
submerged and could take in nothing until sherry revived
her.

The setting was that of one of the old drawing-room
comedies of the years between the wars. The french windows, the chintz-covered sofa and chairs, were all in the
right stage places and so was the white bearskin rug before
the hearth, the ormolu clock on the mantelpiece and the
French mirror on the wall. The flowers were perfectly
arranged and placed at all the strategic points. Mary
waited for the parlour maid in her black dress and flimsy
apron to come in and announce that dinner was ready. It
unnerved her when a Swiss girl performed this office but
she was restored to her comedy again by the dining-
room with its oval mahogany table, pink shaded lights
and oil portraits. Of whom could they be likenesses, she
wondered, aware of an aristocratic profile, a sword, a periwig, and a parakeet perched upon a white wrist. I'd give
a good deal, she thought, to see the real forebears of these
two.

Mr. Hepplewhite was an astonishment. The back view
she had seen getting out of the car had predisposed her to

expect the round red face and hearty manner of the conventional self-made man, genial and self-satisfied in what he had achieved. But Mr. Hepplewhite's front view was not at all like that. His fleshy face was smooth and olive-skinned, he had firm beautifully moulded lips and a profile like a Roman emperor on a coin. His grey hair was thick and wavy, his plump hands white and well kept, one of them adorned with a sardonyx signet ring. He had fine dark eyes which looked straight into Mary's as he talked to her, giving an appearance of great candour, and his voice was clear and well produced and at the same time caressingly gentle. There was no sense of strain about him for he was entirely relaxed in his part. There was little to suggest it was a part; only his back view and the fact that his signet ring was just a little too large. He was an enthusiastic host and talked with knowledge and intelligence upon every subject that came up; although, as Paul had said, he did not listen well. He never looked at his wife but now and again her eyes turned to him, nervously and with a naked adoration that made Mary want to weep. She realized that Mr. Hepplewhite was an extremely clever man. She did not know if she liked or disliked him for he did not allow her to find out. His presentation was too dazzling for her to be aware, as with Mrs. Hepplewhite, of the person behind the personage. Perhaps there wasn't one. Perhaps Mr. Hepplewhite was dead. It was a startling thought. But he had got a different back view and she found the remembrance of it oddly reassuring.

It was also reassuring to turn to Roger Talbot beside her, and look at Joanna across the table, for a more serenely normal couple she had never met. Roger, she found, was an architect with an office in Westwater. Joanna was a rosy brunette with work-roughened hands and that very special attractiveness of a comely young woman who takes no interest in her appearance. Her black dinner dress had probably done her for dinners ever since she had married, and showed to perfection the contrast between the rich tan of arms and neck and the dazzling whiteness of the skin that was normally covered by her high-necked short-sleeved jumper. She had a delightful friendly smile and Mary was quite sure she had been at Roedean and later had been a games mistress. She liked her but could not visualize her as mother to that strange little Edith.

2

The Talbots took her back to the village and asked her to come in for a cup of tea. "One needs it after a Hepplewhite evening," said Joanna, leading the way through the open gate in the wattle fencing of their garden. The house was contemporary and Mary was thankful it stood well back in its garden and could not easily be seen from the village green. Contemporary was a word that stood for everything she disliked in the way of architecture and furniture; box-like houses with too much window and furniture poised on inadequate legs; and that just shows, she said to herself, that I am now old. The garden was also contemporary. There were asphalted paths and beautifully kept grass, and here and there a little pointed evergreen tree, looking in the moonlight as though it had been cut out of green tin, stood up starkly, but there were no flowers and no trees apart from the old mulberry close to her garden wall. She could see that there was a vegetable garden behind the house where a vast amount of things to eat grew in neat rows, but again there were no trees. No wonder the children had preferred The Laurels, for children, she thanked heaven, were never contemporary. Their manners unfortunately could some-times be so described but not the children themselves, for like the very old they were ageless in their unself-consciousness.

The ground floor of the house consisted of what Mary believed was called, in contemporary houses, the living-space. Finding her way round the half walls from one area to another always made her feel as though she was wandering round a maze, but with no hope of finding any core of privacy when she got to the end. Yet this maze was fun, and so were the queer reptilian plants that sprang from scarlet pots to claw one wall of the living area, and the large painting that hung against the other. She had not the faintest notion what the picture represented but it was splashed with red and orange and emerald green and was bright and gay. There was a staircase with airy treads and no visible means of support, and a central chimney of rough-hewn stone that soared up through the house like a tree trunk. The furniture was reduced to a minimum and as curiously shaped as the reptilian plants, and there was a good deal of space and brilliant light. Close to her, on top of a bookcase, a hamster was curled up fast asleep in a wooden cage with stairs, a sight as astonishing as though a Beatrix Potter picture had appeared in the midst of a modern action painting. The house was striking as well as fun but it was an astonishing apparition to appear in Appleshaw and she wondered what Jane would have thought of it. She could also understand Edith's passion for the little things.

"Did you design it?" she asked Roger.

"I did," he said with pride. "If you're building a house in a village like Appleshaw then build it of your own period, right up to the minute, and don't try and ape old places like The Laurels and Orchard Cottage. To my mind there's a sort of dishonesty about it. Cowardice too. One should have the courage of one's own convictions in one's own generation and not cower back into the past. Do you like Jo's picture? Sunset in the New Forest."

So Joanna was a painter, not a games mistress, and had probably never been near Roedean. It is good for me, thought Mary, to have come to this country backwater. It is possible that I shall learn more about the modern generation here than I could have done in London. How very odd. "The country," she said to Roger, "isolates things. Even modernity. I believe I shall come to appreciate this house better in Appleshaw than I would have done if you had built it at Wimbledon."

"You don't appreciate it yet?" he asked with twinkling eyes.

"I don't think it's a very good setting for the hamster," she replied lightly, and then, half to herself, "Nor perhaps for Edith."

She had thought of Joanna as being in the kitchen making the tea, and had forgotten that the kitchen area was separated from her only by a low wall of silvery wood crowned by a row of pots containing the kind of ferns that like steam. She was suddenly aware of Joanna looking at her through the green ferns. Her brown eyes were troubled, and they stayed troubled after she had carried the tray round the ferns and they were drinking their tea.

"You've seen Edith?" Roger asked Mary.

"We met last Sunday morning in my garden. No, don't protest, and don't tell Edith not to come into the garden. I want her there. And the others too. I told you before, I like children."

"Mummie, I want a drink!"

The imperious cry of a small boy sounded from upstairs and Joanna said, "You go, Roger. Did Mr. Hepplewhite send them anything?"

"Toffees and Lindt chocolate," said Roger, and Mary noticed that his pockets were bulging. "Hepplewhite is an odd man, Miss Lindsay. I suspect him of being devoid of the usual human affections yet he always sends gifts to the children."

He went away up the airy stairs two at a time and Joanna turned instantly to Mary.

"I love children so much," she said breathlessly. "I imagined that because I'd had two myself I knew all there was to know about them. I didn't realize how blessedly ordinary my own two are. I didn't realize how ordinary I am. And Roger. I imagined that because we are artists we are unordinary, intuitive and so on. But of course it doesn't follow at all. It's the kind of picture you paint, or the kind of book you write, that makes you unordinary, not just writing a book or painting a picture. Don't you think so?"

Mary had discovered during the evening that Joanna was inclined to lose herself in abstract discussion and she brought the conversation gently back to what she imagined it was supposed to be about, Joanna's failure with her adopted child. "How old was Edith when you adopted her?" she asked.

"Five. Her mother was a school friend of mine. We were at Malvern together. Anne and Rupert were killed in a motor smash. There were no near relatives to take Edith and so we did. She took our name. We were awfully fond of the little scrap and we thought it would be the best thing for her. But it's not worked out right and I don't know why."

She was near tears and Mary said, "It *will* work out right,

for what else could you do? The inevitable thing is always
in the end right. Why was she called Edith?"

"It was Rupert's mother's name. He was devoted to his
mother and she died a little while before Edith was born."

"What was Rupert's work?"

"He was on the stage. Charming and queer and brilliant.
Edith's like him."

"Brilliant?"

"No. That's the queer thing. The children go to a good
day school. Roger takes them on his way to work. Next
year we want Rose and Edith to go to boarding school together but Edith is doing so badly she'll never make the
grade. She doesn't get on well with the other children either
and she keeps being sick. The doctor can't find any reason,
but he's worried and he suggested I keep her at home for
the rest of this term and teach her myself. But I can't teach
and she doesn't respond to me at all. She's such a funny
shut-up little thing. Forgive me for pouring this out to
you, the very first time you come to see us, but I felt suddenly that it would help to tell you."

"Would you like me to teach her?" asked Mary. "I
taught when I was young. I'm old-fashioned now but I
have teaching friends who will send me the right books and
help me to get up-to-date. I'd do it for my own pleasure
because I like teaching and I love children. Would you like
me to try?"

She was instantly filled with dismay. Whatever was she
doing? Soon Rose would need coaching in a few subjects
and then Jeremy would feel left out. Before she knew where
she was she would be running an old-fashioned dame's
school. And she had come here to seek solitude and retirement. She had spoken without premeditation, on one of
those impulses that come behind you like a wave and lift
you off your feet before you know where you are.

Joanna's face went an even brighter pink and tears came
into her eyes. "Would you really do it? It would be marvellous for Edith if you would. But how can we let you do
such a thing? May I talk to Roger about it?"

"Yes, of course. Don't be in a hurry to make up your
minds. Just remember that I'd love to do it if you'd like
me to."

"You would understand Edith," said Joanna. "I don't. I'm so hopelessly ordinary."

"So am I. Perhaps I shan't get on with her any better than you do."

"You will. Paul Randall does. He's good with children. It's a shame he has none. They couldn't afford a child. Valerie says it's broken her heart to have no baby."

Mary looked at Joanna, but saw no sign in the charming pink face of the dryness of tone she thought she had detected in the voice: nothing to reinforce her own conviction that when people said their hearts were broken they were really entirely indifferent. She said, "May the children come and have tea with me? I'd like Edith to get accustomed to me and the house. Sunday?"

"Yes," said Joanna. "Thank you very much. I wish there was something we could do for you."

"I want a cottage tabby cat," said Mary. "And I want it rather quickly to prevent Mrs. Hepplewhite persuading me into a white poodle."

"I'll see to it," said Joanna. "Mrs. Croft's Susan is expecting. I'll see Mrs. Croft at once."

Roger came back and they talked of the difficulty of circumnavigating Mrs. Hepplewhite's kindness until Mary rose to go. She walked slowly back towards The Laurels, her thoughts flying ahead of her. This flight of the thoughts, like homing pigeons, was a new experience. The house came into view, low and solid, its thick walls and steep roof and air of having settled down deeply into the earth making it look eternally strong. The white chimney in the centre of the roof towered like a unicorn's horn, a magical thing. She had not seen her home before from this angle and she was as excited as though she were an explorer finding a new land.

She went indoors to the parlour and sat for a little while thinking of Mrs. Hepplewhite and her adoration of an indifferent husband, of Edith, and of Paul deprived of children. Living here is like being with the concentration camp people again, she thought, and then was horrified by the idiocy of what she was thinking. That had been fearful and degrading suffering, this was just a few people gathered together in one place with their normal human problems.

It was because that had been the most worthwhile period of her life, and so was this, that the two communities had come together in her mind. She stretched out her hand for the diary and sat for a while holding it. But she did not read that night. It was late and she was tired. Presently she put it away and went upstairs to bed.

CHAPTER VII

I

"THERE'S no need to take Martha," said Joanna.

"We are taking Martha," said Rose. The hamster was already in her arms and she shut her mouth firmly upon the statement.

"Very well," said Joanna. "But you must take Martha's travelling basket with you and then if Miss Lindsay doesn't like Martha she can go in her basket."

"There's no need to take the basket," said Edith.

Jeremy, when united with his sisters against authority, was silent but stood like Napoleon with his hands behind his back.

"Good-bye darlings," said Joanna hastily. "Be good."

They smiled at her kindly, dismissed her from their thoughts and ran to the gate. In a moment they were out of sight but she could hear their voices excited as those of chattering starlings. She stood upon her doorstep once more digesting the knowledge that she could not manage her children. Miss Lindsay, she believed, would be more successful. How did these tall, poised women who could command obedience with the lifting of an eyebrow get like they were? Was it something they ate? But would even these olympic ones be able to manage their own children if they had any? Joanna doubted it and went back into the house in a more cheerful frame of mind.

The three walked down the lane slowly, savouring the great occasion. They were going inside The Laurels, the house that for years had lain brooding beside their garden like some fabulous golden beast with many eyes and a towering horn sticking out of his forehead like a unicorn. At least that was how Rose thought of the house. It was not impossible to go inside a beast, Jonah had, but it was an unusual thing to do and she had no idea at all what it would be like inside. That was what made the visit so exciting and was why Martha had to come too. She did not like to enjoy things unless Martha could enjoy them also.

Jeremy felt differently about the house. For him it was not a beast but a sailing ship, and the boy in the pond was the boy who kept the lighthouse. From the trusty ship Mulberry he looked across the green rolling sea to the golden galleon, fo'c's'le windows blinking in the sunlight and the mainmast towering up into the sky, and his longing to be the captain of that ship was only a little less consuming than his longing for food. The Mulberry was a nice old thing but it was not his own, he had to share it with the girls. That other ship would be his own once he could board it. No one, not even his mother, knew about his passion for the sea and ships. There had been a day some while ago when the children had gone to have tea at the Manor. Rose and Edith had been out in the garden with Mrs. Hepplewhite and Mr. Hepplewhite and Jeremy had been in the library. Mr. Hepplewhite had taken him on his knee and shown him pictures of sailing ships, for which he had so fiery a love that Jeremy had caught alight too. From that day onward the garden of The Laurels had been for him no longer a garden but the sea.

Edith, more imaginative than the other two, was less imaginative about the house because for her it had a subordinate value, it was a jewel-case lined with dark velvet that held the little things. But she had always been fascinated by the door in the wall and she was longing to walk up the steps and ring the bell and watch the door open. "This is one of the special days," she said. The others nodded but they did not know what she had seen this morning. She had woken at dawn to find the full moon still shining and the owls calling, but right up in the dark yet shining sky a lark had been singing. Night and day had been perfectly balanced, greeting each other. She had known then it would be a special day in Appleshaw, the most unlikely people greeting they knew not what and not knowing they'd done it.

The children were now facing the green door and Rose spoke first. "*I'll* ring the bell," she said. "No, *I* will," said Edith. Jeremy said nothing because for him there was no door. The bottom step, upon which he stood, was the pinnace that had brought him alongside. It rocked gently beneath his feet. Presently, from far up, the rope ladder would descend. Edith seized the bellpull quickly and fiercely and pulled it out to its farthest limit. Rose, hampered by Martha, was not able to stop her. She kicked her briefly, and then smiled, for she was not a child to bear malice. The bell, which had now been repaired by Bert Baker, operated smoothly and could be heard ringing far away in the beast's stomach, the ship's hold, the velvet depths of quietness. "Don't come too soon!" Edith called voicelessly to Mary. She need not have done so for Mary understood these things. She came to the door with measured and mysterious tread, opened it slowly but wide and stood smiling down upon the little group on the steps.

Edith was looking remote and Mary knew instinctively that she must give no sign of recognition. Ignoring Edith she smiled at the two rosy faces and the grave furry countenance looking up at her with such profound consideration that she felt her smile becoming unsteady. Then the sandy, freckled boy began to smile too. The right-hand corner of his mouth gave an upward quirk, his button nose wrinkled up and his eyes screwed shut while entrancing creases folded themselves across his fat cheeks. Then the creases smoothed themselves out, the grey eyes flew open and were full of light. Mary saw with pleasure the tousled head, the suit of crumpled green linen stretched rather tightly over the aldermanic front, the scarred knees and scuffed brown sandals. Joanna, she realized, was not a mother who tormented her children with too much tidiness. "It's Jeremy," she said. He nodded, accepting and recognizing her, as she had recognized him, as someone without whom he would be the poorer.

And Rose? Being older her intuition was not so acute and she was not quite sure yet. She was lovely in her faded cotton frock, her warm brown eyes looking gravely into Mary's. Then her pink face began to glow and a quick smile came and went leaving a dimple in her right cheek. "Rose," said Mary. Rose nodded briefly, and said looking downwards, "This is Martha."

Mary bent to the hamster who was now sitting on the top

step. It sat up on its hind legs, its front paws folded de-
murely across its breast like an old lady's tippet. It had a
grave benevolent dignity.

"And Edith," said Rose, continuing her introductions.
Edith's face was pale and still but her eyes were dancing.
She and Mary shook hands with formality and then the
children and Martha followed Mary through the tunnel of
wistaria into the hall, where now wallflowers glowed in the
silver tankard on the bamboo table. Mary was aware of
stillness and a sigh behind her and she felt an intruder in
her own hall, too large and too old. She wished she could
turn into a spider and scurry up to a dark corner of the
ceiling and hide there. But all she could do was go into the
kitchen without looking at them, saying as she went, "Tea
is in here. Come and join me when you feel like it." They
did not join her for a full ten minutes. Where were they?

Rose was in the beast's magical stomach and it was
velvety dark just as she had thought it would be. And the
beast was moving, slowly stretching himself, yawning,
tossing back his head with the tall white horn. He had only
been waiting for her to come to him to go somewhere.
Presently he would trot, then canter, then gallop, then leap
for the sky, taking her with him. She had a moment of
delicious panic and shut her eyes, clasping Martha to her.

Jeremy found the darkness of the hold entirely satisfying.
Ahead of him worn stairs sloped away into the shadows. At
the top of them was the quarter-deck where he would
presently pace up and down with his telescope under his
arm. He was moving towards them when he was arrested
by the smell of toasting buns, and paused, his nose twitch-
ing. The delicious aroma was drifting from a half-open
door under an archway at the top of two stone steps. Instantly he forgot about the quarter-deck and ran up the
steps and through the door and Rose followed him.

Edith was left gazing at the wallflowers in the silver
tankard, which only she had noticed. It was a few minutes
before she followed the others into the kitchen.

"We are having tea in here," said Mary, "because my
dining-room is all upside-down."

They had never had tea in a real kitchen before, only in
the work area, and they were thrilled by the space and the

dresser and the big old table piled with good things to eat, savoury things such as they loved, twiglets and paste sand-wiches and sausages on sticks. The only sweet things were the buns that Mary was toasting on the Rayburn but they liked sweet things if they were toasted. The tea was a great success and appetites large, Martha imbibing milk from a saucer and sitting up on her haunches and holding twig-lets in her paws in a most enchanting manner. When no one could eat any more Mary showed them the house; the mossy parlour where the little things had been removed from their place in the window, the dining-room and spare rooms left by Bert Baker as fascinating scenes of devasta-tion, and her own room filled with light. She let them go where they would for as long as they would, for she saw that all three were playing private games inside their heads. Or at least Rose and Jeremy were. She was not sure about Edith who whispered something about singing.

"Singing?" asked Mary. "It must be a wireless some-where."

"It's inside the house," said Edith.

For a moment they were alone together in Mary's room, for Jeremy was motionless at the landing window, gazing out over vast spaces, and Rose had gone down to the kitchen to find another twiglet for Martha.

"What sort of singing?" asked Mary.

"Chanting," said Edith. "Like in church but more beautiful. Listen."

Mary listened but she could hear nothing, not even a thrush. She shook her head. "I can't hear it," she said.

"That's because it's gone now. It comes and goes."

" 'Where should this music be', " quoted Mary, " 'i' the air, or the earth? It sounds no more'."

"That's nice," said Edith, her face lighting up. "Are you saying poetry?"

"Shakespeare's *Tempest*."

Edith slipped her hand into Mary's. "My daddy said poetry like that when he put me to bed."

Mary knew she was not speaking of Roger and she asked, "Do you remember him?"

"Yes. Could you teach me to say that sort of poetry?"

"Wouldn't it be too like school?"

"No! I don't like school. I wish I could do lessons with you."

"We'll ask Mummy if you may. We must go down to the parlour now and play games with the others."

"I'd rather stay here."

"We must go and play with the others," said Mary. "Do you know what I found in one of the drawers in the desk in the parlour? Chessmen. They are almost as beautiful as the little things. Look." She opened one of the doors of her wardrobe and inside were the little things gleaming under the glass shade.

"No one knows they are here but us," whispered Edith. "I like secrets. Do you?"

"No," said Mary. "I don't," and realized as she spoke that this was one of the differences between youth and maturity. You were adult when you no longer cared for secrets. Then looking at Edith she saw the child's face had blanched. She had touched some wound. "Let's go down and find the chessmen," she said.

In the parlour she set them out on the table and the children gathered round. The chessboard had squares of ebony and mother-of-pearl and the men were red and white, marvellously carved. Mary had never seen chessmen so beautiful and the children had never seen them at all. She explained the moves to them and Edith and Rose were quick to learn but Jeremy was young for chess and he was soon bored. Out of the tail of her eye Mary saw him disappear over the window sill, a green figure instantly absorbed in the sea-green of the conservatory. It was as though a small wave had rejoined its element. She let him go for the outer greenness seemed his milieu just now. And he'd be safe in the garden. The latch of the garden door was difficult and beyond his reach.

He did not even try to reach it for he was in a sailing boat and for him there was no door. The garden wall was a high wave, curved to break, but his little craft went up it, hovered dangerously at the top for a moment and then slithered down on the other side. The old wall was in need of re-pointing and there were hollows between the bricks that took his prehensile toes and fingers comfortably, but he was not aware of them, nor of the bruises he sustained on the other side, for one is not bruised by the sea. As he ran through the lychgate and across the churchyard the tang of it was in his nose and there was salt on his lips. The freshening wind filled the white sails and the small ship danced over the waves. He had seen the other ship from Neptune's quarter-deck. He had known at once who she was, the *Victory*, and her captain was his friend. She was home from the West Indies with spices in her hold.

He climbed over the stile in the low wall that divided the churchyard from the bluebell wood and struck uphill to the right, up the hidden path that he and Rose and Edith had discovered last spring. It led from the Manor to the church and must have been well trodden in the days when the Manor servants, and on fine days the squire and his lady, used it Sunday by Sunday, but now it was so lost beneath brambles and fern that only a child could have found and followed it. Jeremy followed it as unconsciously as a hare or a badger would have followed its path to form or set, and was equally unaware of the westering sunlight and the green-gold mist about the boles of the trees. But he was aware of the blue sea washing about his boat.

The trees thinned and there was a green lawn and bushes of forsythia and cherry. Behind the old house with its array of tall chimneys was banked a splendour of white cumulus cloud, like the sails of a ship. It was this that he had seen from Mary's landing window. "*Victory*," he whispered, and set his course for an open window beside a magnolia tree.

2

Just inside the window Mr. Hepplewhite sat at the writing table in his library. When he had bought the house from the old squire's distant and indifferent heir he had bought some of the furniture too, the portraits in the dining-room and the contents of the library. Except for the laying down of a few Persian rugs and the hanging of sherry-coloured velvet curtains he had not allowed his wife to lay a finger on the library. The high moulded ceiling was still smoke-dimmed and the panelling that showed between the bookcases was pickled black with smoke and age. The room was steeped in its own unchanging and unchangeable smell; the wood smoke and tobacco smoke of centuries and the smell of old leather. The sunlight in this room was always liquid amber, the shadows strange and soft as the feathers of a vast, ghostly, night-dark bird. The library gave Mrs. Hepplewhite the shivers but Mr. Hepplewhite was satisfied by it.

So few things in life had satisfied him, nothing really except this room and the sea. Children did not so much satisfy as trouble him, because he had none, but he hungered for their company just as in the midst of a busy day in the city he longed with a sharp pang for nightfall and this room. The only child Hermione had produced, a son, had died at birth. Something wrong with her. His resentment was still deep. At one time he had had a yacht but it had taken too much time from business and he had had to give it up. Business was what supremely mattered to him and he was a single-minded man. This room did not distract him from business for its quietness gave him a power of concentration that even he had hardly known before. Within it he was like a bee sucking at the honey of the gold. The room, its mystery curved about him like the beauty of petals, made no protest. Like the flower it was helpless, and it had sheltered many passions in its day.

Mr. Hepplewhite rapidly added up a column of figures and wrote down the breathtaking total without a tremor. His handwriting was strong and thick and he favoured a very black ink. He laid down his pen and sat back in his chair, his large handsome head slightly bowed forward, his dark eyes hooded. Should he do it? It would be the most audacious gamble of his life, and the most risky, both for himself and others. He stood to win or lose the biggest fortune yet.

It was not now the lust for money itself that consumed him, though he liked money, it was the lust for power. The power and the gold were the same. Gold. In his mind he still used the old-fashioned word though there were no sovereigns nowadays. But there had been gold when he was a boy. He'd not seen it when he'd sweated in the basement kitchen but he had seen it when he'd been bell-boy, and later a waiter in the club. He'd seen them pay bills with sovereigns, seen them fish up a handful of loose silver from their pockets as though it were no more than a handful of gravel. He had loathed them, loathed the sight, sound and smell of them, sleek, soft-spoken, cigar and wine-scented, soap-scented. He'd longed to fling the soup in their smooth faces. He'd had his own ways of doing things to them; an extra dusting of pepper in the soup, a crack of open window directing a draught on to a bald head, an obsequious manner verging on the insolent. As a small boy in his kitchen period, in bed at night with his brothers in their basement bedroom, apprehensively eyeing the bugs on the wall, he had planned hideous tortures for them. And bided his time.

And then something happened that changed him. In his early waiter period his father was hanged for murder. Partially crippled by a stroke, and a heavy drinker, his father had for many years been a feeble creature and how he could have summoned the strength to cosh the policeman, even though the drink was in him at the time, only his son Fred understood. His father had driven a hansom cab. He'd driven the lordly ones, received the flung coins from men who'd never bothered to look in his face and thank him, and he had loathed them and bided his time. And then, drink-fuddled, had mistaken the poor devil of a copper for one of them and struck out from the deeps of the vast hatred he'd handed on to his son.

Fred's ambition was now changed. Not to bide his time while he let the loathing fester, that led to the condemned cell, but to be one of them. Beat them at their own game. Look, sound and smell like them, and coax the gold out of their pockets into his not by force but guile. He had gifts useful for his purpose. From his paternal grandfather, a little Jew who had done well with a second-hand clothes shop in the East End, he had inherited cunning, a good brain and a fine head for figures. From his mother, a game-keeper's daughter who had gone into service at the local manor, accompanied her family to their town house for the season and had the misfortune to be beguiled by the black eyes of Fred's father, he had inherited good looks and stamina. Of himself he possessed keen observation, self-confidence, and somewhere deeply buried in him a child-like belief in the possibility of the impossible, that sublime belief that makes a man of genius and a man of faith, and he set himself to do what he wanted with no doubt at all that he would succeed.

From the moment of his decision his manner towards the lordly ones subtly changed. He studied their individual tastes and served them with considerate care. He never forgot an order and he was always on hand when wanted. He helped the old ones in and out of their coats with infinite gentleness and was the soul of tact with the slightly tipsy. He received his increasingly large tips, which he saved, with grateful humility. Though the youngest he was soon the most popular waiter in the club. It only needed one of the older members who happened to be staying there, an important old person on the stock exchange, to fall sick and be tended by the solicitous Fred for the upward climb to begin. He became the old gentleman's valet, employing his free time in educating himself with astounding success. Then he became his employer's personal secretary and right-hand man and upon his death was left a considerable sum of money. After that he never looked back.

Dolly helped him. He had married her while he was still a waiter. At the time he had been not only in love with her but grateful to her for marrying him, for she was more than a cut above him. She had progressed from her father's flourishing pub to the halls, and from there to a musical comedy chorus. She was enchantingly pretty and a good actress, with a soprano voice of piercing quality. It was the opinion of all her friends that Dolly could have married a lord, but instead she fell in love with a slim young waiter and on his wedding day he actually felt humble, for the first and last time in his life. She taught him many things; niceties of manner and deportment that she'd picked up from the young men who took her out to supper after the show, small courtesies and graces that had touched and pleased her. She would have taught him other things as well, unconsciously, had he been capable of learning them; honesty, loyalty and long-suffering. But these, so noticeable in her, he did not notice. It was not that he turned from such things but that he simply did not notice them. They had nothing to do with his overwhelming purpose.

He soon fell out of love with her because she rather

quickly lost her prettiness. She began to put on weight, to look tired and strained, and the social advantage she had had at the beginning was soon lost. She kept up with him but she was not the actor that he was. Completely self-centred, he had always dramatized himself, but she had not. She had consciously to build up a part. She knew how but the strain of the ceaseless effort told upon her. He did not leave her for she was useful. She understood his ways and his needs and gave no sign that she was aware of his infidelities. Her love made no claims upon him and he was not incommoded by it. He saw to that.

Should he do it? The fact that it was a nefarious project did not trouble him but he was aware that a man may tempt his luck once too often. Yet his flair for a good thing had never let him down yet. Why should it now? Was his nerve failing him? The mere thought, touching him lightly, instantly stiffened him, for failure was not a word that existed in his vocabulary. His jaw set and he reached for the bell that should summon Julie, his secretary and the present object of his affections. Then he checked. Better keep even Julie right out of it. Then he smiled and touched the bell. If he had a weakness it was that while his infatuation for them lasted he trusted these pretty girls too much. And, in Julie's case, was inclined to underrate her intelligence. He never supposed they understood a word of what he was dictating. And he hated writing a letter as much as he hated telephoning. He liked all such menial tasks to be performed for him. Julie came, cool and slim, her white eyelids obsequiously lowered. Her skin was like milk. She was an enchanting creature.

"Take down a couple of letters," snapped Mr. Hepplewhite. "I want to get them off my mind now. Be done with them. Ready?"

She sat beside him and he dictated the letters. She went into the next room and typed them and brought them back for him to sign. As she turned to leave him again her bare arm brushed his coat sleeve. He did not look up, for he kept his private and professional lives in watertight compartments, but the slight touch tingled through his body. She was a clever girl. The door closed soundlessly behind her but the quiet of the room was subtly disturbed.

He sorted his papers and locked them away in a drawer of his writing-table. Raising his head he became aware of a small woodland creature patiently waiting outside the open window. Jeremy was a very ordinary small boy but against the background of lawn and beech wood and flowering shrubs, all caught in that most magic moment of low and level sunlight, he did not seem earthly and Mr. Hepplewhite suffered a profound shock. It pitched him suddenly into another dimension. In the depths of the wood he heard a bird calling and a flowering branch stirred in a breath of wind. The child's face, that in the moment of shock had seemed to him unreal in its innocence, became more real than anything he had ever looked upon, yet at the same time elusive and lost, himself, yet lost to him. He looked only at natural things, a flowering branch, shadows and sunlight and a boy's face, yet the experience had a quality unknown to him and he was tossed with sorrow, and yet at the same time aware of danger. The man he had made over so many years was in danger. With an effort he fought back the sorrow. It receded and he was once more within the self and experience that he had willed. He looked down and saw his hands lying on his blotter, his signet ring and fountain pen. He was extremely tired. He was not often tired, for he was a strong man, but the pressure of business had been very great lately, the pressure of this big decision to be made.

He looked up and the child was Jeremy. "Hello, son," he said. "How long have you been there?"

"I hid in the magnolia tree till you weren't busy any more," said Jeremy.

"Come along in," said Mr. Hepplewhite. Jeremy came to him and he took him on his knee. "What were you wanting, eh? Those pictures of the sailing ships again?" Jeremy nodded and Mr. Hepplewhite set him down while he fetched the books, volumes of illustrations of eighteenth-century merchant vessels and ships of the line, Nelson's ships among them, that had belonged to the old squire. His own delight when he had found them was still vivid to him but he had not shown the books to anyone except the boy.

"I sailed here," said Jeremy, when he was once more

seated on Mr. Hepplewhite's knees. "I sailed in my little boat from my big ship to your ship."

Mr. Hepplewhite accepted this statement as fact and nodded gravely. Sharing with them their belief in the possibility of the impossible, and having proved it true, he never laughed at children's fantasy. That was why they liked him. He would not have called it fantasy any more than they did. It was as real as their faith. "Good voyage?" he asked.

Jeremy told him about it while Mr. Hepplewhite turned over the printed part of the book before them to find the pictures, but when the pictures were reached he fell breathlessly silent. Such marvellous sails rising one above another like towering white clouds, such splendid figure-heads, carved poops, flags flying in the wind and seas with curling waves like the edges of pastry on a tart. And wonderful names like *Neptune, Victory, Mermaid, Garland* and *Illustrious*. Mr. Hepplewhite told him the names of the sails and explained how they were set to catch the wind. Then he told Jeremy about his own boat. It has been called *The Swan*.

"Did it fly fast?" asked Jeremy.

"With power and beauty," said Mr. Hepplewhite. He hesitated, then unlocked a drawer and took out a small paperweight, a crystal ship with sails set. It was an expensive little treasure that he had seen in a Bond Street window and bought for himself on the day that he had returned from his first sail in *The Swan*. He had not looked at it since he had sold his boat. It had never been his habit to give many gifts but since he had lived in this house he had frequently found himself doing so, and he gave the ship to Jeremy. "Here you are, son. You can keep it."

With the exquisite thing sparkling on his grubby palm Jeremy gazed in stillness and silence. The colour rushed into his face, then ebbed away. When at last he looked up he was still speechless but that quirk had come at the corner of his mouth. His eyes screwed shut as his fat cheeks creased, then opened full on Mr. Hepplewhite's face, blazing with adoration.

Watching him, Mr. Hepplewhite was intensely moved. He pinched Jeremy's ear. "Good boy," he said. "Now put it in your pocket. Take care of it, mind, and when you are older you can give it to some other boy, as I've given it to you. Now let's get back to the book. Look, here's the *Agamemnon*. She was one of Nelson's. Sixty-four guns."

They bent over the pictures and the minutes flew. Mrs. Hepplewhite, passing by in the garden, saw their two heads together and went quietly back into the house to telephone to Joanna that Jeremy was safe and should be returned in due course. There were tears on her cheeks when she had finished and she dabbed at them with her handkerchief.

"What's the matter, Mrs. Hepplewhite?"

Mrs. Hepplewhite swung round. It was that hussy coming down the stairs. But for the effort of her will Mrs. Hepplewhite's mind would have used a much stronger word than hussy to describe Julie. But calling names did not alter a situation. Mrs. Hepplewhite did not know how one could alter a situation such as hers, but certainly not by venom. She clutched at her dignity and smiled at Julie, who had the most extraordinary habit of always appearing from nowhere just when she was at her lowest ebb. It couldn't be done on purpose, because how could Julie know? But perhaps she did know for hate has its sensibilities as well as love.

"I am tired I think," said Mrs. Hepplewhite. "The spring is lovely but tiring. Don't you think so?"

"I don't feel it so myself but then I am young," said Julie in her warm husky voice, a voice like chocolate sauce poured over ice cream, a sweetly masking voice. "Poor Mrs. Hepplewhite. You'll have time to lie down before supper. Shall I take the quilt off your bed?"

"No, dear, thank you," said Mrs. Hepplewhite, and tried to turn away, for Julie was standing in a flood of sunlight that illumined to perfection her flawless skin, the perfect curve of her breasts and the long sculptured line from hip to knee. But it was an effort to look away and she felt blindly for the handle of the drawing-room door, loathing her clumsiness. Inside she stood listening for she could not be certain if Julie had gone. One could never be certain. She moved like a sunbeam, weightlessly. Mrs. Hepplewhite, as she sat down in the armchair by the window, felt all weight.

She tried to relax and admire the garden and the beauty of the room where she sat. She always tried hard to appreciate it all for she realized her good fortune. Her lines had fallen to her in very comfortable and pleasant places but her inward misery was like a glass wall between her and the good things about her. She could see them but when she put out her hands to them she met that cold wall. And then again she sometimes wondered if the country really appealed to her. Or the old house either. When she was alone it frightened her with its spookiness and oppressive silence and she had to rush about and be on committees and things to get away from it. But Frederick liked it. Being the squire appealed to him. Of course there were things she liked, her lovely clothes for instance, and the power to do good and be kind to others. She loved being kind and Frederick was generous about the amount of money he allowed her for clothes and charities. He was always kind to her. Why could she not adjust herself to a common situation? Other women did, many of them with graceful humour. Why must she hanker after the impossible? It was she who was abnormal, not he, for she loved him now as she had loved him at the beginning. To love this man was her life. She had to love him.

Why? You needn't. Why suffer when you needn't? Only a fool suffers unnecessarily.

It was the first time the idea had ever occurred to her and its impact was so strong that it was like a voice speaking.

Be like the other women, laugh and be indifferent. Or have a row and then divorce him. Indifference. Anger. The poison or the knife. It doesn't matter which you use. Either is equally lethal. Love dies. Then you can enjoy things again. You're not old yet. You've got time.

But if I ceased to love him I should be dead inside, she answered, for it is I who love him, I myself, Dolly Barnes. I am not anything but loving Frederick.

You fool, said the voice, you fool.

She was aware of conflict, strange and deep, and then it seemed to cease and she thought she had decided. Angry with Frederick she could not be but she would be indifferent. She would not care any more. Let Dolly die. She'd always been a fool anyhow. Life held a great deal for Mrs. Hepplewhite.

She slumped back in her chair with a sigh of relief, but just as she was relaxing into a blissful state of utter blankness the door flew open and Elise, her Swiss girl, burst in. Elise, though extremely efficient in her work, was as noisy as Julie was soundless; though sometimes Mrs. Hepplewhite thought she was noisy on purpose, just to be different from Julie whom she loathed. She came across the room now scattering console tables in her wake, then picked one of them up and placed a little tray of tea beside Mrs. Hepplewhite, whom she loved, and on whose side she invariably was.

"Hot and strong as you like it," she said. "You like it better than sherry. You don't really like sherry. Drink up, Mrs. Hepplewhite. That Julie! That bitch! She tells on you to me! Tells me you were crying. How dare she. She's a bitch!"

Elise's enchanting broken English somehow robbed her language of offence while taking nothing from its incisiveness. In the blankness of Mrs. Hepplewhite's state emotion stirred again, profound relief that Elise had spoken it out loud to her. In gratitude to Elise she looked up in her round face and saw it flushed with rage, the brown eyes snapping, the untidy curly dark hair standing up on end. Elise was a darling. There was no indifference about Elise. Anger, yes, but not anger like a knife. Anger like a sun-burst. She was alive to her finger tips.

Will you separate yourself from Elise?

While she mechanically poured herself out a cup of tea, and added a lump of sugar, she realized that it had begun again, strange and deep. It was not over after all. She had not decided. This was another voice and she was being given another chance. If she became indifferent she would be like Julie, who did not care in the least what suffering she caused.

You've only given yourself one lump of sugar. Dolly took three.

Mrs. Hepplewhite discovered that her slumped position in the arm-chair had caused her corsets to dig in most uncomfortably. She sat up, braced herself to accept their discipline once more, and helped herself to two more lumps of sugar. She turned to Elise and smiled. "Thank you, dear," she said. "I am more grateful to you than you know."

After Elise had taken Jeremy home Mr. Hepplewhite was again alone in the library. For once they had no guests this weekend and he'd be having the evening meal alone with Hermione. No need to hurry. It was dusk now and though the Manor House thrush was still singing the owls were calling down in the wood. He liked the owls. This morning he had stood at his window at the first light and there had been a lark singing in a sky that still held the shining of the moon, and the owls had been calling as the lark sang. Odd how he'd come to love the country. He supposed it was his mother in him. Through the open window the air blew fresh and cool, like well water. There had been a well behind his grandfather's cottage, the game-keeper's cottage in the woods where he had stayed once with his mother, and the water, welling up from a deep spring, had been the purest and coldest he'd ever known. He'd liked to hang over the edge of the well and breathe in the cool scent of the water. He could see that boy leaning over the well, his dark hair standing up stiffly on the crown of his head. He could see him as clearly as he'd seen young Jeremy at the window a short while ago. The two boys seemed one. Mr. Hepplewhite no longer felt tossed about, pitched into another dimension, though that moment and this one were as united as the two boys. He had been shaken then. But now it seemed that he was gently per-suaded. The scent of water. He had forgotten there was such a thing. Perhaps only children were aware of it. He couldn't ever remember feeling so tired. He stretched out his hand and rang the bell.

When Julie appeared he said, "Those two letters. I've changed my mind. Bring them back and I'll destroy them."

"They're posted," said Julie. "I imagined you would want them to arrive on Monday morning first thing."

"You posted them? But I've told you time and again not to post letters until I tell you." He glared at her, then re-laxed. "You little fool! There's no Sunday post out from the village after three o'clock."

She smiled at him sweetly. "I sent Archer into West-water to post them." There was a trace of mockery in her smile and the sight of her, so utterly a part of the world of his attainment, restored him to what he was accustomed to regard as sanity. The two boys vanished like dew in the sun and if he had been capable of blushing he would have blushed.

"All right," he said. "You took a lot upon yourself but in this case you were right. The thing needed clinching. But don't use your imagination again, Julie. There's no place for it in business. Imagination and over-fatigue. Avoid them like the devil."

3

Mary was tired after the children had left and after supper she took the diary upstairs with her. In bed with the oil lamp burning beside her she listened for a few moments to the owls calling, and then she wondered about the singing that Edith had heard. She, listening then, had heard only silence, but in a child's life and mind there are no empty spaces. Stillness, silence, are quickened for them either by Keats's world of the imagination or by heaven or, and she smiled, by mischief. Where had that child Jeremy got to? When she had taken Edith and Rose home his mother had been unperturbed by his disappearance. Jeremy, she said, always turned up. What had stirred Joanna with relief and joy had been their mutual decision that Edith should leave school and start lessons with Mary in a week's time.

She turned a fresh page of the diary. Between her first reading and this one the entries had been chiefly concerned with getting settled in the house. The old vicar, whose name was Benedict Carroway and who still wore a white stock and a top hat to go about the parish, had lent her his carriage in which to go shopping. Driving in it to West-water she and Jenny had found there stuffs for curtains, damask hangings for her bed, a carpet to match, and a mossy green carpet for the parlour. She described these purchases with delight and Mary could picture the West-water of those days, the gentle traffic of carriages and governess carts up and down the winding streets, the leisurely shoppers in their long skirts, and enchanting hats poised on high piled hair. And she described the squire, Sir Charles Royston, and his little wife who still wore her hair in ringlets with a white lace cap on top. In contrast to the vicar, whose rosy face was clean-shaven apart from white side-whiskers, Sir Charles was hirsute. A long grey beard flowed down over his chest and his hair curled upon the collar of his black velvet smoking jacket. He sat all day in his library writing a history of Greece that never got finished and left the running of the estate to his son, re-ferred to by everyone at Appleshaw as Mr. Ambrose, a vague and kindly man who never looked himself except dressed in tweeds and accompanied by a cloud of dogs. Dressed for dinner he looked like someone else, someone whom he very much disliked. Sir Charles's grandfather had built the Georgian manor house with money brought to him by his heiress wife, and reading about them Mary re-membered the two portraits. The much older manor house had been burnt down some years before and the Roystons had lived in a farmhouse in the beech woods until the heiress restored them to their own again. Cousin Mary's descriptions captured her diary entirely through the re-maining weeks of October and the first half of November, when they abruptly broke off. They did not begin again until after Christmas. Mary found herself at New Year's Eve when she turned the page.

"I was indoors for a month before Christmas. I got very tired, settling in, and though there are not many people here I had to get to know the few there are. But they are so different, these few, from Mother's friends. I think they would all be called rather odd people. When Lady Royston came to see me after I was better and said, 'Was it liver, dear?' and I answered truthfully, for I'm always going to speak the truth here, 'It's my mind. I get very afraid,' she only said, 'Camomile tea the last thing at night,' and did not seem to think me peculiar. She came again next day with a small box which she put into my hands. Inside was a minute blue glass tea-set, too small for dolls, about the right size for fairies, 'I've loved it a long time,' she said. 'I thought you might like it too.' And then she went away before I had time to thank her properly. And two days ago Sir Charles came to see me and brought me a Christmas present of red and white carved chessmen, and taught me how to play. 'Send for me when you want me,' he said. 'There's nothing like chess when you feel low.' And so now they all know about me and I don't mind because this is a place close knit in family affection. When you pass through the lime avenue you come to a world within a world, a place enclosed. The enclosure has nothing to do with enchantment, for it's not a fairy world. It has to do with obedience. That was one of the things I found out when I was ill.

"It's odd, but this time what I went through was a double thing, two strands twisted together of black and gold. There was the bad thing, fear and darkness pressing in, and there was the glad singing of love, the 'yes, I will' that is my song. I had not known before that love is obedience. You want to love, and you can't, and you hate yourself because you can't, and all the time love is not some marvellous thing that you feel but some hard thing that you do. And this in a way is easier because with God's help you can command your will when you can't command your feelings. With us, feelings seem to be important, but he doesn't appear to agree with us.

"What else did I learn? I found out what the dark walls are and why, like Job, I must repent in dust and ashes.

"It was a dream I had, a little while before Christmas. It had been my worst day, after a sleepless night, and one of the worst things about it was that I had stopped being aware of the double thing. I did manage to say, 'yes, I will', but I think I only said it three times and each time saying it was like lifting a mountain, so reluctant was I. It had been a cold dark day. There had been a light sprinkling of snow but with no sun to make it sparkle it had seemed not beautiful but bitter and sad. It was dark so soon that at four o'clock Jenny drew my bedroom curtains. For I was in bed, where I'd been for a fortnight. Bed did not help my insomnia at all but it seemed to make it all easier to bear and Jenny didn't worry me to get up. She brought me some tea and I drank it, and then I asked her to leave me alone and she did. I heard the clock strike five and I thought, Soon it will be Christmas and I shan't be able to enjoy my first Christmas in my own home. I was very sorry for

myself. I thought, I can't bear it. I was lying on stones and
the walls were moving in. And then, and that was the third
time, I said, 'yes, I will'. But it didn't help. The walls
moved in nearer and as they closed right round, trapping
me, I screamed.

"I don't suppose I really screamed. What had happened
was that I had fallen asleep at last and drifted into nightmare. I was imprisoned in stone. I knew then what men
suffer who are walled up alive. But I was able to think and
I thought, Shall I scream and beat against the wall or shall
I keep my mouth shut and be still? I wanted to scream
because it would have been the easier thing. But I didn't.
And when I had been still for a little while I found myself
slowly edging forward. There was a crack in the stone.
The hardness pressed against me upon each side in a
horrible way, as though trying to crush me, but I could edge
forward through the crack. I went on scraping through and
at last there was a glimmer of light. It came to my feet like
a sword and I knew it had made the crack, a sword of fire
splitting the stone. And then the walls drew back slightly
on each side of me, as though the light pushed them. I had
a sense of conflict, as though the darkness reeled and
staggered, resisting the light in an anguish of evil strength.
It had a fearful power. But the light, that seemed such a
small beam in comparison with that infinity of blackness,
kept the channel open and I fled down it. There was room
now to run. I ran and ran and came out into the light.

"I had escaped. I was so overwhelmed with thankfulness
that I nearly fell. I sank down on the ground and sat back
on my heels, like children do sometimes when they are
saying their prayers and are tired. It was ground, not
stone, it was a floor of trodden earth. The stone walls were
still there but the light had hollowed them out into a cave
and they no longer frightened me. There was a lantern in
the cave and people were moving about, a man and woman
caring for a girl who lay on a pile of hay. And for a new-
born child. As I watched the woman stooped and put him
into his mother's arms. An ox and ass and a tired donkey
were tethered to the wall of the cave, and their breath was
like smoke. I was not surprised for the strange changes of
a dream never surprise me. It was like one of the nativity

scenes that the old masters painted only not tidy and
pretty like those. The girl was exhausted, her clothes were
crumpled and the sweat on her face gleamed in the lantern
light. The man was dusty and tired and not yet free of the
anxiety that had been racking him for hours past. The
woman was one of those kindly bodies who turn up from
somewhere to lend a hand in times of human crises. She
made soft clucking noises as she gave the baby to his
mother, and the two women gave each other a long look of
triumph before the girl bent over her baby. He was like all
new-born babies. He looked old and wizened, and so frail
that my heart nearly stopped in fear, as it always does when
I see a new-born child. How could anything so weak survive? His thin wail echoed in the stony place and then was
stifled as he sought his mother.

"They've not come yet, I thought. All the prettiness the
artists painted isn't here. No angels, no shepherds, no
children with their lambs. It's stripped down to the bare
bones of the rock and the child. There's no one here. And
then I thought, I am here, and I asked, who am I, Lord?
And then I knew that I was everyone. I wasn't solitary.
Everyone was me and I was everyone. We were all here,
every sinner whose evil had built up those dark walls that
held the child like a trap. For looking round I saw that the
cave of the nativity was very small. The walls were pressing in upon him close and hard and dark like they pressed
in on me. And the old claustrophobic terror was back on
me again, but not for myself. I remembered the rocks of
the wilderness and the multitude of sinners surging in,
selfish and clamorous, sick and sweaty, clawing with their
hot hands, giving him no time so much as to eat. I remembered the mocking crowd about the cross and the thick
darkness. I remembered the second cave, the dark and
stifling tomb. Two stony caves, forming as it were the two
clasps of the circle of his life on earth. And I remembered
Saint Augustine saying, 'He looked at us through the lattice
of our flesh and he spake us fair.' Shut up in that prison
of aching flesh and torn nerves, trapped in it. . . . The
Lord of glory. . . . I remembered the sword of light that
had split the rock of sin, making for me the way of escape
to where he was at the heart of it. At my heart. At the heart

of everything that happened to me, everything I did, everything I endured. He was not the weakness that he seemed for he had a sword in his hand and all evil at last would go reeling back before it. He had entered the prison house of his own will. And so he was not trapped and nor was I. There was always the way of escape so long as it was to the heart of it, whatever it was, that one went to find him.

"The shepherds were coming. I could hear them singing, a homely rough singing and a little out of tune. And the high sweet piping of a shepherd's pipe. I shut my eyes and listened and it came nearer and I woke up.

"But the singing continued. It was carol singers not far from my window. There was the bass rumble of a few men's voices and the piping of small boys. It was the choir. They were singing one of the oldest of the carols, 'The Holly and the Ivy', the old folk tune that has been part of the English Christmas for so many centuries. I listened to it and I was at peace, and knew I would soon be well again. In the pause between this carol and the next I got out of bed and went to the landing and called out to Jenny to find my purse in my escritoire and give the boys their Christmas tips. Then I went back to bed again and listened to 'While Shepherds Watched', and then to the music dying away in the distance as they moved off to other houses round the green. And then I began to think. I remembered how rebellious I had been, and how I had told the old man that I had done nothing that called for dust and ashes, and he had replied, 'No?' I hadn't realized then just how vile my own sin is and that every sinner must bear the pressing in of my sin, as I bear his, in penitence. And I thought that the dust and ashes of the suffering that results from sin is purging if offered as prayer for each other. It may take me my lifetime to know the vileness of my own sin, and perhaps not even then, perhaps not till later, but until I do know I will not know God. Oh yes, I will know his goodness, it will come to me now and then like a touch, like a breath of fragrance, and I will find his presence at the heart, but not himself entirely. Not heaven.

"I slept well that night, no longer aware of the pressure of the walls for they had vanished, but of the very different pressure of protection. Not pressure at all really but shelter.

And the next day the old Vicar, Mr. Carroway, came to see me. I'd refused to see anyone while I was ill except Doctor Partridge, who has a bristling ginger moustache and rides to hounds but doesn't seem to know much about sick people, but I was glad to see Mr. Carroway. I don't think he knows much about sick people either, and if I'd asked him to say a prayer with me I am sure he would have been much embarrassed, but his kindness and courtesy, his rosy face and white whiskers seemed very much in place in my beautiful room.

" 'My house is old isn't it?' I said to him. 'Especially the hall and the archway leading to the kitchen. That bit seems to me to be older than the rest.'

"His face lit up and he sat forward with his finger-tips placed together, which is his habit when he is pleased about something, and I remembered that his hobbies are church history and bees. 'Part of the Cistercian monastery,' he said. 'Alas, there's nothing left now but the abbey church, our church, and a few walls and doorways built into the old houses round the green, and the bees and mulberry trees. The monks were famous for their apiary. I've never known a patch of country that had so many bees as Appleshaw. The lime blossom and the orchards bring them. That lime avenue led to the abbey gateway. This house, my dear young lady, was once the infirmary. Your hall, so far as I can make out from the plans, was the infirmary chapel.'

" 'Then that explains it,' I said.

" 'What does it explain, my dear?' he asked.

" 'The fact that Appleshaw is a place enclosed. And monks take vows of obedience, don't they? This is a very obedient place, close-knit in love.' Mr. Carroway became even pinker in the face than is natural to him and looked on the floor for his top hat, which he had left downstairs. 'And one feels in this house the shelter of God's hand. No wonder, if it sheltered the sick.'

"Mr. Carroway rose to go, with courteous murmurs, and I told him he'd done me a lot of good, which was quite true. My hall had been the infirmary chapel. I made up my mind I would buy an old table or chest, altar shaped, to have in the hall, and I would always have flowers on it. And if that was a sentimental idea I didn't care. Being ill makes you feel what well people call sentimental, but what you feel is none-the-less genuine whatever they call it.

"Christmas in this place was so familiar, as though I'd always lived here. What is it that makes one place more than another home to one? Not length of stay. I think it is compatibility. I want God and so did the monks. The unseen spirit of a place has its deep desire and if it's the same as yours then your small desire goes down like an anchor into the depths."

Mary closed the diary and murmured to herself, "Like as the hart desireth the water-brooks." She put out the lamp and lay waiting for sleep. The owls were calling greetings to each other. Probably hunting calls really, for nature was never as agreeable down below as it seemed on top, it had the two strands, but they sounded like greetings. This had been a very special day.

CHAPTER VIII

I

MARY had not realized until now the importance in the life of countrywomen of small social occasions. Going out to tea, to lunch, to sherry, to the Women's Institute, varied their routine and gave them the illusion that they lived at the hub of things. But we don't, thought Mary. The Bennetts and the Eliots visited just like this. If it wasn't for the wireless and television and our cars there'd be no difference at all. Who would have thought that the lime avenue carried one back to this archaic leisure? But that's England still. Just a few miles away from the main road, down this lane or that, you come to another world, and I expect all the worlds at the lanes' endings are quite different from each other. When they are not I hope I'll be dead.

The bell rang and she took off the apron she was wearing to sweep out her reconstituted spare room and went down to open the door. It was half past three so it was going to be a social occasion.

The moment she saw them she knew who they were. The walk had been too much for them. Colonel Adams was trembling on his sticks and Mrs. Adams was short of breath. Mary thanked heaven that the two little arm-chairs were in place. She brought them into the parlour and installed them there and after a moment or two left them to recover while she got the tea. It grieved her that they had bothered to call on her. Why could they not have asked her to come to them? But she realized, when she was back in the parlour with them, that it would not have occurred to them to summon others to their presence, as though they were people of importance, and they wished to honour her at whatever cost to themselves. They had taken a most exhausting amount of trouble, for their misshapen old shoes shone with polishing and the Colonel's shirt and Mrs. Adams's white silk blouse, thin as a cobweb with much laundering, were snowily clean. Their neatness and exquisite manners, their sincere kindness as they asked her gently of her welfare and desired that she should be happy here brought her so near to tears that she could scarcely answer them. They had brought with them into her room the atmosphere of their particular brand of courage. Cousin Mary's tough valiance, the courage of a fighter, was alive in the house already, but theirs was different. It was a delicate thing, the distillation of suffering that was never mentioned because courtesy forbade such a thing, and not even interiorly dwelt upon because again their bone-deep courtesy kept their interest and attention moving outward. Paul had asked her to love them. It would not be difficult.

Mary had been practising her cooking and there were scones for tea. And she had sent to London for her favourite brand of China tea which she fancied had given pleasure to the Staffordshire teapot, for it seemed lovelier than ever. The old people were delighted as children and now and again they looked at each other that each might delight in the pleasure of the other. And they looked at Mary, the eyes of each gently thanking her for giving such pleasure to the other one. The vine leaves rustled in the breeze that blew through the open door of the conservatory, and the faint scent of the blossoms was shaken into the room. Mary had a fancy that the apple tree outside the west window was leaning its elbows on the sill. The little things sparkled and glowed under their glass case at the south window and they talked, among other gentle topics, of them.

"Miss Lindsay was so fond of them," said Mrs. Adams. "Always when I came to see her she would show them to me. She would forget she had shown them to me before and show them all over again. But I was never tired of seeing them."

"You weren't afraid of her?" asked Mary.

Mrs. Adams was surprised by the question. "Not at all. She was always gentle with us. In her good times she and my husband used to play chess together."

"She could play quite a good game," said Colonel Adams. "She'd rap me over the knuckles with her fan if a move of mine annoyed her yet there was always a gentleness. She had a special costume for chess-playing, two black velvet skirts one over the other, a red knitted shawl, mittens and of course the fan. She felt the cold I think. She always kept a poor fire."

Mary's heart lurched. Had Cousin Mary kept a poor fire that she might have more money to leave to little Mary? And how was it that she had been so gentle with Colonel and Mrs. Adams and yet had so frightened Jean Anderson? When the time came for them to go she would not let them walk back. Her car was outside the house and they gratefully accepted her offer to drive them home. As they were crossing the hall Colonel Adams stopped and propped on his two sticks asked, "Do you play bridge, Miss Lindsay?" There was wistfulness in his tone and Mrs. Adams was looking at her with anxiety. Mary replied, "Yes I do. I enjoy it. But when Mrs. Hepplewhite asked me to play the other night I told a barefaced lie. I said I did not play."

Colonel Adams chuckled. "I think you were wise. Had you said yes you would have had time for little else. But if you would occasionally do us the honour of joining the Vicar and ourselves in a game we would keep your secret. The Vicar plays a tolerably good hand. A little hasty, but he is a hasty man. Excellent but hasty. One's character tends to affect one's bridge."

"I shall be afraid to play with you, Colonel Adams, if you can deduce my character from my bridge."

He had set himself in motion again. "I think you need not fear. You are very like your cousin."

"Tom!" ejaculated his wife in dismay.

"I did not refer to the slight occasional mental aberration," said Colonel Adams calmly. "That was a passing thing, of no consequence as regards essential character, though to her, poor lady, doubtless a sore trial."

"We have one of the bungalows in Abbey Fields," said Mrs. Adams as the car circled the green.

"Abbey Fields!" said Mary with delight. "I've only just found out about the abbey."

"Oh, yes. A Cistercian abbey. The Vicar knows a lot about it. It was destroyed at the time of the dissolution of the monasteries but the church has always remained. This is our bungalow, Miss Lindsay. Holly Cottage. Oh, Tom, look! It's Charles!" She turned to Mary with her small

face alight with joy. "It's Charles, our son. He does sometimes turn up to see us unexpectedly. And there was no tea
for him and the door locked. Did you lock the door, Tom?"

"No," said Colonel Adams. "Not worth while. Nothing
to steal. He could get in."

His reaction to the presence of his son was different
from that of his wife. She was irradiated with pure pleasure
but he was weighed down with apprehensive sorrow. Yet
when Charles came out of the gate of Holly Cottage to help
him out of the car his face was creased with a tenderness
almost more maternal than his wife's. "Hullo, Charles, how
are you? This is Miss Lindsay. She's been kind enough
to bring us home after a most delightful afternoon. Miss
Lindsay, my son."

They smiled at each other but regardless of them Mrs.
Adams was out of the car in a flash, and reaching up to kiss
her tall son. "Are you well, dear?" she asked him. "Can
you stay?"

"Emily," said her husband, "you have not thanked Miss
Lindsay for that excellent tea."

She turned round, her face pink with her happiness.
"Thank you, Miss Lindsay," she said like a child. "Thank
you."

Mary smiled and drove straight up the hill to avoid the
backing and turning that would have kept her longer with
them. She drove to the lime avenue and parked her car on
the grass at the side of the road. She got out and went
through the trees to a gate that looked out on a field full of
moon daisies and vetch and feathery swaying grass. But
leaning with her arms on the gate she saw none of it. How
had they come to have a son like that? Magnificently good-
looking, and rotten.

Gradually she became aware of the moon daisies and the
scent of the lime flowers that were just beginning to
blossom. Today's sunshine, after rain in the night, was
bringing it out. She turned round and looked up at the
bunches of pale green, not unlike her vine flowers. The
scent too was not unlike, though the scent of the vine flowers
was delicate and this was strong and powerful as the vi-
brating hum of the bees who were gathering the honey.
The sunshine, striking down in rods of light through the

ceiling of green leaves, was gold as that honey. There was goodness here, in scent and sound and splendour of light, and if it gave no explanation of man's tragedy it gave reassurance. At least it gave reassurance to her at this moment, when it was not her own suffering that oppressed her. The thing had not got its fangs into her own flesh, darkened her own mind or twisted her own nerves. If it had would it have been possible for her to know anything of this reassurance? Did Colonel Adams know it, or that son of his, or Paul? She would have to be of their company before she would know.

She drove slowly homeward. She understood now the possessiveness of the trees. The visible walls of the abbey had been destroyed but their foundations, unseen beneath the meadows and orchards and gardens of Appleshaw, still encircled a plot of ground that had been accounted holy and had been intensely loved. How many human root ends, she wondered, were now pinned down beneath those stones, like the old Vicar's beneath the walls of Oxford? Cousin Mary's, without doubt, to be joined one day by her own. She saw them in her mind's eye, white and wormy but tough as ivy, holding the old stones firmly down in the earth, never to be moved.

She was passing the second cottage on the green, Honeysuckle Cottage, trim and brightly painted but less sophisticated than Orchard Cottage, when the door flew open and a stout little woman shot out of it gripping a kitten by the scruff of its neck. As she ran down the path of her minute garden she gave her head a skilful jerk that shot her spectacles down on her nose, and looked at Mary with smiling but burning interest over the top of them. When she reached the car she jerked them back again, for they were intended for close inspection. For more distant curiosity she gathered more information without them. It was Mrs. Croft, the district nurse whose friendliness as she bicycled past in the lime avenue had so delighted Mary on the day of her arrival.

She reached her arm through the open window of the car and dropped the kitten in Mary's lap. "Tiger. I'm pleased you should have him. Susan, my cat, is a tortoiseshell but that old rake of a tom at the Dog and Duck, that

Percy, he's tabby. Fathers all the kittens for miles round. You getting settled? It's a nice old house. I spent a lot of time in it, looking after the old lady. She didn't want to go to a home and the doctor didn't force her. Wants a lot doing to it. I see you've Bert Baker there most days. Find him satisfactory?"

Mrs. Croft had sparkling brown eyes behind her glasses, an infectious merry smile and a flow of conversation that was almost equal to Mrs. Hepplewhite's. But her talk did not submerge the victim for it was like herself, brisk and cheerful with a dancing rather than an adhering quality. She had small, broad, capable hands and footsteps that were wonderfully quick and light. Her head was permanently cocked slightly to one side, like a listening bird, so interested was she in the human species and all it did and said. Not Mary imagined, in what it thought. Those who possessed that type of curiosity, she believed, carried the head straight but thrust a little forward. Those with no curiosity at all sagged badly.

"He's very satisfactory. When he's got the house in order for me I hope you'll come and see it. I'm settling in well but there are a lot of mice, so thank you very much for Tiger. Isn't he rather young to leave Susan?" Tiger had swarmed up her and was now spread-eagled on her chest, screaming wildly.

"Not at all," said Mrs. Croft briskly. "He can feed himself and knows what to do with a box of earth. Boiled fish and bread and milk at present. Better unhook him or he'll pull the threads of your jumper."

Unhooking Tiger was no easy matter for his minute claws were curved like scimitars and as sharp as needles. Having disentangled him Mary held him up to look at him. His soft round body was tabby but the absurd tail had a bright orange tip and the small triangular face was snow-white, with a pink nose, surmounted by large bat-like ears. The saucer-eyes were blue. Though there had been dogs and cats in the family when she was young it so happened that Mary had never owned an animal of her own before and a ridiculous thrill went through her. "No other cat was ever quite like this," she said.

"You get some queer mixtures," agreed Mrs. Croft.

"Now don't spoil him. No sharpening his claws on the cushions, now, or sleeping on your bed. And don't over-feed him or he'll grow to the size of his father, and if he should be poorly at any time let me know."

They parted with mutual appreciation and Mary went home with her little cat, feeling suddenly more cheerful. That ruined man, and Tiger. The same world held them both. The tragic capacity of the human race for going off course was a little balanced by the integrity of the animals who were always obedient to the law of their being. We were meant to love like that, thought Mary, simply because that's our law and we were told to obey it.

2

"I'm on to a good thing this time, Dad," said Charles.

Mrs. Adams had gone to bed directly after supper, tired by her outing, and Colonel Adams and his son sat together in the little sitting-room. Only one small shaded lamp burned on a bookcase and Colonel Adams was glad that in the dim light he could not see his son's face clearly. He could see the outline of his finely shaped head and strong shoulders, and the play of light and shadow that the perfect bone structure of the face made into a mask of beauty, but that was all. The mask made him feel that he was sitting here with the small boy whom Charles once had been, the most beautiful and charming of his children, a wonder child whom everyone had adored, himself not least. Charles had been born just after the First World War, the result of his profound joy in his reunion with Emily, for he had been serving abroad and had not seen her for two years. But he himself had been a very sick man at the time and Emily had been worn out by the war years. They'd hardly given the boy a good start and they'd spoilt him abominably. He could see that now but at the time the marvellous charm of the little boy, his abnormal sensitiveness and physical delicacy that had caused him to weep heartbrokenly at the least breath of criticism, and shriek when punished, had made it difficult to be severe with him. Charles lit another cigarette and the spurt of flame illumined cruelly the sly weariness of his face. His father's grief went through him like a sharp physical pain and he shifted in his chair.

Parsons when they preached did not stress sufficiently the weariness of sin. That was its chief punishment, he believed, for sensitive temperaments like that of his son. You could be a cheerful sinner if you were tough but you had to be tough.

"Arthritis bothering you, Dad?" asked Charles solicitously.

"Nothing to mention," said Colonel Adams cheerfully. "Tell me about this new thing."

"You know that chap I told you about once, Tony Richards?" said Charles. "We shared digs together once. Well, he's starting a garage and he wants me to go in with him. It's a new thing for me but I think it's a sound proposition. Now don't smile, Dad."

"I wasn't smiling," said Colonel Adams, and indeed he was not for Charles's new things were never any smiling matter. There had been so many of them that his father had lost count of them, and lost hope that the next would have more permanence than the last. And so, he thought, had Charles. But there was a doggedness about Charles. It was his saving grace. He always picked himself up and went on again. "Who is financing this?" he asked.

"Well, that's the trouble. Tony is about as broke as I am. He's gone off today to tackle an uncle of his. The old boy is something in the city and he's got the dough."

"And you've come to tackle me," said his father; without bitterness, merely making a familiar statement.

Charles lit another cigarette and his hands were unsteady. "You can't do much, Dad, I know, but if you could lend me enough just to keep me for a month or two I'd be very grateful. Just until we're started. I'll pay you back later for this is a sure thing."

Colonel Adams got up and moved on his two sticks to the writing-desk in the corner of the room. He lowered himself to the chair that stood before it, laid his sticks on the floor and took his cheque book from a pigeon-hole. He wrote out a generous cheque slowly and laboriously, for his fingers were as stiff as the rest of him. Everything he did nowadays took a very long time and each task seemed sometimes almost insuperable as he turned to face it. Well, that was old age and to be expected. He tore out the cheque.

The small balance which he had at the bank was now practically gone and he did not know what he would do if Charles did not pay him back; and Charles had never yet paid him back. But he could do nothing else. He had given this man his life and he loved him. Raising his head he saw the photos of his other sons, that Emily kept on the top of the desk that she might look at them when she was writing her letters. Not so good-looking as Charles but decent men whose lives would have been his pride. And they were dead. He got up and journeyed back to the fire, smiling cheerfully at Charles, whom the slowness of the whole affair had reduced almost to screaming point.

"Good luck to you, boy," he said as he gave him the cheque. "Starting back at once, or can you stay a day or two?"

"I'd like to stay a day or two if you and Mother will have me."

"Good. I'll smoke a pipe with you before I go to bed."

Charles glanced round and saw that a battered wireless set that he had once given his parents was still in existence. He switched it on. "Do you mind?" he asked and his father shook his head. It saved them from having to talk. Tomorrow things would be easier. They settled back in their chairs, wrapping themselves in smoke. The light music that came from the wireless, marred by the grating noises of the worn-out instrument, could hold the attention of neither and their thoughts wandered miserably.

Colonel Adams remembered that it had begun right back in Charles's idle prep-school days, when he had failed to win a scholarship. The other boys had done so but his public-school fees had had to be paid for with great difficulty out of the always inadequate family funds. He had done fairly well at first and his father's hopes had risen, but when he was sixteen he had been expelled for misdemeanours of which his mother still knew nothing. She still believed he had been sent home because a mild attack of pneumonia had weakened his lungs.

Colonel Adams had not known what to do with this shamed and penitent and so charming boy back on his hands. For Charles was always penitent, even as life went on to the point of despair, yet always at the mercy of himself, hopelessly weak and yet with that streak of doggedness in him which enabled him always to go on. For the next four years he had tried various things. He had worked on a farm first and when dismissed had not told his father but had gone to London and worked as a waiter, a taxi driver, and finally as scene-shifter at a repertory theatre where he occasionally played small parts. He was sympathetic and superficially clever and at first people liked him and he did well. Yet always his weaknesses reasserted themselves and he failed yet again. His worst failure had been the war. He had hailed it, and so had his father, as his chance to escape from himself. And for a while, lifted up by enthusiasm, he had done that. But when the real test came he broke. Only the influence of his father's army friends caused the verdict of a court-martial to be no worse than dismissal from the army and incarceration in a nerve hospital. His shattered nerves were genuine and it was when he came out of hospital that his drinking began to undermine his health.

Yet for the last seventeen years he had kept going with his father's help and since the war they had never lost touch with each other. When Charles had been in hospital Colonel Adams had visited him with untiring patience, and when his other boys had died he had tried to bear his grief without bitterness. He did not deceive himself into thinking that Charles felt much love for him or for his mother, for he came to see them only when he wanted money, but his son's need of him was a link that he valued for without it he would have lost the boy. He cherished a notion that if he did not actually lose Charles he might yet one day save him. In harbouring that notion he knew that in all probability he deceived himself, but without some small deception somewhere the strongest man can scarcely live. Not in old age.

The music ended and Charles got to his feet. "You like to go to bed early, Dad, I know. I'll get some fresh air before I turn in."

His father smiled at him. It was not closing time yet. After Charles had been to Appleshaw and gone away again Jack Beckett, by special arrangement with Colonel Adams, sent the bill for his drinks to his father. It was a pretty large bill but Charles was generous and liked to stand drinks all round. Jack was silent about this private agreement between them and always would be. The inhabitants of Appleshaw had summed Charles up pretty accurately, though his parents had confided their troubles to no one and he himself was always on his best behaviour when he visited them, but they did not talk about him to each other for there was an unexpressed conspiracy between them to keep Charles dark. It was a way in which they could express their affection for his parents, a form of loyalty to them.

"Go and get your fresh air, Charles," said Colonel Adams. "It's disgraceful, the early hour your mother and I turn in. Lock up behind you when you come back."

3

Charles went out into the wonderful freshness of the night. The first stars were out but the afterglow was still in the west. The trees, in full leaf now, were outlined against it in rounded shapes of velvet darkness. The grass in the meadows was ready for cutting and every light stir of wind brought the scent of it. Charles walked slowly and in desolation. The ugly sound of his footsteps in the silence was as intolerable to him as the nagging headache that beset and confused him. The state of his health scared him at times and tonight fright pushed against him like the walls of a den that has grown too small for the beast inside. When this nightmare sensation came upon him he knew he must get a drink quickly and he quickened his pace.

"Charles!"

Hovering at the gate of Orchard Cottage in her light dress she looked like a moth in the dusk, and like a moth that had settled on his arm he wanted to shake her off, for he was tired of her now and tonight every desire he had ever had was fused and narrowed down to this one thirst for a drink. But he had inherited his father's courtesy and held to it with stubbornness. He wasn't quite a swine yet, he would tell himself. He moved towards her. "How are you, Valerie?"

"Not very well," she said plaintively. "I'm so tired always. You're looking wonderful, Charles."

In the dusk he did look magnificent, and as she had never

noticed in him anything she did not want to notice Appleshaw's conspiracy of silence upon the subject of Charles had kept him enveloped in the veil of romanticism she had dropped over him at their first meeting. Had anyone told her that she had led a sheltered life and was not yet adult she would have been outraged. Yet it was true. She had married a good man very young, he had taken care of her, and the quiet places where he insisted upon living had given her no opportunities for anything beyond the loveless virtue that had sickened Charles of their affair almost as soon as it was well started. She had imagined herself romantically in love with him, she still thought she was, but what she loved was the fantasy picture of a faithful wife denying herself the grand passion of a lifetime for the sake of a worthless husband whom she was too loyal to desert. Charles, who from long experience was shrewd about women, had found her out very soon and had not attempted to pursue the affair to the usual *dénouement*, for which he was very well aware she lacked the courage. And she was scarcely worth the effort. He disliked effort and she was negligible. All he wanted to do now was to end the thing with the minimum of unpleasantness.

They stood one on each side of the gate and her hands were on his shoulders. They rested lightly and were white and thin. And her face too was white in the frame of dark hair. In the dusk she had beauty and the last flicker of his old feeling for her unexpectedly spurted up. He saw them suddenly as a tragic couple, suffering through misfortune rather than from fault, and his self-pity reached out to enfold her with himself in its pitiful satisfactions. He stepped over the low gate and took her in his arms and they clung together.

"Come with me and have a drink," he whispered urgently.

She looked up, for it was not the whisper she had been expecting. "At the pub? No. Paul's there. Charles, what are you doing on Wednesday?"

"Nothing particular."

"Then let's go out together. I've told Paul I'm going to the hairdresser but I needn't go. I'll pick you up in the morning in my car. We'll meet in the lime avenue, like we did before, and have another of our great days. Do you remember that day in the autumn when we picnicked in the woods? Do you remember, Charles?"

"I remember," said Charles tenderly and wondered if she was referring to that tedious day when they had sat on hard beech roots in an east wind, drinking coffee that tasted of the thermos, and she had told him the story of her life. It was curious how he always seemed to be sitting on a hard seat in a draught when women told him the story of their lives. A self-absorbed woman was impervious to discomfort, a man never. "Not a picnic this time," he said firmly, "I'm in funds at the moment. We'll eat at some decent place and then see a flick. All right?"

"Heaven," she whispered. "Ten o'clock on Wednesday?"

"Right," he said and kissed her again, cursing himself for a fool. It had been easier to say yes than no and he always mechanically did the easy thing, even when it meant walking straight back into the situation he'd just been trying to get away from. Anyway it would get him away from his father's company. "Bye-bye till Wednesday, then, if you're sure you won't come along to the pub?"

"But Paul's there."

"What of it? Is he one of those jealous blokes who pull a woman round by the hair if he catches her in another man's company?"

"No, but I've been so careful to keep you apart. You've never met him."

"I'd like to."

"Why?"

"Curiosity."

She was horrified. To her there was something indecent in the thought of lover and husband confronting each other. In the magazine stories she read they were always kept in watertight compartments until the fatal day when the husband came home too soon from the office and there was trouble. She didn't want trouble. She wanted the twin glow of romantic passion and romantic martyrdom to wrap about her chilling spirit. "No, Charles," she said.

"Bye-bye," he said again, withdrawing himself gently from her clinging arms. In the lane he stopped to light a cigarette and she called to him again, but he seemed not to hear and went on to the pub. She went back into her cottage with shaking knees. Now there was bound to be trouble.

The pub was pleasant at this hour but Charles was scarcely aware of it until he had grabbed a drink from Jack Beckett and downed most of it. Then, his elbow on the counter, he looked round him, returning friendly greetings. He liked Appleshaw and he liked this pub. It was as near home as anywhere he knew. When he was away he often saw it as he saw it now, with the lights on and the dusk deeply blue beyond the uncurtained windows, the haze of tobacco smoke drifting up to the rafters, a ring of kindly faces smiling at him and the huge striped mound of Percy the cat heaped on the counter. He smiled round upon them all, Jack Beckett, Joshua Baker, Bert Eeles, Tom Archer the squire's chauffeur and one or two others. The tall man with the dog he did not look at again after the first glance for his mind recoiled from him with fear. Not of the man himself, for in that one glance he felt the quick pull of attraction, but of the fact of suffering. He'd suffered in the war, piteously and without courage, and now the thing seemed to be always lying in wait for him. Just when he was most lulled to safety it would confront him again in the sound of the ambulance bell, faces in a doctor's waiting room, a dentist's instruments. His body was at all times a timid mass of quivering nerves and he drank to quieten them, staving off the outcome. One could always stave things off for one more day.

And now here was this man Paul Randall moving towards him with his drink in his hand and speaking pleasantly. It was odd that a man who had suffered so much should have such an air of well-being. The recoil and the attraction broke over Charles together, with Paul's inexorable advance upon him, and then he was through and in quiet water, in pleasant conversation with an agreeable stranger.

"Odd I've never come across you here," he said. "And I'm here most evenings when I'm at Appleshaw."

"I'm not often here at this time," explained Paul. "I pub crawl before supper most days, after supper is my working time. But work's not going well at the moment." Then he quickly changed the subject, for he seldom talked of his work, and never to comparative strangers. Why should he do so now, to this man of all others whom he suspected of upsetting Valerie? His suspicion might be mere fancy, but when Charles Adams was at Appleshaw Valerie was exhausted and excited, more than usually resentful of him, her small deceptions more obvious and heartless as though she put them out like a smoke screen. He had avoided Charles, hating his fears and hating himself for having them, trying not to believe them and yet aware that they were there quite independently of anything in himself, for he was not a jealous man. And here he was speaking to this man of his work.

Because he was connected with it. This was the man in his book. He had seen him standing at the bottom of his bed and had identified himself with him, as though he were every man. As though he were sighted he could see the dark face and the apple tree fallen in the orchard. Since he was this man, the protagonist, he did not need to be told that war had helped to fell him, the first or the second or both, for it had not been so he would not have been the protagonist. Strange, difficult love stirred in Paul, hard like the birth pangs of this book that would not come alive, and pity, because this man, felled, had been apparently unable to bear fruit. Yet it was laid upon me to bear fruit, thought Paul, and it must have been laid upon him. It always is. There's something he does and goes on doing that corresponds with my writing. I'd like to find out what it is for if you understand people you're of use to them whether you can do anything tangible for them or not, for understanding is a creative act in a dimension we do not see.

With the surface of his mind he was talking to Charles about nothing while the other thing was going on at a deeper level. And a third part of him looked on and laughed. You crazy fool. What would normal people think if they knew what went on in a writer's mind below the surface? They'd think him even more round the bend than they had previously supposed if they could see the witches' cauldron of images and memories boiling up from the subconscious, impressions whirling in from without, ideas and insights bursting up like bubbles and gone again before they can be seized. And the hopelessness of the business, the whole infuriating, exhausting, fascinating business of grabbing something out of the turmoil and imposing upon it some faint shadow or rumour of the order, pattern and rhythm of the world.

Damn it that I've got to like him so much, thought Charles. And Valerie's got no use for him. She's a fool. And I'm a fool that I have got into this mess with her and he's a fool to have married her. She's one of those sticky women, not a moth but a bur. They've no pride, these stickers. Another woman, a woman of the type that brought the parents home, would be gone at a touch. Why do I always attract the stickers?

"Who's the new woman?" he asked Paul. "I forgot to ask my parents. Tall, wears her clothes well. Must have been a smasher when she was young. Easy on the eye even now."

Paul told him, set down his empty glass and turned to go. Rage was boiling in him at the man's tone, and with it dismay. He had been seeing a good deal of Mary lately, but why this rage? The thought of Charles and Valerie together had made him grieve, but not boil.

"Stop a minute," said Charles with an urgency that Paul could not refuse. He stopped and turned, Bess with him. The feel of her head under his hand steadied him. Bess was always a steadying influence. "Will you come for a walk with me one day?"

Paul was silent a moment and then agreed. "Wednesday?" he asked.

"No, not Wednesday. Friday? Two-thirty?"

"Yes," said Paul. "Good night."

He went out and Charles turned round to order another drink with a sigh of relief. Randall was attractive yet uncomfortable company at one and the same time. Even though he could not see it was easier to have another drink in his absence.

CHAPTER IX

I

THE clock on the mantelpiece struck the half-hour. "Half past twelve, Edith," said Mary, and closed her book.

"That clock's fast," said Edith.

"There's the church clock striking now," said Mary, smiling. "There's no gainsaying that. Pack up now, Edith. You've worked well this morning."

"It wasn't work," said Edith. "Not Shakespeare. Maths is work but not Shakespeare or history. I like words and people from right back in the past. I like old things, like the tree in Nightingale Wood, the one by the ruins of Fox Barton, where the well is."

Mary was delighted. One of the joys of being with children was that in their company one recaptured the sense of the strange and the flavour of the unknown. "The tree in Nightingale Wood. . . . The ruins of Fox Barton, where the well is." The place was far removed in green shade, moss-scented and cool. "Is Nightingale Wood the one beyond the Dog and Duck?" she asked.

"Yes, but Fox Barton is at the other end of it. The way to Fox Barton is down Ash Lane. You know Ash Lane because the door in your vegetable garden leads into it." It was the door through which Mrs. Baker came and went but Mary had been so busy that she had actually never explored beyond it. "Let's not do indoor lessons this afternoon. Let's go to Fox Barton and do nature study."

"My car's in dock today," said Mary.

"But we don't need to drive there!" said Edith with a touch of scorn. "We can walk."

Mary's heart quailed for she was no walker. She was urban-minded and car-legged. But Edith's face, flushed with joy and already so changed, could not be refused. "Very well," she said. "But it must be a real lesson walk. I've got a botany book and we'll take that, and we'll take our tea."

145

Edith slipped off her chair. "I'll be back at two. We'd better start early for it's quite a long walk to Fox Barton."

She climbed over the window-sill into the conservatory and vanished, for she journeyed to and from her lessons by way of the garden and the mulberry tree rather than the road. Mary pressed her fingers to her temples. She was suffering nowadays from a habitual slight headache. It had been an effort to start teaching again and the young, both human and feline, had such boundless energy. She glanced at Tiger where he lay sleeping in a patch of sunlight on the floor, but she dared do no more than glance for contemplation of his slumbers sometimes ended them. Even with the brief glance one eye opened with a blue glint and the orange tip of his tail twitched ominously. Mary beat a hasty retreat to the kitchen. Just a boiled egg, she thought, while she packed the picnic tea, and several cups of black coffee. Then she'd have time to put her feet up before they started.

Edith was back at ten to two, wearing her blue jeans and her blue sweater, and armed with a rucksack. Mary, whom the act of putting her feet up had sent into exhausted slumber, had barely recovered consciousness, but Edith packed the tea into the rucksack and they set out. As they walked under the apple trees in the kitchen garden to the door in the wall Mary did not tell Edith that she had not yet found time to open it and go through it to what lay beyond. Edith would have gone beyond before she had been at The Laurels an hour. Mary was ashamed of the procrastination of her advancing years and was ashamed that she was not confessing her shame. It was an inwardly humbled woman who preceded Edith into Ash Lane with confident grace, as though she did it every day. And of this too she was ashamed.

Ash Lane was narrow and deeply sunken between steep banks crowned with hollies and hawthorns, with a big ash tree not far from Mary's gate. As it went only to the woods the hedges had not been cut down and the trees arched overhead. Ancient and bird-haunted, the place imposed a silence and Edith spoke only to point out to Mary treasures that she might have missed, the rose-colour of a chaffinch's breast in the branches over their heads, a butterfly, long-stalked toadstools of pale lavender growing among the wet mosses in the ditch and trails of creamy wild roses and honeysuckle. Now and again there was a break in the trees upon each side, a window that showed a glimpse of sunlit fields and far blue hills, and once the left-hand hedge ended altogether in wooden palings with beyond a group of thatched cottages and gardens full of flowers. "The middle one is Mrs. Baker's," said Edith. But Mary had known it was by the sparkling cleanliness of its windows and the perfection of its garden. She would have liked to have gone in to see if Mrs. Baker was there but Edith was striding on and she had to keep up with her. But she was less tired than she had expected, the cool beauty of the lane affecting her like a drink of water. She was almost surprised when she found tall trees on either side, the softness of beechmast beneath her feet and in her ears the ringing call of birds in a high wood.

The track was not lost in the wood, though the low-growing hollies and brambles crowded in upon it, for the trees themselves did not press in. It remained a lane and looked as though it was trodden daily for here and there were the prints of enormous feet. A troll, thought Mary, for they looked too big for a mere man. They went on until Edith said, "There's Fox Barton," and Mary could see it half hidden and half revealed by the great beech stems, standing in a clearing in the woods.

They came to the edge of the clearing and stood gazing, Edith as silent as Mary, for every time she saw Fox Barton it was as though she saw it for the first time. It was a small house, built of the same silver-grey stone as the church, with narrow mullioned lancet windows and a steep stone-tiled roof. There was no glass in the windows, though iron bars had been fixed across the lower ones, but there was a stout oak door, left slightly open, and the place still had a look of great strength, like a rock in the woods. Moss and lichen patched the roof and where the walls were free of ivy ferns grew in the crevices of the stones. There were a few stunted apple trees in the clearing, and rose briars running wild, remains of a garden that had been here once, and there was a huge old thorn tree beside a well. It did not need the small stone cross over one gable to tell

Mary that Fox Barton had once been a barn, or perhaps a guest house, belonging to the abbey. She would have known because her mind instantly linked it with the lime avenue. Here there had been another entrance to the domain of the abbey. The old deep lane was as old as the abbey church.

"Can we go inside?" she asked Edith.

"I'm sure Mr. Baker wouldn't mind."

"Mr. Baker?"

"This is where Mr. Baker bodges. He makes his chair legs here. He can't be here today because it's all silent."

"Then we won't go in."

"I'm sure he wouldn't mind."

"We won't go in," said Mary firmly. "We'll have our tea under the thorn tree by the well and perhaps he will come back and ask us in." Not a troll, she thought, but Mr. Baker. Does Paul ever come here? The thought that he should do so brought with it a sense of joy, for already this place had her in its grip, and her friendship with Paul was now of the type that takes it hard if love of places, books and people cannot be shared. A short while ago she had rather shyly asked him if she might read his poems. He had not seemed to mind and had given them to her. She had found them well written, full of anger and compassion but free of either despair or illusion, and they had carried her some way towards the understanding of him that it seemed to her so imperative that she should have. For love alone doesn't go far enough, she told herself. It must be charged with understanding. That's where I failed before.

She was looking at the thorn tree, and suddenly dismay struck through her, like a flash of lightning striking through the trees of the summer wood. God help me, she thought, remembering the happiness of their recent meetings and seeing them suddenly irradiated with this new and marvellous light. Not now. Not at my age. Not now, at fifty, to love as I could not love when I was younger. You fool of a woman! Just to think such a thing could be possible shows what a fool you are. It's not possible. This is a place that goes to one's head, that's all. It goes to one's head.

"I'm awfully hungry," said Edith.

"Forgive me," said Mary. If the child had not spoken she

believed she would have stood here struck by lightning indefinitely.

> "*Fear no more the lightning-flash,*
> *Nor the all-dreaded thunder-stone;*
> *Fear not slander, censure rash;*
> *Thou hast finish'd joy and moan;*
> *All lovers young, all lovers must*
> *Consign to thee, and come to dust.*"

The words, flashing into her mind, were a salutary reminder that she was growing old. Yet as she led the way to the well under the thorn tree she did not feel it.

She and Edith sat on the grass beside the well and spread out their picnic tea. As they ate they were silent at first, for a robin sang in the thorn tree over their heads and when they looked up they could see his pulsing throat. In the wood a woodpecker was laughing and wood doves were cooing. The way by which they had come was hidden from them by the angle of the house and the great trees stood all about the clearing walling them in with the impenetrable magic of legend. They could see aisles in the wood, sun-shot leaves, green ferns and brambles, but they no longer believed they could move among these things in their bodies. All of them that could enter that wood was there now. Only their grosser part sat beside the well and would live here, they supposed, for ever, since for their bodies there was no way out through this wood. The prospect was not disturbing.

"If we lived here always we could eat the apples and drink the well water," said Edith.

"The well," said Mary, and she got up to look at it. When she leaned on the parapet and looked down a cool breath came up into her face, for it was spring water, living water. Its surface mirrored her face, and a few white clouds behind her head reshaping themselves in the blue of the sky, but in broken ripples that were the faint stir of its life.

"If you put your head down you'll find the holes in the wall where they used to keep their butter in hot weather," said Edith. "Mr. Baker showed them to us once when we came here with Mother."

Mary slipped her hand down through the ferns that grew inside and found the small square apertures. It moved her

strangely to think how many women's fingers had groped
through the ferns, as hers were doing, feeling for their
hidden treasure. It surprised her to find the little doorless
larders empty now. The cool breath of the living water,
the scent of it, increased the sense of shame that had been
with her all the afternoon. She turned round and sat down
on the parapet facing Edith.

"I want to tell you, Edith. Today is the first time I have
been in Ash Lane. Well, I've been busy, so perhaps I'm
not to be blamed for that, but I am to be blamed that I
walked through the door as though I'd done so every day for
weeks. I wanted you to think I had. I deceived you and
deception is stealing because it takes away the truth. Forgive me, Edith."

Edith was looking away from her. Could a child understand such a very feminine bit of vanity, of compunction?
Suddenly Edith jumped up and came to her, flinging herself into her arms and sobbing wildly. She held the child
but in utter bewilderment. What had she said to provoke
this primordial grief? It seemed vast and hopeless, like
Eve's in the garden when she knew what she had done. She
asked no questions but waited and presently Edith stopped
sobbing and was silent.

"What is it, Edith?" she asked at last.

"I stole them," whispered Edith.

"You what?"

"Stole them."

"What did you steal?"

"Queen Mab in her coach and the little blue tea-set."

"Tell me about it," said Mary.

"When the old lady was ill I used to go and kneel in the
conservatory and look at the little things. I pretended they
were mine; especially Queen Mab and the blue glass tea-
set. And then one day Mother said the old lady had sold
her oak chest. And that night I had a nightmare, and the
next morning I went to see if the little things were there.
They were still there and the window was open." She
stopped and began to sob again.

"And so you took Queen Mab and the tea-set to keep
them safe from being sold like the chest," said Mary. "If
I had been you, and nine years old, that's just what I

should have done." Edith looked up at her astonished and speechless, her face red and blotchy with her tears, the most bedraggled-looking child Mary had ever seen. "Yes, I should. It was unthinkable that Queen Mab and the tea-set should go away to some dusty shop in a town. They'd have died there. When I was your age my Cousin Mary, that's the old lady, offered to give them to me. But I wouldn't have them. I lived in London and I couldn't take them from the green parlour to London."

"Then you don't think I'm awfully wicked?" whispered Edith. "You don't think I'll go to hell?"

Mary laughed. "No, I don't. It's like this, Edith. Why you do a thing is more important than what you do. And so stealing because you love is really better than not stealing because you don't. Not that I am advocating stealing exactly. This question of good and evil is very compli-cated. Life has been very difficult for us all since Eve ate the apple. Let's wash your face with the well water. I'll lean over and dip my hankie in. Where are Queen Mab and the tea-set now?"

"In a box inside my handkerchief case. I'm always frightened that Mother will find them and ask questions. You're quite sure I shan't go to hell?"

"Quite sure. What will you do with them now?"

"Bring them with me when I come to lessons tomorrow and put them back again with the other little things. And I'll share them with Rose and Jeremy if you want me to."

The depth of her own relief astonished Mary. "That's a good girl! Now it's over and you haven't got to think of it again."

Edith cried again in sheer relief, and then let Mary bathe her face. Then they laughed together, each aware of buoyant lightness, as though a tangled string had snapped and they floated free. It was while they were packing up the tea things that they heard a trampling in the wood.

Their minds knew who it was but for a few moments their imaginations took charge and they looked at each other, tingling with expectation. It couldn't just be a man in a place like this. It was Behemoth, or a giant, or some old monk of the abbey who had never died, and he had a third eye, or some characteristic that lifted him above the rut of ordinary men. Yet when he came into sight, striding through the beechmast and the hollies, Mary thought that no creature of legend could have suited Nightingale Wood more perfectly than Mr. Baker. For the last of the bodgers was no ordinary man. That great lean height, the long straggling moustache, the powerful prophetic stride and the enormous trampling boots beneath which the obstructions of the wood seemed to sink into the ground, were all attributes of a figure so majestic that even Behemoth would have looked ordinary beside him. For this wood would not have been Behemoth's own, and would have dwarfed him to the proportions of an outsider, while Mr. Baker was in his proper milieu, in the woods that were his home and his life, his kingdom and his world. Technically this wood probably belonged to Mr. Hepplewhite, in any other sense Mr. Baker held it in direct tenure from his God.

He did not check his advance when he caught sight of them, he tramped on, but as he came across the clearing his eyes flashed like cold blue jewels and the sunlight glanced off his face as though it were polished stone. He seemed to have a shield slung round his shoulders and to be carrying a sword, and it took Mary a couple of minutes to realize that his armour was a sack of wood and a saw laid in rest against his shoulder. He did not deviate in their direction. After that one blue hard glance he dismissed them as unworthy of his attention and tramped on through the door of Fox Barton into the inner sanctuary of his trade and life.

To flee was Mary's first impulse, to apologize her second, and being a courageous woman she obeyed her second. After a decent interval she came with Edith to the door, waited until the work had stopped for a moment and called out, "Mr. Baker, may we come in?"

There was a moment of complete silence and then Mr. Baker growled, "There's naught to see but what you've seen already."

"We have seen nothing," said Mary. "We would not come into your workshop without your permission."

There was another pause and then, "You may come in if you've a mind."

They came in under the archway into Mr. Baker's workshop. It must once have been the kitchen of the farm for the wide hearth, the spit for roasting and the bread oven in the wall were still there. A doorway from which the door had gone led into another large room, now in ruins though showing the remains of an Adam fireplace and oak stairs with a fine balustrade. But the ceiling of both rooms had disappeared and the staircase ended in shadowed space beneath a vaulted roof. Mr. Baker's workbench was the missing door, a solid slab of oak supported upon sawn tree trunks. Mr. Baker stood before it shaping a chair leg that was revolving in a primitive lathe, the power supplied by a bent ash sapling fixed beneath the bench. Finished chair legs were piled in baskets and upon a shelf were other things that Mr. Baker had made; breadboards, wooden spoons, rolling pins and small wooden dishes; and the stone floor was littered as deep with wood shavings as the floor of the wood beyond with beechmast. Through the narrow window the honey-coloured sunbeams slanted down, and a couple of butterflies. Birdsong rang in the place, rising to the great roof and echoing there. The wood had so quickly taken the place to itself that Mary found it hard to visualize the busy farmhouse life, and even more difficult to think of the squire's family here. For this must be the house in the beech woods where the Roystons had lived until the heiress had rebuilt the manor house. Probably she had come as a bride to this house, and her husband, the man with the periwig, had installed the Adam fireplace for her. She had sat beside it with her parakeet upon her wrist and had had her harpsichord in the window. Did Mr. Baker ever hear the tinkle of her harpsichord?

Looking against Mr. Baker she imagined not for he was a man with a one-track mind. He was already deeply absorbed, deftly shaping a chair leg, and she and Edith might not have existed. Yet she dared to ask him a few questions.

"Do you send them to a factory, Mr. Baker?"

He answered, though without looking up. "Aye. There's still a small factory that takes 'em. When that closes down that's the end."

"And these lovely things, spoons and dishes. Do you sell them?"

"To a shop in Westwater. Take a look at the room through there, ma'am. At your age, Miss Edith, you should be outside playing in the sun."

They were dismissed from his immediate vicinity. He had not spoken rudely, merely with reluctant firmness, as a man does who knows he must guard his loneliness even at the expense of his courtesy. Edith chased the butterflies back into the clearing while Mary went into the parlour. The remains of a plaster garland of flowers still clung above the fireplace and she picked up a fragment that had fallen to the floor. It showed a flower with a bee hovering over it. She held it in her hand and looked at it, grieving for vanished loveliness. Her grieving seemed to stop time for she lost her human awareness of it as a moving thing and it became instead a still depth of grief. Yet why grieve because a fragment of fine living had passed away in a small house in a small wood, upon an unimportant planet lost in the vastness of space? The myriad stars remained. And for the moment Mr. Baker's chair legs, and the slanting sunbeams and the shavings on the floor. Beauty not so much vanished as dissolved and reshaped itself, as she had seen the reflected clouds reshaping themselves behind her when she had leaned over the well.

There was a voice in the workshop, speaking from the depths of sorrow, from the past. It was John's voice. She was not at all startled. She put the fragment of plaster in her pocket and listened, distinguishing no words, only the tones, the rise and fall of them, the dissolving and reshaping of their music. She turned towards the door as he came through it, lifting her hands to lay them on his shoulders. She had never cared about kisses. Her greeting to him after a parting had always been her hands resting lightly on his shoulders. It was not until she felt the rough tweed of his coat under her fingers that she knew it was not John. She withdrew her hands gently and without embarrassment. "I am sorry, Paul," she said. "I thought you were someone else. I am bemused in this place."

"One is," he agreed easily, as unembarrassed as she was. "I am sorry he died."

"Do you feel the same here?" she asked. They had moved to the window, Bess moving with them, and she leaned back against the stone embrasure, for she found herself suddenly incredibly tired. From where she was she could just see the well and the thorn tree. "I mean, do you feel that here time becomes a well?"

He was opposite her, Bess beside him. "I've felt like that for years. When I lost my sight I lost with it the sense of time rushing by. The well is within me and memory springs up with force."

"More than personal memories?"

"A good deal more. But then I expect that's the way with all writers."

She looked at him, studying the lines of his face intently, identifying herself with him in much the same way as she was coming to identify herself with her home, her gaze upon it a recognition of unity. Then she looked away, ashamed that she should so take advantage of his blindness. The sound of Mr. Baker bodging seemed to come from far away and the sorrow begun in her by the sight of the broken fragment of plaster was now welling up as blood does when a wound is not staunched. She was well aware that her love for this man was not going to be staunched, for it was no more in his power to satisfy it than it had been in hers to satisfy John's. And now John's grief was her own, and she had never remotely guessed that he had felt like this. The grief came both from the future and the past, for the well was foresight as well as memory, it was both hers that was to come and his that was past and they were not distinguishable. Was this identification what men call empathy? It needed all her strength to steady herself against the surge of feeling that seemed to be sweeping not only through herself but through the wood and the old ruined house, like wind but without sound or outward disturbance. The disturbance was all inward, pulling her and the world about her to pieces to reunite them in a new pattern. With a great effort she tried to remember what Paul had been saying, and to answer him. "You mean you tap ancestral memory?"

"And the memories of people who are in some way near to me. And sometimes the memories of places. I have written stories about this house that I could swear I've not imagined." He laughed. "But how am I to know? Memory and foresight and imagination are so tangled up. Were you well received by Joshua Baker?"

"Mr. Baker likes to work alone," said Mary, "but he can tell one so without offence. Or is it only women who impede his genius? You can be here with him and he doesn't mind?"

"He's not a ladies' man," agreed Paul, "and he's got used to me. Poor chap, he's had to, for Bess and I take this walk more often than any other. We could take it in our sleep. In fact I often do. I see it then."

"You mean in dream?"

"Yes. My dreams are very thrilling. Full of colour. It's an odd experience to know places and people in your waking hours and see them in your sleeping ones."

"I expect the separation increases the deeper knowledge you spoke of once before," said Mary. "How is Valerie?"

"She's been tired. But she's having a day in Westwater today, shopping and so on. That always does her good. Gets her away from me."

She was aware again of his helpless bewildered sorrow over Valerie, and there was nothing she could do except turn from what was going wrong to what was going right.

"I've been reading your poems, Paul. It sounds so tame to say that they are finely wrought and I like them. Yet what else could one have said even to Coleridge? What would you have said to him about Kubla Khan?"

"That I was sorry that chap interrupted him so that he couldn't finish it."

"Then I'll say I'm sorry for all that interrupts you, for all the hindrances and sorrows. If I could I'd take them away."

He quickly and impetuously turned to her and she knew she had touched him on the raw. Then he turned back in quick command of himself. "Thank you. But it was probably just as well that chap did turn up. The promise is magnificent but Coleridge might have disappointed us later on. Even the great ones never tell us all that we hope they will. They grow old and die and haven't expressed it yet. Even with Beethoven it is still only the promise."

Edith had come in and once more inflicted herself upon

Mr. Baker. Sounding through the sound of his lathe, like birdsong through wind in the trees, came her voice talking to him and his grunts in occasional reply. Mary had not heard her talking in this way before, with such effortless and happy ease. Paul heard it too. "You've set that child free in some way," he said. "What have you done? Love's not enough."

"Not without understanding."

"Not even with it. I understand Valerie as well as love her." He spoke roughly and it seemed to Mary as though he were tearing the peace of the place to pieces. "And patience added is not enough. There has to be some sort of violence."

" 'The kingdom of heaven cometh by violence'," quoted Mary. "But Edith, not I, did the violence. To herself. She forced herself to tell me something that was worrying her, I hope because she loves me. But you can't force your love to be violent, Paul. You must wait till it breaks through in its own strength."

"One may wait too long," muttered Paul. He moved his heavy shoulders impatiently and with Bess beside him led the way back to the other room where Edith, silent now, stood entranced beside Mr. Baker. He had finished his chair leg and was now holding in his hand a shallow bowl made from cherry wood, turning it over and over and searching it for imperfections. His huge hands looked like blocks of wood but his fingers were as sensitive upon the bowl as the fingers of a violinist upon the strings. No roughness escaped them. He began to smooth the bowl, slowly and carefully, his grim face ennobled by absorption. They watched him for a few moments, asking no questions, for they thought him oblivious of their presence, but as they went out through the archway he suddenly growled, "You can come again, ma'am, if you've a mind. I can't abide a chattering woman but you've shown yourself a quiet body. Miss Edith too. Mr. Randall and Bess, they're always welcome."

Mary murmured her astonished thanks and looked back once from outside the door. Mr. Baker sat enthroned, his great boots half-buried in the shavings at his feet, as though in leaves, and the slanting sunbeams clothed him in dusty glory. She felt a deep thankfulness that there were a few men still left alive who were kings in their own right.

The walk home had Edith at its heart. Her happiness was so great that wherever she was, running ahead of the two grown-ups, stopping behind to pick flowers or walking beside Bess, she was the centre. The whole beauty of the day seemed to flow into her and out from her. Thinking back to her own childhood Mary could remember some such experience as she believed now to be Edith's. Conviction of sin, the first, a thing most terrible to a child, sorrow and difficult confession and then release. There was no joy like release. Paul too, while talking to Mary, was very conscious of Edith. The three of them, the man and woman and the child, had a rightness that both delighted and tormented him. He'd always wanted a child but Valerie had always been ready with a first-rate excuse. First there had been the war. A baby would probably be killed in an air raid. And then there had been his health. How could they hope for a strong child? And now there was their poverty. How could they afford one? And she was afraid. She had never said she was but he had always been aware of her fear. He could not force her and so by her wish they had not been lovers for some years now. He had resigned himself, he thought, but now, emotionally stirred by his admiration for another woman, by Edith and the beauty of the summer day, he found himself longing for her again. They reached the door from Ash Lane to The Laurels and stopped to say good-bye.

"May I read some more?" Mary asked. "I should like to read all you will allow me to read."

"You'd be bored to distraction."

"You know I wouldn't."

"I'm sorry. I know you wouldn't and I'll take you at your word. Come on, Bess."

"Won't you come in and let me give you some tea? Edith and I had eaten all the picnic one by the time you came."

"Thank you but I'd like to get home. Valerie may be back."

Mary wished him good-bye and accepted the thrust serenely as the first of many. But she felt exhausted as she and Edith walked through the kitchen garden.

"We never had the botany lesson!" said Edith. "We never even brought the book!"

2

The hours spent by Mary and Paul in the woods, the bloom of legend upon them and drowned in quietness, had been restless for Charles and Valerie. For one thing she could not get Paul out of her mind. She had scarcely been ten minutes with Charles, after she had picked him up in the lime avenue, before she began thinking of Paul. Meticulous as his housekeeper she had left a cold lunch ready for him and told him where to find it. Had he listened? "I hope Paul will find his lunch," she said to Charles.

"Forget it!" said Charles impatiently. "You're spending the day with me, aren't you?"

"Yes I am," said Valerie softly and moved a little closer to him. He had insisted on driving her car for he hated being driven by a woman. He drove well but extremely fast. "Not so fast, darling," she whispered.

He accelerated slightly for he was in a rotten temper and the pressure of her shoulder against his, the perfume of her scent in his nose, no longer gave him the slightest pleasure, merely irritated him. He had been a fool to let it begin again. The sense of guilt, that always oppressed him when he was at Appleshaw with his parents, was heavier than ever now that he had met Randall and liked him. It had never been his habit to consider the feelings of husbands, which he regarded as none of his business, but Randall was different. He felt curiously connected with the man, involved with him. And involvement was a thing he avoided like the plague.

"What'll he do all day?" he asked. "Work?"

Valerie opened her eyes, which she had closed partly to avoid her nervousness over Charles's driving, partly in an effort to recapture the sense of being young and beautiful that she had always felt in his company. "Paul? Just moon about. What work he does he only does at night. He'll probably stuff the cold ham I left into his pocket and go out to the woods. He's bone lazy, you know."

"So you have frequently told me," said Charles. "How does he find his way about in the woods?"

"He's got Bess and a good bump of locality. The blind have, you know. They develop marvellous powers People pity them but they needn't."

"No?" inquired Charles dryly, and then after a pause, "As it happens I don't pity Randall. I shouldn't presume."

"For heaven's sake, Charles!" ejaculated Valerie. "Are we to spend this heavenly day together arguing about Paul?"

"Who began it?" inquired Charles. "And if this is a heavenly day keep your eyes open, woman, and look at it."

"I didn't mean heavenly because of flowers and sunshine, I meant heavenly because we are together."

"I take you. But I thought flowers and sunshine were supposed to be an added bloom upon the rapture of young love?"

Though her eyes were closed again she knew he was looking at her and wondered if she was looking as young and beautiful as she felt; or was trying to feel, for there was a sense of strain in it all today; and she was aware of the mockery.

"You're hateful, Charles!" she flashed.

"I am," he agreed. "Let's stop somewhere and have a drink."

They stopped at the next pub and after that they managed better. In Westwater he bought her an expensive pair of ear-rings out of the money his father had lent him and then they lunched in an hotel and laughed and talked in something of their old style. They went to a flick and he did not repulse the hand she slipped into his. Yet all the time he was thinking, what damned fools we'd look if the lights went up, and he thought that growing old, if you've neither wisdom nor stability, does make a fool of a man. Shows you up. And despair took hold of him. It was lightened by the thought, Dad's no fool. He seemed for a moment or two to share his father's wisdom. It fell over him like a cloak and provided a modicum of shelter.

Valerie, eating chocolates while Charles smoked, wondered if Paul had gone to Nightingale Wood. He had told her about it soon after they had come to Appleshaw, and had wanted to take her there. "It's the sort of place you want to share with someone else," he had said. She couldn't remember now why she hadn't gone, she hadn't wanted to for some reason or other, some good reason of course. Suddenly a suspicion scorched across her mind. Was he sharing it today with Mary Lindsay? He'd been for a walk with her once before. One way and another he seemed to see a lot of her. That hateful woman! She slaved for Paul, she was the most marvellous wife, and this was all the thanks she got. The film was very affecting and tears of self-pity welled up. She reached for her handkerchief and dabbed at her eyes.

"What's up?" asked Charles.

"Sometimes I think you don't care about me as much as you did," she whispered. "It's been wonderful, finding each other. It's still wonderful, isn't it?" She nestled closer to him for contact between his body and hers had always sent a thrill through her. It did not come today. His body felt curiously heavy and sullen against her shoulder, though he returned the pressure of her hand.

"This is a rotten film," he said, regarding a close-up of an enormous embrace with an equally enormous nausea. "Let's get out. Let's go to that place on the river. You know. We went there once before. And have a drink."

They drove to the place on the river and sat in the garden watching the swans. Valerie had tea, and sugar cakes which made her feel slightly sick after the chocolates and the swaying speed of the car, and Charles had several more drinks. He had to nerve himself to end this thing. It had become ridiculous. Yet he had still said nothing when Valerie began to fuss about getting back to cook Paul's evening meal. And he must. He couldn't do it in the car and have a weeping woman on his shoulder. They'd land in the ditch. "Don't fuss, Val!" he said impatiently. "Paul doesn't strike me as the kind of chap to make a stink if his chops are five minutes late."

She looked at him sharply. "How *does* he strike you? You met him at the local, didn't you?"

"Not at all what I expected from your description. Quiet, easy sort of chap. We're going for a walk together on Friday."

She was horrified, all the magazine stories she had ever read rising up and circling round her like a cloud of bats with warning squeaks. "A walk together? Charles, you can't do that!"

"Why not?"

"Well, you can't, he doesn't know about you and me."

"I bet he does. He's no fool."

She was on her feet in agitation. "Of course he doesn't know. If he knew he'd have made a scene."

"He's no scene maker. Don't be a fool, Val. Sit down."

"No. It's not chops. It's casserole and it needs a good hour."

She was walking quickly towards the car and he could only follow her in mingled exasperation and relief. He hadn't done it, and now, he couldn't. Another day. A little later. But once in the car exasperation triumphed over relief and he drove far too fast and not at all steadily. As they whirled through the lanes Valerie was frightened. He was, she thought, a little drunk. And he looked sweaty and hot. How could she have thought him so marvellously good-looking?

"Let me drive, Charles," she said sharply, hating him for her fear.

"Little fool," he muttered.

"Stop, Charles! I must drive. If you don't stop I'll make you."

He laughed and drove on, with his elbow out to keep her away from him. They passed a cottage, lurched round a corner on the wrong side and confronted an oncoming car. Charles wrenched at the wheel and they mounted the grass verge and crashed into a telegraph post.

It was what is called a minor accident and after a few moments of bewildering confusion Valerie was aware of herself being helped out of the car, and then she was standing on the grass crying but unhurt. But Charles, it seemed, was hurt, for the occupants of the other car, a man and a woman who were strangers to her, were fussing over him where he lay on the grass. No one was fussing over her and she cried so bitterly that the woman came over to her.

"Don't worry, my dear. He's all right. Just concussion and a broken collar bone, we think. My husband is a doctor. Your car is rather knocked about but you two are all right. Come and see your husband. You'll see for yourself he's not badly hurt."

But Valerie shook her head and looked the other way. She hated illness and injury and she didn't want to look. Her crying took on a hysterical note and the man said curtly over his shoulder, "Take her into the cottage and tell them to give her a cup of tea. Plenty of sugar."

She was taken into the cottage and a dear old woman gave her tea and made a great fuss over her and she began to feel better. A policeman appeared from nowhere and took notes. The doctor telephoned for an ambulance and it came and took Charles to hospital. The doctor went with Charles and his wife drove her to Appleshaw. "Put me down here, please," she said when they got to the green. "My cottage is quite close."

"Is there anyone at home to look after you?"

"Yes," said Valerie. "Put me down here, please. And thank you very much."

Paul would be in and she did not want this woman letting it all out to him. She wanted to tell him herself, carefully. She had seen Charles walking along the road and given him a lift. Rehearsing what she would say she stood at the front door fumbling for her key in her bag. Paul opened the door quietly from within while she was trying to find it. She looked up and saw him there.

"What is it, Valerie?" he asked. "What's happened?" He took her arm and pulled her into their little sitting-room and then suddenly took her impulsively into his arms. "You've been in some sort of danger, haven't you?"

She began to cry again. "The car. It ran into a telegraph post."

"Are you hurt?"

"No."

"You're sure?"

She nodded, her face pressed against his coat, not willingly but because he was holding her so tightly that she could not help herself. "If I had been hurt," she said irritably, "you'd be just about killing me, holding me so tightly. Paul, let go. I want to put the casserole in the oven."

"Damn the casserole," he said. He picked her up and put

her gently on the sofa. He took off her shoes and sitting at
the bottom of the sofa held her small cold feet in his hands.
Her feet were always cold and he had done that sometimes
on their honeymoon. He had been so sweet then, in those
days before he became blind and nervy and obstinate, and
she began to cry afresh as the memory swept over her.
"Don't cry, Val," he said. "Do you want a cup of tea?"

"I've had it," she sobbed.

"Then stop crying and tell me what happened. Were you
with Charles? Was he driving?"

"Yes."

"Is he hurt?"

"Not badly. He's gone to hospital. Coming back from
Westwater I saw him walking along the road and offered
him a lift."

"Don't lie to me, Val," he said fiercely, and the hold of
his hands tightened on her feet. "You've the right to spend
the day as you like, of course, but not the right to lie about
it. Tell the truth for God's sake. You've nearly wrecked
our marriage with the lies you tell yourself and me. Do you
think I don't know about the times you tell me the matches
are in one place when you've put them in another, or that
Bess is ill when she isn't, or all the other little cruelties you
think up? It doesn't matter so much about the lies you tell
me, they're like the pinpricks of a child, but the lies you
tell yourself go as deep as death. If you tell yourself you're
one sort of woman when you're another sort you'll land up
by being no sort. Just a nothingness. No one exists unless
they know themselves. Valerie, pull up for God's sake.
Do you think I want to lose you?"

"I do not," she said. "Hardworking housekeepers are not
easily come by these days."

She watched, with a half-smile on her lips, for that slight
tensing of the muscles of his face that came as he constrained
himself to silence. It was a look that both maddened and
satisfied her, maddened her because she could not wring a
retort out of him, satisfied because she knew her thrust had
gone in. But it did not come. Instead he flared into anger.
"You silly little fool! That's not what I meant. I don't
care a damn about your housekeeping and life might be
pleasanter if you did leave me."

"Paul!" she cried, divided between fury and an anguish of hurt pride.

"I haven't finished. Pleasanter but pretty pointless. I don't only live to write, as you think, I also live to hold you up if I can till you come alive again."

She burst into floods of tears. "Paul, you're hateful! Storming at me like this when I've just has this awful shock. I feel most dreadfully ill!"

"Come to bed then," he said and pulled her up from the sofa into his arms. He did not say he was sorry. He was not sorry. The afternoon with Mary, stirring him so deeply, and the joy of the release he had shared with Edith, had brought about release for him as well. All the pent-up anger and grief of years surged up in a flood of power. Without a false step he carried Valerie upstairs and put her on her bed.

"Send for Mother," she sobbed. "I want to go to bed for days and days and have Mother."

"No," he said firmly. "Neither of us gets on with your mother. Stay in bed as long as you like. But you'll jolly well stay there, not keep getting up in your dressing-gown playing the martyr. If I get stuck over things I'll ring up Joanna."

"You're not to, Paul. I've got some pride if you haven't."

"I'll get you some more tea and some aspirins. That'll quiet you down."

"It's your fault if I'm upset."

"Yes it is. But you'll be all right after a good rest. And I'll ring up Fraser."

She raised herself on her elbow. "You won't! You know I can't stand him."

He flung an arm round her and kissed her and the power in him made her feel she was gripped to a dynamo. Then he went downstairs and she heard him ringing up Dr. Fraser.

3

It was a long time since anything so gossip-worthy had happened at Appleshaw and details of the affair were not wanting, for the policeman who had taken notes turned out to be their own policeman, Ted Barnard, visiting his aunt at the cottage. People could not help enjoying the gossip but they were sorry too because of Colonel and Mrs. Adams. They took it quietly but they aged a good deal and they got very tired going backwards and forwards to see Charles in Westwater Hospital. He was slow in recovering for the concussion turned out more serious than they had thought at first and the shock brought back the nerve trouble of the war. Their friends were good to them, taking them in and out by car. Mrs. Hepplewhite was especially kind, driving them herself in the Bentley with Tania placed on Mrs. Adams's lap to console her. They were very exhausted on Mrs. Hepplewhite's days but not so tired when Mary or Joanna took them, but somehow it usually seemed to be Mrs. Hepplewhite. She was so eager and one could not hurt her. She was so extraordinarily kind. She came to see them at the cottage too, her arms full of flowers. Arranging them after she had gone made Mrs. Adams so tired that she couldn't sleep at night. Mrs. Hepplewhite took flowers to Valerie as well, and held Paul's hand in both hers to show her silent sympathy. Not that she was exactly silent but she did not refer to what had happened. Her talk flowed under and over it and embedded it in jam. Her tact was as overwhelming as her kindness. But Paul was not overwhelmed, only amused. He knew what the sympathetic pressure meant. He had never supposed that Hepplewhite was a satisfactory husband. In Mrs. Hepplewhite's thoughts he and she were now twin souls, locked together in understanding. Gravely he would return the pressure and bow her from the gate with a courtesy that brought the tears to her eyes.

Valerie was in bed for a week for Dr. Fraser said she was anaemic and run down as well as shocked. The rest was something she was supposed to enjoy but it was frightful lying and listening to Paul laughing downstairs with the other women. One or other of them always seemed to be there, Joanna mostly but sometimes Mary or Mrs. Croft. They prepared dainty meals for her and carried them up, Mrs. Croft with the cheerful briskness of the professional nurse, Mary with grace and smiling dignity, Joanna matter-of-fact and kind, but all of them equally maddening. They knew all about her and Charles now and were think-

ing the worst and enjoying it. They were flirting with her
husband and enjoying it. Their food choked her and she
ate very little of it, at least while they were there. When
they were not there and Paul brought her up a tray with
delicious left-overs she thought it her duty to get her
strength back. She had begun by disliking Joanna the least
of the three but ended by almost hating her.

Upon the last day before she got up Joanna came in after
tea to put the trays ready for supper. She sent Paul out for
a walk and came up to Valerie's room.

"Look here, Val, I want to talk to you," she said, shutting
the door firmly behind her, and sitting on Valerie's bed she
tucked her feet up.

"I've got an awful head," Valerie murmured.

"I dare say. You don't eat enough. Now look, Val.
When you get up you'll feel weak. Let Paul help you. I've
simplified the arrangement of the kitchen and he knows
where everything is and can find his way about perfectly
well."

"You've rearranged my kitchen?"

"I had to. The way you had things it was so confusing
that Paul couldn't possibly manage in it. Now he can. Let
him do things. He'd be happier if you let him do more."

"So you think I don't make my husband happy?"

"I didn't say so. Now don't fly off the handle because
there's something else I must say."

"What?"

"You'll be thinking now that all of us know about your
friendship with Charles. Well, some of us knew before you
had that smash. You can't keep things dark in a village as
small as this one. But what I want to say is this. No one
supposed for a moment that the affair was serious. You
know what I mean. We knew you wouldn't be such a fool,
especially with a man like that."

"Like what?"

"Like Charles."

Valerie looked blank. "He's so distinguished," she said.
"Like his father."

"Unfortunately not," said Joanna. "He has a sort of look
of his father sometimes and he might have looked like him
if he hadn't been just no good at all."

"Charles? No good?"

"Surely you knew?"

"No."

"But how could you not know? It's so obvious. Val, what a child you are!"

Valerie flushed scarlet and the tears came into her eyes. Had she really cared for the man? Joanna wondered. She was ready with her sympathy but Valerie's next remark scattered it.

"What a fool you must all think me!"

"Never mind, Val. It's over now. Forget it."

Valerie forced the tears back, for she was too humiliated to cry. Joanna kissed her and went away and her anger at the motherliness of the kiss, the kindness as to a child, kept her going until bed-time. But the next day, downstairs in the sitting-room for tea, she felt sunk in humiliation. How could she go on living with everyone thinking her such an ignorant fool and with her wonderful romantic love, that had seemed like a round golden ball, sunk to the proportions of a little sordid pebble? And she had not even got Paul now. Mary Lindsay had taken him from her. She had deliberately set out to steal him. Now she had lost the two of them, both lover and husband. No story that she had ever read had ended like this in total loss.

After supper Mrs. Hepplewhite came with a huge armful of roses and carnations.

"She's a bore!" said Valerie, exhaustedly contemplating them when she and Paul were alone again. "I've not enough vases."

"She's a darling," said Paul. He was in the arm-chair, contentedly smoking, Bess at his feet, but he got up. "I'll get something for them."

Valerie collapsed upon the sofa and listened. He was moving about the kitchen as though he were sighted. She had never allowed him in the kitchen because it drove her distracted when he bumped and fumbled, and she had not had the patience to simplify things for him, as Joanna had done. Besides, she did not want him there. Joanna was maddening! He came in with the kitchen bucket, filled with water. "Here you are, Val. Stick the flowers in here for now. You can deal with them in the morning."

He put the bucket carefully beside the flowers, but he had filled it fuller than he knew and some water slopped over on to the carpet. It was the last straw and she burst into tears. He sat by her on the sofa and flung an arm round her, but without alarm. That sense of release and power was still with him, and with it the joyous conviction that nothing just now could go very wrong. Rarely, these times came, tossing one up like a lark from the earth, and one continued to go up until the meridian was reached. One had to come down again but there could be quite a long spell in the sun before the impetus was spent.

"Why are you crying now?" he asked her. "Is it Charles? Are you in love with him?"

"You wouldn't care if I was!"

"I care very much. Tell me, please, and tell the truth. You don't know how much it matters to both of us that you should tell the truth."

He held her more firmly, his heart beating so hard with the urgency and risk of this turning point that she could feel it, and moved her hand that she might feel it beating under her palm. She had done that in the old days and now she did it again, a reflex response of memory, but in spite of her wretchedness an echo of the old thrill came back. She felt weak as water, and as though her limbs were dissolving, and flowing away. She tried to move her hand but she couldn't. She left it where it was, the strong beat sending answering hammer strokes through her own blood. Paul pulled her closer so that her head was on his shoulder.

"Tell me," he said. It was not a plea but a demand. He had lifted her clean above deception and evasion and she answered truthfully, "I thought I was. I'm not any more."

"Then why are you crying? Because people are talking about you and thinking you a little fool?"

"Not only that."

"What else?"

She struggled suddenly but he did not let her go. She felt a ruthlessness in the pressure of his arms and answered in anger, "What right have you to blame me for Charles? If I'm a fool so are you."

"I haven't blamed you for Charles. And why am I a fool?"

"Can't you see that woman's out to get you?"

"You mean Mary. I like her and she likes me and she likes my work. That's all. You answered me truthfully and I've answered you truthfully."

"Not all as far as she's concerned. Your work! It's you."

He considered this. "I honestly think not. It would be absurd."

"Of course it's absurd. She's probably even older than she looks. But women can be vampires at that age. It's their last chance."

The word vampire as applied to Mary dissolved him into laughter against his will but he was careful to hold her closer while he laughed. "I mean absurd because of my deficiencies, not Mary's age."

"You're attractive."

"You think so after all these years? Val, you're a sweetie."

She relaxed like a child and said, "I'm so tired."

"Let's go up then."

"Aren't you going to work?"

"Not tonight."

They shut up the cottage, put Bess out and let her in, and went upstairs. At her bedroom door she said, "Good night, Paul," and went in and shut it. He answered her gently, accepting the closed door, but some time later he strolled into her room with his pillow under his arm. She was lying in the centre of the double bed reading a magazine. He dropped the pillow on the bed. "Val, I'm fed up with this," he said. "Shove over."

She looked up at him in astonishment and then moved over.

CHAPTER X

I

THE hot summer days slipped by and the gardens grew parched with drought, and then there was a thunderstorm in the night and after that it rained and went on raining, and Mary felt as though she had fallen through the surface of a river, sunk down and found herself still alive in a dim green underwater world that had an even greater intensity of life than the sparkling one that had vanished.

The house, vacated now by the last workman, was marvellously calm and she found herself gazing in awe at the green light that lapped over the ceilings like water, and at the pools of silver that lay on the floor when the clouds broke at sunset. Looking out of the windows she saw the garden green and wet and dim, the drenched flowers hanging heavy heads. The birds sang rapturously because the drought had broken and their voices, and the voices of the wind and rain, seemed spell-binding around the house. The boy in the pool looked intensely alive, as though it were he who had spun this web of music about her, keeping her house-bound. She did not want to break it for she was experiencing a new intimacy with the house now that she was so dependent on it for warmth and shelter. It talked to her in the tick of the grandfather clock, in the creak of the old boards and the scurrying tap of the mice who had evaded Tiger. Edith came daily for her lessons, so quietly happy that her journeys through the shadows and the greenness had a smooth serenity like the comings and goings of a silver fish. And Queen Mab's coach and the tea-set were back in the parlour. When Mary lit the fire on chilly evenings the blue glass cups and saucers sparkled like sapphires under the crystal globe. When she was alone in the house Tiger came with her wherever she went, striding at her heels, and when she was busy he would play silently, leaping at moths, prancing on spiders, or lying languidly on his back playing with his own tail, an apparently boneless creature, shadowy and soft, so graceful as to seem fluid. Yet the bones were there, and fiery new life within the softness.

Mary too was conscious of fire. It burned inwardly, renewing and warming her but at times wounding her too, so that it seemed that her life flowed away and yet returned to her again, describing a circle that had Paul for its centre. He was unconscious of her life about him for his writing had come alive again and so, he hoped, had his marriage. About the first resurgence he was quite sure, about the second not so sure for Valerie was unpredictable. But she was at least his wife again and in the relief of it work went well. He came to see Mary as often as he could without rousing Valerie's jealousy to fever point; there was good, not harm, he instinctively knew, in keeping it moderately warm, at blood heat. He loomed up out of the rain with a dripping Bess and bundles of manuscript under his macintosh, and Mary dried Bess and gave him tea by the parlour fire, and undertook to read more of his work; a play, a new chapter of his book, another poem. He had found in her what he had never had, a sympathetic but intelligent critic. She could wield the pruning knife mercilessly yet at the same time she watered the roots. They talked much of his work, little of Valerie, yet she knew about Valerie and in this thing as well as the other she struggled to channel all her energies into the one outgoing power of desire. She scarcely knew what this power was, and did not give to it the name of prayer, but she did realize that her desire must be for his fulfilment and nothing else. When he left her she was exhausted yet when the morning came she could go on.

Her absorption in Paul was not making her unaware of anyone else. She found herself very sensitively aware of Cousin Mary, Edith and Jean Anderson. But above all just now of John. She began talking to him, not with her lips but in her mind, as she moved about the house and in bed at night. Sometimes she spoke of Paul and his work, hardly separating the two men in her mind, and at other times of their days together in the past. In the years after his death she had been afraid to think of him too much, partly through sorrow and partly through shame, because she had been so inadequate, but now she thought of him constantly and was coming to understand him much better. Yet she remained unaware of what was happening, as at the turn of the year one can remain for a while unaware that the light is strengthening.

2

The rain stopped. Jean Anderson woke up one morning in her usual waking state, a depression that never failed to frighten her though it was so familiar. There followed the struggle to speak. It was extraordinary how hard it was to do so, when all day long speaking to him was her salvation and delight. But in the early morning dumbness was upon her like chains. She would lie sometimes for ten minutes, knowing there was a way of escape but unable to take it. It was not so long today. It was only a few minutes before she made the effort that always seemed so impossible, and said, "Please will you help me. Illumine my dark spirit with thy light. Then shall my night be turned into day." After that she was no longer imprisoned, and she heard the voice. "It is Thursday."

A sense of warmth crept over her. Thursday was the day that she and Mary went out together in Mary's car but it had been so wet lately that they had either had to cancel their outing or go shopping, and Jean hated shopping, even with Mary, because of the noise. Last night, longing for some sunlit hours with Mary, and for a drive they had planned to the Roman road across the downs, she had prayed that it might be fine again. Her brother said it was childish to pray about the weather because it obeyed the immutable laws of nature. God did not go messing about with his own laws and she was only wasting her time. But it confused her to try and think what she could pray about and what she couldn't. She had to pray about everything or she couldn't live, and it was surprising how the fine days came, and the cat had her kittens safely and she was able at all times to obey.

"Look out of the window."

She obeyed. Huddling her dressing-gown about her she drew the curtains and looked out. From her high east window she could see over the garden to the country beyond. The sky was veiled in silver and swathes of mist lay over the fields. The trees and the quiet cattle stood knee-deep in it but the lifted crests of the trees were illumined, as though some glory was preparing. She watched as the mist thinned and brightened. She did not cease to watch yet when it happened her eyes had not been able to observe the moment of miracle. All she could say was that the sun had not been there and now it was, a ball of pale gold hung like an apple against the silver sky. Suddenly every blade of wet grass below her, every leaf and twig-full of crystal lanterns, caught on fire and the robins began to sing. For a few moments the sun was hers and then with grateful joy she gave it back to him again.

At breakfast her brother said to her, "I couldn't find it in any of the Westwater antique shops."

"What, dear?" she asked absently, because she was intent upon pouring out his coffee without spilling it.

"Good heavens, Jean! You know perfectly well that I spent most of yesterday in Westwater looking for that Queen Anne card table of the Adams's. Then I went to supper with Fraser and when I got back you'd gone to bed."

She remembered now. A few days ago he and Mary had played bridge with the Adamses and the Queen Anne card-table with the candle sconces, their most precious possession, had not been there. They had played their bridge on a deal table brought in from the kitchen. No one had commented upon the loss but Mary and the Vicar had known what had happened. Charles, getting progressively worse in the noisy hospital ward, had been brought to the quiet of the private ward by his father's command. The card-table must have been sold to pay for his room and the Vicar had set himself to find it and buy it back. The fact of the old couple playing bridge on their kitchen table had upset him more than anything had upset him since the upset of leaving Oxford. Also it was an insult to the game to play it on deal.

"James, I'm so sorry to have forgotten," she said, and slopped his coffee into the saucer, for his tone had been sharp. But the memory of the sunrise was still with her and she managed not to be tearful.

He took the cup without comment but sucked his cheeks in and out, as was his habit when suppressing comment. The suppression of comment was always difficult for him

and the movement of his facial muscles was an outward and
visible sign of an inward and spiritual victory.

"It's Thursday," he said. "Don't you go out with Miss
Lindsay on Thursdays?"

She smiled at him. His congenital antipathy to women
had not caused him to be predisposed in Mary's favour and
for some while she had been referred to as the Lindsay
woman. But he had discovered her to be intelligent and
capable, her conversation easy without distressing fluency,
and at times even well informed. What she saw in Jean he
couldn't imagine but she had certainly done her good. So
now Mary was Miss Lindsay. She would never be Mary to
James Anderson for he did not wish to be James to her. He
shared with certain primitive tribes the conviction that
once you yield your name to another that other has power
over you. Only a spaniel bitch he had once kept had had
power over James Anderson. No woman, ever.

"Yes, James," said Jean.

"Going today?"

"Yes, James."

"Then get her to take you to Thornton. There are a
couple of good antique shops there. Of course I know it's
like looking for a needle in a bundle of hay but there's
always a chance."

Jean looked down at her plate so that he should not see
her face. Thornton! It was such a noisy little town, noisier
even than Westwater because the London Road went
through it. And they had set their hearts on the peace of
the downs. But James wished it and she must obey.

"Yes, James," she said. "We'll go to Thornton."

3

"We'll go the long way round, by the river," said Mary
when she was told of their misfortune. "I haven't much
hope of finding the card-table but we'll try."

The day was so lovely that Jean soon forgot her disappointment over the downs. Mountainous clouds were
piled upon each other, snowy mass upon snowy mass,
dazzlingly luminous, the lakes of sky between them deeply
blue. The clearings in the woods were brilliant with willow
herb and by the river the wild irises had hung out their

golden banners among the reeds. Sometimes pheasants called in the woods and once a kingfisher flashed across a stream between the alders. It was a serene countryside, tidy and comfortable, the meadows and woods giving place sometimes to gentle green knolls crowned with silver birches and cypresses, with chestnut avenues leading to hidden houses. It had no wildness and majesty was in the sky alone. I would tire of it, thought Mary, if it were always summer here. But winter is coming with the great winds and the snow.

Jean chattered of the hens and the cat and the sunrise this morning. Mary never found her talk trivial because she herself was not trivial. Her lines of communication might be crossed but behind the confusion she knew things. Much more than I do, thought Mary, and stopped the car at a gate that gave them a view of a church tower among orchards, a loop of the river flung round it and a sharply green hill behind rising against the tremendous clouds. "Does this satisfy you?" she asked.

"Yes, but it's almost too much. It was easier this morning when there was only the sun hanging like an apple in the mist. I could give that as though I had taken it off the tree. Well, so I had. It was given me on the tree."

"What tree?"

"The world."

"I thought you must mean that tree in the Garden of Eden."

"They are the same," said Jean. "And if Eve had given the apple back to him it would have been all right. It was eating it that led to motors."

"Motors?"

"James says that the internal combustion engine is the root of all evil."

"Aren't you enjoying my car?"

"I'd enjoy it more if it was a dogcart."

Mary laughed and drove on. When they reached Thornton they found the narrow high street packed with traffic. There was an aerodrome not far away and jets screamed overhead. Mary was inclined to think that the Andersons were right. Of all the evil things that man had plucked from the tree of the knowledge of good and evil machinery was

possibly the worst. It had destroyed bodgers, with all that
meant in terms of human dignity, and without these ghastly
planes bombs could not be dropped.

The first antique shop yielded no results, except a slight
cessation of noise when they got the door shut. The second
was down a quiet side street and behind it was a paved
court cool with ferns. There was no Queen Anne card-table
in the shop but the assistant, in the absence of the owner,
suggested that there might be in the storeroom beyond the
court. Would they like to come through?

In the long dim room beyond the ferns the floor was so
irregular that the dead centuries leaned together in the dusty
sunlight. Cracked mirrors were propped against bow-
fronted chests of drawers, wig stands against console tables,
high-backed chairs lurched drunkenly and tallboys had
their heads back against the wall. They looked sad and
poor, polish gone and surfaces cracked, listless and weary
as Mary had seen very old people look. With one glance
she knew they would not find the beautiful Queen Anne
card-table here but to satisfy James Anderson they had to
look. The shop bell rang and the assistant left them.

Mary was looking at a wig stand, wondering who had
used it, thinking how strange it was that it should be here
still and its owner dust long ago, when from the far end of
the room there was a crash and a cry. She turned quickly
as Jean came towards her white and trembling.

"What is it, darling?" she asked. "Have you broken
something?"

"Yes, a golden mirror with cupids. The glass is broken."

"Well, never mind. I'll buy it and have fresh glass put
in. I'd love a cupid mirror in the parlour."

"It's not just that." Jean trembled so much she could
scarcely formulate the words. "It's the coffin. The very
one. When I saw it I stepped backwards and the glass went
over."

"What coffin?"

"The one she tried to put me in."

"Where is it, Jean?"

"Over there. I can't go back."

Mary took her out into the ferny court and made her sit
on the seat there. Then she went back into the store-room

to the far end where the mirror lay smashed on the floor. There it was, an old chest of dark oak with the lid up. Even before she got near it Mary's heart gave a lurch. Then, coming near, she saw what had horrified Jean. On the inside of the lid, carved with a rather too realistic cleverness, was a skull, and near it, very small, the initials W. H. The front of the chest was carved with interlaced strappings forming a cross in the centre. Even before she stepped forward and shut down the lid Mary knew what she would see on top. A bird with spread wings. Her knees were giving way and she sat down on a Victorian piano stool opposite the chest. How was it that it had not been bought? It was a bit knocked about, and the new panels that had replaced broken ones had possibly destroyed much of its value, but even so it was a wonderful thing. Probably prospective buyers had thought that skull unlucky. Where had Cousin Mary got it from?

She went back to Jean who was still white and shaky. "I love the glass," she lied, for she had not even looked at it. "I want to arrange about having it mended. Would you rather wait outside in the car?"

Jean nodded and Mary took her out to the car. Then she went back to the shop. It was her fortunate day for the owner had come back. They argued over prices and it astonished him that such a knowledgeable woman should give in so easily. She produced her cheque book then and there and the chest and the mirror were hers, to be sent to her when the mirror had been mended.

They had brought tea with them for Jean did not like the noise and confusion of tea-rooms. It was while they were having it at the edge of a wood that Mary said, "Jean, that wasn't a coffin, it was an oak chest."

"A coffin *is* an oak chest," said Jean sensibly. "And it's the one she tried to put me in."

"Who? Not my cousin Mary Lindsay?"

"Yes, but don't call her Mary Lindsay. I can't bear you to have the same name as her."

"She was a good woman, Jean. She was only peculiar sometimes because she was ill."

"It's more wicked than peculiar to try and put live people in coffins."

"If that's what she did it was both wicked *and* peculiar, but I am quite sure you are making a mistake. Won't you tell me about it?"

"No," said Jean obstinately, and she had to put her cup down because her hands were shaking.

"Jean, you must tell me," said Mary. "I am very sorry but you must tell me at once."

She had already discovered that when Jean was in one of her obstinate moods she would not yield to persuasion but if commanded she obeyed at once with a sweet and touching reasonableness. She did now, folding her hands like a chidden child.

"It was not long after we came. I hadn't seen Miss Lindsay but I was frightened of her because people said she was odd. And I am terrified of odd people because I'm afraid of getting like them."

"Oddness isn't catching. One doesn't catch things unless there are germs attached."

"There are germs attached to anything you're frightened of," said Jean with a return of obstinacy.

"Go on telling me about the chest," commanded Mary.

"We hadn't been at Appleshaw long and I was on my way to visit the cottages in Ash Lane. James said I must. And I had to pass The Laurels. I was always frightened of that door in the wall because once when it was open it looked like the grave of Lazarus yawning in the rock. I tried to walk past it quickly but my feet dragged and I couldn't. And then the door flew open and she ran out like a spider; you know that horrible way spiders run as soon as a fly or a bee touches a thread of their web."

"Yes. Go on."

"She ran out so fast, a skinny old woman in a long black dress, and she gripped my wrist. Her fingers were so thin but they were strong. She spoke to me but I was too terrified to understand what she said, except that I was to go inside and see something. She pulled me up that passage, and the leaves were whispery and dim, and the hall beyond dark. Only the flowers on the coffin were bright and pretty, but she took them away with her free hand and lifted the lid of the coffin and there underneath was that skull."

"What did you do then?" asked Mary.

"I tried to pull my hand away but she held on and I knew she was going to put me in the coffin. I cried out, I think, and somehow I got away and out of the house. I don't remember how. I only know I got out."

"And you went home?"

"Oh no, I went on to visit in Ash Lane."

"But weren't you dithery at the cottages?"

"Indeed I was. I couldn't say anything. But I had to go. James had told me to go."

"You didn't go to The Laurels again?"

"Not till I came to call on you. James didn't tell me to, not till he told me to visit you. He did Miss Lindsay himself. Parish visited her I mean."

"Jean, she didn't want to put you in the chest. She wanted to show you her treasures. It was her way of welcoming you to Appleshaw. What she said to you at the door was, 'Come in and see my little things.' She had a lovely collection of tiny treasures. I'll show them to you one day. And she wanted you to see her marvellous old chest. She thought of it as an altar, not a coffin."

"An altar?"

"The hall used to be the chapel of the monks' infirmary. Your brother will tell you this. I have her diary and I read in it only a few weeks ago that she was hoping to find a chest or table to put against the wall where the altar used to be."

"Poor old lady!" said Jean after a silence. "Do you think she was hurt that I ran away?"

"If she was it's all over long ago."

"Nothing is ever over," said Jean. "You thread things on your life and think you've finished with them, but you haven't because it's like beads on a string and they come round again. And when something bad you've done to a person comes round again it's horrible, for if the person is dead there's nothing you can do."

"I have thought lately that sometimes there is," said Mary. "When it comes round again then if it is possible to give what you failed to give before to someone else. You will have made reparation for we are all one person."

"People only? Or all of us?" Jean's hand, with a gesture calm and serene for such an agitated person, seemed to indicate the birds calling in the wood behind them, the sheep in a high field on the skyline and the cats at home.

"Scientists say we are all of one substance," said Mary. "The Bible says we come from the one God and await the one redemption."

"I'm always full of reverence when I look at my hens," said Jean.

It seemed to Mary that the whole world laughed with her and in her rather alarmingly visual memory the image of the skull was subtly changed. In a lesser degree the carving had shocked her too. The mockery of a skull's grin always shocked her and she had wondered how Cousin Mary had tolerated it, hidden in the hall and why she had wanted to show it to Jean, apparently with affection. But seeing it now in her mind's eye the mockery was gone. It was merely amused, as though to those still in possession of a skull death could show only the profile of the hard bones, yet laughed to think how differently he appeared to those upon his other side.

4

Mary sat up late that night with the diary. She had been reading it slowly and steadily, passing with Cousin Mary through the first few years at Appleshaw, years of alternate illness and respite, so much at one with her cousin that she seemed to be learning with her how to accept the first with hope and the second with wonder and gratitude. Cousin Mary hoped her journey through periods of dark and light was like that of a Swiss train toiling up the mountainside, in and out of tunnels but always a little farther up the hill at each emergence. But she could only hope that this was so, she did not feel it. It seemed to her that she did not advance at all and that what she was learning now was only to hold on. The Red Queen in *Alice Through the Looking Glass*, she remembered, had had to run fast merely to stay where she was, but doubtless she had run in hope disdaining despair, and hope, Cousin Mary discovered, when deliberately opposed to despair, was one of the tough virtues.

And when respite came could there be anything more marvellous than the sunburst of light? What was life like,

Cousin Mary wondered, for those who seem to live more or
less always on an even keel? For them too there must be
the swing of the pendulum, for nothing living could escape
it, but the self-pity of her youth began to leave her as she
considered their relative joys, only so far up because it had
been only so far down, in comparison to her sunbursts.
They would never reconcile her to the abyss, nor was it
right that they should since the abyss was evil, but the
sombre backcloth increased joy to the point where wonder
and thankfulness merged into a clarity of sight that trans-
figured every greeting of her day. She opened her window
in the morning and saw a spider's web sparkling with light
and was aware of miracle. Sitting in the conservatory with
her sewing she knew suddenly that the sun was out behind
the vine leaves and that she was enclosed within green-gold
light as in a seashell. She dropped her sewing in her lap
and was motionless for an hour while the light lay on her
eyelids and her gratitude knew no bounds. Standing inside
the willow tree she looked up and a thrush was there, so
close to her that she could learn by heart the gleaming
diapason of his breast, the sleek folding of the wing feathers,
the piercing bright glance going through her like lightning.
They were alone in the world, he and she, and presently he
was alone and she was only a pair of eyes of which she was
no longer aware. He did not fly away until some sound
disturbed him for the creatures were not afraid of her while
she walked in light, though they feared her in darkness.
Once she held up her finger to a butterfly and it alighted
there, and though it soon flew away again her finger wore
the sensation of airy lightness like a jewel until nightfall.
She grudged herself to sleep on the moonlit nights for she
could not bear to lose a moment of the moon's serene companionship. These and other greetings she recorded in her
diary. "They are more than themselves," she wrote, "and
when the wonder grows in me I am more than myself.
Whenever I am conscious of this more than ourselves I
remember the old man in the garden at home, looking at the
butterflies in the buddleia tree, and how the butterflies
seemed to shine on his face, or something in him shone on
the butterflies, I didn't know which. I may have imagined
the light but I didn't imagine the more than ourselves.

That's real enough, and when I am conscious of it my wonder and gratitude clap hands together and what is caught up from me is more than either. If any words come to me then they are those of the old man's second prayer, 'Thee I adore'."

After that entry there were several descriptions of village doings, in which in her good times she could sometimes take part. Tea parties, games of chess with the squire, Sunday-school outings and cricket matches on the green. It was in the midst of these jottings that Mary found what she was looking for. They were decorating the church for the harvest festival and Cousin Mary was sent to the vestry by Mrs. Carroway to find a ball of string.

"She told me it would be in the chest," she wrote. "I didn't know what chest and I didn't like to ask because she was getting a little irritated; the dahlias were weak-kneed and would not stand upright. I went into the vestry and looked round and at first I couldn't see any chest, and then I saw it in the dark corner under the north window. I went over to it and stood looking down at the closed lid, dark like water and with a greenish tinge because of the yew tree outside the window. It seemed to me that the water stirred, or that wings moved. It was only the reflection of the branches of the tree lifting in the wind but the movement caught my attention and I looked closer and saw that a bird with outspread wings was carved on the lid, like those symbols of the spirit that one sees in stained-glass windows. I lifted the lid and inside, just beneath the bird in flight, was a skull. Both were beautifully carved and were enclosed in a circle of the same size and design, so that I realized that one was not to be considered without the other. They were a unity, like a two-sided coin. The front of the chest was carved with a typically sixteenth-century design, interlaced strap work forming a cross in the centre. It was riddled with woodworm, the carvings broken in places, some of the panels cracked. Seeing it like that made me want to cry and I stood looking down at it as though it were someone I loved ill in bed. Then I suddenly remembered what I was here for and I rummaged inside it, among torn old hymn books, broken candlesticks and all sorts of rubbish, until I found a ball of string.

" 'Couldn't you find it, dear?' Mrs. Carroway asked when I brought it to her. I apologized and finished the pulpit for her, tying the weak-kneed dahlias to the heads of the twelve apostles, and presently Mr. Carroway came along, rosy and smiling, his hands clasped behind his back, to see how we were doing.

" 'Very tasteful, Miss Lindsay,' he said. It wasn't true for I don't know much about arranging flowers, and nor does he, but Mr. Carroway is always courteous.

" 'That chest in the vestry,' I said, getting up and dusting my knees. 'Where did it come from?'

" 'Chest?' he asked.

" 'The one under the north window.'

" 'Ah yes,' he said vaguely.

" 'Come and see,' I said, and to his dismay I took him by the arm and led him to the vestry. I had already discovered that his interest in church history includes the fabric of the churches but not their furniture. Nor does his passion for bees extend to the flowers that are the reverse side of bees. He has a two-track mind, which is more than most of us have, but the tracks are narrow. Yet I think he was stirred when I told him I was sure the chest was sixteenth-century, and he agreed with me when I said it must once have been a treasure of the monks. He put his spectacles on and had a good look at the carvings, and he seemed a little ashamed of himself that he had not had a good look before.

" 'I fear I have noticed little apart from the general dilapidation,' he said, 'brought to my attention by the churchwardens. They have it in mind to replace this chest by a cupboard, a more convenient receptacle for the hymn books and such odds and ends as accumulate from time to time in a vestry.'

" 'And what are you going to do with the chest?'

" 'There is a room in the tower where we occasionally deposit such derelict furnishings as we have no further use for. Brownlow, that's the people's warden, is averse to throwing things away. They might, he thinks, come in useful at some future date.'

"I made a mental note to visit the room in the tower as soon as possible, and I did some quick arithmetic in my head and then I said, 'Mr. Carroway, may I give the cup-

board to the church? I would like to do that as a thank
offering because my health has improved so much since I
came to live here.'

"At first he was courteously hesitant, wondering if he
ought to accept my offer, but he was very pleased and when
I assured him I could well afford it he agreed that I should
give the cupboard. Then I asked if I might buy the chest
from the church because it was just what I wanted in my
hall, and at this he was horrified because of its dilapidated
state, but I persisted and he said he would discuss the
matter with the churchwardens.

"Well, in the end I got it. The cupboard was installed
and Mr. Entwistle borrowed the squire's gardener's hand-
cart and fetched the chest. Jenny wouldn't have it in the
house for a moment, because of the woodworm, so Entwistle and I took it right away to Nightingale Wood, to Mr.
Abraham Baker the bodger, who is a woodcarver as well
as a bodger and can do anything with wood. It was one of
those early November mornings that are as beautiful as any
in spring. There was gold everywhere, drifts of it on the
elm trees, flakes of gold under our feet, gold dust on the
hedges, liquid gold in the refracted falling light. For the
sun today broke through pale and luminous clouds. It was
a gentle day with no wind. Entwistle trundled the cart
with the chest in it and I walked beside him. He whistled
sometimes, answering the robins, and sometimes we laughed
and talked together. But we could be silent when we
wished for we were good friends.

"The wood, when we reached it, was almost frightening.
Trees look taller in the autumn than at other times and the
beeches towered to such a height that their red-gold seemed
to lift and lift and have no ending. Yet in spite of the glory
above many leaves had already fallen and lay drifted about
the silver trunks and the low darkness of the hollies. The
bramble leaves, tipped with fire, seemed to leap out of the
golden wash like flights of birds or butterflies. The smell
of the wet leaves and moss was sad and strange yet marvellous to me.

"We came to Fox Barton, the ruined farmhouse where
Abraham Baker has his workshop. I love the place and hate
to see it falling to pieces. The ceilings have gone long ago

and soon I am afraid the plaster garlands in the parlour will fall to pieces with the damp. Abraham Baker's grandfather, a farmer, lived here as a young man but when he married his wife couldn't stand the loneliness and the ghosts and he sold it. The man he sold it to, a recluse reputed by Mr. Entwistle to be very odd, lived alone in it for many years and then he couldn't stand it either and he went to America. He had not kept it in repair and it was so dilapidated that no one else wanted to live there, and so Abraham Baker's father quietly moved in and used it as his workshop, for he was a bodger too.

"Abraham was hard at work when we went in, a giant of a man with a grim seamed face and a long grey beard that he buttons inside his shirt when he is at work lest it get caught in the lathe. This keeps him with his chin permanently tucked down and his great broken nose much in evidence. His son Joshua was with him today, a strange lanky child with bright red hair, terribly shy. Abraham is not shy but he does not speak unless it is necessary. He did not speak while I told him about the chest and asked him if he could repair it for me and get rid of the woodworm. But when I had finished and Entwistle showed him the chest he suddenly stopped work. He came over and looked at the carving and ran his huge hands over it. Then he lifted the lid and smiled with delight at the sight of the skull. I had never seen him smile before and it was a remarkable sight for his smile is huge as himself, an enormous mouth registering delight. 'Why does it please you so much?' I asked.

" 'Fine bit of carving,' he said. 'And hidden like. Folks don't do hidden work so much these days.'

"I told him about the hidden carvings in cathedrals, marvellous work hidden from all knowledge but that of its makers and God. He nodded and told me there was a carving like that in Appleshaw church, on the right-hand side of the door leading to the tower. 'I ain't one for church-going,' he said, 'but I go at harvest to see the veges. The wife, she always sends a vegetable marrow for the font and I always sits at the back of the church where I can see the marrow, and one year I tipped me 'ead back an' give it quite a crack on that there carving. I 'ad a look at it later.

Well, you can look at it for yourself if you've a mind. Cost you a pretty penny to have this repaired. Look at this 'ere.' Some of the carving on the front of the chest, riddled with worm, came away in his hands and a trickle of wood dust fell to the floor like water.

" 'I don't care what it costs,' I said recklessly. 'If you have to carve fresh panels I shan't mind. Is the lid all right?'

" 'Naught wrong with he,' said Abraham. He had lifted the lid again and was holding it with one huge hand covering the bird and the other the skull, the circle surrounding each hand, and I thought suddenly of the hands of the Creator holding life and death. And then I thought of the hands of the man who had carved the lid holding the finished thing, and thinking it was good, and in my mind he was identified with Abraham.

"Something touched me and it was the nudging elbow of the lanky Joshua. He was standing by me holding something in his hand. He glanced solemnly up through the mat of red hair that hung down over his eyes, smiled and opened his hand. Inside was a treasure that he had, a large conker carved with his initials J. B. 'What you doin' of, nudging the lady?' roared Abraham suddenly, and aimed a good-humoured blow at one of Joshua's protruding ears. The child ducked expertly under the workbench and hopped up behind it, grinning, his shyness suddenly gone, and all the way home I remembered how he had shown me his conker.

"That was weeks ago and it is nearly Christmas and this morning the chest came home. Abraham has an old pony and cart and he and Joshua brought it. They carried it in with Entwistle's help and put it in the hall against the wall and we all stood and gazed. It was a day of frosty sunshine and the chest, now oiled and shining, seemed to gather all the light to itself. Mr. Baker had done a marvellous job and the two new panels he had carved himself were scarcely distinguishable from the original work. I did not try to distinguish them since Mr. Baker and the first craftsman were one man in my mind. I tried hard to thank him but it was difficult to find the words.

"Something touched me and again it was the elbow of the

child Joshua. He had nothing to show me this time, he just wanted to smile at me. But I realized I had something to show him and leaving the other three talking I took his hand and led him into the parlour. Lady Royston's gift of the blue glass tea-set gave me the idea of making a collection of tiny treasures and I have quite a number of them now, under a glass case on a table in the parlour window. People have found out about my collection and they bring me things for it. Doctor Partridge brings me something whenever I am ill and I am sorry now that I said he did not know much about sick people for he knows they like presents. I showed my little things to Joshua and watched his face and I think my enjoyment of his face just about matched his enjoyment of my little things. I gave him one of them, a dwarf with a red cap. He held it in his hand for a moment or two and then shook his head and gave it back. I understood how he felt, that it belonged here with the others. To take one away was like taking a jewel out of a crown.

"We went back into the hall and Abraham was standing there alone with his hat in his hand. He's so tall that his head nearly touched the rafters of the ceiling. I asked him how much I owed him for the chest and he handed me a bit of dirty paper. When I had read what was on it I gasped, for he had not charged me nearly enough for all that labour. 'It's not enough, Mr. Baker,' I said.

"He seemed to grow even taller as he told me with great dignity that he had enjoyed the work. I realized that I could not argue the point without wounding him so we shook hands with mutual respect, and I went to the door in the garden wall and watched him and his son drive away in the funny little cart.

"And now it is the dead of night and as I can't sleep I am writing this in bed. In my mind's eye I can see Abraham's huge hands holding the skull and the bird together as though they are one thing. To me they are the symbol of so much, body and soul, time and eternity, death and life beyond death, even of the two halves of my own life, the sick times and the times of respite. The chest is a fitting thing to have in an infirmary chapel. It might have been carved by the infirmarian himself.

"The clock has just struck two and I am thinking, as I often do, that in monasteries all over the world monks are saying their night offices as once they did here in the church across the way. The sick in this house would not have been able to get so far and the infirmarian would not have left them, but he would have gone to the infirmary chapel, with any monks who were well enough to leave their beds and any who were here to help him with the sick. I feel quite sure about this, and I know the words of many of the prayers and psalms they would have used. I asked Mr. Carroway what they would have been and he didn't know, but he was ashamed he didn't know and he found out for me. Sometimes I say one or two of the psalms myself and imagine I am saying them verse by verse with the infirmarian. I know which I shall say tonight, the fifty-fourth, 'An offering of a free heart will I give Thee, and praise Thy name, O Lord, because it is so comfortable'."

CHAPTER XI

I

AUGUST came and Joanna and Roger and the children went to the sea for a fortnight, and while they were away Catherine came to stay with Mary. She was not fond of children and Mary chose the moment of their absence to ask her, for the three were increasingly with her. Or rather with the garden, which they had taken as theirs again. Whenever she saw a small figure upon the wall behind the copse she went indoors, and Rose and Jeremy did not seek her out until they were hungry and wanted ginger biscuits out of the tin on the kitchen dresser. Edith sought her out often, for love's sake, even though lessons had ended for a while. When the Talbots came back again Paul went to stay with them while Valerie went for a holiday in Switzerland with her mother. She thought she did not want to go for it left Paul with only the Talbots' garden wall between himself and Mary. But he insisted and she went, for she found herself continually giving way to him nowadays. She was not at all well and he took advantage of her lassitude to bully her, or so she told Joanna as she helped her pack. "You want to go to Switzerland," said Joanna briefly.

For Mary the three weeks of Valerie's absence went like a flash and yet seemed three centuries. The weather was fine again and Paul asked if he might work under her willow tree. He wanted to teach himself, he said, not to work by night only, for late hours disturbed Valerie.

"The children come into the garden," Mary warned him.

"They won't be as bad as Joanna's hoover. You don't appear to have a hoover, Mary."

"Neither Mrs. Baker nor I are mechanically-minded."

"Thank God for that."

"Why do you think under the willow tree would be a good place to work?"

"I'm aware of those cool bending branches and their

shadows as though it were night. 'Dear night, this world's defeat.' Night gives one the freedom of the cloister."

"I'm asking about it because if you want to work under the willow tree you must ask Edith's permission. It's her place."

"I'll ask her," said Paul.

Edith said he might. She was flattered that a book should be written in her place and established herself and Kipling's *Just So Stories*, that Mary had given her for her birthday, in the green shade of the conservatory. Mary, sitting at her desk and reading the earlier typed chapters of Paul's book, looked up often, delighted in the sight of her dark head beyond the open window. She was as absorbed in her book as the man under the willow tree in his, and Mary was so absorbed in both readers that she seemed to have them in her blood. The man, the woman and the child. But not her man or her child. And yet they were hers, in her veins. No, not her veins, that were only the high roads of her body. They walked the roads of an inner hidden country and in that country they were her own.

Sitting at her desk one morning she remembered the day she had come here, and the sense of penetration she had had, reminding her of the Indian boxes one within the other and the small gold one at the centre. And she remembered being in this room as a child and trying to make herself small enough to get inside Queen Mab's coach; and then being in this room at evening, waiting to read the diary, and feeling herself at the heart. Life was full of these intuitions that one must get smaller, go farther in. The golden box was so deeply within that it was hard to find, yet it contained an entire country and was, she supposed, the only luggage one could take with one if there was anywhere to go beyond death. For much of her life she had believed there wasn't. Yet in this place she had had so many intuitions of a door. The lime trees in the avenue, guarding the abbey gateway that could no longer be seen yet was still there. The door in her own garden wall that had seemed to her as a child to be the entrance into the inner world of a picture. And often in dreams she had opened a familiar door and found beyond not what she was expecting but something so beyond description that it could not be accurately remembered on waking, though it held one all the following day like light. Dreams were all nonsense, people said, but she had come to believe there was sometimes a true thread woven through the middle. Have I come to believe there is a door? she asked. She had just finished a chapter of Paul's book and closed the cover that contained it. Her hands folded upon it she asked the question again. Have I? She felt the beginning of a great astonishment, cut short by a child's voice.

"I've finished it. I've read my favourite three times." It was Edith in the conservatory.

"What is your favourite?" asked Mary.

"The kangaroo who kept on running."

"Why do you like that one best?"

"I like the kangaroo. He didn't want to go on running but he *had* to. He *had* to grow his hind legs."

"Well, I know I have to go across to the church to look at the carved corbel on the right-hand side of the door that leads to the tower. Would you like to come with me?"

Edith jumped up eagerly. "Climb out through the window," she commanded.

As they crossed the lawn, their footfall they thought light as dew, a curtain of willow was pulled back and Paul asked, "Mary, did you finish chapter ten? Is it all right?"

"No," said Mary. "Edith and I will only be gone a few minutes and when I get back I'll tell you what I think is wrong."

"And will you read my letter to me? I had one this morning but I didn't want to ask Joanna. It's her washing day."

"Yes, I will."

"Mother gets het up on her washing day," said Edith as she and Mary crossed the green to the church. "Why do you want to look at that corbel?"

"It is beautifully carved. In church at a service one cannot see things properly and I thought we could look at it together."

"Good," said Edith. "I don't like it that next week it will be all of us." For it had turned out as Mary had thought it would, and next week she would be running a dame's school; for Rose needed coaching in a few subjects and in case Jeremy should feel left out he was coming along too. "And I don't want to go back to school in the autumn."

"But you must. You're well now."

They were walking through the churchyard and Edith kicked savagely at a stone in the path. "You're getting as bad as Mother. It's always must, must, must."

"Then say 'have', like the kangaroo. You have to go back. It's asked of you."

"What do you mean, it's asked of me?"

"You know quite well what I mean."

Edith sighed and abandoned her ill temper, for she did know. She'd had to tell about the little things.

It was cool in the church and they slipped into a seat and sat down gratefully. There's more to the coolness of an old church than thick walls keeping out the heat, thought Mary, there's the coolness of history. Looking back from the claustrophobic congestion and satanic noise of the modern world the past appeared so uncluttered and quiet. Piers Plowman saw all the people of the world sitting in a field, a mere handful, a gatheration of starlings, and beyond the field what spaciousness and peace. The old church held that as well as the spaciousness of an undreamed-of future. The Norman arches of the nave, washed with the pale green light that came through the high, small windows, narrowed to the distant glimmer of the chancel. The only stained glass the church possessed was in the east window. It was old, with deep jewel colours of blue and crimson that spilled down on to the altar. Peering under the darkness of the arches one could see the Victorian marble memorial tablets surmounted by urns, angels and coat of arms, and a tomb with an iron railing round it where a knight lay on his bier with his rusty iron sword chained to the railing.

"Is this where you sit when you come in the evenings?" asked Edith.

"Yes," said Mary. "I sit here with Miss Anderson." It was a seat at the back of the church and next to a pillar. Jean, sitting beside the pillar, could almost hide herself behind it. "Where do you sit in the mornings?"

"Over there by the knight. Jeremy likes it there."

"He likes the knight?"

"It's the mouse he likes, a particular mouse that is his

mouse. The mice nest behind the knight. Rose likes it there too because she can see her hat in the brass eagle. We only wear hats on Sundays so a hat is special. What did you say we'd come here for?"

"To see the carved corbel beside the door to the tower. Let's go and look at it."

Behind the font two steps led up to the door to the tower, small and low under its stout little Norman arch. The corbels seemed to Mary to be of later date. The one to the left bore a coat of arms of three bees and a cross-handled sword, the one to the right showed the head and shoulders of a monk. The features were worn but something about them, the fact that one eyebrow was higher than the other, the ways the ears stuck out, was highly individual. "I think it was a portrait," Mary said to Edith.

"Of himself?" asked Edith.

"Perhaps. The old craftsmen did portray themselves sometimes."

Behind the monk's head was a garland of thorn branches that hid his shoulders and it was easy for Mary to put her fingers through the lattice work of thorns and feel what was behind. Something was carved there. She withdrew her fingers and made Edith feel.

"What is it?" she asked.

"Bunches of little flowers," said Edith. "Like hawthorn, I wish we could see them."

"They haven't been seen since the carving was put in its place," said Mary. "They will never be seen. Now let's go up to the room in the tower."

Beyond the door was a spiral staircase and they climbed up it. The door to the tower room no longer existed and pale green light shone down to meet them. "It's like climbing up inside a tall green reed," said Edith.

The room, when they reached it, seemed still a dumping ground for things that no one wanted, as it had been in Cousin Mary's day. There were some broken chairs, tin receptacles for flowers such as Mary remembered seeing years ago on graves, torn hassocks pouring out their sawdust, and kindred rubbish The sunlight, falling through the green glass in the narrow lancet window, illumined humanity's dislike of parting with anything that might one day come in useful; only the need for a burst hassock or a broken flowerpot had somehow not arisen and here they were still. Down below in the church the sun moved slowly over the old flagstones, as it had always done, the knight's sword was chained to the iron railings and the mice nested behind his tomb. Over their heads in the tower the old clock ticked, ancient and remorseless. Mary's pleasure turned to sadness. The tower, that had seemed a green reed full of sun, was peopled with anxious ghosts, and the church below rustled with them. They were being driven in and in upon the quiet places and they were afraid.

A sudden ugly clatter almost made her cry out as though it were the fall of cities, but it was only Edith knocking over a pile of the old tin flower holders that were stacked against the wall. "Sorry," she said. "I tried to take one out that I thought would be useful and they all fell over. Look, someone's carved their initials on the wall."

Mary went to look. The letters W. H. were deeply carved within a rough circle. Edith traced them with her brown forefinger as though incising them more firmly on the wall, but neither she nor Mary said anything. They climbed down the turret stairs again, Edith carrying the bent tin mug she had filched for Jeremy's paint water. On their way out Mary stopped to look again at the monk's head. It struck her now that the encircling thorn branches made him look like a man in the stocks, yet the mouth smiled with a wry humour.

They parted on the green. Edith went home and Mary crossed her lawn towards the willow tree, in outward possession of her usual serenity but inwardly humbled and terrified. Her love for Paul now had her in a grip that frightened her. She was afraid, quite simply, of the pain, and she was also afraid of betraying it. She had lived in a difficult and dangerous world and had discovered how to manufacture the armour called for by difficult situations and how to wear it with confidence. But though she had felt deeply over many things there had never been anything like this to batten down; it was like trying to put a lid on a volcano. With her armour cracking it seemed as though the years that had gone to the making of it were falling away too, leaving her helpless as a child, with a childish and most humiliating longing to run for shelter. Only there was nowhere to run.

Unless it was to humility. As a man she now wanted Paul with human urgency, but as an artist she drew back from him. During these weeks of working together she had had hard work not to let her criticism, that he wanted and needed, be beaten down by her awe of his emerging power. She had discovered the daemon in the man and she believed that he too was discovering what it was that had driven him for so long. These last weeks they had been looking together at a calm pool, watching its waters first disturbed and then parting as the dragon with the shining scales heaved itself from the depths. She had watched not only with awe but with humble withdrawal, as though he were not of her clay, and he had watched with a mounting self-absorbed excitement. There was selfishness in his excitement and she recognised it. He was not naturally selfish but all men are selfish in the grip of a daemon. That too would perhaps provide her with a sort of shelter.

Though she made no sound crossing the grass he knew she was there and lifted a branch of willow. She bent her head and went in. Bess, two chairs and the table with his tape recorder almost filled the little place yet she had a feeling of emptiness. Paul was smoking and Bess was asleep. "Have you finished the book?" she asked with surprise.

"For the first time through, that's all. But the first time through is a profound relief, like knowing you've reached the turning point of an illness. Tell me what's wrong with the chapter you've been reading."

She told him and he accepted her criticism. "You know the book is good," she said.

"I know it will be when I've had another go at it. But when I say good I only mean the best I can do."

"Have you felt so confident before?"

"I don't feel my usual despair about this book, nor about that play you sent off for me a few weeks ago."

She saw the letter on the table and picked it up. "It's from your agent."

"It's too early to hear anything yet."

She opened the letter and glanced through it. "No, it's not too early. I'll read you the letter."

It seemed to her strained nerves that she read it in a silence in which Appleshaw itself was listening. She saw the face of the monk with the thorns round his neck and she fancied that his smile broadened into a triumphant grin. Having finished reading she could no longer trust herself to speak. It was a detective play, written before she had come to Appleshaw, but she was a *Who Dunnit* addict and she had suggested alterations which had given it added punch and excitement. Paul laughed, the sound exploding joyously, and held out his hand to her. She took it and he swung their linked hands backwards and forwards in boyish high spirits. "It will probably come to nothing," he said.

"Why say that when you know it won't?"

"Placating fate I think. Valerie comes back tomorrow. What a gorgeous bit of news to greet her with."

"She will be pleased," said Mary. One o'clock struck and he got up, for Joanna preferred punctuality though she was adjusted to its absence. "I'll come with you to the door."

They walked across the lawn to the wistaria tunnel. It had been so hot that the green leaves were already tipped with gold. Paul stopped.

"Mary, what can I say? I realize how much you've helped me."

"It's been a happy partnership."

"It's been like dew coming down on dry earth, or like dead bones living."

Mary laughed and opened the door in the wall. "You exaggerate, but we've enjoyed ourselves. Come round to-morrow and we'll take your tape recorder and manuscripts back to the cottage."

She shut the door behind her and went quickly into her cool, dark hall. She would see him tomorrow but he would not be the same man tomorrow. What he had said about the dew had truth in it for somehow renewal had come to his marriage and his work, and so to himself. He was different now and would be increasingly so as success came to him. Though not less in stature he would be perhaps less lovable. Though never to her. She would achieve shelter and steadiness and would suffer less with the passing of time, but she would carry this with her until she died. She found she was looking at the oak chest, now in place in the hall, and once again she remembered the monk with the thorns round his neck. She turned away and went upstairs to wash her hands for lunch. Her feet felt like lead on the stairs. But at the top she remembered John, and half expected to see him come towards her out of the shadow. "It is you I love in this man," she said to him, "and I love him as you loved me. The thing is mutual now, and so strong that I do not think I am any longer a land-locked sea."

2

The next morning Paul visited Charles for the third time. After Valerie had gone away he had asked Dr. Fraser to take him with him on his hospital days and to leave him with Charles while he visited other patients. Not even Mary had known of his visits for he had managed not to coincide with anyone else. The first visit had been pure embarrassment for both of them for he had been unable to explain to Charles why he had come. How could he say, "I have not come in a spirit of pious forgiveness because you flirted with my wife, got drunk and drove her into a telegraph post, I've come because you look like a chap in a book I'm writing." This would have sounded odd to Charles in any case and in view of the fact that Paul was blind, stark mad. And so the first visit had remained an embarrassment and the second had not been much better at first, though later they had achieved ease, even a sort of happiness together. This one went very differently for as soon as the preliminaries were over Charles asked bluntly, "Why do you come?"

"We didn't get that walk we'd promised ourselves."

"Things have changed a bit since then, haven't they?"

"As regards myself, for the better."

"You mean Val is thoroughly fed up with me?"

"Yes, she is, and I'm enjoying the rebound."

"Good," said Charles and he meant it, but his embarrassment was not relieved. Let him think me mad, thought Paul. What does it matter? And he took the plunge.

"I don't come to see you for any reason connected with Valerie. That's all past. I come because I'm writing a book and you're the chap in it." He was aware of blankness like an empty bucket and tried again. "That must sound mad to you. The book's about myself really, though I didn't know it till that night at the local."

"I don't know much about writing books," said Charles, "but if you think this chap in yours is like both you and me then you've made a mistake about one of us. Of course I don't know what you think about yourself, or me, but if you think there's the slightest resemblance between us then all I can say is, I'm more capable of writing this book than you are; that is if a rudimentary understanding of character is necessary to the writer's craft, which I was under the impression it was."

Paul laughed. "Probably you could have written it better than I can. Shall I tell you about it?"

"I might see more light if you did."

Paul told him about it with an ease that astonished him. Was it relief from loneliness that was making him so garrulous with Mary and Charles? With Charles, of course, it was like talking to himself. With Mary it was much the same, for she could have been that companion who is to a man the other half of himself. That was why rage had seized him at Charles's way of speaking of her at the pub. At some deep level of existence she was his woman as Valerie his wife was not. The knowledge had come lately like a flash of lightning, with burn and shock. Then he had accepted the knowledge and let it take its place with the fact.

He came back to awareness that there was now something in the bucket. "A diatribe against war in fact," said Charles. "There are so many. Do they do any good? Is there anything now that can be done about our fate except to rail at it? By the common man I mean. The V.I.P.s of course are like a bird in a bush mesmerized by a snake, so mesmerized by horror that it just hops nearer and nearer. The common man, that's you and me." He seemed pleased by this and smiled. "But can we do anything?"

"Rail," said Paul . "Scream at the bird from behind."

"Is your book a powerful scream?"

"I hope so. The common man of our generation knows what he's talking about."

"Yes. I don't know as much about it as you do, you know. I wasn't in the war for long. It's true I've been a mess since, but then I was a mess before. People talk a lot of ballyhoo about suffering improving you. I should say that what it does is to underline what you were before. It did that to me. And probably, in a different way, for you. No, I can't blame what I am on the war."

"The last one. What about the one before?"

"Good lord, I can't go back that far! And I still don't see why you recognize me as the chap in your book."

"I don't think I can explain really. Say I recognize you and always will and leave it at that."

"I'll be glad to," said Charles simply. "I'm always coming back to Appleshaw. Don't move away from the place when you're a V.I.P. yourself."

"Is the job your father told me about still waiting for you?"

"Yes. I'm starting in ten days' time I hope. There's Fraser out in the passage. Damn!"

"You sound better. Go on with the good work."

"Yes. You go on with the book. It won't do any good but go on with it and good luck to it."

"Good luck to your new job."

"It's not much of a job. Just something to be going on with."

Outside in the passage, waiting for Dr. Fraser to finish with Charles and join him, Paul thought they had laid a good deal of emphasis upon mere going on. It was of course a stark necessity, unless one wished to be a beatnik. He imagined it was what made Charles tick. His religion in fact. If he could get to the end without having thrown in his hand he would have kept his integrity. No one could wish man a greater gift than the power to avoid apostasy.

CHAPTER XII

I

It was Saturday afternoon and Mr. Hepplewhite decided to go for a walk. The decision was momentous for he never walked. Like all the lordly ones he shot, that being the natural activity of the species, and he played golf to keep his weight down, and these pursuits involved walking, but walking for walking's sake had always seemed to him an act of insanity. What was the point of it? Muscles could be stretched in more intelligent ways and the beauties of nature could be more conveniently observed from the window of a car. There was of course this question of wanting to be alone. On a golf course there were other men. A car did not take one to lonely places and legs did. But he could be alone in his library. Shrugging on his macintosh in the hall he realized with something of a shock that he had not wanted to be alone out of doors since his childhood. Not until this afternoon.

Mrs. Hepplewhite, her needlework in her hand, had come to the door of the drawing-room. "Are you going out, Frederick?" Her eyes went to the fine drizzle outside the window and then came back anxiously to his face. "What is it, dear? Indigestion?"

"No," said Mr. Hepplewhite shortly. Mrs. Hepplewhite took a few tentative steps towards him. He was troubled in mind. He never confided in her but she knew the signs. Irritability and a queer sort of emergence of Fred, the young waiter she had married. It was difficult to say in what this emergence consisted. A slight intonation of the voice, a look in the eyes, a movement? She could not analyse it and emergence was the wrong word, for it was more of a memory than an emergence. It came so seldom for Frederick was hardly ever troubled. His business affairs were always triumphantly satisfactory. Was it Julie? He had come home last night without Julie and had announced briefly that he had dismissed her. He had

dismissed a pretty secretary before, when she had gone stale
on him, and turned to the next with renewed enthusiasm.
But Julie she believed had gone deeper than the others. It
was hard for her to express sympathy, with her heart singing for joy at Julie's downfall, but she did most truly grieve
that he should be troubled and she put her hand timidly on
his sleeve. "If you're going for a walk may I come with
you?" He gazed at her in astonishment, for she never
walked either, then shook her hand from his sleeve,
grabbed his stick from the stand and disappeared into the
rain.

He strode steadily through the village, for his walk had a
purpose. In order to keep hold upon faith in his own sanity
he had had to think up some sort of reason why he should
tramp through woods in the rain. Looking at his estate map
this morning he had noticed that he had never been to Fox
Barton farm. It was only a ruin, his bailiff had told him, and
the lane that led to it was too narrow for his car or shooting-
brake. He had shot in Nightingale Wood but he had never
happened to come near the farm. All the same a landowner
should know every corner of his land. Once he had seen Fox
Barton practically every yard of his would be in the possession of his memory. His memory? He forged across the
green without seeing it, his powerful shoulders straight and
his mouth grim. His hands were on this place and it was in-
conceivable that he could lose his grip upon anything that
was his. Yet he had thought Julie was his until he had
seen her the other night at the bar at the theatre with
Lawson, his enemy, and with him in that unmistakable
way. And then he had discovered that leak of a bit
of information; not important as it happened but there
might have been other leaks and Lawson was damned
clever.

He scarcely noticed Ash Lane as he tramped down it and
only at the edge of the wood did he become aware of his surroundings. It was November and the beech trees still
carried their leaves. The fine drizzle was no more than a
drifting veil and it was almost dry and strangely warm under
the weight of gold. Sometimes a single leaf floated down
and fell into the beechmast below like a drop of rain into
the sea, to be lost there, but otherwise there was no move-

ment. And no sound, not even of his own footsteps on the moss and soft earth.

He had come to the farm before he realized it for its gold-lichened roof and silver-grey walls were hardly distinguishable from the wood around it. The mist was wet on his face again as he crossed the clearing, cool as the spray that had so often drenched him on board his boat. He came to the door and found it locked. He pushed hard, hoping the lock would break, for the place was his and the resistance angered him. He banged on the door but there was no answer, only silence and the drip of trees. He went to the right-hand window but though the glass was gone he could make no entrance through the iron bars fixed across it. He shook them but they were as unyielding as the door. He could only look through them. He saw the workshop with the shavings on the floor, the workbench and lathe, the chair legs and Mr. Baker's artefacts upon the shelf. He saw no beauty in their wooden shapes and wondered that anyone should think them worth protecting with these bars.

Then after a while the workshop captured his attention and held it. He realized slowly that a man spent his working life there. It was his world, as much to him as a great factory to its owner, or as the vast web of high finance to the men who spun and schemed within it. But this world upon which he looked through the bars had a stark simplicity. The man who worked here was not dependent upon other men. There was nothing here to entangle or betray him. The primitive lathe, the wood of trees, his own vision, brain and muscle, the silence, were all he had. Mr. Hepplewhite stood and gazed until it seemed the scene he looked upon had burned itself into his mind. It was utterly unfamiliar to him and yet he recognized it. Men whose blood was in his veins, his mother's people, had lived this way. He stood and looked and nostalgia became a sort of despair. He went quickly to the other window and shook the bars there, trying to banish the misery with anger. But he could not recapture the anger, he could only stand there looking in. This was no workshop, only an emptiness, but he saw the gracious ruined stairway, the Adam mantelpiece and the broken plaster flowers upon the floor. He vaguely remembered the Vicar telling him that the squire whose portrait hung in his dining-room had rebuilt the manor house. He had not been sufficiently interested to ask where the fellow had lived in the meantime. It could have been that the man who in later life had spent his evenings where he spent his, in the library at home, had sat here before this hearth, reading or listening to his wife playing the harpsichord. His books would have lined the walls, the smoke from his pipe drifting its blueness across the gold and crimson of their bindings. That past too was now in his blood. He looked in upon the man and again he looked so long that he was bemused.

Coming back to himself he was aware of the iron bars in his grasp, cold and wet, and claustrophobia gripped him, as though they were keeping him in instead of out. He stepped quickly back, aware of the blessed space of the clearing about him. He was ashamed of his momentary panic but he did not look again through the two windows, he walked to the end of the clearing and looked instead at the old thorn tree. For a while it held his attention with its twisted strength. Most of the leaves had gone but it glowed deep crimson with berries. Then he saw the well and did not know that he'd walked to it.

There was a small boy leaning over the edge of the well, sniffing the scent of water, feeling the cool breath on his face, feeling down with one hand for the cavity behind the wet ferns where the butter was hidden. He found it but the butter was not there today. There was an emptiness. He peered down the well, expecting to see his own brown face. But there was a fair-faced boy down there, snub-nosed, freckled and red-headed. There were two small boys and it was morning. The sun shone and the birds sang.

A few moments later, sitting on the parapet of the well but with his back to it, Mr. Hepplewhite was in the grip of rage. Had Julie been here he could have murdered her, yet it was scarcely against her that he raged, or even against his own incredible idiocy that he had allowed the little bitch to know too much. His fury now lay deeper than those surface things, though possibly the savage laceration of his pride and his emotions had laid him open to it. It had to do with those two rooms at which he had been looking through the bars, with the well and the two boys. For the first time in his life he had seen with vividness a picture of a world that had gone, the craftsman's world, the world of the Adams' garlands about the hearth and the books upon the wall, of the wells of faith and the innocence and perception of children. Even he, a child of the slums, had once perceived the scent of water. Had he lived in this place a hundred years ago he would not have sat here now, one of the richest and most successful men in the country yet facing defeat like the crashing of ice-floes about him, and sickened of the whole business to the marrow of his bones. It was not his fault. If he had made himself what he was he'd not made the so-called civilization that had not offered him, as far as he had been able to see, any ladder to climb other than the one he had climbed. Other men had built up this vast crashing screaming madhouse and now it was falling down upon the lot of them, the innocent and the guilty alike. Sitting perfectly still he cursed these guilty ones, exhausting himself with hatred and despair.

He staggered to his feet at last and found that a watery sun was shining. He turned and looked down into the well and saw a gleam of it caught in the water, and was pleased he had seen it, as though the seeing was to his credit. He thought suddenly that perhaps the men he had been cursing felt much as he did himself. Helpless. Trapped. Innocent yet guilty. For now his rage was spent he found that he did somehow feel guilty. He remembered that evening in his library when he had momentarily wanted to destroy those letters. Something had occurred then. There had been some occurrence in a timeless dimension, a voice or movement neither heard nor seen. He had no explanation of what had occurred but he did know that he had deliberately chosen to be deaf and blind. And not for the first time. All his life he had been for ever stabbing something out as one extinguished the glowing end of a cigarette. That yielding to Julie had only been the last refusal of many. Each in its own place had possibly been just as disastrous yet at the time apparently so inconsiderable, and so immediately forgotten. It must be the same with all men. And so the sparks were stabbed out and darkness gathered and one man's darkness, since one man is many men, was the darkness of the world.

Striding across the clearing he was angry again. The thing, whatever it was, had no right to demand this watchfulness. If it had anything to communicate then let it blaze and thunder the news across the heavens for all men to see and hear. This was no world for whispers and intuitions. It might have been once when the monks lived here, or when the woman who had played the harpsichord in that room had dropped her hands in her lap to listen. Possibly the old anachronism who now toiled at his craft in that workshop knew a thing or two. No one else did nowadays. They'd no silence. Little by little it had been stolen from them. Raging at the thieves, raging at whatever it was, if anything, that would not speak out, he began to feel more like himself, his sense of guilt overlaid by returning self-confidence. By the time he reached the lane he was even jeering at his own fears. He'd been in tight corners before and rounded them. He'd always been a lucky fellow. He was almost cheerful by the time he came out on to the green and saw Mary and Valerie at the gate of Orchard Cottage. He raised his hat to them and called out a greeting, then went over to them.

"You look well, Miss Lindsay." Mary acknowledged the fact of her good health and thought how expertly he did it, his glance lingering upon her face just long enough for her to know that he complimented her upon her looks as well as her physical well-being, before moving on to Valerie with a kindling enthusiasm. "And you, Valerie? I've never seen you look better. Feeling fine are you? May an old friend congratulate you? Splendid."

Valerie flushed but met his glance steadily, as though daring him to interpret her flush as one of embarrassment. It was actually of annoyance for every face she met now was wreathed in congratulatory smiles. From the way everyone was behaving anybody would think there'd never been a baby expected in Appleshaw before. Nor of course had there been, except among the gipsies and farm labourers' wives and people like that. Jeremy had been born before the Talbots came here and the rest of the village people were old. It was maddening to have everyone rejoicing so selfishly in her misfortune, with never a thought for her suffering and peril. Serve them all right if she died.

"Will you come in and have a cup of tea?" she inquired of Mr. Hepplewhite with weary dignity. "You too, Mary."

Mary, who had come to return a basket, returned it and excused herself. Mr. Hepplewhite did likewise and they turned away together, a little too quickly, for they missed the drooping exhaustion of Valerie's figure as she returned to the house. Mr. Hepplewhite came with Mary to the door in the wall of The Laurels, left wide open for the first time in his experience, and was caught by what he saw. There were still a few wistaria leaves left, and the pale sun lit their transparency to gold. The front door was wide open too and he saw the gleam of gold chrysanthemums in a pot on an old chest. Beyond was only deep shadow and an intimation of warmth and safety. The façade of his recent self-confidence suddenly cracked and with inward terror he knew it for what it was, a mere façade. It fell and all else with it.

"Won't you come in?" said Mary gently. She was aware of some change in him and aware too that for the first time in their acquaintance she liked him. He shook his head, for he was now outside safety, turned away and then swung back.

"The boy," he said gruffly. "Jeremy. He's not been to see me lately. He's all right?"

"Quite all right," said Mary. "He had a bicycle for his birthday."

"That's it," said Mr. Hepplewhite, accepting the fact that he could not hope to compete with a bicycle with matter of fact humility. "When you see him give him my love will you?"

"I will," said Mary. "Good-bye, Mr. Hepplewhite."

"God bless you," was his surprising answer and she was left looking at the upright departing back in a bewilderment touched by incomprehensible sorrow.

2

"Anybody would think I was some sort of Punch and Judy show," said Valerie angrily to Paul, as she wheeled in the tea-trolley. "What's that you've got?"

He had been in London for a week, staying with an old friend who had just driven him home, seeing his agent about

his play and some book he had written. She had been
pleased about the play but not particularly interested. She
did not suppose it was any good. And she had thought him
heartless to leave her at such a time. Her mother had come
but had been entirely maddening. Having suffered acutely
for some years from grandchild-starvation her mother could
now think of no one but herself. Her discovery, when they
had been in Switzerland together, that in due course if all
went well she would become a grandmother had revealed to
her daughter the essential egoism of her mother's nature.
Her anxiety lest Valerie should have a miscarriage had not
been entirely on her daughter's account. Valerie's conten-
tion that all men were brutes and Paul in particular, taking
her by surprise like that and giving her no chance whatever
to take preventive measures, had merely led her mother to
express disapproval of preventive measures and then to
smile tenderly and hope that nice woman, Mary Lindsay,
was taking proper care of Paul.

"It's Joanna who's seeing to him," Valerie had snapped.

"I mix them up," her mother had replied dreamily. "I
don't mind if it's a girl or a boy though it would be nice to
have a boy with a look of your father about him."

"Do you realize, Mother, that I'm in my thirties? I'll
probably die."

"Nonsense. Aunt Dorothy had her first in her forties.
There was no trouble. An hour and a half. And Margaret
Brown. Thirty-nine. He came in the ambulance. A lovely
little boy. Or was Margaret's a girl? And then there was
Hester."

Her mother had run on like that all the time, a smooth soft
flow of selfishness, both in Switzerland and at Appleshaw
while Paul had been away. It had been a relief to part with
her, and get Paul back, full of proper concern for her. She
had been lying down when the car bringing him home had
stopped at the gate, and she had not got up because she
did not want to have to offer his friend tea. There weren't
any cakes because beating them up was bad for her, and
she was not going to offer bread and butter only and be
thought a bad housekeeper. But the sound of Paul's voice,
of Bess barking, had sent a thrill of delight through her, so
warm and quick and astonishing that she had not been able

to suppress it. She had still been shaken by astonishment when a few minutes later she had come down to greet Paul. In his arms she had felt herself almost melting with relief, as though some danger had threatened him. He alone now understood her. Only he was truly concerned for her. She had felt suddenly that they stood alone together against the hostile world, guarding each other with their bodies for the sake of each other and also because of this other who was to come into it.

But she had forgotten that now. "What is it, Paul?" she asked again.

He handed her a box. "Take it upstairs and look at it."

"But I've just made the tea."

"It won't take you a moment to look at that."

With mounting excitement, for she had seen the label on the box, she ran upstairs. The tissue paper inside rustled in her fingers like a rustle of gold, so rich and precious was its message. And there was gold beneath it, a housecoat of amber and russet and pale green, silky and marvellous. She put it on, looked at herself in the mirror and caught her breath. For she looked wonderful. It must have cost a fortune for it took a fortune to make an ageing woman look as she looked now. Was Paul mad? They were poor as church mice and the baby was coming. Yet Paul had never been reckless about money. What had happened? The explanation was knocking at the back of her mind, persistent and humbling. She went downstairs again, her head held high, rustling at every step.

Paul was aware of the rustle, and the faint scent of new silk. "You've got it on," he said, hoarse with anxiety. It hurt her that he should be so scared. Had she in the past been so difficult to please that having clothed her in the sun he should still shrink from her displeasure?

"I don't know what to say, Paul," she said. "I've dreamed of having a garment like this. What do you say when you're dressed in dreams?" The answer was so unexpected, so unlike her, that he crimsoned with shock and relief. "How did you get it? Did you go into the shop by yourself? Let's have tea. Tell me while we have tea."

"There was a woman I got to know in town, an actress. I asked her where to go and she told me. Then I took a taxi and went there. It seemed a small place, sort of quiet and silky, with a thick carpet your feet sank into, like beech-mast. There was a woman there with a quiet silky voice, like the shop, and I told her about you. I told her what colours suited you and I described you. Then of course I had to leave it to her."

"How did you describe me?"

He described to Valerie the girl he had married, not the woman whose present likeness had been stamped upon the screen of his mind by her edgy voice and the stifling dust that had seemed sometimes to settle upon them both, the mental fall-out of her discontent. It was for the first woman that he had bought the housecoat, and for the child's mother. They had come together in his mind, blotting out that other woman, a fused and radiant image lit up by the passion of his gratitude.

He discovered that Valerie was crying. "Not in that frock or coat or whatever it is," he implored her. "You'll spoil it. Is it only what's to be expected in your interesting condition or is something the matter?"

"I don't look like that any more."

"It's what you look like to me, and what you are in your-self. The thing suits you, doesn't it?"

"Yes, Paul, it does."

"Well, there you are then. If it was matched to my description, and suits you, then my description was accur-ate, for it was a very clever woman who sold it to me."

Valerie laughed and dried her eyes. "I bet she was! They are in those soft silky places. And in shops that are very quiet they charge the earth. Poor lamb, the shock you must have had when you heard the price!"

"It wasn't a shock," said Paul cheerfully. "The moment I went in I felt that sort of religious feeling that there is in places where they fleece you. I didn't mind. Nothing is good enough for my wife."

"Paul, you're different. Reckless and happy. It was an actress, you said, who sent you to that place?"

"Yes. Do you think she was in league with the woman in the shop?"

"Obviously. Paul, is it the play?"

"The play and the book."

"Both accepted?"

"Yes. From now on, Val, life's going to be easier for you."

"But how do you know they'll succeed?"

"There's such a thing as the law of demand and supply."

"Who's demanding?"

"The baby."

"What a child you are! When the baby comes there'll be two of you."

He was suddenly serious. "Val, I'm not supposing that from now on our life is going to be a sort of prolonged happy ending to an up and down story. The state of the world is as ugly as ever. Our human nature is still what it was. I only mean that no desert is so dusty as not to have an oasis here and there. What's that psalm? 'The pools are filled with water.' Don't you think we're coming to an oasis now? I feel we are."

She did not cry any more but gripped his hand for a moment under the trolley. Then to her utter astonishment she heard herself say, "I'm glad we're having this baby."

A strange deeply buried desire to please him had welled up from somewhere, but she felt winded and dazed. What she had said was something she could not go back upon, something she must keep to, and with one brutal twist it had stripped from her mind the comfortable delusion that she was a martyred woman.

CHAPTER XIII

I

APPLESHAW was shaken as though by an earthquake. At first they could not believe it, as they would not have believed it if the green had suddenly cracked open and swallowed the church. It was true that the news made headlines in all the morning papers, and that was the first that most of them knew of it, but the events that hit the headlines had never hitherto had any connection with Appleshaw and it took them a long time to grasp the fact that this one had. There it was, in print, with photographs in the picture papers. Mr. Hepplewhite had been arrested. According to temperament, incredulity and shock turned to dismay, sorrow, excitement, even pleasure. How are the mighty fallen! The dramatically-minded could not help a feeling of aesthetic satisfaction, and those who were not in the red were aware of their own financial solvency shining like a halo behind their heads, enormously to their credit. But not Colonel and Mrs. Adams. There was no room in their minds for anything at all except grief for Mrs. Hepplewhite. Nor was there in the Vicar's.

"The poor woman must be visited," he said to Jean. His tones were those of ultimatum and his fierce eyes went boring through his sister's head.

Jean had just taken up a shovelful of coal to mend the fire and she dropped the lot. The room swung round her and she thought she was going to faint. No demand made upon her had ever been worse than this, no spiritual struggle more fierce than the one which brought her with the help of God to the whispered words, "Yes, James. Do you want me to go now?"

"What? You? Good heavens, no! I must go myself. Don't wait tea."

"Put your muffler on, dear," said Jean to the closing door. Then she heard the front door bang and knew she was alone. She sank into the nearest chair as faint with relief as a moment before with terror. Reprieved from the impossible! She knew now how Abraham had felt when he had not had to sacrifice Isaac after all. But poor James. She believed he had been nervous. His voice had sounded very jerky when he went out.

James Anderson's stride was also jerky as he stormed up the hill. What an appalling kettle of fish! Mrs. Hepplewhite of all people. She'd weep. Now this was just the sort of thing that had made him dread becoming a parson. Weeping women. Fashionably dressed women. Fashionably dressed women weeping, with their powder melting, if that was what powder did, and their lipstick running down. He was fortunate of course that so far only the country griefs had come his way, the sorrow for the one who had had his life, for the happy release, with prosaic reliance upon the will of God and childlike pleasure in the new black clothes, none of which had embarrassed him at all. But this! Would he have to visit Hepplewhite in prison? Of course he would. Now may God Almighty help me! James Anderson ejaculated mentally. Good heavens, am I here already?

To his astonishment the door was opened to him by Mary Lindsay, cool and competent, and the realization that she, not he, was evidently in charge of this affair so flooded him with relief that his tense, gaunt frame relaxed upon the doorstep like an icicle in sunshine, and Mary's eyes twinkled. Unwinding his muffler in the hall he found he did not object to the twinkle, nor to the competence, though as a rule he disliked competence in women. So few women could exercise competence without fuss. As she disentangled him from the last few yards of his muffler, which had stretched considerably through the years, and gave him the necessary information, sugar-coated with a little tactful instruction, he could for the first time believe that she had held the positions of administrative responsibility assigned to her by gossip. Certainly the present situation, which included himself, was being administered very well indeed.

"Elise fetched me a couple of days ago, after Mr. Hepplewhite had gone," said Mary. "Mrs. Hepplewhite was at first prostrated, and no wonder, and asked for me. She seems to have lost touch with her own relatives. She is now quite in command of herself and being a humble woman hurt pride forms no part of her grief. She doesn't want sympathy. She is loyal to her husband, and devoted to him, and to speak of his merits comforts her."

"Merits? Tell me a few."

"They will occur to you. But what will please her best of all will be the fact that you've come and she can talk to you. If she asks questions tell her the truth."

James Anderson found himself in the drawing-room. Mrs. Hepplewhite was on the sofa with her feet up, Tania on her lap, a bottle of eau-de-Cologne and a large photograph of Mr. Hepplewhite on a table beside her. The November sun showed him that she had a bad headache but she was well dressed as ever and her make-up had been carefully applied. He felt inclined to cheer, noting the slightly defiant angle at which she held her head and the even greater defiance of the photograph so prominently displayed beside her. She held out her hand with something of a regal gesture, as though daring him to pity her, but she was pleased to see him and came to the point at once.

"I'm glad you've come," she said. "You're the only person I can ask. Sit down here, please. Has my husband done anything wicked? I've read and read the papers but they are so confusing. I can't understand at all. I expect Mary knows, she's so clever, but though I love her I can't ask her. It would be disloyal to Mr. Hepplewhite. But I can ask you because you're a clergyman. What exactly has he done? Whatever you tell me will make no difference to my love for him, but I would like to know if you think he has done wrong. The papers have said some horrible things. One of them said he was nothing but a common thief."

"He has certainly done wrong, Mrs. Hepplewhite. He has defrauded a good many people of a great deal of money. But I wouldn't call him a common thief. He did not deliberately set out to steal other men's money, as a common thief does. He gambled with it. I have not the type of mind that can grasp the complicated financial affairs of big business but so far as I can gather it was a daring and brilliant gamble. Had he brought it off he, and other people too, would have made fortunes. But something went wrong and he failed. And so he is execrated."

"So if he had succeeded he would not have done wrong?"

"Not in the eyes of the world."

"But in your eyes?"

"Yes, I should have thought he had done wrong. The money was not his to gamble with, and it represented the prosperity and happiness of other people."

"Other people are ruined because of what he did?"

"Perhaps ruined is too strong a word, but they will suffer."

"I'm sorry," said Mrs. Hepplewhite simply, and then after a pause, "I must do something for them."

The typical kindness touched him but that she should think that anything she could do would ameliorate even the fringe of the devastation touched him even more. It was like a child trying to empty the ocean with a toy bucket. Yet the same criticism could be levelled at every individual attempt to ameliorate or withstand the titanic evils of the world, and the puny efforts had to be made because it was all one could do. And if there were enough children with enough buckets. . . .

"I agree with you," he said. "We will talk about it later when the situation is clearer."

"They call my husband an adventurer, too."

He perceived that everything they called Mr. Hepplewhite was sticking into her like Sebastian's arrows, and grieving that they should have reached the wrong target he tried to comfort her. "That word has two meanings, Mrs. Hepplewhite. If you take it in the favourable sense it means that your husband loved adventure for its own sake. I think that's true."

"You mean like discovering the North Pole and climbing Everest?"

James Anderson replied that in different circumstances he was sure Mr. Hepplewhite would have done both those things. The reply was, he hoped, truthful, for given a certain number of circumstances anyone could doubtless do anything. And then suddenly he had a queer mental vision of Mr. Hepplewhite plodding through a blizzard, his head down against the whirl of snow, a massive dogged bulk of obstinacy. "Your husband is a man of great strength," he said. "And, I think, of resurgence. One cannot imagine him doing anything with a storm except eventually getting the better of it."

Mrs. Hepplewhite brightened, and then the gleam of light passed as she asked, "How long will he be in prison?"

"I don't know. Possibly for some years."

"It's a long time," she said. "But it will pass. I suppose I ought to want him to be sorry, repentant, yet do you know I don't really want him to be anything different from what he is. I've always loved him just as he was however unhappy he made me."

This was suddenly too much for James. He ought to be saying that they should wish for repentance but just now he couldn't. What she said was so utterly true of human love at its deepest, blindest and most heartbreaking. All he could say was, "I am sure you will find, when you get him back, that he is still essentially himself."

He left her and said to Mary, as she let him out, "That is an extremely good woman."

"But you knew that before, surely?"

"Possibly, but without the humility to recognize my knowledge."

"And Mr. Hepplewhite?"

"He will emerge. The power to do that is of course a virtue. You are staying here?"

"For the present," said Mary. "I've even brought my cat."

"When you first came here I should never have suspected you of a cat. Good day."

Now what does a cat symbolize, Mary wondered as she shut the door on him? Domesticity? Decay, like pears going mushy? Anyway I've got the cat. She remembered Tiger with acute pleasure and then turned back to the front door as the afternoon post shot through the letter box.

She took Mrs. Hepplewhite the post and went to fetch the tea trolley. When she wheeled it into the drawing-room she found her in a flood of tears so desperate that Tania had betaken herself to the hearth rug. I never did like poodles, thought Mary briefly, and conquering her native distaste of elderly women in tears she knelt down and put her arms round Mrs. Hepplewhite. The time-honoured phrases came to her quite easily. "Do you good to have a good cry, my dear." And then later, "What you want now is a cup of tea."

"It was in my stars," said Mrs. Hepplewhite huskily, accepting the cup of tea. "It was in my stars that we should be great friends. Do you remember that day I called on you and told you I knew we should be friends?"

"I remember," said Mary, and had a moment of alarm. She had always liked to choose her intimate friends, not have them thrust upon her. Yet why should she have things as she liked them? She abandoned the alarm. "Was there bad news in your post, Hermione?" she asked. It was the first time she had used Mrs. Hepplewhite's Christian name.

"Oh, my dear, call me Dolly!" Mrs. Hepplewhite begged her with another quick burst of tears. "No, not bad news. It was that *he* called me Dolly. Fred. I've had a letter from him. Just saying that he'd like me to go and see him. Just that but calling me Dolly. I thought he'd quite forgotten that he used to call me Dolly. That was my name when we got married, my real name, but when we began to get on in life he didn't like it any more. He didn't like anything that reminded him of the early days, and being poor and so on. He told me to choose something more dignified. So I chose Hermione. I saw it in a newspaper and thought it was dignified. But I'd like you to call me Dolly."

"I'd rather go on calling you Hermione," said Mary. "It suits you."

"Why, dear?"

"Did you ever read *The Winter's Tale*?"

"That's Shakespeare, isn't it? No, I don't read poetry. It muddles me. Why use lots of unnecessary words just so as to get a rhyme at the end of each line?"

"Well, the woman in it is called Hermione. She was not well treated by her husband but she won him back in the end."

"You mean . . . you think . . . ?"

"Yes, I do."

"But Mr. Anderson doesn't think people ever change very much."

"A man is not a different person just because he becomes aware. Oh I know it must seem like metamorphosis when the eyes of a blind man are opened, but he's the same man. We grow, mercifully, and growth is just awareness of more and more."

"Could you read me *The Winter's Tale*? I love your voice and all those words might make some sort of sense if you spoke them."

"I'll read it to you," Mary promised. "Won't you tell me about the days when you first met Fred?"

For the rest of the day Mrs. Hepplewhite told her and no poet at his most eloquent had ever had more to say. There was even a lyric quality in Mrs. Hepplewhite's description of her early years, when Dolly Arnold had been living within her own milieu like a fish in the sea. The sweet ease of those days had invested them with a poetic glow of beauty. For each of us, Mary thought, where we rest and are at home is beautiful. But our conception of home changes as awareness grows and would she be happy now in the Edgware Road and the Gaiety Theatre?

"Would you like to go back there?" she asked.

"Where, dear?"

"To the Edgware Road."

They were in Mrs. Hepplewhite's bedroom now and it was night. She shook her head and looked out of the window at the winter trees, their dark sculptured beauty motionless against the starry sky. "No. I don't think I'd like the television aerials or the noise of the traffic. Not now. But I'd like a little house or a bungalow. All modern, with gadgets." Her voice dropped to a whisper. "There's going to be one for sale in the village. Julie told me. The Howards are leaving. It's only two doors off from those dear Adamses."

Now may heaven strengthen the Adamses, thought Mary. Aloud she said, "You could let this house."

"If Fred agrees I'll sell it," said Mrs. Hepplewhite. "And my jewels and the Bentley."

"Won't you miss the Bentley?"

"No. I've always longed to travel by bus with all the other people. It's lonely in the Bentley. And I can give the money to the people who will be poor because of Fred."

Mary knew with James Anderson that it would be as a drop in the ocean, but she agreed. "Shall I stay with you until you sleep?" she asked. She had been doing that these last few nights, sitting by Mrs. Hepplewhite until her sleeping tablets took effect. But tonight she was sufficiently convalescent for the terror of loneliness to be less severe. "With Tania on the bed I'll be all right," she said.

2

Mary escaped with thankfulness to her own room next door, feeling loneliness to be the supreme blessing, but she was too tired to sleep and when she was in bed she put her dressing-jacket round her shoulders and reached for *Mansfield Park*. The house was centrally heated, which should have been ideal for reading in bed, yet she missed the slight tang of cold that her bedroom at The Laurels had nowadays. It was invigorating and invested a hot water bottle with a pleasure keen as itself. But *Mansfield Park* failed to hold her. Fanny was good but she lacked the serene depth of Anne Eliot and Jane Bennett. Mary found her a rather tiresome little creature and putting her gently aside turned to another. It was Cousin Mary whom she found she wanted.

So this blessing of loneliness was not really loneliness. Real loneliness was something unendurable. What one wanted when exhausted by the noise and impact of physical bodies was not no people but disembodied people; all those denizens of beloved books who could be taken to one's heart and put away again, in silence, and with no hurt feelings. Cousin Mary was one of these, coming and going in the pages of her diary, yet greater than the others because when she went it was not into nowhere. Mary knew that now. One morning, waking out of deep sleep, she had, like James Anderson a few hours ago, humbly recognized her knowledge, and known herself mistaken until now, and a follower of the path of least resistance. For unbelief was easier than belief, much less demanding and subtly flattering because the agnostic felt himself to be intellectually superior to the believer. And then unbelief haunted by faith, as she knew by experience, produced a rather pleasant nostalgia, while belief haunted by doubt involved real suffering; that she knew now by intuition, soon probably she would know it by experience also. One had to be haunted by one or the other, she imagined, and to make the choice if only subconsciously. She was ashamed that subconsciously she had chosen not to suffer.

And so here I am, she thought. I came here to get to know Cousin Mary and John and I do know them better than I did. While they lived in this world I knew little even of John. I know more now for T. S. Eliot was right when he said,

> "*And what the dead had no speech for, when living,*
> *They can tell you, being dead: the communication*
> *Of the dead is tongued with fire beyond the language of the*
> *living.*"

Complete knowledge I cannot hope for until I am with them again but I know the essential thing about them, that they're alive. And because they live, so does God for without him what would be the point of life beyond death? Life is a reaching out for something or someone. That is its definition. We choose one thing and then another to reach for, climbing to a new rung on the ladder as awareness grows, but they are all only symbols, even human love at its highest and most redemptive. And so now I know, without cataclysm or vision, simply living among the people here, loving them, and growing in the soil of this place.

She opened the diary and the first words she read startled her profoundly. "I am at the Manor." The date was ten years later than that of the entry which had told her of the finding of the old chest. There had been intervening entries, all valuable to Mary because deepening her knowledge of Cousin Mary, but containing nothing of relevance to her own life in Appleshaw. "It is because Jenny has had to have a holiday. I've had a bad time this winter. Jenny got worn out looking after me and Dr. Partridge said she must go away for a rest. And so I came here. I was invited and there seemed nothing else to do, but until a few days ago I didn't know how to bear it that as well as injuring Jenny I had to be an anxiety to the dear old couple here, and a nuisance to their servants. I was very wretched, for the aftermath of this last bad time has been horrible.

I have been despairing, not because of my illness, because I have found meaning in that, but because of the burden I am to other people and because I was convinced that everyone must be shrinking from me. And so, hating myself, I shrank from them and that created a new sort of loneliness. I was alone with self-hatred and that is utterly vile.

"But that was when I first came. I feel different now because of a book I read. I am writing this sitting in the library window, thinking of Sir Charles and Lady Royston but no longer with despair darkening my love for them. That's gone. They must be very old now. I thought they were old when I came, because I was young then and to the young, people in their seventies seem to have one foot in their grave. Now they must be in their eighties. Yet they are very nearly as vigorous as ever, though smaller and somehow more concentrated, like the residue of perfume in an empty bottle. Or like this February weather, winter but so marvellously alive and warm. They have driven out in the carriage to pay a call at a distance, and Mr. Ambrose is out shooting, and so I am alone in the house except for the servants, and the old blind spaniel who is sleeping at my feet. He and I, both of us cracked pitchers, have a fellow feeling for each other and are always contented together. And I love the library better than any other room in the house. I love the smell and feel of it and the throng of happy ghosts who I like to imagine are with me here. It always surprises me that they don't step visibly from the books they wrote. When I take only one book from the shelves the whole lot of them seem to me to be tinglingly alive, not only the man who walks beside me as I carry his book to my chair. Craftsmen are deeply united, I think, and rejoice in each other's artifacts from one generation to another.

"But today I am here not to read but to write about the book that is lying in my lap, and about one of the craftsmen, William the Hunchback. I cannot understand now how I've been so long in finding out about him, since I've known him so long. Some years ago I went to the tower room to poke about among the rubbish but I did not connect the W. H. I saw carved on the wall with the W. H. carved inside the lid of my chest, or the ugly humorous monk with the thorns round his neck with my infirmarian, or realize that it was himself he had carved at the bottom of the stairs leading to his workshop in the tower. The book on my lap, which I found a week ago, and in which I read William's story, is one that was given to Sir Charles by the Rector who was here when Sir Charles was a young man. The Rector, Gervase Jackson, wrote it when he himself was young so it's an old book now and all the s's are f's and I had hard work to make it out. It's a short book, part of a Latin book which Gervase found in the library of his Oxford college. The whole book, he says in his preface, was a long history of the abbey with a selection of stories about personalities connected with it, some probably true, others perhaps mythical. The most picturesque of these Gervase removed from the original work, like plums from a pudding, and translated into English. It did not take me long to find the one about William and though Gervase in his preface placed it in the perhaps mythical list I know it is true. I'll write it out again here, very shortly, just for my own joy. It's a double joy for not only, thanks to Gervase, do I now know William better but he has shown me something I did not understand before. And nor did he before it was shown to him.

"William was his name in religion and he took it because William was the first lord of the manor of Appleshaw who at his death bequeathed a large tract of land and much of his wealth to the Cistercians, that they might build an abbey round the church that held his tomb. His full name was William de Garland and he went on the disastrous Second Crusade and was knighted on his return. His Coat of Arms was a cross-handled sword and a beehive, for according to legend he was a fine apiarist, and the abbey kept his Coat of Arms as their own. William the monk had another reason for wanting to bear the knight's name, for in his boyhood he had worked for the lord of the manor of his day, Sir William Roche, who had built a Tudor manor house within the ruined walls of the first Sir William's castle, and Sir William had been good to him. For he was not only hunch-backed but, as the old book says, 'mightily misshapen, with short bow legs and long arms that hung down, sickly and very plain of countenance', so much so that other children were scared of him, or laughed and threw stones. And he himself, neglected as he was by the uncle whom he lived with and knocked about by his horde of healthy children, grew to be as scared of the human race as a hunted leveret. And a hunted wild creature he might have been until the end had not Sir William rescued him one day from a crowd of jeering children, taken pity on him and given him work to do at the manor. He was dog-boy first, and later he was promoted to help with the horses, and then to be bee keeper, for he was wonderfully clever with all animals and wild creatures and they loved him greatly. When any animals in the neighbourhood were sick or injured he was sent for to care for them for he had knowledge of healing herbs and hands gifted with healing. He would have liked to care for human creatures in the same way but to his grief they continued to shrink from him, and so he continued to shrink from them. He was a skilful carver in wood and stone and in this work he found pleasure, and despite frequent sickness of body he did not manage too badly, whatever his inward sorrow, until such time as Sir William had a bad fall while hunting and received injuries from which eventually he died.

"Then did grief and despair take hold of the hunchback, for his love and life had been centred upon his master. His only comfort were his bees and soon they too were taken from him, for Sir William had left no heir and the manor passed to another family, the Roystons, who brought their own servants with them. They were repelled by William's appearance and dismissed him. He went into the woods and lived there alone for some months, finding shelter in bad weather in one of the abbey barns, that had in early days been a guest house, and marked the boundary of the abbey lands upon the north. Kindly villagers brought bread and left it by the well beside the barn, and he gathered berries and edible fungi, for he would never kill wild creatures for food, and somehow he managed to live.

"Then one day in early spring he suddenly appeared among the stonemasons who were enlarging the abbey church and with changed and smiling countenance offered them his services, and laboured with them until the work was completed. Then with the same cheerful face, quite changed from the man he had been, he presented himself before the Abbot and asked that he might be accepted as a lay brother. He was put in charge of the bees, and later made infirmarian, and the Abbot gave him a workshop in the tower where in his spare time he could continue to use his skill with wood and stone. He lived until old age, dying just before the dissolution of the abbey, and was reckoned at the time of his death to be a very holy man. He himself however deemed those mistaken who called him holy, declaring himself to be a great sinner saved from despair only by the mercy of God that came upon him in the vision in the wood.

"He delighted to tell this story and believed implicitly in his vision. When it was suggested to him that he had imagined what he saw, he said, dream or vision, what did it matter? Whichever it was his God had by its means lifted him out of his despair. He had, he said, that afternoon in early spring, taken shelter in the barn from a sudden drenching thunderstorm. Around sunset the rain ceased and he went outside to get himself a drink of water from the well under the thorn tree. He came out into a dazzle of gold and to the east, where the last of the storm clouds made a violet bruise in the sky, there was a rainbow. The trees were rosy with the swelling buds and the grass sparkled. The birds were singing and the first primroses were in bloom around the well. Yet there was no lightening of his darkness as he stood looking at them, only a deepening of it. Caught in this web of beauty he felt himself a thing of horror, ugly and dirty in body, mind and soul. He wished he could tear himself out of the shining web, that he might no longer defile it. And then the thought came to him, why not? On the other side of the well was the thorn, a young tree but with stout branches, and inside the barn there was a length of rope. For a short while after he would continue to defile the web and then he would be found and buried and the fair earth would be quit of him.

"He looked hard at the tree, seeing it already as his gallows, and then found that he could not look away. There were no green leaves yet to veil the starkness of it, it was still a winter tree, and the thorns looked long and sharp. He looked deeper and deeper into the tree, into the heart of it, trying to see himself hanging on the tree, and presently, with horror, he did. And then, staring as though nothing of him now existed except his straining eyes and thundering heart, he knew it was not himself but another. And he knew who it was. He would never, afterwards, attempt to describe what he saw. He could not. But he did say that he believed the fair Lord of life had accepted a death so shameful of deliberate intent of love, so that nothing that can happen to the body should cause any man to feel himself separated from God. And he said further that fearful though the sight was it was not what he saw that made him cast himself down upon the ground, with his face hidden in the grass, and weep. It was that the Lord of heaven, giving himself into the hands of men, that is to say into his hands, to do with what he would, had by his hands been broken. This he said he had never sufficiently considered, and now, considering it, his heart broke. A little later he was able to stop weeping and lifting himself up from the ground he dared to look again into the heart of the tree. It was as it had been, a bare winter tree full of thorns. But he knew now that he need never hang there, since another had chosen to hang there in his place, ridding the world of his ugliness by taking his sin into his own body that it might die with him. For he saw now that his true ugliness had been withdrawn by his Lord while he wept. His misshapen body remained but men would not again shrink from him. What they had shrunk from had been his own sin of self-hatred, that had made him like a beaten cur in their presence. Why should he hate himself, since God had loved him enough to die for him? He would go back into the world, and smile at all the folk in it, and love them with the same love, and they would no longer shrink from him. When their bodies were sick they would even put themselves gladly into his hands, as the creatures did. He held out his hands and looked at them, remembering how they had treated his Lord. He would make reparation, now, to those other men who mysteriously were his Lord, with his hands. But that was not enough. The least he could do, he, Adam, the man who had so brutally done what he would when his trusting Lord put himself into his hands, was now to put himself into his Lord's hands to be done with what his Lord willed. He held out his hands towards the tree, empty to his human sight yet containing all he was, and said aloud, 'Into thy hands'.

"The rest of the story I will copy out in the words of the old chronicle. 'His prayer ended then did Brother William get upon his feet right joyously, and going to the thorn tree he plucked therefrom a curved and thorny branch and set it about his neck as though it were the halter from which his Lord had saved him. Yet he plucked it from the tree not as a halter but as a yoke, for now was he the thrall of Christ, yoke fellow with his Lord in the bearing of the cross. And he went forth singing into the wood and came in the last of the evening light to where the masons were still working upon the church, and he came in among them as eager to be with them as the bee is eager for the honey, and asked if he might work with them on the morrow. The wideness of his smile and his eagerness for their company attracted them mightily, but they laughed much at the comical appearance of the man, and at the notion that the weak and misshapen little fellow could turn mason. He laughed with them, no wit abashed, and then he showed them his hands, broad and strong, and asked if they were not the hands of a craftsman skilled in the carving of stone. So they said he should work with them on the morrow and they found him then as skilled as he had said. Great was his joy in this work, and great also, after he became a brother, was his joy in the care of the sick. And they were as eager to give themselves into his hands as he was to serve them. This he would say was as God willed it, for he is among us both as he that serveth and he that is served.'

"When I had finished reading the story for the first time I was ashamed of my despair but I also had a new joy and a new sense of direction. I must use my hands more, I thought. I did not mean it literally for I am stupid with my hands, I can't carve or paint and even the seams I sew are never straight. What I meant was that I must build something up for somebody, make something to put into the hands of another when I die. But what could I make, and for whom?

"I was wondering about this when the old spaniel began to thump his tail on the floor and then the door opened and

Mr. Ambrose came in surrounded by the usual cloud of dogs. Mr. Ambrose is red-faced, awkward and inarticulate. How he comes to be the son of his charming and most articulate parents is a mystery. Yet no one has ever been contemptuous of Mr. Ambrose. His heart, they say, is in the right place. I like Mr. Ambrose immensely and though he seldom speaks to me, and generally blushes furiously when I speak to him, I am somehow aware that he likes me. He came up to my chair, knocking into the furniture as he came, blushed purple, laid a small box on my knee and said, 'For you.'

" 'For me?' I asked. 'A present, Mr. Ambrose?'

"He nodded and whispered hoarsely, 'Saw it in the window. Thought you'd like it.'

"I took the lid off the little box and lifted the cotton wool inside. At my elbow Mr. Ambrose was breathing as heavily as though he had been running a race, and all the dogs were trembling and taut with eagerness about me. Mr. Ambrose is so united with his dogs that they share his every emotion. Under the cotton wool was something small and white and delicate. I picked it up and my breath caught in my throat so that I could not speak. It was a carved ivory coach, about the size of a hazel nut, and inside was Queen Mab. There are no words to describe the loveliness of that coach, like a sea shell, or the beauty of the little queen's face half-smiling beneath her tiny crown.

"I held it in the palm of my hand and it seemed to be all that there is. With a flash of knowledge I knew that Mr. Ambrose had in truth put into my hand all that there is, all he has. He does more than like me, I know now. For years he has more than liked me and I suppose deep inside me I have more than liked him. Abnormality may forbid the normal course of love between man and woman but it does not preclude the love, as normal people so often seem to think, it merely drives it underground to a great depth. This gift in my hand told me more about the inarticulate man beside me than if he had talked about himself for a week on end. That he should have noticed this tiny thing in a shop window, should have liked it, told me what he was. That he should have known that I would like it told me how much he knew about me. I could have wept only what

I was feeling strangled tears. But the increasing heaviness of Mr. Ambrose's breathing, the rising anxiety of the dogs, told me that I had to do something, say something, and something simple that Mr. Ambrose would understand. I held the little coach against my cheek and then I got up and took Mr. Ambrose's hand and laughed for joy. And it really was joy though a moment before I could have wept. I was so glad that he had found the way to tell me, even if he himself was largely unaware of what he had told me, and I was so happy for us both that we had this hidden love. At the sound of my laughter his face was wreathed in smiles and all the dogs relaxed into tail-wagging relief. Then the old butler came in with the tea tray and Mr. Ambrose and I had tea together and talked about my collection of little things.

"When he had gone and I was alone again I sat and looked at Queen Mab and I saw that she had a child's face, and suddenly I knew what I was going to make, a home for the child. Not just the little carved ivory child but for the child whom this toy represents and who will one day come into my life. I cannot even imagine yet who she will be but I feel sure she will come. I have often wondered who will live in The Laurels when I die. My next of kin is my sister but a house like The Laurels, a place like Appleshaw, would neither of them mean anything to her. If The Laurels went to her she would only sell it. But now I see what to do. This child, my child, will come and she will have The Laurels and all I possess. I will set to work to make the garden as lovely as I can. I will plant flowering shrubs and rose trees and make a waterlily pool, and find a cupid or a dolphin boy to watch over it till she comes. And I will take great care of the house for her. She will love my little things. It is for her of course that I have been collecting them. I didn't know that until now. I feel one with her, as though we were the same woman. She will find great happiness in all that I have prepared for her, and, in her, so shall I. 'They that sow in tears shall reap in joy.' Perhaps she will even reap my faith, as I believe I have reaped that of the old man."

There the entry ended and Mary closed the diary, put it on her bedside table and switched off the light. But she did not sleep. She lay awake thinking how the threads stretched back and back into the past and away into the future, and how one's own small web of life trembled on these threads. For most of the time one was unaware of them yet they were the lifeline. And she thought how marvellous was the tapestry of human oneness and that in a place like this one could know it. In a city the multiplicity of threads forced a whirling confusion on the loom but here the simple pattern and the slow weaving made purpose more discernible. She considered these things to keep herself from thinking of the child whom Cousin Mary had planned and built for, and who had been with her for only a few hours on a spring day. That was all she had had of the child. I cried when I left her, thought Mary, so why did I not ask to be taken there again? Even after Father had died why did I not demand that Mother let me go back? I didn't know what I meant to her, of course, but surely I ought to have known. I think I did know when I said good-bye, but my knowledge was so quickly covered. Children are such creatures of the hour. They uncover again later in life the things that were important to them, but at the time, as one thing flows upon another, they have eyes only for the immediate thing. But she could not comfort herself with meditation on the nature of children. The fact remained that she, so important and precious to Cousin Mary, had been with her in this world for only a few hours.

But the last person she thought of, before she finally fell asleep, was not Cousin Mary but Mr. Ambrose, who had lived and died in this house. . . . To be succeeded by Mr. Hepplewhite. . . . She thought for a little of the two men, Mr. Ambrose in his rough tweed coat, inarticulate in his cloud of dogs, and the smooth financier. They represented two worlds and between them was the deep chasm that during the years of her lifetime had cleft human history in two. Though in point of time she and Mr. Hepplewhite were together on this side of the chasm yet he appeared now misted and distant. It was Mr. Ambrose who was close and real to her. She drifted into sleep and dreamed she was a small child walking with him in the woods, hand in hand in the midst of the cloud of dogs.

CHAPTER XIV

I

A WEEK before Christmas the cold, bitter and iron-grey, clamped down upon London. Charles, who had slept only towards morning, woke about nine o'clock hardly aware of his surroundings, for his morning dream still encompassed him and retained its extraordinary vividness. He had been walking on a warm summer day in the Appleshaw beech woods with a man who was sometimes Paul and sometimes a stranger, a queer little fellow with a humorous ugly face. The two seemed in some odd way to be the same man because the conversation flowed on unchecked whichever one of them was beside him. Half-awake he had no memory of their talk, only of the delight of the companionship he had enjoyed and the warmth of the summer sun. Then the warmth drained away, leaving him shivering under his inadequate blankets. Awake, but with eyes closed, he still saw the face of the odd little man, but now it was no longer a face of flesh and blood but carved in stone, and about the neck there was a wreath of thorns. It was familiar. He'd seen it before. But where? He did not bother to think where for full consciousness rolled upon him. He tried to escape from it and could not. He lay rigid and knew himself awake.

He was alone for Tony Richards had walked out on him ten days ago, leaving him in possession of their flat but broke. The garage idea had crashed with the financier uncle, who had been deeply involved in the Hepplewhite affair and one of the many temporarily overwhelmed in its avalanche. He'll struggle out, thought Charles, and so will Tony, they're tough. I shan't. I've had enough. He'd known he couldn't go on yesterday, a day he had spent in a fog of self-loathing. A failure like himself defiled life and the best thing he could do was to tear himself out of it. He was of the same opinion this morning. Going on was the strong habit of his life but he had forgotten that now. His misery had reached such a pitch that it had blotted out not only habit but memory, a darkness of annihilation admitting consciousness of nothing but the necessity of escaping from it. He had to get out. He raised himself on his elbow and then dropped back again, not from any failure of will but simply from the inertia and exhaustion that were part of the weight of his despair. The gas fire was there, and the shilling on the mantelpiece above it, but he would have to block up the crevices of the draughty little room with newspaper and for the moment the effort of it was beyond him. He rolled over on his back and shut his eyes. Why could not men do what animals did? When life became impossible they simply lay still and died.

There was a bang on the door, and then another, thundering impatiently. At first his dulled mind registered the noise without curiosity, then mechanically he rolled out of bed, went to the door and opened it. An indifferent postman thrust a registered envelope at him, with a pencil and scrap of paper. He scrawled his signature, banged the door on the departing postman and sat down on the side of his bed, the letter in his hand. The post. It took ten minutes of staring at it before bewildered surprise stirred feebly. For no one knew where he was except Tony, and he had parted from him with a bitterness that precluded further contact. He never told his parents where he was, for fear the old man should visit him, and he had not told Paul. For he'd seen in the paper that Paul's play was a success and Paul himself the latest literary lion. Good luck for Paul was what he had hoped for but paradoxically now it had come he had suffered a savage revulsion of feeling, as though Paul in pulling himself out of the rut of misfortune that had held them both had left him behind deliberately. He had written no line of congratulation for it would have looked like toadying to the fellow. So no one knew where he was. So what? He was incapable of caring and flopping back on the bed he shut his eyes again.

But presently the memory of his father thrust upon him. It came again and again as though someone were trying to wake him. Was the old man dead? That, possibly, if he'd seen it in the paper, would have made Tony write to him. A childish panic seized him as though he were a two-year-old who had woken up alone in the dark, and he rolled out of bed and grabbed the letter.

It contained sixty pounds in notes with a covering type-written letter. Charles looked at it stupidly, his mind registering nothing. Then he looked at the signature. Paul Randall. How had he tracked him down? And the fool, to send a sum like that through the post in notes. Had he never heard of money orders? It was just the sort of fool thing he would do. Anger gave Charles a sudden clarity of mind and he could read the letter. "I've had the devil of a job to find you. Why this hibernation? It was only a fluke that I got hold of your address at last. Valerie and I were in town last week and a man in my play brought along your friend, Tony Richards, to a party. You told me of him and I remembered the name and asked him for your address. Just a coincidence but I'd have spent a rotten Christmas if Richards and I had not coincided." There was a good deal more, friendly and tactful. The letter ended, "Best wishes for a happy Christmas".

That phrase, and the careful tact, further infuriated Charles. A happy Christmas! Was the man mad? He'd be happy all right, with success and money, a wife and home. He was like all the rest, as soon as good luck came his way he'd built it about him like an ivory tower and now he just nodded out of the window at the poor devils down below, and threw a few coins down to salve his conscience. But if he thinks I'll touch his conscience money, raged Charles, he's very much mistaken. Yet what was he to do with it? He sat stupidly on the side of his bed, looking at the notes in his hand. Pay the rent? There were several weeks owing. Or post the money straight back to Paul? Yes, get a money order, to teach him the right way to go about these things, then post it and come back and finish the business. That would pay him out all right.

He found that he was slowly dressing, and then stumbling down the stairs, the notes in his pocket. Out in the grey street, shivering in the wind, he forgot what he had come out for and was thinking of the stone man. Where had he seen him? His mind fumbled at the question, round and round, unable to leave the problem. It was like one of those maddening tunes that play themselves over and over

in the mind when one is feverish. Over and over. Where
had he seen the stone man? The wind came round the
corner of a street like a knife and hungry and cold as he was
it bent him over as though it had plunged its steel into his
body, pushing him back into the shelter of a shop entry.

He straightened and waited a moment to get his breath.
Beyond the plate glass lights shone on holly berries, and garlands of tinsel and greenery made a glitter of softness over
the hard rectangular shapes that filled the shop window.
They were like blocks of stone. Stone. Who was the stone
man? Holly. Christmas. One thing suggesting another his
mind groped back to the last time Christmas had had any
significance for him. Some years ago he had actually gone
home for Christmas. It had been the only Christmas he had
ever spent at Appleshaw and he had nearly passed out with
boredom. But it had pleased his parents. He'd been broke
at the time and it had been necessary to please them for
he'd wanted money. He'd even gone to church with them
on Christmas Day. He was suddenly back in Appleshaw
church, filing out with the congregation at the end of the
service. There was holly everywhere and the lights shone
on the red berries, and upon the wreaths of greenery that
softened the old grey stone. It was then that he had seen
the stone man at one side of the door that led to the tower
stairs. He had stopped a moment, arrested by the man's
face, but the people behind had carried him on with them
and in five minutes he had forgotten about the fellow. Profound relief swept over him, almost like the relief of pain
ended, simply because he had remembered where he had
seen the stone man, and relaxing he saw that the rectangular
shapes were television sets. Television. That was a rotten
old wireless he had given his parents that Christmas. He'd
picked it up cheap, secondhand, just to make Christmas at
home less embarrassing for himself, and had been shamed
by the old people's pleasure in it. The thing was more or
less worn out now yet they still listened to it, his father
especially. There was a television set in the window marked
fifty-eight pounds. That letter had not been to tell him
of his father's death but to bring him sixty pounds.

Afterwards he had no clear recollection of walking from
the shop to the post office, but when he got there his mind

was clear. He bought a money order and a stamped envelope and borrowed two pieces of paper from the man behind the counter. He had an agonizing moment trying to remember the name of the wireless shop at Westwater but it came to him suddenly as though spoken in his ear. He wrote a letter and asked them to deliver a television set to his father by Christmas day, and he enclosed a note of good wishes to his parents to be sent with it, and posted the letter. With the loose change in his pocket he had almost three pounds left. He went out into the street and dizziness overwhelmed him. He had scarcely eaten yesterday. In this state he'd not get home. There was an espresso bar almost next door to the post office. He went there and got himself a large cup of hot sweet coffee and a couple of sandwiches. Sitting alone in a corner he ate and drank and as the warmth spread in his body he remembered the warmth of the summer day in his dream, and the two men who had seemed one man. Shutting his eyes he saw first one face and then the other, not in the least alike but stamped with the same quality, something indefinable yet as clearly to be recognized as that quality of light that differentiates the real jewel from a fake. His bitter thoughts about Paul had vanished. He was a good chap and he was intensely grateful to him for now his parents would have a Christmas gift to remember him by. It would soften the blow.

Would it?

It was as though a voice had spoken in his ear. In his despair he had not remembered his parents, for nothing had existed except the necessity of escape. Now his mind was suddenly flooded with memories, a chain of them reaching back into childhood, even to a forgotten memory of being carried on his father's shoulder through a garden, and the ecstasy of knowing himself taller than the hollyhocks. Even, he felt vaguely, farther back than that, back to the memories of other men whose lives were in some way linked with his. Forward to other men. It was a chain he could not break without injuring not only his father but the past and future. He could not tear himself out. Therefore he must go on. He had always known he had to and he could not understand now that refusal of a few hours ago.

He tried to think what to do next. He must go back to the

flat, fetch the bare necessities and leave the rest in lieu of the
rent. Then disappear and lead the usual wretched between-
whiles existence, a doss house at night, washing up at some
hotel while he searched for a better job. The same old dreary
round. Yet this time he felt more hopeful than usual. It was
not that he had any hope of being a different sort of man.
From what you are there is no escape, he knew that, but it is
possible to live in such a manner that the burden of what
you are bears less heavily upon other people. And in that
he vaguely felt there might be help for himself, too. He'd
write to Paul and thank him for his gift and when he was
more or less on his feet again he'd go and see his parents,
not to ask for money this time or to get free lodging but
simply to see them. As he walked back to the flat he was
thinking of the bar of the Dog and Duck and its homeliness.
It would be good to be there again with Jack Beckett,
Joshua Baker, Bert Eeles and the rest. And Paul. He remembered their first meeting there and the thought of Paul
gave him a sense of extraordinary strength. And also,
strangely, did the thought of the stone man.

2

Mary had made several plans for her first Christmas at
Appleshaw but then none of them materialized. That, she
thought, was the way of Christmas plans. There was something disruptive about Christmas and not only in the merely
material way. The original Christmas had proved exceed-
ingly disrupting to the entire world and the tremors
of the original event vibrated through every life year by
year.

She had thought Catherine would spend Christmas with
her but Catherine had formed a poor opinion of Appleshaw
at her first visit and preferred to go to her brother at York.
Mary was secretly relieved for she felt she needed to be
alone with the pain of her love for Paul and the joy of her
new-found faith. Yet the two seemed united for she would
not have chosen not to love Paul and she did not suppose for
a moment that anything worth having, and she now knew
faith to be supremely worth having, was ever easy to have.
She had wondered once if the human love she had longed
for, and now knew, was symbolic and she realized with the

approach of Christmas that the love of God contains the human power of love in its supernatural state. It was that that burst forth two thousand years ago and disrupted the world like a tidal wave.

But rejoicing in the thought of aloneness she suddenly realized that Mrs. Hepplewhite must spend Christmas with her. Instead of wallowing in what she had hoped would be a spiritual experience she must wallow in the warm flow of Hermione's conversation. The realization was bleak, and her first taste of the extraordinary contrariness of the will of God. Mrs. Hepplewhite, invited, clasped Mary in her arms in tearful relief and pleasure and said she would come for a week.

She came and at first Mary wondered hourly if she would survive, for now that the first shock was over Mrs. Hepplewhite was finding intense relief in the conversational recapitulation of her troubles. From the beginning to the end they rehearsed it all and then went back to the beginning again. Mary could expect no escape in packing up Christmas gifts in her bedroom, or in a little lonely washing up, for wherever she went Mrs. Hepplewhite came too, loving, helpful and verbose. There was relief in the occasional presence of Mrs. Baker and the Christmas visits of neighbours, bringing gifts and invitations, for though the conversation continued the impact of it was shared. And two of these visits Mary by some miracle was able to receive alone.

She was dusting the oak chest in the hall when Mr. Baker came prophetically tramping through from the kitchen and stood beside her. Wordlessly he proffered a bunch of Christmas roses from his garden. Though he said nothing he held them out with both hands as though showing her their incomparable beauty, and suddenly the years swung back and beside her was a lanky redheaded child showing her his conker. For a moment she could not speak, then she thanked him and spoke of the beauty of the flowers. "I will put them in a silver tankard here on the oak chest," she said.

Mr. Baker's Adam's apple worked mightily and then he said, "Glad to see this chest back in its place again. Funny how you found it."

"Mr. Baker, there's a little thing I want to give you," said Mary. "Please will you come into the parlour."

He followed her to the table in the window and watched while she took the glass shade off the little things. She picked up the dwarf with the red cap and gave it to him and said, "I want you to have it. I think my cousin Miss Lindsay would have wanted you to have it."

She watched him, wondering if he would once again refuse the gift, but this time he seemed to feel differently about it for a broad grin creased his face and taking the dwarf he sat the tiny creature on his huge palm. It was beautifully carved and she saw he was delighting in its workmanship; and also that he was remembering his first meeting with the dwarf.

"Thank you kindly, ma'am," he said, using the phrase he would have used in his boyhood, and pocketed the dwarf. "I wish you the compliments of the season." And he tramped out of the parlour. Mary could understand why he felt, now, that he could take it. He and she as children had felt the collection of the little things to be something secure and eternal, and therefore not to be pulled apart. Edith had not felt that and nor did he, now. Nothing today was secure. The urge to share what one had quickly, while one had it, was imperative.

Her other visitor was Paul. She was in the kitchen garden hanging out dish cloths and the door leading to Ash Lane was open. Something warm, soft and strong pressed against her knee and looking down she saw it was Bess, and Paul was with Bess.

"She saw you through the door and brought me in," said Paul.

"Come into the kitchen where it's warm," said Mary. "I'm alone for five minutes. Mrs. Hepplewhite has gone to the post."

"It might be ten minutes," said Paul hopefully. "In the week before Christmas there can be as many as six people at a time in the Appleshaw P.O. It can be quite a serious congestion. What a pungent Christmas smell!" There were mince pies in the oven and a pot of chrysanthemums on the dresser. "Are you happy, Mary?"

"Why do you ask me that?"

"Because I want you to be."

"That means," said Mary smiling, "that you are happy yourself."

"It would be a poor show if life seemed good to me and not to my friends, wouldn't it? I don't think just now I could put up with that."

"Does success seem so good to you, Paul?"

"Not in all ways. I miss things. I miss the lonely struggling; it took one deep. And the fruit of it crowned with success looks to me rather as your statue in the garden would look with a silly hat on his head, a bit meretricious. But I like the money. I want it for Val and the baby. And I like it that people now want my work. But I don't like them knowing so much about me through what I write for it makes me feel naked. I want it both ways of course, to be wanted and anonymous at the same time. But on balance it's good. And it's better still that Val is well and wants her baby. And it's Christmas at Appleshaw. It's extraordinary that with the world in the state it's in one can, so to speak, climb inside Christmas at Appleshaw and for a week or so be allowed to forget it. Appleshaw even more than most country places has the scent of water in its air."

"The scent of water?" asked Mary.

"I don't mean that literally. 'For there is hope of a tree, if it be cut down, that it will sprout again, and that the tender branch thereof will not cease. Though the root thereof wax old in the earth, and the stock thereof die in the ground; yet through the scent of water it will bud, and bring forth boughs like a plant. There's one thing blindness did for me, gave me a braille bible. My father gave me one. If I'd kept my sight I'd never have read the Bible as I have for I haven't many braille books."

"What is the scent of water?"

"Renewal. The goodness of God coming down like dew. Mary, it is most alarming, the way you make me talk. I don't talk to anyone else as I do to you. I'd be ashamed to."

Mary was suddenly aware of wealth and when he asked her again, "Well, are you happy?" she replied with absolute truth, "Yes I am."

Mrs. Hepplewhite was heard talking to Tania in the hall. He laughed, kissed Mary briefly and yielded to Bess's tug upon her harness. Bess could not stand Tania and towed him rapidly out of the back door.

"Darling," said Mrs. Hepplewhite, entering from the hall, "you promised to read me *The Winter's Tale* and you never have."

"We'll read it tonight," said Mary.

After supper they sat in the lamplit parlour with Tania and Tiger dozing before the fire, and talk gave way to the quietness engendered by good poetry perfectly read. Mrs. Hepplewhite could make little of it but she was aware that in likening her to the Hermione of the story Mary was paying her a compliment, and after all the years of struggling so inadequately in Fred's victorious wake that brought respite. Mary thought her adequate and she could relax the tension. She folded her hands in her lap and tried not to fall asleep, or alternatively not to let her thoughts wander to Fred. When she had seen him the other day he had kissed her. To her great relief he had not seemed changed except for being strangely quiet. . . . Quiet. . . . She started awake again to find the room as quiet as Fred. And so was the night. The snow had not come yet but outside was the windless stillness of frost under the moon and stars. While Mary was reading of the rosemary and rue that keep seeming and savour all the winter long they heard the carol singers outside. The air of "The Holly and the Ivy" did not seem to break the quiet at all, merely to thread through it, and when later the bells began practising for Christmas Mary's reading kept them as a triumphant background to Hermione's restoration.

After she had said good night to Mrs. Hepplewhite in her room Mary went back to the parlour, for she was not sleepy. Sitting before the fire she thought there was a great deal of happiness in the village just now, with Paul's success and Valerie's expected baby, the Adamses joy in their television set and a few other like happenings. And, as Paul had said, in spite of outer darkness at Christmas one was justified in trying to get inside it. With the bells quiet again she fancied she heard the air of "The Holly and the Ivy" floating disembodied round the village, echoing the music of centuries of past Christmases. Cousin Mary had heard it in that way at her first Christmas here, which for her too had been happy.

There was only one more instalment of the diary and now seemed as good a time as any in which to read it. She knew what she was going to find even before she turned the page.

3

"She has come," wrote Cousin Mary. "She has actually been with me here, in her home that I am making for her. We have been together here and though I cried when she went away this has still been the happiest day of my life. It was strange how I saw the announcement of her birth eight years ago. I never look at the births, marriages and deaths column but that day, picking up the paper casually, my eye was caught by a familiar name and there she was, Mary Angela Lindsay, the daughter of my cousin Arthur Lindsay whom I used to play with when we were children. His parents went abroad and I did not see him again but we had been so fond of each other that I never forgot him, and I doubt if he forgot me. The thought came to me that in calling his daughter Mary he was remembering our childhood. I wrote to him to congratulate him and said how much I would like to see the child. He wrote back politely, after the lapse of a few weeks, but made no reference to my seeing the baby. At first I was hurt and then I remembered that he was a busy doctor and my sister had told me his wife did not like our family and that he had been very much absorbed into hers. Twice during the following three years I asked if little Mary could be brought to see me but I wrote to her mother, thinking it right to do that, and each time she wrote back making some excuse. I realized of course that she and Arthur knew about my illness and I thought that they did not want the child to come. I was heartbroken but I accepted what I imagined to be their ruling. It made no difference to the fact that Mary was my child. I knew she was. But just lately I have been so much better that I wrote once more, to Arthur his time, and I reminded him of our times together in our childhood and I actually said I wondered if he had remembered me when he called his daughter Mary. This time he replied at once, in so friendly a way that I am afraid I wondered if his wife had showed him the previous letters. And only a fortnight later, two days ago, he came with Mary.

"She is a marvellous child, gentle, very intelligent, with clear-cut features unusually delicate for a child of that age. I think she will be a beautiful woman. At first I could see that she was frightened of me but she was not frightened of the house. Though she said little I saw that she loved it, and at lunch time I saw her eyes go often to the window, looking at the garden. After lunch Arthur went for a walk and I took her into the parlour to show her the little things, her little things. It was then she ceased to be afraid of me. She loved them, and of course the ones she loved best were the blue glass tea-set and Queen Mab in her coach. When she was holding the little queen, absorbed in her, I looked from the fairy face to the child's and they were so alike. I longed, desperately, for Ambrose. Next time she comes, I thought, he must see her. I would have given her the tea-set and the little queen, for she wanted them badly and they are hers, but she refused to take them. I did not force them on her for they will be safer here and it won't be long, I hope, before it is all hers. I say, I hope, for I am very tired of being ill. Thinking it would not be long I thought I would tell her that I had made this home for her, but just as I was beginning to tell her the door opened and her father came in. It was tea-time already. The afternoon had gone like a few minutes. Then they had to go and Mary and I both cried at parting. If Arthur had not said he would bring her again I don't think I could have borne to say good-bye.

"Yet though I am sure Arthur is a man of his word I am haunted by the fear that I may not see her again. And that Ambrose will never see her. I have had a growing sense of isolation lately. It is as though I stood alone in the centre of a bare room and all round the walls are pictures of houses, gardens and cities. There are men and women laughing and talking inside the houses, children playing in the gardens, people hurrying up and down the streets, but the doors of the houses do not open to me, I cannot join the children at their games or walk with the busy people in the streets. They are too distant from me. It is the nightmare of the stone walls the other way round. They no longer close in, they recede. And so I am afraid that Arthur may not again bring Mary to see me."

The diary broke off there and did not begin again until

six months later when there was a short entry, the last in the book.

"I was right, for two months ago I saw in the paper that Arthur was dead. It was a great shock to me but I managed to write to his widow to condole with her, and a month later I wrote and asked if Mary could come and stay with me. I had no answer to either letter. I understood. To Mary's mother I am the skeleton in the family cupboard and she does not think I would be good for the child. I expect she is right but even though it is for Mary's sake it has taken me two months of struggle to be able to accept her decision and the struggle made me ill; but now, two days after Christmas, with the house wrapped in snow like a child in a white fur cloak, I have accepted it and I am no longer ill. I am sitting in front of the parlour fire after tea and the curtains are drawn. There is the smell of burning wood and the scent of chrysanthemums Ambrose brought me for Christmas. They are gold and cream and deep crimson, and he must have despoiled the greenhouse and infuriated the gardener. The day he brought them I could only go through the motions of gratitude, so great was my depression and so far away did he seem, but today the scent of the flowers is as close to me as though it were the lining of the white fur cloak. Both scent and silent whiteness are invisible to me yet I hold them about me closer than my own breathing.

"This change, this reversal, happened to me in the middle of the carol service on Christmas Eve. Jenny had not wanted me to go to the service, indeed she had refused to take me because she did not think I was fit to go, but I fought her like a naughty child. It was the first time we had had a snowy Christmas since the first one in this house and I remembered, though far off, my dream of the cave in the rock. The old stone church was the nearest thing to a cave I could think of, indeed they were one in my mind, and I was determined to be there. So we went and I was almost crazy with eagerness to get inside, but when I got there I didn't find what I was wanting. I didn't find either the cave in the rock or the intimate cosiness of a village church on Christmas Eve. I was in some crypt or dungeon, or in a clearing in the frozen forest, and it was dark and bitterly cold. Framed by the arches of the crypt, or the shapes of

the frozen boughs, were little pictures, very bright and gay.
I saw shining candles and red berries, elf-like children with
furry caps upon their heads and a crowd of people like a bed
of tulips, but all so distant, like the scenes of microscopic
busyness in the snowy background of a Dutch painting.
There was music too, but so far away that it might have
been harp music fingering at the thick walls outside the
crypt, trying to come in, or wind at the edges of the forest.
Close to me there was nothing but the icy spaces of my
loneliness and a misery that no one could understand. I sat
shivering with the cold, sometimes stumbling to my feet or
sinking to my knees in obedience to Jenny's hand pulling
or pushing me, and far away I heard her sigh and knew that
this misguided expedition was turning out just as she had
feared it would. I tried to realize what I had learned in the
years behind me, the flashes of understanding that had
irradiated my times of respite, and to furnish the void with
them, and I did remember the forgiveness and love of God
waiting at the heart of all experience, and the adorable
radiance of being shining out from all created forms, and
the hands that gave and received. But I only remembered.
None of it was real, only something I remembered imagining. I had thought before that I knew what despair meant,
but I hadn't known. I knew now, I don't know for how
long, for perhaps only a few moments. It passed and I
found I was standing half turned in our pew, looking over
my shoulder at William the Hunchback's carving of himself. We were at the back of the church, where Jenny had
carefully placed me in case I should disgrace her, and I
could see him clearly and easily. He looked highly amused,
and I turned my head away again quickly in anger and out-
rage, back to the emptiness.

"A change had come over it. The chill had become an
indescribable freshness and the emptiness was filled with
what I can only call vast spaces of liberty. They were waiting, blue and warm, already faintly irradiated with the
growing sunlight, and were not only outside me, as I had
thought, but inside me too. I was being hollowed out,
emptied, and filled with this newness. The little pictures
of people and scenes had vanished now but I no longer
needed them. I had forgotten them. All I wanted was that

the thinning walls of my bodily life should let me go, cast
me out like a captive lark freed and flung from a window.
And I thought, this is death, and it seemed that I sang
already.

"But it wasn't. I was singing, but it was a carol, and
about me were the candles and the holly, the elf-like
children and the tall people like tulips in a border. There
was no emptiness any longer but people pressing upon me
in so friendly and so close a fashion that they seemed a part
of me. I loved them and welcomed them back, though it
was so short a time ago that I had loved and welcomed the
sun-warmed spaces of liberty. I knew that in another
dimension the two were not mutually exclusive but existed
together. I also knew that it had happened again. The
experience of that other Christmas years ago had repeated
itself and I was well.

"Now, sitting in front of the fire, I have asked myself, did
I really die? No, of course not. Then were the two ex-
periences, this one and the other when I found the cave in
the rock, merely the hallucinations of illness? No, for they
healed me. They also illumined my mind for they showed
me something of the extraordinary reversals of God.
Everything he touches is changed, death to life and emptiness to liberty, and not only changed but changed into himself since he is himself reversal. And so it seems to me now
right that the two people who mean most to my life, the
old man who gazed entranced at the butterflies in my
parents' garden and the child Mary, should have been
physically the most parted from me. With both there was
only the one meeting, yet they are now more to me than even
Ambrose or Jenny. I never grieved that I did not see the
old man again and I will set myself to learn not to grieve
because I shall not see Mary again. The broken relation-
ship, touched by God, is whole and perfect as it could not
have been if there had been the normal sequence of human
misunderstandings. I am so thankful for all I have learned
here, for the treasure hid in a field. It's not the final
treasure, it's merely a shadow of coming knowledge, not
knowledge itself. For that I must wait. How long? Perhaps so long that I shall go through the thing that I dread
most of all, senility, and become so old and childish that I

shall forget all I have learned. But then will come reversal
again with loss turned to restoration and decay to renewal
at his touch."

That was the end. If there had been another volume of
the diary it was lost, but Mary felt sure that Cousin Mary
had written nothing further. For forty years more she had
lived in this house but what she had suffered and learned
while she waited for deliverance was something about
which she was silent. Mary found that she did not regret
the silence for it gave dignity to Cousin Mary. The silence,
she was sure, had extended to the old lady's daily inter-
course with those about her. There had been almost a
note of querulous complaint in the words "a misery which
no one could understand", but Mrs. Baker had said, "She
never spoke of it", and Paul had said, "She never complained." Not even to her diary. She had progressed
beyond the need of it.

Mary had, as she hoped she would, suffered in the reading of the diary. She had wept sometimes during sleepless
nights, but after this final reading she was left with a sense
of triumph with regard to Cousin Mary, and with regard to
herself a queer but certain knowledge that she had somehow
transcended time, shared her cousin's experience and con-
soled it.

CHAPTER XV

I

THE snow did not come at Christmas, and only a light sprinkling in January, to Appleshaw's relief, for with influenza decimating the ranks the removal of Mrs. Hepplewhite from the Manor to her bungalow was a major undertaking. Mr. Hepplewhite forbade his wife to sell the manor for an old age spent in his library was something from which he definitely refused to be parted, and for which he was prepared to work with renewed energy when he was free again, but it was let for a term of years. Appleshaw was surprised to find itself glad that Mr. Hepplewhite hoped to return one day. They had always felt him to be something of an anachronism, and feared in his person an intrusion from an age they hoped might pass them by if they could keep their heads stuck in the earth for long enough. But now he was more missed than feared. He had not tried to pluck them from their green shade, indeed he had in his own fashion loved it too. They saw that now and began to feel very fond of the squire. The papers had been at great pains to dig out his past history and it had been the greatest service they could have done him, for in the indulgent eyes of Appleshaw, stealing that levelled out such gross injustice was scarcely stealing at all. And meanwhile Mrs. Hepplewhite was delighted with her bungalow, and loved travelling by bus, Colonel and Mrs. Adams were deeply happy with their television set and the knowledge that Charles had given it to them, Jean was looking forward to another year of Mary's friendship with quiet content, the chrysanthemums that Mary had promised herself were doing well in the conservatory and the Randalls' change of fortune was like a lambent light upon the grey landscape.

Only Mrs. Croft was not entirely satisfied when Mary encountered her at her garden gate a couple of days before Candlemas.

"I've six snowdrops out," said Mary triumphantly. Mrs.

Baker had told her that country snowdrops must be in flower by Candlemas and watching the tight upright spears in her garden day by day she had been afraid The Laurels' snowdrops might fail in their duty. But they had not let her down.

"Showing white?" asked Mrs. Croft.

"Right out," said Mary. "Heads dropped down and out."

"Mine have been out for a couple of days," said Mrs. Croft. "The wretched things. Don't mention snowdrops to me. There's always a snowfall the moment they drop their heads." She glanced up at the grey sky. "Look at that, and I've a baby due."

"The Randall baby? I thought Valerie was going to hospital."

"She is, and in any case it's not due yet. No, it's a gipsy baby. The caravans are down at the far end of Abbey fields. Gipsy babies always come in the middle of the night and generally in a storm. Thunderstorm, hurricane or blizzard. Any sort of disturbance. It's all the same to a gipsy baby. They're elemental little things, like kittens. Tiger shaping well? Well, dear, I'll say good-bye. I mean to get to bed early tonight."

Next day the snow began to fall, large, slow flakes drifting on a light wind. The sky was leaden and the earth crouched beneath it drained of beauty. All the light and loveliness were in the snow itself, in the movement and glimmer of the flakes large as wild white roses, in the tide of whiteness flowing slowly over the dark earth, like moonlight or the surf of a soundless sea. Mary moved through her day entranced, for this was not only her first snow at Appleshaw but her first country snow. After she had rescued her six snowdrops from the garden she stayed indoors and gazed out of first one window and then another, watching how the whiteness outlined the church windows and the ledges of the tower, how it lay on the shoulders of her cupid in the garden and crept along the branches of the apple tree outside the parlour window. There were sounds at first, Bess barking, the early return of the next-door car bringing the children home from school before the roads worsened, voices of people crossing the green, but with the approach of twilight they one by one fell away. Even the light wind dropped and no longer murmured in the chimney. When Mary at last reluctantly drew the curtains she shut herself in with a silence so living that she moved about the house or sat by the fire as attentive to it as though she were listening to John talking, or Cousin Mary, or to some other music still just beyond her human hearing. Or for some arrival. Who's coming? she wondered. There was expectancy in her listening but no impatience.

She went to bed early and lit the oil stove she had purchased with the first cold weather. She thought she would keep it alight in this her first snow, especially as Tiger had favoured her with his company. When she was in bed with her lamp out, and the little cat asleep on her eiderdown, its glow gave her a cosy feeling of nursery comfort and warmth. The flame had a murmuring voice but no louder than the ticking of her watch, and neither voice could so much as finger the garment of the silence. She did not at once sleep deeply yet she was not aware of weariness. She dozed and woke again and saw the light shining on John's photo and on her six snowdrops in a vase beside it, and smiled and slept once more.

She woke slowly from her dream of the moving shadows and the candlelight shining on the snowdrops on the altar. It had been hard to tell which had been the shadows cast by the cowled figures, long shadows that ran up the wall in the flickering light and were lost in the smoky gloom of the vaulted roof, and which the men themselves, their hands in their sleeves, their heads bent as they chanted. There were only a few of them, men who had been sick but were now sufficiently recovered to be able to take their part in the first office of Candlemas. Though she could not see their faces the men themselves were very real to her, especially the tall monk who stood before the altar and the short one with the bowed shoulders. It was she who was unreal for she cast no shadow. She looked for her shadow and could not find it and feeling a little afraid began to wake up. But the light still shone on the snowdrops, the chanting continued, the tall man turned and smiled at her and he was John. Slowly the reality to which she was accustomed asserted itself; John's photo and the snowdrops in their vase, the familiar outlines of her room. But the chanting continued and lying in her bed she listened to it. When, again with a little tremor of fear, she remembered that Edith had listened to the same thing it was gone. She heard only the clock striking two and then a cock crowing, that first mysterious deep of the night cock-crow that always thrilled her. Yet, with midnight past, it was a new day.

She was beginning to develop the country dweller's seventh sense about the weather and so she knew without going to the window that the snow had stopped. One of Cousin Mary's reversals had taken place. The leaden clouds had all been transmuted into whiteness and the stars were shining in a clear sky. Unexpectedly the cock crowed again and a dog barked. Mary sat up in bed, once more with that feeling of expectancy, but the dog did not bark again and she lay down and fell deeply asleep.

2

The urgent call beneath her window woke Mrs. Croft at once and she was out of bed instantly. This was what she had expected, her clothes were ready on a chair and her bag, packed with all she needed, stood on the floor beside it. With her dressing-gown hugged round her shoulders, for it was bitterly cold, she opened the window a little way behind the curtain, called out, "Wait where you are. I'll be down in a moment," and banged it shut again. Reuben Heron, the gipsy father, was a dirty fellow whom Mrs. Croft very much disliked, and she was not going to waste precious time going downstairs to let him in; nor have him and his dog dirtying her carpet while he waited. Let him stay where he was. Do him good. She dressed quickly and soundlessly, for no good nurse ever drops anything, so soundlessly that she was able to notice the stillness outside. That was odd she thought. She had expected a blizzard. And now she came to think of it she had been aware of a glory of stars before she dropped the curtain again. She had never known a gipsy baby to arrive in a dead calm before. Very odd. She took her torch, went downstairs and let herself out into her snowy garden. There was the softness of a dog's fur against her legs and a man's hand gripped her arm in a relief so strong that it nearly broke it. "Nurse! Come on! Valerie's started!"

"Mr. Randall!" she ejaculated. "Well I never! I thought it was the gipsy baby that's been due a week."

"It isn't. It's Val's baby. The phone's out of order. The snow I suppose. So I can't get the ambulance. Anyway it would never get her to Westwater in time in this weather. Nurse, you've been an hour dressing."

"I have not," said Mrs. Croft tartly but breathlessly, for he was rushing her down the garden path as though it were broad daylight and he could see every stone. "Five minutes. Now there's no need to get in a state, Mr. Randall. I know it's early but that's all to the good with your wife the nervous type. Less time for her to work herself up before-hand. There's nothing wrong with her and she'll have an easy time I shouldn't wonder. Is your mother-in-law there?"

"She was coming next week. No one's there. Val's alone."

"Did you phone the doctor?"

"I tell you the phone's dead. Good lord, why didn't I use yours?"

"Mine's dead too. I tried to put a call through last night and couldn't. Now don't take on. As soon as I've seen your wife comfortable I'll pop over the Talbots. If their phone's gone Mr. Talbot can go for the doctor. It's not far. And Mrs. Talbot can give me a hand; though many's the baby I've delivered singlehanded. How did you find the way to my cottage?"

"Bess brought me."

"She's a good dog. Here we are now. Your sitting-room fire's out I see. I'll light it up again later and make you some hot coffee. Now I'll pop up. Nothing to worry about, remember."

Paul could not see her bright eyes and flushed and happy face. She might complain but there was nothing Mrs. Croft enjoyed more than delivering babies. Especially if the doctor came too late.

3

Mary was in the middle of a late breakfast when the bell rang. When she had opened the door it seemed to her for a moment that history was repeating itself for on the steps stood three children and a hamster. But the bare brown legs, the cotton frocks and the crumpled green linen suit had given way to Wellington boots, thick coats and mufflers, so that even the slim Edith looked almost as broad as she was tall. Martha, held in Rose's arms, was dressed in a pink shawl. Behind them were no longer the green and gold of a spring day but the marvellous glitter of sun on frost and the branches of trees borne down by their weight of snowblossom; great magnolia chunks, may bloom and blackthorn in arcs and drifts; and so still spring, Mary thought, midwinter spring burgeoning in a silence empty of birdsong yet filled with unheard singing. It was as though the second movement of Mozart's flute and harp concerto had just died away on the air but the echo remained crystallized in frost.

She was aware that the children were tingling with excitement and that Rose was offering her a letter. "From Mummy," she said. "The phone's dead and so's the Randalls' phone and Mrs. Croft's. But the Vicarage phone's all right. Daddy telephoned from there in the middle of the night."

"It was morning," said Edith. "It's morning after twelve. Daddy telephoned at two-thirty."

"Silly!" said Rose. "It's night while it's still dark."

Edith no longer minded when Rose knew best and allowed this to be washed off by the sparkling glory of the morning. "We're spending the day with you," she said joyously to Mary. "Meals and all. Daddy's trying to get to work himself but wouldn't risk taking us to school. Mummy's at Orchard cottage helping with the baby. It's all in the letter."

"It's a boy," said Jeremy. It was his first remark and even while she eagerly opened the envelope Mary was aware of his deep satisfaction. Counting Martha he had until now been outnumbered three to one. She looked down at him and smiled her congratulations but his thoughts had now been diverted in another direction by the aroma of toast and coffee and his nose quivered like a rabbit's. "Breakfast?" he queried.

"Come along in," said Mary.

"But we've had ours," said Rose.

"I need help with mine," said Mary. "Come into the kitchen and eat some more and tell me all about it."

In the intervals of the children's chatter Mary read Joanna's letter. The words, "quick and easy and all's well", were set to music in her mind, rippling up and down invisible harp strings. There was something special about this birth, she told herself. All birth was a miracle but this new life seemed to be shining out into the snow like light and for a few extravagant moments the boy seemed to her the whiteness of the snow and the sparkle of the frost. She saw in her mind figures about the child, men and women of Appleshaw past and present and to come, and the light in their eyes was reflected from the child. Just another baby, she kept reminding herself, struggling after a modicum of common sense. But he was not just another baby. He was the future. She had come here to recapture the past and in so doing she found the future shining on her face. She got up eagerly from the table when the children had at last finished. "Come and pick flowers for Valerie," she said. "My conservatory is full of them."

Under the vine branches she and Edith and Rose stripped the chrysanthemums of their flowers, red and white, tawny and bright gold. She remembered Mr. Ambrose cutting the Manor chrysanthemums for Cousin Mary and smiled to herself. Laughing and talking neither she nor the little girls noticed that Jeremy was no longer with them.

He had followed them no farther than the hall, where he put on his Wellingtons again and his coat and muffler. Then he opened the front door, turned right and plunged gloriously into the deep snow. It was the sea! He struck out for the bottom of the garden, using only his left arm to swim with because his right hand was deep in his pocket holding a treasure that he had there. He reached the rock where the boy who kept the lighthouse stood looking westward and climbed up beside him. Now he could see his good ship *Neptune,* and her sails were so white that they dazzled his eyes. Blinking, Jeremy turned away and looked in the direction of the other ship that he could not see from here, the *Victory* whose captain was away. For a moment he remembered Mr. Hepplewhite very vividly, and the nice smell of his library and the big books with the ships in hem, and his hand tightened upon the treasure in his pocket. I will write a letter, he thought, and tell him to come home again. And I will tell him about the boy.

Then he said good-bye to the lighthouse boy, leapt off the rock and swam at great speed towards the door in the wall, for the excursion down to the lighthouse had been a digression, not the purpose of the present exercise.

Out on the green he considered that he was on dry land again and his swimming hand, now stiff and purple with cold, was thrust into the left-hand pocket of his coat. He went rather slowly across the green, kicking up glorious fountains of snow as he went but rather absently, his right hand gripping the thing in his pocket tighter and tighter, but as he approached Orchard Cottage eagerness came uppermost and he almost ran up the path. He removed his Wellingtons at the front door, then opened it and went inside. It was warm and cosy in the tiny hall and he stood listening. From the kitchen he could hear women talking, his mother and Mrs. Croft. He avoided them and went into the sitting-room. Paul was there, asleep in the arm-chair. He shook him relentlessly awake and when he had got him thoroughly aroused laid his left hand firmly on his knee and said, "I have come to see the boy."

"What?" asked Paul.

"I am Jeremy and I have come to see the boy."

"Not at this early hour," said Paul.

"It is not early. I had two breakfasts hours and hours ago and I have come to see the boy."

"But Valerie is asleep."

"I have come to see the boy."

As his wits returned Paul gradually began to understand what this event, a thing of awe and glory to himself, promised Jeremy. There was no other boy in his home and such female companionship as was to hand he had possibly found somewhat lacking in understanding; as had Paul himself in the past. They were drawn together in sympathy but Paul was also dismayed. "The boy's new, you know," he explained to Jeremy. "Very new indeed. It will be some time before he can play with you."

"Of course he's new," said Jeremy with a touch of scorn.

"He only came last night. But he'll grow and I've come t
see him."

Paul already knew that Jeremy had strength of characte
beneath his usually placid good humour but he had no
realized before that his obstinate determination was of th
corkscrew variety. It seemed to come boring down into hi
fatigue, withdrawing his resistance like a cork. "All right,
he said weakly, his heart pounding with trepidation at th
thought of the two women in the kitchen. "But we must no
wake Valerie. If you let out so much as a squeak I'll ski
you. Let's take your wet coat off."

This proved a difficult operation and tugging impatientl
Paul found a cold balled-up fist stuck in one of the sleeve
of the coat. "You're growing out of this," he said. "Ope
your fingers."

"I am holding something," said Jeremy gravely.

"Then pull hard. Now you're out. Don't make a soun
or you'll bring your mother and Mrs. Croft out on us."

Hand in hand the man and boy crept up the stairs. Pau
opened Valerie's door a crack and heard her say cheerfully
"I'm awake, Paul."

"Stay there a minute," Paul whispered to Jeremy, an
went in. Valerie's voice had sounded as young as thoug
she were a girl again.

"I've got him here. In bed with me. Nurse said I coul
have him for a few minutes while she was downstairs. I'm
feeling fine now and I'm glad I'm not in hospital for yo
scarcely see your baby in hospital. Come here and feel him
He's wonderful. Small but perfect." She took Paul's han
and held it under the shawl against the warm baby, and jus
as her youthful voice showed him a picture of her happy fac
so the feel of the baby seemed to unite him with his son a
closely as though at birth the boy had passed from Valerie'
body to his soul. When a few hours ago Mrs. Croft ha
given him the baby to hold he had been able to feel nothin
but layers of impersonal wrappings, and mixed with relief
sense of agony because he would never see the boy. Now
he no longer minded. This was his son, under his hand
and this was his wife united with him in adoration. "W
mustn't spoil him," said Valerie at last. "But it will be har
not to."

Suddenly Paul remembered Jeremy, patiently waiting outside, and told Valerie about him. She had always thought she did not like the Talbot children but now she laughed softly and called to him to come in.

Jeremy advanced and inspected the baby. He nodded once or twice as though confirming the newness. "I'll have to wait," he said with resignation, "but he'll grow." He placed his left forefinger within the baby's minute hand which promptly closed upon it. His slow smile spread over his face and unclosing his right fist he disclosed a marvellous little crystal ship which he handed to Valerie. "It was mine but now it's for him," he told her, "but you'd better keep it."

Valerie took it with an exclamation of delight and held it in her palm, trying to describe it to Paul. But how could she describe such a perfect thing? It sparkled on her hand like clear water momentarily caught by the frost and lit with its fires, and glowed with reflected colour. She said to Paul, "It's a new little ship sailing out on living water."

Also by Elizabeth Goudge in Coronet Books

All these books are available at your bookshop or news-agent, or can be ordered direct from the publisher. Just tick the titles you want and fill in the form below.

CORONET BOOKS, P.O. Box 11, Falmouth, Cornwall.

Please send cheque or postal order. No currency, and allow the following for postage and packing:

1 book—10p, 2 books—15p, 3 books—20p, 4–5 books—25p, 6–9 books—4p per copy, 10–15 books—2½p per copy, 16–30 books—2p per copy, over 30 books free within the U.K.

Overseas—please allow 10p for the first book and 5p per copy for each additional book.

Name ....

Address ....

....

....